THIS
RAVENOUS
FATE

THIS RAVENOUS FATE

HAYLEY DENNINGS

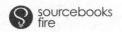

sourcebooks
fire

Copyright © 2024 by Hayley Dennings
Cover and internal design © 2024 by Sourcebooks
Jacket art © Colin Verdi
Jacket design by Nicole Hower
Internal design by Tara Jaggers/Sourcebooks

Published by Sourcebooks Fire, an imprint of Sourcebooks
P.O. Box 4410, Naperville, Illinois 60567-4410
(630) 961-3900
sourcebooks.com

Cataloging-in-Publication Data is on file with the Library of Congress.

Printed and bound in the United States of America.
MA 10 9 8 7 6 5 4 3 2 1

For Black girls everywhere—
you are enough.

"I've known rivers ancient as the world and older than the
flow of human blood in human veins.
My soul has grown deep like the rivers."
LANGSTON HUGHES

"Through thickest gloom look back,
immortal shade,
On that confusion which thy death has made."
PHILLIS WHEATLEY

PROLOGUE: THE FIRST

S HE WAS REMADE WITH SPITE. THE FIRST OF HER kind, her humanity stripped away and pumped full of poison and depravity in a laboratory. She was pushed to the brink of death, but pale hands, thorny and unkind, kept her from tipping over the edge.

Death had become her.

She searched for a familiar face in the darkness and cried when she could not find it. Once a giver of life, now a breeder of death. Carnage was now her only child. The one she had borne had succumbed to the venom, would never feel sunlight on her face again.

Death would have been kinder.

Blood trailed in her wake like the veil of death's bride. She was as new as America, a reincarnation of its greatest evils, comfortable in corporeal sin.

Death would kneel to her.

She took the name of the doctor who had taken her life and drained him of his blood. She liked the way the *V* name rolled off her tongue, sharp like vengeance. But her spite remained. She was a victim to the curiosity of the New World, which ground out mercy and reason. They bred beasts with their tools and made monsters out of men, then left the illness of ignorance to fester, century after century.

First there were multiple beasts, but their numbers dwindled in just a few days once they showed their strength. The colonists put their guns to the mouths of the beasts or burned them at stakes, claiming to eliminate original evil with them. Only she remained, sticking to the shadows, never to be found. As colonists hunted her, they spread stories that spun into folklore the longer she evaded them.

For years she hid and became a myth, but she never forgot the taste of human blood.

Eventually, she grew ravenous.

A pit of hunger opened within her as the New World folded into steady colonies. The Revolution left bodies behind, but they only satiated her for so long. She wanted new blood. The Civil War unleashed new traumas, and she nursed the victims of more physicians who tore women's bodies apart. Her venom spread and new beasts arose. She was no savior, but instead a mother who sought an end to her anger and pain. As the years passed, she and other reapers learned to control their hunger to avoid a second gruesome death at the hands of fearful humans.

After the Great War, the world clung to debauchery while soldiers returned home empty and politicians grappled with solutions for the universal suffering. People scrambled for distractions from the chaos, lighting their houses up with parties, spilling illicit liquor into open throats, all while jazz rose like a spiritual symphony around them. Thrill seekers flowed into cities, and corruption reared its ugly head. Gangsters fed the greedy hands in New York, but the hunger for more never ceased. They celebrated being alive despite the devastation that surrounded them.

The mother reaper watched, her hands curling into fists. A promise of violence spilled from her lips like blood.

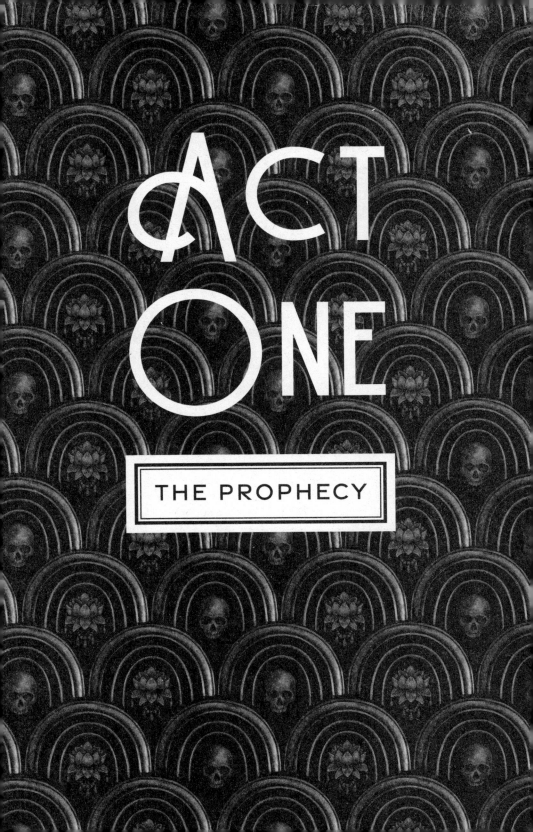

ACT ONE

THE PROPHECY

1

AUGUST 1926

ELISE FOUND THE WORLD MORE BEAUTIFUL WHEN she closed her eyes.

Melancholic jazz music rode the soft sea breeze around the pier, each note lingering like a clandestine kiss. Quiet and unseeing, Elise felt the most herself. Her other senses opened up and softened the edges of her anxieties, making her feel grounded.

Then she opened her eyes. Chelsea Piers came into view around her, the massive docking ocean liner just beyond the piers' entrance ablaze with the glow of the setting sun. Her pulse thundered in her ears and the jazz notes grew fuzzy. Trying to purge the clamminess from her earlier panic, she wiped her hands across her skirt, then stepped toward the waiting car.

Once finished loading Elise's luggage into the trunk, Colm, her family's driver, helped her into the automobile. "Your ship docked late. My apologies, Miss Saint, but we're in a race against the sunset. Your father is already in a mood." He glanced at her through the rearview mirror as the engine roared to life. "Welcome home, by the way."

Elise thought facing her father again sounded worse than being out after the sun went down. As far as she was concerned, the house in Harlem was no longer her home. Not in a city full of monsters who craved the taste of her blood. Monsters like the one her best friend had become.

The car turned north, and though the sky over Manhattan darkened, the streets were still full of people, hats held down against the evening breeze and faces twisted with fear.

Colm stepped on the gas. To settle her nerves, Elise peeked into her bag for what she knew was the fifth time that hour. The letter with the lovely golden seal of the Paris Conservatory was still there, staring back up at her. Her fingers plucked at the loose threads on her coat seven times, her chest growing tighter while the residential buildings of Riverside Drive whipped past her window. They quickly neared Sugar Hill. Elise wondered how much had changed in five years. Whether Layla was even still alive—

Colm cursed in the front seat as he hit the brakes. Pedestrians rushed the intersection the car was trying to cross. "Everyone wants to be close to Saint territory at night," he explained.

Elise nodded. When she was younger and word had spread about her family's reaper-hunting services, it seemed like new neighbors introduced themselves to her father every day. Some wanted to bargain with him for more of his steel bullets; only the ones made with the alloy he'd devised could reliably kill the reapers. Others wanted protection. The empire went from just distributing Saint steel to hiring ex-military who needed jobs and training young men around the neighborhood who were brave enough to hunt reapers. Back then, Elise enjoyed the fullness of their home. People who desired to enter the Saint inner circle brought with them some of her life-long friends. Though none, not even Mrs. Gray, with her scientific advancements and a tentative hope for a better future, were as special as the Quinns, who had been the ones to welcome the Saints to New York. But friendship wasn't enough to keep people safe.

The business grew larger every year, though the number of reapers seemed to keep up. Elise almost couldn't believe her father had gone from a steelworker in Texas to a top steel manufacturer and distributor in New York.

The car crossed Amsterdam Avenue into the Sugar Hill neighborhood, the noisy traffic fading. The Saint mansion stood on what had once been a block of brownstones, which had been leveled on Mr. Saint's order. Now the iron gates of the Saint estate rose before them, guarded by two of the Saint security officers, their silver badges and guns glinting in the dying light as they moved to let the car in.

Elise waited while Colm opened her door. But he suddenly shoved it shut again as one of the guards called out, "Miss, this is private property—"

Elise looked out the passenger window to see a brown-haired young woman standing just inside the gate.

"The monsters are in my neighborhood, and you must do something about them," she told the guard.

For a moment the young woman looked so familiar, a bitter name lodged in Elise's throat, and her heart lurched. But when she turned to get a better look, Elise realized she saw a stranger—not the girl she had left behind years ago, bloody and bruised.

The Saint guard tried to lead her away from the gate. "Tomorrow we'll send a patrol over—"

"No. They must be dealt with now," the woman snarled. She stepped toward the car and her sharp eyes met Elise's, her lips pulling back to reveal fangs. Elise scrambled back in her seat, though the car door separated them. Bloodlust swirled in the woman's dark irises, her veins bulging and ripe with hunger. But other than her shining eyes and fangs, the reaper looked utterly human. "*Murderers*. Layla Quinn will be avenged—"

A gunshot cracked through the air. The reaper's head exploded, and her body collapsed onto the pavement.

"All clear. Someone clean it up," a guard ordered.

Elise let out a shaky breath and shoved the car door open, avoiding the bloody mess at her feet. As she stumbled out, a gentle voice halted her panic.

"Relax, Lise. She's dead."

Elise looked up. "Sterling," she breathed. She could hardly believe she was looking Sterling Walker in the eye after five years of only exchanging letters. Blood covered her friend's shirtfront, and he held his gun arm steady, but he still smiled. He had gone from a young boy seeking refuge in their home to one of the Saint's leading reaper hunters.

His thumb traced a cross over the handle of his gun, then he lowered it. "Welcome home, Lise." Sterling leaned toward Elise, his amber eyes glowing in the dusk, and kissed her cheek. He had always been beautiful with his smooth brown skin and perfectly styled curls. But Elise thought he looked even more beautiful now. She eyed his gun, knowing every day he worked as a reaper hunter, he put his life on the line for the citizens of Harlem. And for her father.

Elise swallowed. Her music studies had kept her father content for this long, but she had no idea how it measured up to the bloody work his people did for him every day.

Elise wanted to hug Sterling, but the blood kept her back. "Are you all right?" she asked.

"I'm perfect. As always. The blood isn't mine; I've been on a patrol. I've still got an hour or two left of work, but I wanted to catch you as soon as you got home." That overly confident grin of his hadn't waned, and Elise was glad. People said distance made the heart grow fonder, but time also changed people. And she wasn't sure she could handle Sterling changing. Not when everything else in her life had changed so abruptly.

Elise glanced over at the body by the gate. "The reapers know I'm back now." She couldn't even bring herself to say Layla's name out loud.

Sterling shook his head. "Just that one. Whichever guard let

5

her onto our street is getting fired. Though I will admit, it's getting harder to tell the reapers from us. Good thing I caught her just now, otherwise the whole Harlem reaper clan might know you're here. We can't have that."

The mansion seemed even bigger than Elise remembered. It still stood, proud and lavish, with the marble columns and pristine hedges fronting the house. The Saint empire seal, with its image of a lotus flower and the North Star, was set into the brick floor of the front veranda. Colm had placed her luggage around the seal, not a single trunk or bag touching the embossed brass. Superstition ran high in the Saint empire, and it was not limited to the hunters who traced the shape of a cross over their gun handles.

The front door swung open. "Lisey!"

Elise hardly recognized her younger sister standing there, eyes bright. Gone were the chubby baby cheeks of a four-year-old: Josi was still little, but *so big*. When she flew into Elise's outstretched arms, Elise felt right at home. "I missed you so much, Josi."

"Mama said you were coming soon, but she didn't say when—"

"*Josephine.*" A stern voice broke in as their mother approached. "Back to your lesson, please."

"I'm sorry, Mama." Josi ducked her head and went to her mother's side. The light had gone from her eyes, which made a painful lump rise in Elise's throat.

6

"Claude is waiting for you. Go now," their mother ordered.

Josi shared one last look with Elise, then disappeared into the house. Her mother's attention finally settled on Elise. "Oh, Elise…"

Elise blinked. A tight smile found her lips, and she nodded. "Mother." Her skin prickled with unease as her mother's sharp eyes roamed over her, stopping at the scars on her throat. A fresh pain filled her eyes, and Elise had to steel herself to keep from looking away.

"Welcome home, my love." Elise accepted her mother's stiff hug and followed her down the hallway. "Heavens, I'm already exhausted. Your arrival was nearly catastrophic. It's distracting Josephine." Her mother paused at the bottom of the grand staircase. "She's worried about the reapers returning for you. I can't do this again."

"It won't happen again," Elise said quietly. She peeked over her mother's shoulder to see Josi sitting restlessly with her tutor. "She's been writing me about how excited she is to audition for the Paris ballet school. How have her practices been?" Elise asked.

Her mother's lips tightened into a flat line. "She has not been practicing. There's no time."

"What do you mean?" Josi was only ten years old. She could not possibly have that many responsibilities. "Mother, the instructors in Paris are much stricter than the ones we have here. Josi needs to be perfect—"

"*You* are here to celebrate the ten-year anniversary of this empire, Elise. Your priorities should be set on being perfect for your father. People need to see that the heir of this business is focused on—" Her mother sucked in a sharp breath and looked away. She reached up to push an imaginary loose curl behind her ear. "Let me worry about Josephine. You worry about yourself." She proceeded up the stairs.

Elise trailed behind. *Heir.* Elise didn't feel like the heir of the Saint empire. No, that role should have gone to someone whose name their family brought up only once a year, when they had enough time to prepare for the rolling pain that came with her memory. On the stair landing, Elise stared at the massive family portrait for the first time in five years and a shudder passed through her. The vibrant paint strokes could not conceal the absence haunting their family, the ghost that brought ruination to their memories.

"Your father is entertaining some new partners at the Savoy tonight," her mother called from the top of the stairs. "We will meet him there later."

Swallowing hard, Elise nodded. "Father is not home?" The news struck a chord of hurt in her, knowing she had been worrying about what he thought of her, yet he could not be bothered to be home for her. Another part of her felt distinct relief that she could put off facing him for a few hours.

"No, something came up at the factory."

Elise opened her mouth to say something, but her mother was already halfway down the hallway. She shook her head and continued to her room. Much to her disappointment, someone had pulled it apart, rendering it nearly unrecognizable from the state she had grown up in. Though the blood from her last night there was gone, thankfully. New white drapes identical to the ones she had when she was little surrounded her four-poster bed, which was still adorned with countless throw pillows and silk blankets. It was all recognizable enough, but she knew they were replacements to erase the bloodshed that had once filled her room. Even the books, the pictures, the records, the letters—the things that made her *her* were missing. The old Paris Conservatory music box she had wished on and wound up every night after piano class was gone, too—the main thing that had drawn her to Paris willingly, before Layla had given her no choice but to flee there. Elise had left so quickly all those years ago, she didn't even get to pack up her most precious belongings. And now they were gone. Her throat tightened with disappointment as she reached into her closet and picked out the nicest dress she could find.

The heart of Harlem came alive that night at the dance hall, and Elise stood witness to its allure. The music of the jazz band pulsed around her, shaking her bones and pounding between her heartbeats. The dance floor was a spectacle, and the lights strung throughout the club seemed to chase every sequin and crystal woven into the attire of the partygoers. The attendees were taking a risk to be out during prime reaper hours, their drunken haze and the threat of danger amplifying the thrill they sought.

Those who did not dance talked, their sharp voices carrying through the crowd. Politicians conferred with gangsters, their wallets pressed to their palms and spilling cash between their fingers. Actresses draped themselves over the tables, blowing out hot smoke as they twisted pearls around their necks and spoke of their dream roles. Stoic heiresses forced smiles and lifted their chins to ensure their jewelry caught the light. Money, class, and diplomacy mixed to create a bacchanal of chaos, the most dangerous cocktail.

Prohibition had been in effect for six years by now, but many had learned how to skirt the selective enforcement, especially in Harlem. An owner of such a glamorous establishment would be well connected and able to fend off, or pay off, any legal suspicions. People came to clubs in Harlem for more than just dancing, and tonight, it felt like everyone was at the Savoy, drinking and dancing beneath the cut glass chandelier. Racial integration occurred in the search for liquor and urban thrills.

Elise narrowly avoided colliding with a couple dancing the Charleston and bumped shoulders with Sterling.

"What do you think of the Savoy so far?" he asked. "It opened while you were away." He lifted a couple drinks from a passing waiter's tray stacked high with crystal glasses. "I'm assuming the clubs are not as colorful in France,"

"You assume wrong," said Elise, taking a glass from him. Admittedly, the Savoy Ballroom was glorious so far. As her eyes traveled over the vibrant crowd again, she spotted her mother and Josi near the tables. Her younger sister wore an expression of pure awe. She clapped wildly, silk bows in her hair stirring while she watched a row of costumed dancers over on the bandstand stage. Nearby stood her father, Tobias Saint, patriarch and leader of the ever-growing Saint empire, in deep conversation with a business associate.

"Elise, if you're not going to drink that, please allow me—" Sterling couldn't even get his words out before Elise downed her drink.

She wiped the back of her hand over her mouth and grinned. "Champagne is much better in France too." Elise's gaze slipped past her friend, finding her father's cold eyes staring right at her. His jaw had gone tight, and not a hint of warmth touched his expression. Then, almost as soon as Elise had caught his eye, her father turned, a smile cracking across his face while he continued the conversation with his companions.

Ice spiraled down Elise's spine. She breathed in deeply, trying to settle her nerves, but the thick air and the heat it carried made it nearly impossible. Sterling nudged his elbow into her side and nodded toward the dance floor. "Dance with me."

Elise shook her head. She had put off greeting her father for long enough. "I want to check on Josi first." She left Sterling by the edge of the dance floor and made her way through the crowd to her family. When Josi saw Elise, her face lit up, and she rushed right into Elise's arms.

"My angels," her father crooned. He looked the same as Elise remembered him—tailored black suit, silver cuff links glinting. The exhaustion in his black eyes betrayed the time more than his face. He turned back to his associate, an older Black man with a severe expression. "This is what I fight to protect," Elise heard him say.

The half-hearted acknowledgment stung, but she supposed it was better than his usual overbearing attitude.

Josi tugged on Elise's arm. "I want to go by the bandstand so I can see the dancers better!" She had begged to come tonight, and Elise never had the heart to tell her no. They began to make their way across the crowded dance floor. Elise's eyes scanned the crowd, stiff hands on Josi's shoulders to steer her clear of any commotion, but her sister seemed completely unfazed, bouncing along with the music. As they got closer to the stage, Elise's dress felt heavy. With each step brushing against the silk hems of the nearby revelers or catching on their jewelry, it felt less like luxury couture and more like an extravagant trap.

Suddenly, Josi's shoulders slipped from beneath Elise's fingers. Elise gasped, "Josi!" She tried to rush after her, but someone collided with her. Feathers from a woman's boa went up Elise's nose and into her mouth. For a moment, her world went black, and the music swallowed her panicked shriek.

"Oh, heavens, I'm so sorry!" the woman said as she finally drew away. By now, Elise had lost sight of Josi, and the crowd seemed to close in on her. But she finally spotted her sister, her white dress a beacon. The showgirl dancers formed a neat line at the edge of the stage, blowing Josi kisses.

Elise almost thought it was sweet. But then she saw the dancers' faces; what should have been radiant brown skin beneath the lights looked pale, as if their blood had been drained. Their eyes held a vacant stare in the bright stage lights. The sound of the crowd faded around Elise, and time seemed to slow as the dancers' bloodred lips stretched into wide slashes against their pale faces, teeth gleaming. One reached forward, hand outstretched toward Josi. Elise saw the dancer's eyes go black, a glimpse of fangs behind her sanguine-slicked smile.

A familiar face flashed in Elise's mind, sending her back to her blood-soaked bedroom five years ago, Layla crouching over her with dripping fangs and a ravenous snarl. She was too close. Josi would be next.

"Josi!" she shrieked. She stumbled, crashing into a waiter. His tray toppled over, and champagne sprayed the air.

The sound of shattering glass jolted Elise's senses back to the present. Only a few nearby guests stopped their dancing—the rest of the ballroom carried on, the music drowning out the commotion. On the stage, the dancers were shuffling away, feathered fans covering their faces.

Elise felt a strong hand clamp onto her shoulder. "Careful," her father muttered as he took her hand and helped her over the glass and champagne-soaked floor.

"Father—" she started, but he shook his head, pulling her out of the crowd. He waved to his guests to bid them goodnight. And while his smile never wavered, his grip grew so tight around Elise's hand that her fingers were numb by the time they made it out of the Savoy.

Elise could not hide her relief when Colm finally pulled up with the car and her father released her hand. She took her seat between

Josi and Sterling, and her parents sat opposite them. The moment the door closed, the smile dropped from her father's face.

Elise's heart rate picked up. "Did you see the reapers? They were there, weren't they?"

Her father snapped his focus to her. "What did you say?" he demanded.

"The dancers onstage… I saw the way they looked at Josi, and they had fangs—"

Sterling stiffened beside her. Even Josi lowered her gaze.

"There were no reapers," her father said.

"But—"

"Surely, Elise, you do not believe I would put my family in danger, do you?" her father asked.

Elise shook her head. "No." She noticed her mother's hand resting calmly on her father's shoulder.

"Then I assure you, there were no reapers in there." His tone softened and he leaned forward, taking her hands into his own. "It's possible that because of what you went through, you are seeing these things. You cannot trust these anxious thoughts. They will show you danger even when it does not exist."

Elise's heart beat so hard, her chest ached. She took a few deep breaths, forcing that familiar anxiety down, and nodded.

The car lurched forward into the night, darkness pressing around them from all sides.

2

LAYLA LOVED WHEN THE WORLD WENT DARK AND the city became hers to command. Shadows clung to every corner, creating perfect pockets of darkness to lurk in. Normally, Layla would stay close to the ground, weaving in and out of the shadows, but tonight she stood above the gloom.

She kneeled on the edge of the roof. The toe of her boot scraped the low wall that stood between her and a massive drop as she watched the pedestrians scattered around the streets below, their shouts and whistles ringing up through the air. Even this high up, Layla felt like one of the masses.

The roof shook beneath her feet with the rumblings of a party just below. Lights poured out of the skylight and they lit up the low-hanging clouds.

"Good lord," Mei said behind her. "One of these days, they're going to collapse the whole building."

"It's not a party if there's no blood," Layla muttered. She backed away from the edge of the roof and turned to look at her clanmate. Mei, like Layla, was dressed to blend into the night, black clothes clinging to her slim frame. The wind blew a few strands of Mei's dark hair into her face; as she swiped them away, Layla could see her hand shaking slightly.

Layla frowned. "You should really go back to the lair—"

"No, we need to get this over with. And I find it insulting that you think I cannot control my hunger," Mei said sharply. The shadows beneath her eyes stretched so deeply, they looked almost purple. What used to be delicate veins barely visible beneath her skin now bulged against her neck and hands, black and bitter with the need to feed. Mei bit her lower lip, and her fangs pierced it, drawing blood.

Layla narrowed her eyes. "You know Valeriya hates when we wait this long to feed—"

"And she hates not settling debts even more," Mei hissed. She began to say more, but the air filled with a new scent. It was fresh and human, tinged with a bit of raw apprehension. Both girls straightened their stances and listened for steps coming up the fire escape ladder. One by one, six men climbed on to the roof and approached them.

Layla studied the lapels of their black coats for their gang affiliation until she saw the diamond tattoos on their necks just above their collars. They were one of the smaller gangs and tended to use excessive violence to prove a point. In a city rampant with organized crime and most gangs bootlegging liquor, territories crossed often. Today, the Diamond Dealers had a blood dispute with the Harlem reapers. But Layla wasn't going to let them take anything back from her clan.

The one who was clearly the leader tipped his hat brim lower and spread his hands by his sides. "Where's our money?"

Layla lifted a brow. "Good evening to you too," she said.

The gang leader let out a sharp laugh. "No, it's not a good evening, because if it was, I would have my money. When you hunt my men, you pay up. Blood for blood. That's how it works."

Mei glared. "We did not hunt on your territory. If reapers killed your men, they were rogue and not of any clan. Certainly not ours," she spat.

The gangster moved his coat back and pulled out a silver revolver. The rest of his men stepped forward, brandishing their own weapons. Mei remained quiet by her side, though agitated and trembling.

"I could pay your clan leader a visit. But that didn't go well last time, did it? She delivered your reaper friend's head to me as payment for their crimes."

Layla winced. Sometimes Valeryia turned to violence to settle debts when a reaper had killed someone they shouldn't have.

"This is your last chance. Pay up, or I shoot," the man snarled,

The odds of him having Saint steel in his gun were slim. Most gangster's guns were illegally acquired and not specially made with a metal that could actually kill reapers. The Saints sold their bullets for excessively premium prices if they sold to gangsters at all. But regardless of the type of bullet these men had, getting shot would hurt.

Neither Layla nor Mei had money. The best they could do was

sell out whichever clanmate had crossed the gangster's boundaries, but even that was risky. She glanced out at the glittering skyline. Music from the party downstairs still thrummed beneath their feet, making Layla consider the way life carried on despite the atrocities that took place every day.

As Mei lifted a hand to speak, the gang leader pulled the trigger. White light exploded around them, sending Mei stumbling back. The scent of blood filled the air, metallic and bitter.

Layla turned to see Mei pressing her hand to her chest. To a gaping wound right over her heart.

A sinister smile cracked Mei's lips and she lifted a cold stare back to the gang leader as she lowered her hand, letting the blood spill. Layla caught the moment Mei's hunger took over her senses, her eyes going black. She tried to reach for Mei, to stop her, but her clanmate shot forward and pounced on the gang leader.

His blood sprayed as he fell back, and his gun went off, the bullet downing one of his men. The chaos broke out in full as the other men rushed at Mei. But her fangs sank into the throat of the next man to reach her. As a reaper, she was already much faster than a human. But while starving, she was an apex predator, spilling blood her only impulse. In only a few moments, she had taken down three more of the Diamond Dealers.

Layla watched calmly, her arms folded. A starved reaper bred carnage, and she knew intervening while Mei drank her weight in blood would only result in a bloodier battle. She surveyed the blood-bath with vague interest, taking note of each man that fell. But her breath caught when she realized the sixth man wasn't among the dying. Layla raced to the edge of the roof to find him, bleeding and panting, making his way down the fire escape. He glanced up at her and his foot slipped, sending him crashing down the ladder. His hand scrambled to catch one of the last rungs before he could plummet to the dark alley below.

Layla leapt from the roof and landed hard on the first platform, rattling the metal ladder. Her eyes glinted in the moonlight, and she saw the fear flash across the gangster's face. The smell of his blood filled the air, the wound at his side dripping over his shoes and into the darkness below. Layla's fangs pierced her gums as they emerged.

"Help me, and I will let your clan go," the man gritted out.

Amusement lifted the corners of Layla's lips. "I think *I'll be* the one letting *you* go tonight." She stomped the heel of her boot onto the man's fingers. Layla watched him fall, his screams ending in a satisfying choking noise. She hurried down the fire escape, forgoing the final ladder to jump down the rest of the way.

Her bones rattled as she hit the ground, but an electric adrenaline lit her veins at the overpowering scent of human blood. Heat rolled beneath her skin, her body tingling at the thought of the pure human life source running down her throat.

The gangster lay before her in a bloody heap. His breath left him in wet rattles, which only quickened as Layla stepped up to him. She kneeled and pressed her knee into his spine. A pained gurgle left him. Layla almost relished it. But the sound of footsteps approaching had her leaning down and covering his mouth with her hand.

The faint voices grew louder as two young women walked down the alley. Layla could sense their innocence: young blood and desperation all rolled into one. Blood spurted from the gangster's mouth, slipping between her fingers and coating her hand.

"You know nothing," one girl was saying. "I can't believe you're going to France to see *Swan Lake,* and you don't even know who wrote it."

Layla crouched in a pool of moonlight. As soon as the girls reached this part of the alley, they'd spot her if they looked over.

The other girl scoffed, "You don't know either."

"I do."

"Who is it, then?"

Just then, the two girls stepped into the moonlight, and Layla let out a rough laugh. The girls stopped. As Layla stood, their gazes slid over her.

"Tchaikovsky," Layla said.

She lifted a bloody hand to her lips and shushed them, her smile revealing her fangs.

Shrieking, the two girls ran out of the alley.

Layla watched with a bitter smirk. Only a few years ago, that had been her, whispering to her best friend about the roles she dreamed to dance in ballet. Now she stood over a dead gangster, her hands bloody from a fight she hadn't started.

Layla stood and looked up to the roof and shouted, "Mei!" No response. Sighing, Layla hauled herself back up the fire escape and onto the roof. She was met with a bloodbath that had somehow grown since she left it. Blood covered nearly every inch of the rooftop and had even splattered on the illuminated glass of the skylight. Mei was at the center of it all, her body limp and trembling.

She looked up as Layla approached. Blood smeared across her face and trickled from her mouth. Her fangs still protruded, their points digging into her lower lip. The usual dark brown of her eyes was glazed over with a golden sheen, her irises almost entirely black even in the moonlight. Her shirt was tattered and saturated with blood where she had been shot, but the wound was already mostly healed. Still, Mei swayed on her hands and knees, bloodlust ravaging her.

"I told you so," Layla hissed. "Now I have to drag you home so you can sleep this off."

Mei's eyes rolled back into her head, and she collapsed.

Layla groaned. She bent to lift her clanmate into her arms. While the night had taken an unexpected turn, Layla had to admit Mei had done them a favor, despite how risky they left the scene. Their clan would be debt-free and no one's target. For now.

Dawn light spilled across the floor like blood, its hues tinted red from the early sun. The other side of the bed was cold, but the smell of still-drying blood lingered on the sheets. Layla sat up at the harsh sounds of retching coming from her bathroom. "Mei," she called, getting to her feet. A nearby mirror showed bags hanging around her eyes, her dark skin failing to hide the blue marks beneath them. Despite having fed recently, she looked half-starved with her bloodshot eyes and nearly black irises. Their usual golden color had darkened to nearly black. There was no way she would be able to pass as a human, which would make today's tasks difficult.

After scraping her honey-brown curls into a decent braid down her back, Layla pushed past her brain fog to deal with her sick clan-mate. She nudged the bathroom door open and stopped in the door-way. Mei slumped over the toilet, her spine curved while she gagged.

Layla's nose wrinkled at the scent of old rotten blood. She clenched her teeth, fangs almost piercing her gums when Mei turned to face her. Her lips were dark red, eyes bloodshot. Clumps of spoiled blood clung to her chin. Layla sighed. "What did we learn from last night, Mei?" she muttered.

Mei dragged a hand across her mouth and stood, spitting. "Kill a whole gang to get a proper feast."

A sharp laugh left Layla, but she didn't smile. "Valeriya won't be happy."

"Valeriya is never happy," Mei muttered. "We should've brought her a gangster's heart. Maybe that would keep her quiet."

"You ruined them all." Layla glared. Their clan leader was prickly on a good day. But she was bound to show that icy ire they knew all too well when she found out about Mei's bloodlust-driven rampage from last night. They were lucky she had not been home when they arrived last night.

Layla tossed a towel at Mei, then stalked away. "You owe me new sheets." Her bed was a disaster. Blood soaked the side Mei had slept on, and there were tears in the bedding that Layla had only just noticed. Upon closer inspection, she realized there were rips down to the mattress. "You also owe me a new mattress," Layla grumbled.

Mei emerged from the bathroom, rolling her eyes. "If I hunt for you for a week, will you forget it?"

Layla rolled her eyes. "That is a bold offer from someone who just killed an entire gang and would benefit from laying low for at least a month."

"You say that like it's a bad thing. Harlem is better off without the Diamond Dealers running around. Less people to make us their enemies. And now we have their territory," Mei said, pushing her shoulder-length black hair behind her ears. "My instincts saved us an extra payment to the Cotton Club this month."

Layla lifted a brow. "As long as you understand that murder will not fix everything, I can let this go."

Mei scoffed. "You're one to talk."

Like most nightclubs, The Cotton Club looked rather lifeless in the daytime. The floors gleamed with fresh polish, the air heavy with its scent when Layla and Mei walked in before a long-limbed young blond man stopped them in the foyer.

"You know better than to walk in here, Quinn."

Layla knew this gangster: Jamie Kelly, leader of one of Harlem's biggest gangs, the Crooks. Because most people hated them, reapers

23

and gangsters had more allies in each other than with anyone else. Lawless and thirsty for violence, they shared similar territories. But boundaries persisted. Segregation prevented shifting loyalties between reapers and humans and racial mixing.

Jamie blocked the doorway to the club, arms crossed while he stared Layla down. "Your clan still owes dues from last month."

Mei glared at him. "We've brought our *final* payment. We won't be needing your territory to hunt on anymore."

Jamie glanced sideways at Mei. "Do you know something about the Dealers getting killed?"

Layla nudged her elbow into Mei's gut to keep her from saying more. The girl had been a reaper for nearly a decade longer, but when it came to instincts and maturity, Mei might as well have been a baby reaper. At times, Layla felt more like her guardian than her friend.

"Look, we heard about the Dealers," Layla said, passing him a wad of bills. "So until some other gang moves in, that territory is free for us."

"Fine," Jamie muttered. "Is that all?"

Layla cocked a brow at Jamie. "Tell Giana to come home. Valeriya wants a word with her."

"Anything else, Your Majesty?" The slightest hint of amusement clung to Jamie's words and for a moment, he actually looked his age. Layla couldn't imagine how he'd become such a cold gangster at only twenty. He was only two years older than her, but he had already racked up a reputation and body count that had most people scared to approach him. Layla didn't fear him—as a reaper, she didn't fear much, since she was able to rip out the throat of anyone as easily as one might peel an orange. But the law was different for gangsters than it was for reapers. Gangsters worked either outside it, or through it, bribing authorities and threading their business ties to corrupt and powerful judges. They flirted with the law and liked the bite of its warning. To appear in the newspaper was an accomplishment for a gangster, as it only made them more notorious and widely revered. But for reapers, any attention was closer to a death sentence. With hunters constantly out for them, laying low was a part of their existence.

Growing up, Layla had been taught to fear reapers and curse them with the same fury a Christian might condemn the devil with. Never did she anticipate becoming one.

"Tell Giana yourself." Jamie knocked on the backstage door, calling for her friend. When Giana emerged, she looked skinnier than ever, with a dazed look on her face. Her big brown eyes were ringed with black eyeliner and silver eye shadow that matched her fringe dress. With one look at the dark bags under her eyes and the blue veins that bulged on her temples, Layla could tell Giana was overdue for a feeding.

"You need to come home at some point, Giana." Layla noticed the chalky tone of Giana's usually radiant brown skin. "And go hunt."

Giana's lip curled. "Since when did you start commanding me?"

"I'm the only one who sticks around enough to listen to Valeriya and relay her messages. Maybe if you returned to the lair more often, you would have a better standing with the clan," Layla said coldly.

"Well, I'm not interested in letting this *condition* hold me back from my dreams. I refuse to let my life be dictated by such bullshit. At least some of us should still lead a normal life, right? Otherwise our existence is in vain," Giana muttered.

The words stirred a deep fury in Layla. Every good part of her life had been stolen from her by her reaperhood—an affliction dealt to her by the hands of someone she had once trusted. For years she had trained her anger to cool, but it was impossible to put aside an event that had changed her life forever. She still wanted to make the Saints pay for what they had done to her.

But she hated when other reapers tried to act like their lives were normal. There was nothing normal about their tendencies, or the way they were made. Layla was sick of the delusion.

"Mei had an incident. So you need to be extra careful around here, because we cannot afford any more slipups," Layla said through gritted teeth.

Giana's eyes darkened. "Everyone knows about Mei. Jamie's men have been whispering about it all morning. She's the only one in danger."

Layla took a deep breath, forcing the rise of anger back down. "We all stick together. Whatever happens to one reaper affects us all. You know this. No one *here* has your back. Did it ever occur to you how twisted it is to be hired by a club that wants to profit from your talents, but won't allow your own people to be your audience?"

"I must support myself somehow. If I need to dance for the whites, then I will." Giana petted the thick white fur pelt that hung across her shoulders, over her dazzling dress.

Irritation clawed up Layla's spine. But she bit back a sharp response and sighed. "Just come home sometime today."

After Giana had disappeared backstage, Layla turned back to Jamie, who was watching her and Mei with twinkling blue eyes. "Anything else you need to tell us, Jamie?"

A muscle popped in his cheek as he threw her a sidelong look. Jamie reached into his pocket and pulled out a thick piece of paper. On it was the unmistakable Saint seal: the lotus flower and North Star. "The Saint empire's ten-year celebration. I thought you might want to know. You know, because of your little vendetta." Jamie grinned at Layla.

She wanted to smack the smile off his face. "Why do you have this?" Layla demanded.

Jamie shrugged. "My men have more connections than you know of, Quinn. I would worry about what this anniversary means for your little clan."

If normal humans hated reapers, then the Saints had a blood oath with the devil to keep reapers contained. For years they'd been allied with the New York City police to control the reaper population. Though these days it seemed less about control and more about eradication. And Layla had known the Saints, back when her parents were still alive. She had been close enough to Elise once that she was practically considered a member of the Saint family. That was before everything went to hell.

Sometimes she still woke up screaming in fury, from dreams where blood coated her hands after hunting Elise down. The night they'd separated was still fresh in Layla's mind even if it had happened years ago. Her heart had never healed. And she hoped Elise's never did either.

3

I N THE DINING ROOM OF THE SAINT MANSION, ELISE sat rigidly in her white silk gown, pearls weighing on her neck. Her father had insisted on this family dinner but he hadn't yet come to the table.

Just a few minutes ago, she had gone to knock on his office door to tell him dinner was ready, the way she used to when she was younger and would tug him down to the dining room while he tried to guess what would be served.

But her mother had caught her hand and hissed, "You are not to interrupt him. He will come on his own. Go sit down."

Elise's face still burned with embarrassment.

Finally, when the ancient grandfather clock in the corner of the room chimed seven o'clock, their father walked in.

"My beautiful family." His deep voice filled the room. He stopped next to his wife to place a gentle kiss on her cheek before taking the seat at the head of the table. "My beautiful, perfect family. Last night was a spectacle, but *this* is irreplaceable. It has been ages since we had a proper family dinner like this, and we must commemorate the moment." The table wasn't so big that it would keep Elise from reaching across to touch her parents' hands if she wanted to. But somehow her father seemed a great distance away.

"Dinnertime!" Josi cheered.

"*Josephine*—" their mother scolded.

But Mr. Saint just shook his head and spoke under his breath, "Analia." He reached into his jacket and brandished a small black box. "Josi, come."

Josi wasted no time in scrambling out of her chair to his side. Her eyes widened as he opened the box for her. "This is mine?" Josi asked, stunned.

Mr. Saint raised the box so the whole table could see. Inside the box was a silver signet ring, the Saint family seal engraved on the front.

Mrs. Saint nodded her approval. "Remember, Josephine, when you turned ten, you accepted new responsibilities. That includes keeping track of your jewelry," she said to Josi.

Josi slipped the ring onto her finger and danced around the room, her eyes never leaving the new gleaming silver on her hand. A small smile lifted Elise's lips as she watched her younger sister's joy. Then she felt her father's hand on her shoulder, gentle, but firm. He slid a tiny box in front of her, red velvet with gold flowers embossed on the front.

"For you, my pearl," her father murmured. He stood and placed a soft kiss on the crown of her head.

In the box was a signet ring identical to Josi's, but gold. It glowed against the black velvet interior of the box. Elise's breath left her body when she realized exactly what her father was emphasizing with these gifts.

Everyone would see the wearer of this ring for a member of the Saint empire. And with such a well-known symbol, Elise would be recognized everywhere she went. These rings... Their sacredness rivaled that of the one her mother wore. Hers was a wedding band that promised loyalty to her father, while Elise's ring was one that swore loyalty to her family's empire.

"Thank you, Father." Elise smiled tightly as her father took his seat.

He raised his champagne flute. "This weekend, we celebrate a decade of this business as well as ten years of Elise's success with her music." His focus settled on Elise. "I do hope you will have some good news following your auditions, my pearl."

Elise's breath stalled in her chest. Soon, she would announce her acceptance into the Paris Conservatory. She hoped her father would be proud of her. "Perhaps," she said quietly.

Something bright sparked in her father's eyes. "You've survived a lot. It's not easy to go on after such upheaval in your life. But you persevered. And I want you to show everyone that a Saint never backs down. A Saint never kneels. A Saint never falls."

The room seemed to still with the intensity of his voice, and Elise swallowed hard. Darkness shrouded her mother's face while her father shared a look with her, nodding slightly. Mr. Saint cleared his throat. "The Saint empire has become something of a marvel these past ten years. But we must never forget why we began."

Her mother's breath grew shaky; Josi's doe eyes settled on Elise, a deep sadness clouding them. Elise ducked her head as her father continued to speak. "We celebrate our success now, but more than anything, we celebrate Charlotte's life. My Charlotte, taken too early by the greatest evil known to man. Charlotte, my first heir and my true saint."

Mr. Saint rose and walked slowly to the fireplace at the front of the room, where he lifted an ornate box from the mantel. Elise's chest grew heavy as he placed the box in the middle of the table and opened it. Inside sat a silver revolver. All air vanished from Elise's lungs.

It held the same shine it had ten years ago, when Elise had seen her older sister wield it to defend her life. They had been playing chess that night—Charlotte teaching Elise some of her favorite sneaky moves. The windows of the old house—the brownstone on 148th Street where they lived on the first floor—rattled in the wind of the impending storm. Their parents were out; it was rare for both of them to be gone at once, but the Quinns had insisted on treating them to dinner while Layla endured an evening dance rehearsal. Elise remembered her tooth was loose, and Charlotte kept begging to pull it out for her. The moment she let her—the moment the first drop of blood dribbled down her chin—something smashed through the nearest window.

The world seemed to move in a blur after that. Elise could only remember her older sister dragging her into their parents' bedroom, her hand fumbling on the handle of her father's revolver as she pushed Elise into a wardrobe. Elise didn't even know the thing could lock, but she banged on the door from the inside and screamed so hard her voice went hoarse. Still, she could hear her sister's gun firing and the sound of snarling reapers throughout the house. Until finally, her gun stopped and nothing but silence and the scent of blood filled the air.

That first attack from anonymous reapers had spawned fear that altered Elise's entire world. The next attack, years later and by her own friend, had shattered it.

Mr. Saint turned to Josi and Elise, eyes red lined and shining. "Her death made me realize I needed to do more to protect all of you. The bullets were not enough. Now we have trained men who act as protectors of this city—everywhere you look, there is Saint influence. You two carry on Charlotte's legacy. You live because of her sacrifice," Mr. Saint muttered. He traced his finger over the engraved cross on the handle of the gun. "For this ten-year celebration, it's important to establish new ambitions. We have lasted this long building the business on Charlotte's death, but now we move forward with the empire powered by a new life." Mr. Saint looked at Josi, whose eyes were transfixed on the gun. "You never met Charlotte, my love, but you carry her in you. For that reason, her legacy is yours. You are our last Saint, but now you are my first heir."

Elise's breath stuttered out of her. "Josi?" she whispered.

Her sister went to her father and wrapped her arms around his neck, leaning her head against his shoulder, her brown eyes wide on the glimmering future set before her.

Born after her death, Josi had never known Charlotte. But that also meant she did not know the violence that had torn Charlotte's young life from her, and was too young to remember the years of spilled blood that followed. To be attached to such horrors at Josi's young age… Elise hated it. But she also wondered if it was inevitable because of who they were and what their family represented. Elise's first experience with reapers had been a baptism into violence. She'd been introduced to malice before most children; being a young Black girl, vulnerability was inherent, protection nonexistent. Even in a world where there were beasts that fed on blood and drank human hearts dry, Elise often felt less than human, worse than every reaper in existence.

Perhaps there was no hope for Josi either. Josi stared at her new ring with the brightest eyes, as if she held the entire world on her finger. For the Saint empire to one day be this young girl's responsibility made Elise's stomach turn.

"Yes, Elise. Someone must take over the empire when I die. Josi will begin hunter training soon at our base and her lessons will pivot to strategy," Mr. Saint said. "Josi is such a young, new life, the reapers here have no existing strife with her. Unlike you. You have endured multiple attacks. The Harlem reapers still want your blood, Elise. A reaper that tastes human blood never forgets. You were safe in France, where no one knew you, and that is why we cannot risk you being here for longer than is necessary."

Elise's heart pounded.

"Daddy, will I still get to dance?" Josi asked.

Mr. Saint shook his head. "Not anymore."

The Saint empire was bound to eat her little sister alive. Elise thought she might die if Josi's light was extinguished for the sake of this cruel business.

"No fair. Lisey got to do her music in France."

A small chuckle left Mr. Saint. "You will be doing much greater things here, my love."

Heat exploded across Elise's cheeks and behind her eyes. Her father did not care about her endeavors. She clenched her jaw as the letter from the Paris Conservatory burned in her mind.

Elise considered the childhood Josi deserved, slipping away right before them. Gone, like Charlotte's life, before it could even begin.

Layla dreamed of music. But it was not the lilting, delicate music she used to spend hours dancing to as a little girl. It was a haunting melody that she had only ever replayed in her mind while conjuring up images of blood-soaked snow, of her own fingers digging into the feeble throat of her most bitter enemy. It was Elise Saint's song.

The second this thought came to mind, Layla forced herself awake.

After running around the city all day, trying to deal with the mess Mei had created and urging clan members to return for a meeting, she'd had no energy left. But this dream had her jumping out of bed and rubbing her eyes. Layla would rather go days without sleep if it meant not having to confront the demons of her past before she'd been a reaper.

She left her room and made her way to Valeriya's study. No light shone beneath the closed door, but Layla knew her mentor liked to work in the dark. She pushed open the door and was immediately hit with the strong scent of ancient tomes. Somehow, Valeriya kept the pages of hundreds of books intact in the centuries that she had been living. No one was allowed into her study, but Valeriya had made an exception for Layla when she was first turned, and since the boundary had been breached, Layla continued to cross it. She still wasn't sure what made Valeriya take her in that night. She'd been thirteen years old and terrified—not the youngest reaper to join Valeriya's clan, but Layla supposed she must have looked extra pathetic when she'd wandered in that night, with nothing but despair and fear to her name. Valeriya had noticed her tears; she'd shut her drawer full of human hearts and pulled Layla into her arms to comfort her.

A light flashed in the dark now, the striking of a match bringing Layla back to the present.

Valeriya sat at her desk. The candlelight illuminated her beautiful features, the shadows sharpening her cheekbones and making her eyes blacker than the night itself.

"Some Saint men stopped by," she said. "There was a reaper attack a few days ago in the Heights and they think we had something to do with it. Unsurprisingly, they had nothing to say about the Diamond Dealers."

"No one cares about gangsters," Layla muttered.

Valeriya looked at Layla, and her perfume, the haunting scent of crushed roses, filled the room. "I'm sure you are to thank for keeping that bloodbath mostly quiet."

Layla accepted the gratitude with a careful nod. "Did the Saints make any threats?" Giana had never returned to the lair, and Layla tried not to think about her going into a starved, murderous rampage just like Mei had.

"A threat, a promise..." Valeriya held up a letter, sighing. "They will remove this hotel from our possession if the attacks continue. This agreement is hardly a year old, Layla. We cannot afford to ruin it so soon. If we lose this lair, I'm finished. No more managing human-reaper affairs. I've had it with this hell."

Layla flinched. "But the Diamond Dealer territory is open now—"

"Not the point," Valeriya snapped. "There are plenty of animals to feed on, even in the city. No hunting humans as long as we are in agreement with the Saints. We are not rogue reapers."

Layla swallowed. "About that... I have news."

"Speak." Valeria reached for the crystal glass at her side and took a sip. Blood coated her lips as she lowered it.

Layla pressed her palms against the desk so her hands wouldn't shake. "Elise Saint is back. The Saints are having a ten-year anniversary celebration, and there is no way she would miss that," Layla said.

Valeriya lifted a brow. The darkness made it hard to read her face, but the small quirk of her lips told Layla she was rather impressed with the news. "You're sure?"

"Positive." Layla slid the Saint invitation from Jamie onto the desk between them.

Layla still didn't know for sure, but Elise was eighteen now, and she would have graduated from her fancy Paris school. And there was no way she would stay away from her younger sister for this long. If Elise wasn't back in New York by now, then she might as well be dead.

"Do you still want to lie low?" Layla grumbled. "The Saints have been running this city for the past ten years and whatever they are planning now can only make things worse for us. You hate living under their rule just as much as I hate Elise."

Valeriya released a sharp breath. "I know you want to hurt Elise—"

"I want her dead. For what she did, she deserves death," Layla seethed. Before becoming a reaper, such words never would have left her mouth. But after a night that left ghosts terrorizing her dreams, a winter full of blood, and a cracked heart, Layla was no longer the forgiving young girl the Saints had known her to be. And she was tired of letting them run the city while everyone suffered at their hands.

"I never should have told you it was the Saints who caused your ruination," Valeriya said. "You're absolutely vexed by them now." Layla's eyes rolled and Valeriya sighed. "Yes, we need to destabilize the Saints. But, Layla, there is no room for mistakes here. We do not need a repeat of last time."

Layla felt the years of built-up fury finally settling in, ready to be released. She flashed her mentor a bitter smile. "This time I won't fail."

4

"DO YOU THINK LAYLA KNOWS YOU'RE BACK?"
Sterling asked.

Chills traversed Elise's spine at the sound of that name. She glanced in the mirror at her friend, who leaned back in her vanity chair. His tie was undone and his jacket open, but the relaxed energy he radiated did not reach Elise.

Elise sighed. "If she did, she would have made it known by now. I've been home for five days."

Sterling pulled a fan from Elise's vanity drawer and opened it with a snap of his wrist. "I don't know… Reapers are good at sneaking."

Elise turned and snatched the fan from him. "I don't want to talk about her. Tonight is our last night together; let's make the most of it." She adjusted her silver hairpiece for the fourth time.

"Nervous?" Sterling asked.

"Always." Elise pursed her lips. "My father expects my

performance to be perfect, and he wants a ten-year-old to be a perfect representative for the future of the empire. It's a lot."

"Elise." Suddenly, Sterling was in front of her, lifting her chin with gentle fingers.

He was the one who had pulled Layla off a bleeding and traumatized Elise five years ago in the middle of the night. Elise owed him her life, but the best she could give him was her friendship.

Now his hazel eyes met her brown ones, and a dimple creased in his cheek with his smile. "You're a piano prodigy. You will be perfect tonight; you always are."

Elise wished she could tell him she was not perfect. And everyone expected her to be. The expectations weighed her down, her self-worth bending beneath the pressure. Still, Elise nodded at her friend. "Sure, but the reapers—"

Scoffing, Sterling moved his jacket back, revealing two guns at his waist. "I'm not the only one who has come prepared tonight, Lise. You should see the grounds; I don't even think a squirrel could make it inside this place without ending up full of bullets." He squeezed her hand and smiled. "Everything will be fine."

The anniversary party began with a bang that seemed to resound throughout all of New York. In the Saint mansion, the polished floors glittered with confetti and gold licked over every surface. The ballroom chandelier had been replaced just for the party. Instead of brass and glass, gold and crystals hung from the ceiling, gold foiled streamers spiraling out from the center and cascading down the walls.

Elise wore a shimmery jade dress that draped over her body like water over stones. Her eye makeup glittered in the light and she couldn't resist smiling at herself in the mirror, lips as red as the ruby polish coating her nails. Pearls hung around her throat, yet as beautiful as they were, she could only focus on her family ring.

Saint guards stood near every entrance and window, their focus sharp and unflinching on the growing crowd in the ballroom. Elise would never get used to having these strangers around, but Sterling nodded to them as he walked by. For the first time since being home, Elise noticed the tension in his shoulders and a crease between his brows.

A dark-haired woman approached them. Elise, not keen on interacting with a stranger, braced herself until the woman's eyes met hers, and recognition struck. "Thalia?" Elise stuttered out.

Thalia Gray still had the same deep brown eyes that seemed to hold the answer to every problem in the world. She wore not a dress, but a tailored suit with satin gloves. Elise stared at her old friend, taking in every inch of her.

"Thalia, you have a lot of explaining to do," Sterling said sharply.

Thalia flicked her wrist at Sterling, waving him off. "Step aside, Walker. Let me greet my old friend." Thalia pulled Elise into her arms.

"I didn't know you were coming," Elise exclaimed.

Sterling scoffed by her side. "Neither did I. No one did."

"Some people knew. The important people." Thalia laughed and Elise couldn't help but laugh along with her. Sterling, however, remained stiff.

"Is your mother here?" Elise asked, looking around the crowded room.

Thalia rolled her eyes. "No. The bad blood persists."

Mrs. Gray had once been a part of the Saints' inner circle. It was a miracle Thalia's mother let her spend time in the Saint household when they were younger, even when Tobias Saint no longer found use for her scientific endeavors. After Mrs. Gray's working antidote for reaper bites had failed on Charlotte, Tobias Saint dismissed the Grays. But Thalia refused to give up on being Elise's friend.

Elise tugged on Sterling's sleeve. "You wrote to me saying you two were finally getting along." She could still remember their squabbles. The only thing Thalia and Sterling had in common was Elise. She had worried they would kill each other when she was in France.

"I'd call what we did 'stress relief,'" Thalia said.

Sterling's eyes went wide and a dark flush filled his ears. "You cannot be serious."

Thalia flagged down a waiter and plucked a champagne flute from his tray. She held her finger up, sipping the bubbly liquid while Sterling watched her with increasing irritation. Once finished, Thalia lowered her glass and clicked her tongue. "Indeed, I am serious."

Elise exhaled. "I cannot believe this."

"Sterling got too attached. It started taking time away from my research, so I ended it. Whatever our little 'tryst' was."

Sterling clenched his fists. "You leaving for Switzerland for a month without notice was not ending anything. It was disrespectful," he snapped.

"Oh, Switzerland had nothing to do with you and everything to do with me furthering my research. As long as I'm here, I must make up for where my mother fell short. Now, please." Thalia leaned in to kiss Elise's cheek. "It's been lovely seeing you. Good luck tonight." In a matter of moments, Thalia was gone, having disappeared into the crowd.

Sterling sighed. "Elise. I'm going to sound absolutely mad, but I swear, the more hostile she is toward me, the more attracted I am to her."

Elise laughed. "I don't understand you."

"I told you. Madness." Sterling threw a longing look over the crowd. "I'm going to check on the guards. Shout if you need me."

Elise nodded. And with one final squeeze of her hand, Sterling was gone.

She glanced around the room, looking for Josi, but came face-to-face with her mother instead. Analia Saint, dressed in a white dress and layered pearl necklaces, silver comb placed perfectly on her black finger waves, looked like a picture of pure grandeur.

"That's not the dress we decided on, Elise," she said sharply, before she moved on to speak to a guest.

Elise's stomach turned. Being around so many people always made her nervous, but tonight, knowing her family was on the brink of forging a new future for everyone, made her feel especially ill.

Relief washed through her when she finally spotted her younger sister. Josi's curls were fastened into a sleek bun with white silk bows that matched her dress.

"Hi, my dove." Elise tried to pull Josi into her arms, but the girl was far too bubbly to be contained. She grinned, bouncing on the balls of her feet.

"I get to show everyone my ring!" Josi exclaimed, flaunting it. "I'm Josephine Mireille Saint and I am the heir to the Saint empire." Her smile widened. "My sister is going to be the best pianoist in France—"

"It's *pianist*, darling." Their mother had waltzed back over to fuss with Josi's curls. Josi tried to back away, but their mother's grip dug into her wrist. "Where's your coat? Good heavens, you've had it for only a day, Josephine, don't tell me you already lost it."

"It's in my room." Elise gently pulled Josi back. "I'll get it."

Her mother nodded slowly. "While you're up there, please change into the dress we picked out earlier."

It was meant to be a quick stop in her bedroom to put on a new dress. But the sight of the curtains billowing in the evening breeze and her white carpet alight with the glow of the sunset made her pause.

She still remembered jolting awake, the stars bright in the night sky, to hear footsteps nearing her bed. The next moment, her back was on the floor, Layla's hands around her throat. Elise could still feel the pierce of Layla's nails. But the crescent moon scars they left on her neck were the least of her injuries from that night. And even though the ruined flesh above her heart was a constant reminder of the attack, the most pain came from beneath the scars. Ghosts lurked. Sometimes they whispered, sometimes they screamed, other times they were just faint enough to pull Elise's focus and settle under her skin, nudging and pulling at her until she wanted to rip her own flesh to bits. Most days, Elise wanted to step out of her body and watch herself break. She couldn't determine what caused the pain—loneliness, guilt, regret, anger—whatever it was, it was burrowed so deeply in her, Elise feared it would never leave her.

Layla Quinn consumed her thoughts.

Was there something Elise could have done to prevent the violence they shared between them? To prevent Layla from turning into a monster—

Elise's jaw tightened. *No.* It wasn't her fault.

Sometimes Elise imagined what she would say to Layla should they ever cross paths. She wrote it in the margins of her sheet music during practice when she couldn't focus. When the music wouldn't flow from her due to the agony tearing her thoughts apart.

I still feel you under all of my scars. It still hurts.

Over and over Elise scribbled those words, willing them to lose their meaning. But the pain never left.

She wondered if Layla ever felt the same way. If she ever thought about Elise as much as Elise's mind called for her.

Sometimes it didn't make sense to Elise how her feelings contradicted each other. The aching sadness that rushed through her at the sight of her childhood bedroom was followed by a quick burst of fury. Fury at the person that made her afraid of a space that was supposed to be sacred to her.

Elise slammed her window shut. The curtains fell still, and silence filled the room, but anger continued trembling through Elise's hands.

A knock at her door forced Elise to relax. She turned to see Josi, with Sterling standing just behind her.

"Mother sent us to check on you. It's almost time for you to play!" One of Josi's ribbons had come undone, and it hung loosely down the back of her neck. If she noticed, she didn't care. "Oh, and there's my coat. Thank you, Lisey." She pulled the coat over her shoulders and ran out of the room.

Elise couldn't help but smile as she and Sterling followed her sister down the hallway. The back of Sterling's hand brushed against her wrist, and she looked up at him. "I liked being her brother for these last few years, but I am glad you're back," he said.

A gentle laugh escaped Elise. "You can still be her brother. In fact, she'll need you more than ever now." Elise felt the hard ridge of one of his revolvers as he nudged her with his hip. She squeezed his hand. "Do not leave her side tonight."

Sterling nodded. "Of course."

For the first time all week, Elise played for an audience. Her fingers flew gracefully over the piano keys while the song unfurled around the massive room. Hundreds of people watched her, but she paid them no mind. When Elise played, she lost herself in the music. The Bach piece she had chosen to perform for the party was a complex one that she'd stumbled through as a child and eventually dissolved her confidence with each mistake. Now, she played it flawlessly.

The silence that passed after her last note seemed to stretch on for an eternity. But then the room exploded into enthusiastic cheers.

Elise stood and took a bow. As she straightened up, she looked for her father. His smile of approval made her chest feel light with relief. Elise made her way off the stage to stand with her family.

Mr. Saint addressed the crowd with a champagne glass clutched in his hand. "I must say, I don't think I've heard proper music since my daughter went off to Paris," Mr. Saint said. A low chuckle rumbled through the room. "This city prides itself on its music, but it is often overshadowed by the horrors we face on most days. Ten years ago I lost my eldest daughter and founded this empire. Together, we have rid our home of many reapers and I hope, earnestly, that we continue to do so to keep her name and this city alive." Mr. Saint raised his glass. "I would like to open the floor to toasts. First, I begin by blessing my lovely daughter, Josephine, with the duties of first heir to this empire." He threw Josi an endearing smile and she grinned back. "Next, I wish my daughter, Elise, continued success with her musical endeavors." Elise couldn't help but notice that his proud smile had faded and was more strained than the one he'd given Josi. Elise's own happiness wavered as she nodded to him.

Mr. Saint continued, "It is with great excitement and pride that I welcome a new initiative to this Saint empire. We have spent so long eliminating the beasts that plague our home, but now I believe it is time to turn to new avenues of danger prevention. Miss Thalia Gray, a talented, ambitious young scientist whom I have known for many years, has excelled in her reaper research. She is close to developing an antidote to the poison in reaper bites and, with her help, our empire will grow stronger than ever, and reapers will become less of a threat."

Excited murmurs moved throughout the room, and Thalia beamed from her seat a few tables away, lifting her hand to wave at everyone. Elise's stomach flipped. Who cared about piano and music when a possible solution to reaperhood was at hand?

"Lastly, but certainly not least, I announce a partnership with Stephen Wayne, the broker and philanthropist. He actually encouraged me to start this business many years ago when he saw how powerful my Saint steel was against reapers." Elise recognized Mr. Wayne, who stood while impressed gasps sounded around the room. "Mr. Wayne funds a lab for reaper research and advocates for human-reaper legislation. With his and Miss Gray's assistance, I am positive we can make headway into eliminating reaperhood." Mr. Saint beamed, lifting his glass once more. "Toasts and blessings to the future of the Saint empire. Together, we rise."

The party carried on through the night. Though the nine-piece band was still playing strong at ten p.m., Elise retreated to her bedroom with Josi, where they sneaked chocolate-covered strawberries, whispering and laughing. By the time Sterling had come in to check on them, Josi had fallen asleep in Elise's bed, despite the booming music and noise downstairs.

Elise slipped out into the hallway with Sterling. "Very brave of you to skip your patrol shift just to spend more time with me. The estate grounds need you," she teased.

"Not skipping it, just taking an unapproved break. Besides, I have to say goodbye to you. I miss you already," Sterling said.

Elise looked over at her steamer trunk that the servants had packed, waiting near the hall elevator, and her heart ached with the thought of leaving soon.

"We're not complete without you here," Sterling told her. "Josi really needs you. And so do I."

Elise touched his wrist and forced a smile. "I've been accepted to the Paris Conservatory. I must go back."

Warmth lit Sterling's eyes. "Elise, that's incredible. Why didn't you say anything earlier?"

"It's not a big deal. Especially not with the ten-year anniversary and everything else." Elise shrugged. "I'm going to tell my parents soon. I hope my father approves."

"Of course he will." Sterling playfully flicked Elise's chin and she laughed. "I'm proud of you," he said, voice soft.

Just then a high-pitched shriek split the air.

It hadn't come from the party. It had to be Josi.

Blood went to ice in Elise's veins as she and Sterling pushed open her bedroom door. Josi was standing on her bed, shaking so hard the entire frame seemed to move with her.

"What happened?" Elise gasped. It wasn't like Josi to have nightmares, but no one else was in the room.

Sterling lifted Josi into his arms. Fresh tears glimmered on her lashes, brown eyes sharp with fear. "Monster," she whimpered.

Elise and Sterling exchanged looks. "You don't think—" Elise began.

"Let's take her to her room to make sure she's okay," Sterling said, carrying Josi to the door.

"Just give me a moment," Elise said. She got down on her knees and lifted the bed skirt to peer beneath the bed. Just as she had hoped, there was nothing lurking in the darkness. She stood up, sighing, but to her dread felt a brush of cold air. The window was open.

The curtains billowed with the night air. Chills rose on her arms. Elise took a deep breath as she walked to the window and looked out. Aside from a slight sway of the hedges caused by the breeze, nothing moved in her view. She stepped back and closed the window.

Deafening silence surrounded her, the room suddenly too still and the air too tense. Elise froze. She clenched her fists until her Saint ring pinched her palm, then turned around.

And came face-to-face with Layla Quinn.

Cold metal dug into Elise's throat. The reaper held a blade, its silver edge angled right against Elise's pulse point. Moonlight glinted off the knife and illuminated the golden hues in Layla's eyes. Her lips curled into a wicked smile. "Long time no see, *Saint*."

5

PANIC SWARMED ELISE'S SENSES. HER HEART spasmed, her body froze, and for a second, she returned to this very same moment five years ago.

A wild fury lit Layla's eyes. Before, Elise had convinced herself that the feral state Layla attacked her in had been involuntary; the ire in her eyes was the kind that was only conjured up by newly turned, starved reapers.

But today was different. Layla was watching her with pure malice. Elise knew it was not merely an instinctive frenzy but a rage-induced hunt—personal and set to kill.

"Back to ruin more lives, are you?" Layla hissed, fingers tightening on the knife's handle. She shoved Elise back against the wall so hard, Elise's skull snapped with a searing pain. "Mine wasn't enough for you?"

Anger flared in Elise, her chest going hot. She pressed forward, and the blade bit into her throat. The close contact pushed Layla slightly off-balance. It was all Elise needed to back away from her and lift the heavy gold hand mirror from the bedside table. Warmth trickled down her throat, and as Elise raised the mirror, her blood splattered onto the glass.

"You're the one who put a knife to my throat. And you scared my sister. I'll fucking kill you—" A snarl seared through Elise's words. She didn't think about how hard it would be to kill a reaper without proper training and weapons. She didn't think about the force and blessed metal that was necessary to stop an ancient reaper heart. All Elise could process was her own rage, the stifling, burning anger that pulsed through her at the thought of Layla anywhere near her sister. *I will not lose someone else to a reaper.*

Elise's hand tightened around the mirror's handle, then she threw herself at Layla. Layla's nails raked down her arm and Elise was able to graze a sharp corner of the mirror against Layla's cheek.

Sterling came rushing into the room, gun raised. He stepped between them and threw one arm out to prevent Elise from coming forward.

By the time Sterling had a steady stance and aim, Layla was at the window. Her eyes still fixed on Layla, Elise reached for the other gun in Sterling's holster. She pulled the trigger and the window shattered around Layla as the bullet erupted.

The young reaper merely cracked a cruel smile. Sterling's arms closed around Elise as she tried to lunge forward once more. Layla leapt out of the window and into the night.

The drop from the second-story window jolted Layla's bones. Anger blurred her vision. Everywhere she looked, she saw red—vicious, crimson cracks split her focus. But with ire fueling her adrenaline and Elise's blood filling her nose, Layla felt nearly invincible. She lifted her hand, watching the blood drip from beneath her nails. Whatever marks she left on Elise—Layla hoped they scarred.

With a bitter smile, Layla licked her fingers. No matter how many times she fed, the taste of human blood always sent an electric current through her. Elise's tasted even better than she remembered. Layla was half tempted to believe she could pick out every ounce of fear and anger in just a drop of Elise's blood.

"Franklin!" A distant light sparked as a man's voice rang around the dark yard.

Nearby lay the guard Layla had knocked unconscious in order to slip into Elise's room undetected. He stirred as the other guard continued to call his name.

Imagining the look on Tobias Saint's face when he realized his men had failed at their job that night almost made Layla smile. As she stepped over the man, pain shot across her ribs. Lifting her shirt, she cursed. The bullet had grazed her. Though the cuts from the glass and the mirror were already sealing themselves shut, this bullet wound would not heal on its own at normal reaper speed. The Saint steel bullet meant to stop reaper hearts blocked the properties in reaper blood that sped up their healing time. Blood soaked her shirt, already draining her energy.

Normally Layla could go a week without a full feeding, but the lost blood made a fresh hunger rise in her. And the taste of Elise still fresh on her tongue released a frenzied need in her. She wiped the blood off her face, wincing a bit when her cut stung, and stalked off the Saint estate grounds.

A melancholy song from a nearby jazz club greeted her as soon as she made it onto St. Nicholas Avenue.

Gee, but it's hard to love someone

When that someone don't love you.

I'm so disgusted, heartbroken too.

I've got those downhearted blues…

Layla's mind wandered to those old desires of being in a dance studio and letting the music lead her body. It had been years, yet the urges never left her. Layla clenched her fists and stalked forward. With their heads down and gazes averted, no one on the street knew a monster lurked beside them. She wondered how quickly people would scatter if she should pick a target in the middle of the street and rip their throat open with her teeth. The image of blood spraying across the damp sidewalk and over her face made her throat tighten with anticipation. Her fingers twitched by her sides and she smirked.

Such wicked and vile thoughts would send her straight to hell if it truly existed. Layla used to curse herself for every drop of blood she enjoyed, but as the years went on and her days grew longer, her heart grew less tender. It was her nature now, as a reaper, to kill and to consume blood like wine.

"*Watch it*," someone growled.

Layla stopped and stared ahead at the two Black men leaving a club. A white man at the entrance hissed after them. He lifted a cigarette to his mouth, his glare never leaving the two Black men even as they walked away.

Instantly, Layla found her victim.

The second the man realized there was too much wind in the open street for his cigarette to light, he went into the alley. Keeping her footsteps light, Layla followed. She heard him grumbling under his breath, but stopped listening when a slur slipped past his lips.

"What was that?" Layla asked.

The man jerked back, stunned. His mouth hung open and the cigarette dropped onto the ground between them. "Excuse you?" he demanded.

Layla stomped on the cigarette. When she looked up at him, his eyes flashed with fear. The bloodthirsty look in her eyes must have been especially apparent now. Layla made sure he got a good long look. And as realization sparked in his expression, she pounced.

Despite being a full two heads shorter than this man, she took him down in an instant. Her teeth locked around his throat first, tearing into his flesh and ripping out his vocal cords so no one could hear his distress. Smooth muscle snapped between her teeth, and blood flowed into her mouth.

Warmth unfurled in her body, satisfaction reaching a blinding peak as blood filled her. Nothing compared to this feeling. Layla felt as if she had been struck by lightning, the heat searing through her body and igniting her nerves.

The man had gone still already. By the time Layla finished with him, he was completely slumped against the wall, his mouth slack while blood leaked down his shirtfront. Layla knew she needed to clean up the scene, but her hands were shaking too hard, and her concentration was quickly being ravaged by the adrenaline-inducing effects of human blood.

She stared down at the lifeless body, warm blood still dripping from her mouth. "Shit," Layla hissed. She had no one to blame but herself for tonight's carnage. And she would have to pay for it.

6

TOBIAS SAINT'S VOICE ECHOED THROUGH THE hallway from his study despite the closed door.

"A guard was attacked on Saint property. Then there was a murder three blocks away. What am I paying these men for if they are not doing their job?"

When Elise walked in, she expected to see her father still in his dressing gown. But he was fully dressed, his black curls smoothed down, and he had the telephone to his ear.

"Just take care of it," Mr. Saint snapped. He hung up the phone and turned to face Elise. His brow furrowed. "A reaper was close to the estate last night. Too close."

Elise nodded. Last night, after Layla had disappeared out the window, Sterling had wrestled the gun from Elise's hands. She'd wanted to run downstairs and get her father, but Sterling's eyes went wide with fear as they both realized he would have to explain to Mr. Saint why he'd been in Elise's room and not out on patrol.

Then there had been Josi to consider. To Elise's relief, Josi was unharmed, at least physically. Elise had lain in bed with her until she could fall asleep.

"You'll keep me safe..." Josi had whispered before she'd drifted off. "Like Charlotte kept you safe."

The last thing Elise wanted was for Josi to know that her nightmare had been real. And she'd made a pact with Sterling to never tell anyone else what they had seen last night.

Still, she wished there were some way for her father to know that Layla was a threat.

She took a deep breath and set her jaw before speaking. "That reaper... I wonder if it could have been Layla Quinn."

"Not possible," Mr. Saint said. "It must have been a rogue. No reaper who knows the Saints would think to trespass."

"I just have a feeling it was her," Elise said, her voice trembling. "And that it's not safe here."

Mr. Saint stood, his arms folding across his chest while he leaned against his desk.

"This estate is the safest place for anyone in Harlem. In all of New York, actually. We do more than the police by now. I have hundreds of men out there in the city every day, hunting those bastard reapers down—"

"You are not hearing me." Elise's voice broke.

Tobias Saint's shoulders tensed. His eyes, dark and unyielding, roamed over her for a long moment. "I always hear you, Elise. Everything I do is for you and for your sisters and your mother. I must say, it hurts to know you think I don't know what's best for you." Mr. Saint came around his desk so he stood closer to Elise and leaned down. "It was *my* idea to send you to France after that Quinn girl tried to kill you." Elise flinched, but her father continued, unmoved. "You built a beautiful life and started your career in France because of *me*. As far as I'm concerned, the only words out of your mouth should be 'thank you, Father.' I saved your life. I couldn't save Charlotte's, but I saved you. Be grateful for that," he said roughly.

Guilt plowed through Elise. She fiddled with the tie of her robe. "I'm grateful, Father. I really am. I only wish that Josi could have the same. Here, she lives in fear. In France, there would be no reapers with resentment toward the Saints; she could dance and be a normal child—"

"Josi is my only chance at continuing our legacy beyond my death since you must return to France for your music career. I cannot have zero heirs." Mr. Saint went back to his desk and sat, his hands folded in front of him.

Any hope Elise had quickly shattered. She willed her voice to be steady. "Then let me stay here."

"Excuse me?" Mr. Saint asked.

"I want to stay. I don't need to go back to France," Elise said.

Her father looked dubious. "Your career?"

"It's nothing." It hurt to say it. Elise remembered the pride that had burst in her when she received her acceptance letter to the conservatory. Now, she stomped the flame of that joy out, leaving only ashes behind.

As if a switch had gone off in her father, Mr. Saint looked away, his body tense. "You are excused, Elise."

Elise's throat tightened to the point of pain. She swallowed hard as she nodded, blinking back tears. By the time she returned to her room, her face was wet and her chest heaved with sobs. Josi stirred in bed behind her while Elise pulled a stationery box from her desk and sat down to write a letter to the director of the Paris Conservatory.

In just a few minutes, with the meeting of ink to paper, Elise eliminated her dreams and all that she had worked toward for the past decade. But the tears that fell were not for her ruined future. They were for the future she knew she could give her sister by throwing away her own.

And, for the first time in ages, Elise felt relief.

Jamie Kelly swiped a gloved finger down the bloody cheek of a dead man. He glanced up at Layla, blue eyes glinting in the hot sun. "If I take this off your hands, it will cost you."

"How much?" Layla demanded. The man she had killed the previous night was slumped behind a row of garbage cans. Layla was glad to have Jamie take care of the rest of it for her.

Jamie crossed his arms over his chest. The subtle twitch of his lips told Layla there was some trick coming. She had known Jamie since she had first been turned; he was just a fifteen-year-old, getting caught up in crime before he had truly experienced life. They had that in common. Innocence stolen from them at an early age, both of them forced to push themselves to desperate extremes just to survive. Jamie's parents were as good as ghosts. Shell shock had kept his father from holding a job after the war, and while his mother stayed home to care for her husband, there was never enough food in the cupboard and the lights were shut off more than they were on. Jamie paid the bills for some time, then became fully invested as a gangster, moved out, and never looked back.

Years later, Jamie Kelly was hardly a friend, but useful to Layla.

"You're funny, kid," Jamie muttered. "I know you don't have money."

"Wow."

Jamie smirked. "Does Mother Reaper pay you?"

Layla fell silent. Valeriya offered her a home, and that was enough.

"That's what I thought." Jamie nodded to the body, sighing. "I can get my guys to move him. In exchange, I need you to pick something up for me. I'm getting a delivery at the port tomorrow evening."

"What is it?" Layla asked.

"You don't need to know. Just tell them you're there for Kelly. Actually..." Jamie straightened his jacket lapels, his jaw tightening as he grinned at her. "Tell them you're there for Vex."

Layla furrowed her brows. "Excuse you?"

"It's my alias. Police are getting too uptight around here and they're starting to refuse bribes. Not everyone needs to know Jamie Kelly. But Vex… That's more intimidating." Jamie gave her a proud smile.

Unable to hold back anymore, Layla burst out laughing. Jamie frowned at her. "Vex? That sounds like the name of a pretty performer. I bet there's a dancer at the Cotton Club who calls herself Vex. Between this and your gang being called 'the Crooks,' you're not very creative."

Jamie grimaced. "You know, for a little girl, you are so vicious sometimes."

"I'm not a little girl. I'm eighteen," Layla snapped. "If you want me to pick up your package and ask for *Vex*, I will, but I refuse to call you that ridiculous name elsewhere." She started to walk away, still fighting a small smile at the absurd name.

"Quinn," Jamie called.

Layla stopped at the end of the alley. "What?"

"Is 'Vex' really that bad?"

The scent of blood lured Layla more than anything. Sometimes, when she was beyond starved, it was the only thing she could concentrate on; that pulsing, delicious warmth thrumming through the veins of any living being around her. Her senses sharpened whenever blood was spilled, drawing her in like a moth to a flame.

As she neared the Harlem reaper lair, Layla's spine went stiff. Fresh blood assaulted her nose, and she half expected to see a dead body in the foyer of the building. It wouldn't be the first time, especially with so many new reapers seeking solace. She had found herself in a similar situation after attacking Elise. Blood had still dripped from her fingers when she arrived at the front door of the Hotel Clarice as a wounded thirteen-year-old.

Layla looked around now, searching for the source. Tracking sent her to the decrepit row houses a block away from the Harlem lair.

Something felt wrong. Layla followed bloody footprints into an abandoned building with crumbling back steps. Inside, the scent was overpowering. And immediately, she sensed trouble. Blood covered the walls in chaotic sprays, half-eaten organs scattered around the floor—death coated every corner of the room, weaving through each shadow and clouding the air.

She spotted a crouching form in the far corner of the room.

Layla shut the door behind her. The resounding creak jolted the boy to his feet. He hissed, his fangs bared and eyes glowing with malice. Layla knew this look all too well. Every new reaper struggled to control their new urges. This boy was no different. The bright sheen covering his black eyes made them glow almost gold. But deep in his burning desire for violence, Layla saw fear.

Still, he continued trying to size her up. Layla stood just over five feet tall and she was slim, though lithe muscle covered her body after years of practiced hunting. This boy, while younger, towered over her.

Layla lifted her hands, showing deference. "I know you feel like the strongest being in existence right now because you just

fed, but your judgment is just as poor as your adrenaline is high,"
Layla said. "Unless you *want* me to kill you, attacking me is not
worth it."

The boy only continued to glare at her. It might have been more
menacing if he did not still look so young with round cheeks and
maturity barely starting to shape his features.

Layla took a gentle step forward. "I thought you were a rogue
reaper, but you're a *baby*," she said. Scorn twisted his face and Layla
laughed roughly. "Don't worry, you won't be a baby forever. You will
age until your midtwenties, when your brain development stops—"

The young man hissed again, blood-tinged spittle flying from his
mouth. "I'm not one of those *things*. Are they not all rogue?"

"Oh boy…" Layla blew hot air between her teeth. First barrier to
overcome: denial. "Rogue reapers are what we call the reapers that
deliberately disobey every standing reaper and human agreement,
ignore the advice of wiser, ancient reapers, and live as dangerously
as they want, feeding exclusively on humans. They're usually young.
You…" Layla lowered her voice as the boy's eyes darkened. "You just
turned."

The boy shuddered. "No…"

"I know it's a lot to take in. But you are in a highly volatile state
and area, what with being newly turned and police patrolling nearby,
so I suggest you come with me into the lair so you can calm down
in a safe environment."

The boy said nothing, but he did stop hissing. He finally closed
his mouth, and his eyes settled from the feral gold to a more muted

brown. "I can hear your heart beating… It's so slow. Like mine… Am I dead?" he asked.

"Not quite," she sighed. "What's your name?"

"Theo." His voice was rough, but Layla still heard the youth in it. No more than fifteen years old. Sweat covered his brown skin, and he trembled so hard, Layla thought he might collapse.

For a moment, Layla's tough exterior cracked, and a flood of sympathy overwhelmed her. "I'm Layla. Do you remember what happened?"

"I-I don't know why I can't stop. I don't… I swear I didn't mean to hurt her." Theo's voice broke as he eyed the remains scattered around the room.

Layla clenched her jaw. No matter how many times she tried to help new reapers, it never got easier. Their desperation and guilt cut right through to her own, bringing her back to her first days as a damned soul. She tried so hard to avoid those feelings; it wasn't her fault she was changed, it wasn't her fault she had these uncontrollable urges. But it still hurt. It hurt to walk around with a heart that no longer felt like her own and instincts that appalled her, but were as necessary as breathing air.

"I understand what you're going through," Layla said softly. "Were you attacked?"

Theo shrugged. "I don't even remember. I just remember feeling the most pain I've ever experienced in my life." Frantic light suddenly filled his eyes, and Theo trembled harder as he stepped toward Layla. "I haven't even gone home. My parents are probably worried—"

"We can help you figure that out," Layla assured him.

Confusion crossed his face. "'We'?"

"My lair," Layla said. "It's the Hotel Clarice—"

"I need to go home," Theo said quickly. "I need my mother."

Layla pursed her lips. "It's best if they don't see you like this. Trust me."

"What do you know?" Theo said in a low voice. "I thought most reapers just killed—" He gestured to the bloody mess around him. "I'm sure you and your reapers will jump me the second I walk in."

"Watch yourself—"

"I don't need a lecture," Theo snapped.

The sun was starting to set, and Layla was too tired to argue this boy down. He would have to come to his senses on his own. Layla clicked her tongue and retreated toward the door. "Fine. Valeriya probably wouldn't appreciate a newcomer now anyway," she muttered under her breath. "You're more trouble than you're worth." In a second, her hard shell had re-formed, all the guilt she had felt evaporating with her vulnerabilities.

She could offer a hand as much as she wanted, but she couldn't force anyone to take it. Theo was on his own.

7

I CAN ALREADY TELL SO MUCH SUCCESS WILL BE achieved within these walls." Mr. Saint trailed his hand over an examination table, his Saint ring scraping along the polished metal.

Elise's ears grated at the noise. No one else seemed to notice. Her mother surveyed the lab with curious, albeit judgmental, eyes, and Josi stood on her tiptoes to see over every countertop. Thalia Gray and Sterling stood on either side of Elise, Thalia standing tall in a pristine white coat, while Sterling's eyes roamed the room.

The laboratory walls were white, and the yellow and green tinted ceiling lights reflected off the white linoleum floor beneath them. Elise, standing against one of the counters, felt claustrophobic with the scent of antiseptic pressing into her from all sides. She shifted uncomfortably, her gloves creasing while she pressed her hands together.

"Pardon my ignorance, but why have you decided to fund a lab, Mr. Wayne?" Elise's mother asked. "As long as Tobias and I have known you, you've given most of your financial support to political causes…"

Mr. Saint's jaw clenched and he whispered something into his wife's ear. Analia Saint nodded reluctantly and fell silent.

"That's an excellent question, Mrs. Saint," Stephen Wayne began. Elise noticed the expensive watch on his wrist, and it took no genius to know that his suit was of top quality. He wasn't just rich; he was made of money. Elise knew that was what had drawn her father to him when they had moved to New York. Tobias Saint had been just a man with a small metalworks business, hoping for a break. To him, Stephen Wayne must have been a beacon of possibility.

"If I aspire to be anything," Mr. Wayne continued, "it's a man in politics, not a scientist. But scientific research is necessary for ending reaperhood, which, as you know, is my current cause. I do hope the lab meets your expectations. Dr. Harding is a somewhat reserved man, so he is not joining us today, but he's hard at work in the research lab."

Mr. Wayne had been acquainted with the Saint family since before Elise was born; later, it had been Mr. Wayne's money that finally pushed Mr. Saint's business from a modest factory to an empire. Elise understood why he was so important to the Saints; she just wished her father was as interested in making up for lost time with her as he was in touring laboratories.

"From what I've seen so far, I'm impressed," Mr. Saint said.

Thalia grinned. "Just wait until you see the clinic."

Mr. Wayne laughed gently. "That's where Miss Gray spends most of her time."

Elise couldn't help but notice how pale Stephen Wayne looked under the lights. He was almost ghostly, his skin so white it looked nearly translucent. But his smile seemed genuine at least.

He turned to her just then and held out his hand. "I hear congratulations are in order for you. You graduated with honors from your music school?"

Elise smoothed sweaty palms over her skirt, then took his hand. "Yes, sir. Thank you."

"Have you any plans to continue performing?" Mr. Wayne asked.

Elise opened her mouth to respond, but her father spoke instead, "She auditioned for the Paris Conservatory, but is still waiting to hear back from them. We're not worried about it. I know she will be playing full-time in Paris come autumn. She will remain home until then."

Sterling stared hard at Elise, and she looked away.

Relief crashed through her when Thalia suggested they tour the adjoining clinic.

Thalia and Mr. Wayne led the group down a hallway and into a bright room that resembled a busy hospital ward. Visitors filled the entryway, lining up at a front desk. Others occupied cots while nurses tended to them. An antiseptic scent overpowered Elise's senses, and she fought the urge to wrinkle her nose.

"It's so beautiful, I love it here," Thalia breathed, her eyes lit up.

"It was originally supposed to just be a lab, but I suggested we have a clinic attached."

Elise noticed Sterling sharing a gentle look with Thalia, who bit her lip, hiding a smile.

"Excuse me," came a voice from behind Thalia. "I need help." A Black boy who could not have been older than fifteen stepped up to her and Stephen Wayne. His clothes were so loose he appeared to be swimming in them, and his voice quavered as if he was on the verge of tears.

Mr. Wayne held out his hand. "That's what we are here for. What's your name, son?"

"Th-Theo," the boy whimpered.

Elise watched Sterling narrow his eyes and move closer to Thalia, putting himself between her and Theo. But Thalia pushed past him to talk to the boy. "It's okay. You're safe here. What's going on—"

"Miss Gray, he should see Dr. Harding," Mr. Wayne interrupted. His brow creased with concern.

Mr. Saint cleared his throat. "I would like to meet the man who founded this lab. Do you mind if Analia and I accompany you?"

Mr. Wayne nodded. "Please. Join me." With an arm around Theo's slumped shoulders, the man led Elise's parents back to the lab.

Worry crept into Elise, and her heart rate sped up. She didn't realize how hard she was squeezing Josi's hand until she yanked herself away. "I'm sorry," Elise mumbled.

"What do you think is wrong with the boy?" Josi asked.

Thalia shrugged. "He might have been bitten by a reaper."

"*What?*" Elise gasped.

"Reaper bites are common cases here. What most people do not know is that just one bite will not turn them; you have to die with reaper blood in your system as well. But it's better to be safe than sorry. We give them a little pain medication, then send them home with less anxiety." Thalia pushed her hair back from her face, rubbing her chin. "I think it's better to have scared people come here than anywhere else. Other hospitals would...take advantage of them. I want these patients to feel safe," Thalia said.

Elise rubbed her chest, right where the scars marred her skin. Perhaps she was lucky. All she had gotten was Layla's nails. Elise could not imagine the suffering that would have followed if she had been infected by reaper venom—if five years ago, Layla had *bitten* her.

"It's clear they do," Sterling said. "Look at how many people are in here already, and you've only just started working."

Thalia beamed. "My hope is that one day the clinic will be empty, because that would mean there are no more reapers."

Sterling reached forward to tuck a lock of Thalia's hair behind her ear. "I'm proud of you. And you should let yourself be proud too."

Josi sighed. "This is boring, Lisey," she whispered to Elise. "I don't want to be heir if I have to do stuff like this when I'm older." She kicked at the linoleum.

"We're going soon, so stop kicking," Elise whispered back. "And tie your shoe."

Elise considered herself willing to do anything for Josi, but she was glad she didn't have to do that task for her anymore; shoes were so dirty and touching them had always made her hands feel contaminated. Even now her fingers twitched by her sides, already uncomfortable at the thought.

"Ugh, fine." Josi crouched down to redo the laces of her saddle shoe.

Elise watched her sister's hands loop them slowly. Until she noticed something. "Josi, where's your ring?"

Josi paused. She looked up, apprehension bright in her eyes. "Don't tell Mother—"

"Did you lose it?" Elise asked sharply.

"I think I just misplaced it. I didn't mean to—"

"Hey, hey." Sterling stepped between them. "Josi, let's go take a look at that candy out at the newsstand. I've got some nickels."

Josi grinned and followed him toward the front door of the clinic.

"God, he's the best friend a girl could ask for," Thalia said.

Elise almost laughed. "Thalia—"

"I know how it sounds, but we've discussed it and he understands. I want to focus on my work now and I might be selfish, but I'd rather have him as a friend than not at all," Thalia said.

Elise wanted to wince on Sterling's behalf. But she touched Thalia's hand and smiled gently. "I'm proud of you, too, by the way." Elise gestured around them. "This is incredible, and Mr. Wayne says there are stories in the papers about it—"

"Oh, trust me, I'm still earning my place here. Dr. Harding never mentions me when he talks to the papers," Thalia said bitterly. "I almost confronted him about it, but I'd rather not compromise my job. My mother is worried. She believes I'll end up like her, used

73

and discarded. She is a brilliant scientist who made *one* mistake and your father cast her out. As much as I hate to admit it, I have a better chance of making a difference here. Even if it means putting up with Dr. Hardass." She rolled her eyes. "The man is insufferable and barely lets me touch anything, but other than that, the connections here are extraordinary," Thalia said.

"I understand," Elise said. "You've always wanted to change the world."

Thalia nodded weakly. "Of course. Though it's difficult to get people's hopes up only to disappoint them in the end. Reapers are getting harder to differentiate from humans, and other countries are starting to see the United States as a breeding ground for evil. When I was in Switzerland, there were already talks of cutting ties with us because of how we're handling the reapers here. It's starting to feel oppressive. I don't want to let anyone down," Thalia muttered.

Elise understood that all too well. She laced her fingers through Thalia's. "You won't disappoint us, Thalia."

"Okay, that's enough of that. No more emoting." Sterling returned with Josi, who had a lollipop and a red tongue from the candy. "We need to make up for our lost time," Sterling said.

"Jazz club tonight? I can have Colm pick you up?" Elise asked.

Thalia nodded. "Yes, please." She turned to Sterling, who had lifted up a giggling Josi. "Unhand her."

"Unhand me, stupid!" Josi squealed at Sterling.

Elise fell into a fit of laughter, all earlier gloom chased away by her sister's mirth.

8

NIGHT FELL OVER HARLEM, AND THE MONSTERS came out to play. Normally, Layla would join in for a hunt, or help Valeriya settle new clan members in, but since Mei had her covered as payback for ruining her bed, she gratefully lounged on her new sheets and ate chocolate-covered strawberries. A silver Saint ring twisted between her fingers as she chewed, the seal staring up at her with annoying radiance.

Layla smirked and shoved it back into her pocket. Pulling the ring from Josi's finger as she slept had been a last-minute decision. Just something to keep the older Saint girl up at night when she realized reaper hands had touched her younger sister after all.

Only minutes into her peace, she heard a quick knock, followed by a note slipped under her door.

Layla—

Pick up the package at the port at 10 p.m. Ask for Visily. Say you're there for Vex.

Layla stared at the neatly scrawled message for a solid minute. Then she burst out laughing. "I cannot believe this fool." She tucked the paper into her pocket and pulled her coat on. She wondered what to do with the half-finished strawberries sitting on her nightstand. They were one of the few foods she had learned to tolerate since becoming a reaper. But the strawberries would only melt while she was away, so Layla took the bowl with her as she headed down the hall.

Valeriya looked up when she saw her standing in the door to her study. "You brought me a gift?" she asked.

"Yes," Layla said a little nervously. She set the plate down and licked a spot of chocolate off her finger. "It's my strategy to give you gifts because I know I will inevitably make a mistake in the future and this will help you remember you do not hate me."

"You're funny," Valeriya said. She did not laugh; her tone remained completely deadpan. "You just made a mistake and on Saint territory, nonetheless. Mess up again and you'll find yourself on the streets. It would do me better to have fewer reapers to look after here."

Layla opened her mouth to say something. But Valeriya went back to scribbling at the paper on her desk, so she only sighed and left.

Despite Valeriya's frequent coldness, Layla would keep trying with her. Nowadays, Layla rarely trusted anyone. But she trusted Valeriya, no matter how rigid she stayed. Sure, Valeriya took care of Layla, but that was her obligation as an ancient reaper, part of an agreement with the city to keep younger reapers under control. Sometimes Layla wished she would show an ounce of affection. But in moments like these, Layla realized just how starved she must be for warmth. As a reaper, such tenderness was not warranted, or expected. No matter how many years it had been since turning, Layla never got used to the numbness of being damned. Especially after losing parents who had hugged her just because they wanted to feel close to her and who told her they loved her through every word they exchanged with her.

The longer she lived as a reaper, the more distance she put between herself and her past, herself and love, herself and hope. As long as she was damned, the relationships she formed would be too.

Fog settled over the port like a blanket. Layla walked through the thick mist, water droplets clinging to her clothes and hair. The port was almost completely empty, save for a single man stacking boxes on a truck. He looked up at her with stern eyes and settled his hand over his hip, no doubt where he concealed a weapon.

"Who are you?" he demanded.

Layla pulled her hands out of her pockets so he knew she was unarmed. "I'm here for Jamie…" Layla clenched her jaw, resisting the urge to roll her eyes. "I'm here to pick up for Vex. Where is Visily?"

The man stared at her for a long moment. "He's calling himself Vex? Really?"

"That's what *I* said!" Layla exclaimed.

He shook his head. "He can have his package, but tell him to pick a better name if he wants people to take him seriously." The man nodded to a wooden crate on his left side. "There you go, kid."

Layla hauled the box into her arms and left. The sound of liquid sloshing around inside confirmed her suspicions that she was picking up liquor for Jamie. Luckily for her, reaperhood came with the perk of increased strength, so she had no problems carrying what could have been several bottles of the illegal stuff. It was an easy payback task for someone who needed help cleaning up a murder. Sometimes Layla wondered why Jamie was so nice to her. He could so easily ignore her, but he answered her. Every time.

The sound of a scuffle behind her made her stop in her tracks. Layla turned to survey a nearby dark alley. More than likely, it was a reaper, or a drunk person lurking where they shouldn't be. But something told Layla to wait. A familiar scent filled her nose. She set the crate down and crept toward the source of the noise.

A scream split the air around her. It ended in wet choking, like the person was being drowned. Layla tensed, prepared to defend herself, when she recognized the scent. Youth and blood all rolled into one. "Theo?" she called.

A figure slumped out of the alley, and Layla hissed when a hand reached toward her.

Blood plastered the woman's dark hair to her head, her eyes stretched wide with terror. "Help me," she barely managed to choke out.

"Thalia!" a man's voice called out. Then he was there, too, crawling toward the woman. He was as good as dead. The amount of blood Layla smelled in the air told her that before she saw the gaping wound in his throat.

She turned, intending to leave Theo to his hunt. But something on the man's chest gleamed and caught her eye. Layla would know that badge anywhere—the Saint lotus and North Star.

She realized then she'd once known the dying girl—remembered she and her mother would visit the Saint house. Memories flashed in her mind, making her head spin. Her body went stiff and she launched herself into the alley.

Theo's eyes found her and he swiped a bloody hand at her, but she reached him first, slamming him against the wall.

"What are you doing?" she seethed. "Touching Saints is a death sentence. Back off."

But Theo's eyes wouldn't focus on her. "Theo," she tried. Her nails dug into his shoulders so hard she drew blood. Veins popped in his eyes, turning them almost entirely red. Layla had seen reapers so sick with blood poisoning that they hallucinated in a comatose state, but she had never seen anything like this. Theo clawed at her like he was being controlled from the inside out.

"Theo, it's *me*, Layla—"

His nails, long and black, slashed at her. Layla backed away as blood seeped from her middle. He had barely touched her, but it stung like liquid fire melting across her body.

Theo stumbled away from her. He pounced on the two humans still trying to claw their way out of the alley.

Only then did Layla see the bullet hole in his back, right over his heart. But he still stood.

Layla tried to walk toward him, but her entire world swayed and the ground shifted beneath her feet. A roaring filled her ears. Black frayed at the edges of her vision. She finally reached him and grabbed his shoulders, trying to haul him off the bloody bodies. But his strength beat hers. The roaring in her ears intensified, and Layla screamed.

Then her world went black.

9

ELISE GREW TO HATE NIGHTTIME IN NEW YORK, AS everything bad seemed to happen when the sun disappeared and the darkness emerged. She stood in the middle of Lenox Avenue, gloved fingers twisting the pearls at her throat while she watched Sterling balance on the edge of the curb. The last of the evening light had faded, but Elise could still see the blush in his cheeks, rosy as ever in the glow of the streetlights above. Music drifted faintly from the club just down the street, the gentle saxophone notes a smooth rhythm to which Sterling moved. His freshly polished shoes creased as he stepped down and he glanced up at Elise, jaw hard with concern. "Elise. I will descend into misery if I have to wait any longer," he said.

"You are so dramatic. She's probably just stuck in traffic." Elise rolled her eyes, but her gaze drifted down to the bouquet of white roses in Sterling's hand. Despite his nervous fidgeting, he had managed to keep the flowers pristine and undamaged. *It's a congratulatory gift*, Sterling had insisted when he showed up in Elise's room with them earlier that night.

Elise could not wait to see Thalia's reaction to them.

"I just know this is Colm's fault," Sterling muttered, moving next to Elise. "He doesn't know how to drive at night. I always tell him he can go fast because he's driving a Saint car and everyone will understand—"

Elise scoffed, "You might as well run for office with the way you already assume the law should bend to your commands."

Smirking, Sterling gestured to his silver Saint seal, pinned to the front of his suit, then flipped his jacket back to reveal the two pistols tucked into his waistband. "It already does."

"Right," Elise said dryly.

A group of white people came bustling down the street, voices loud and smiles wide while they waltzed into the Cotton Club. There seemed to be fewer Black faces on Lenox Avenue than there'd been five years ago. Now white people were flocking to their neighborhood.

"It feels less like home," Elise muttered.

Sterling sighed. "I'm still getting used to the changes." He eyed a Black couple while they passed the Cotton Club, white pedestrians waiting by the entrance watching them with hard glares cracking their carefully made-up faces.

Elise studied the line of cars parked along the street until she caught a familiar vehicle just at the end of the block. "Sterling, I think they're here."

Together, they walked down the sidewalk, Sterling walking a bit faster than Elise out of excitement. But the car was empty.

"Maybe they went inside already?" Sterling asked.

But Elise knew that couldn't be. They had been waiting outside the club since it had opened; they would have seen Thalia and Colm if they had walked in. Elise stepped away from the car. Her heel snagged on something on her way past the alley behind her, and when she shook her foot free of it, the sound of metal hitting the ground split her focus.

Metal glinted in the streetlights as she looked down, then gasped with recognition.

A silver signet ring engraved with the Saint seal. Jósi's ring.

She picked it up, turning it in the light. As the ring slipped between her fingers, blood smeared across her gloves. Startled, Elise dropped it and it skidded across the ground, into the alley. "Sterling…" she breathed. What she had assumed were shadows spilling from the alley were pools of blood. And when Elise stepped forward, she saw an all-too-familiar face staring up at her, eyes glazed over.

A sharp breath left Sterling. He stood beside Elise, eyes wide and face struck white with horror. The roses fell from his hand into the puddle of blood. Elise could only scream as blood soaked the fair petals, Thalia's lifeless hand outstretched toward them.

10

LAYLA AWOKE IN A BED OF BLOOD. A QUICK assessment told her it wasn't hers.

She did have a considerable amount of scrapes and bruises, though, many of them just starting to heal. Whatever outrageous brawl she had been in last night had slowed her healing process. Of greater concern was the memory loss; she had no idea what caused the injuries. Layla couldn't even remember crawling into her bed the previous night.

Such amnesia was common among new reapers that were still learning to control their voracious cravings for blood. Bloodlust settled over them like a blindfold that blocked out most of their memories, so that they couldn't recall what they had done upon waking up, high on the sensation of fresh feedings. Valeriya called them blood furies. They were what got most young reapers in trouble with authorities. A blood fury could be a death sentence, not just for those who crossed a ravenous reaper's path but for the reapers themselves, if they were caught. Layla's first blood fury had led her to Elise Saint. Then, there had been an insatiable desire for Elise's blood and a craving for the fear in her eyes as she had hunted her in the middle of the night. But now it was like last night had never happened. Her brain skipped right from picking up the box at the port to the present moment, where she sat, confused, in her bed.

The fog blocking her brain was so thick that at first, Layla didn't notice Valeriya lurking by her door. But when she did, she straightened up, alarmed. "Valeri—"

"*Do. Not. Speak,*" her mentor hissed. Ice seemed to settle over the room. "You have one minute to explain why you attacked Saints—"

Layla scoffed. "I did no such thing—"

"Do not lie to me. I'm trying to protect you."

At this, fury heated Layla's blood. She stepped out of her bed and onto shaky legs. "I can protect myself."

Valeriya's glare deepened. She backed away from Layla and pushed the door open. To Layla's sour surprise, the Saint patriarch walked into her room. It had been ages since Layla had seen Tobias Saint, but the calculating aura in his dark eyes remained. Even years later, she was still on the receiving end of his accusations.

Police and Saint guards filed into the room after him, making a semicircle that enclosed Layla against her bed. "We have reason to believe you were present during the murder of Saint associates, Colm and Thalia, as well as one young man," Tobias Saint said coolly.

Confusion creased Layla's brows. She steadied her quickly rising panic with measured breaths and she clenched her jaw. "Why would you believe that?" Layla knew the sight was beyond damning. Soaked in blood, she looked like a rogue reaper.

"You have a history with the Saints. Mr. Saint has informed us that recently you were on their property, threatening the daughters," one policeman said.

Buzzing anxiety gripped her heart, squeezing her so tightly, her breath caught. "And?"

The officer continued, "We request your presence at the station for questioning. You risk losing this hotel. Every agreement we established with your clan will be dropped should we find any of you involved in this murder."

Layla hated that she looked at Valeriya for guidance. Her mentor shifted a quick glance toward the officer awaiting Layla's response. With a heavy sigh, Layla relaxed her shoulders. "Fine."

The police station was full despite it being early morning. Layla was set up in an interrogation room with a dimly lit window on one side. No doubt there were people behind that window, watching and listening to her every move. She wrung her hands together, legs bouncing beneath the table. It made her uneasy, knowing she was unable to see the ones picking her apart.

"Layla Quinn. Where were you last night?" the investigator sitting in front of her asked.

Layla dug her fingers into her thighs. Steel chains burned into her wrists and blood seeped down her arms. A Saint steel, manufactured by the empire to keep reapers under control. Layla wondered what life would be like for reapers had the steel never been made. Police officers would have less power in the streets while reapers wreaked more havoc, no steel cuffs to burn their flesh and steel bullets to stop their hearts. It was the perfect material to bring the empire and the police force together.

Layla's throat went dry as she collected the pieces of her fragmented memory. "I went to the port to pick up a package for someone."

"For whom?"

She fell silent. Turning Jamie in to the authorities would only lose her another ally. The investigator noticed her hesitation and with a slight lift of his eyebrow, he scribbled a few words onto his notepad. Layla let out a frustrated breath. "His name is Jamie," she said quickly.

"Jamie…last name?" the officer asked.

"Irrelevant," Layla snapped.

"Jamie Irrelevant." The officer laughed dryly, his bushy mustache shaking on his upper lip. "This can go quickly if you cooperate, Layla. Listen: *Pick up the package at the port at 10 p.m. Ask for Visily. Say you're there for Vex.* Does that sound familiar?"

Layla swallowed, but remained silent.

The officer cleared his throat. "We found a handwritten note with your name on it at the scene of the crime, so we know you were there. What were you picking up at the port?"

Layla worked her lips between her teeth before blowing out a quick answer. "I can't be positive. I never opened the crate."

Doubt crossed the officer's features. "Where is this crate?"

"With Jamie," Layla said. She shot a nervous glance at the window, then back at the officer, who was still writing things down. "I don't know what you want from me. I did not murder anyone, and I don't know what happened."

"Hmm…" The officer tapped his pen against his chin, thinking. "Now that is a bold claim. Especially for someone with so much evidence putting you at the scene of the crime."

Layla's blood ran cold. The officer leaned forward, and her stomach turned at the intensity in his eyes. "You won't escape this."

The door to the interrogation room swung open, and in stepped Tobias Saint. He wore a smug expression on his face that Layla was dismayed she remembered so clearly from her own childhood. Part of her questioned her own parents' judgment; what had they seen in this man that made them want to build their lives alongside him? Years later, past their death, past the rift that tore them away from her and the Saints, Layla still wondered.

Tobias Saint stood above her with his hands in his pockets. Layla wanted to smack the satisfied smirk off his face. "Moments like these make me regret the clan agreement. I ought to scrap all the developing human-reaper agreements so I can exterminate every last one of you without need for probable cause. It's clear your kind are not fit to live alongside humans." Mr. Saint removed one hand from his pocket, and in it sat a ring. Layla's heart lurched at the sight. "Please explain to me why my daughter's ring went missing after you paid our house a visit, and it was found at the scene of the crime. Now two of my people and a boy, an innocent human, are dead," Mr. Saint said, his voice unsettlingly calm.

Ice funneled through her veins and her breath grew shallow as she watched Mr. Saint. Even her hands, burning beneath the steel cuffs, trembled against the cold metal of the table.

"Theo wasn't human. He was a reaper," Layla said.

Mr. Saint shared an annoyed look with the investigator. "Really?" He nodded toward the officers standing guard at the back of the room. They approached and spread several photos across the table in front of Layla.

The pictures displayed Theo's body, laid out on an examining table, a white sheet thrown over his chest and legs. Some photos were so graphic, Layla almost felt guilty peering so closely at the dead boy.

Until she saw a bullet hole in his back and a memory from last night came rushing back.

She shifted uncomfortably while Mr. Saint stared down at her. "He has a full set of human teeth, no tainted blood, no fangs, no corroded heart. There was even a fang found in Thalia's throat, yet Theo has no gap in his teeth. This young man was as human as everyone in this room." Tobias Saint's lips twisted into a cruel smile. "Except for you, of course."

"Someone shot him. I did not kill him," Layla whispered. "I have never killed for sport; I am not a rogue reaper. If I had fed, he would be drained of blood, and I would have blood poisoning."

"The autopsy will have to corroborate that," Mr. Saint said.

Her teeth dug into her lower lip and she clenched her fists to keep her hands from shaking. Defending herself felt impossible when there was so much evidence stacked against her. The longer she remained in that interrogation, the murkier her own thoughts became. She had seen Theo, cowering in that abandoned house, newly turned. But this boy in the pictures was not a reaper. He was human again. He had been cured.

11

BLOOD SEEPED THROUGH ELISE'S THOUGHTS. WHEN she closed her eyes, the crime scene remained plastered in her mind, as if a picture had been burned into her eyelids. The bloody bodies painted a horrific picture of failed attempts at protection and unearned respite. Colm's throat had been torn out, muscles and tendons exposed to the harsh morning sun. Blood caked his clothes and pooled around him, soaking into Thalia's hair. He reached for her in death, gun abandoned by his side, an effort for protection left unfinished.

"Lenox Avenue is still closed. I suspect businesses on that street will take a hard hit until this case blows over—"

Elise blinked the vision of blood away to see a slumped Sterling in front of her. He sat, one hand on the radio, head tilted to catch every word while his eyes glazed over.

"Sterling," Elise muttered.

The radio continued, feedback growing louder, "*This might be one of the worst reaper attacks Harlem has had in a while, but we can't say we didn't see it coming. New reaper cases have been emerging all over New York and the country with the influx of immigrants. People are now saying not to come to the United States unless you want to suffer. And let me tell you, other countries are surely laughing at us. It won't be long before they invade to sterilize us. Now with last night's attack, I'm starting to think all hope is lost—*"

"Sterling, turn that off," Elise snapped.

Finally, he switched the radio off. The static cut out immediately and he looked at Elise, eyes bright with grief.

Guilt plowed through her. He was hurt just as much as she was—probably more. Elise squeezed her eyes shut, willing her tears not to fall. "I'm sorry," she whispered. The couch shifted beside her as Sterling moved to be closer. His knee brushed hers, and the spark of familiar warmth nearly made Elise fold into herself. Tears burned behind her eyes, the lump in her throat only growing more painful when she saw the redness in her best friend's eyes and the quiver of his lips.

The silence, for once, was welcome. Neither knew what to say, and sitting with their grief together had been the only thing they could stomach doing since returning home.

Sterling inhaled, his shoulders shaking. "I never thought an attack like that would happen to us again."

Elise pressed her face into Sterling's shoulder, finally letting her tears fall. She might have stayed there for hours, his presence softening her pain, if the door had not opened. Her tears stung her face as she sat up and wiped them away.

Her father stalked into the room, bringing, for Elise, a cloud of uncertainty and resentment. A scowl twisted his face, the crease between his brows deepening as he gestured for Sterling to leave.

Sterling gave Elise's hand a gentle squeeze, then left the room. Mr. Saint shut the door after him and turned to Elise, jaw tight. "I cannot imagine how you feel right now. Thalia was a brilliant young woman, and I know she was an even better friend to you."

Hearing Thalia's name made her heart skip a beat, but her breath resumed normally and she stared ahead. As if acting like nothing happened would make that a reality. But no matter how much Elise ignored the death, it remained. Like a scarlet mark in her life, their futures snuffed out in one fateful night.

More tears crested in Elise's eyes. "It's my fault she was there in the first place. I told her to come for a show—" Sobs cut her off.

Pity darkened her father's face. He swiped a gentle thumb across her cheek, wiping her tears away. "Blaming yourself will solve nothing. You spent years blaming yourself and grieving the Quinn girl, and look where that got you. She was not a friend to you. No friend would ever put your life in danger like she did. To think the Quinns tried to convince me that reapers and humans could ever live in harmony… What a hideous goddamn joke." Bitterness seeped into his tone and his voice went hard as he pulled away from Elise.

Elise recoiled. Her father continued, paying no mind to the

distance spreading between them. "Layla Quinn has always held you back. You know your mother wanted to bring you home when you started sending us letters, saying how scared you were all the time in Paris. I can't help but wonder where you would be now if you spent less time crying over that girl and more time focusing on yourself and your craft. Perhaps the Paris Conservatory would have admitted you immediately." Mr. Saint's voice turned cold.

Ice seeped through Elise's body. "Father—"

"The Quinn girl is our main suspect for the murders," Mr. Saint said.

In an instant, anger flooded her senses, turning her body hot. Layla's interference—her threat—had turned everything over in Elise's life. It made sense that she would have done this; she would have left a bloodbath in her wake just to get back at Elise. The air sucked out of her lungs and Elise inhaled deeply, trying to settle her nerves. "She took Josi's ring," Elise breathed. The thought of Layla laying a hand on her sister made her heart stop. Her hands began to shake and the room swayed around her. "She's not safe here. She needs to be sent away somewhere—"

"Josephine is my heir—"

"Maybe she shouldn't be." Elise snapped her mouth shut. The words had tumbled out so quickly, even her father lifted a brow in surprise.

He drew closer to her, his fingers pressed together. "And who should replace her?"

Elise wanted to look away. His eyes held a challenge so great, she felt like she was being led into a trap. But she lifted her chin and spoke softly, "Me."

Her father watched her for a long moment. Then he yanked his shirt collar so his tie loosened around his throat. Unintelligible grumbles left his mouth as he rummaged around in the drawer of the side table before coming away with a lighter and a pack. Mr. Saint lifted a cigarette to his lips and lit it. They stood there in silence while he smoked, his eyes leveled on Elise, the patriarch and his discarded heir staring one another down. Finally, as the smoke sifted between them, he spoke, "Why you? Do you feel guilty about what happened to Charlotte?"

Elise flinched. She hoped the answer would have been obvious. She was his oldest daughter. But perhaps her value to him had been discarded with her innocence the night Elise failed to save her older sister.

"You said it yourself, since Layla has had a taste of my blood, she will always be linked to me. I might be able to get her to talk," she said.

Mr. Saint moved toward her. His dark eyes pinned her to the spot and fear tore through her for a brief moment, her heart pounding, when the hot rage etched into his expression did not ease up. "There is no 'might,' Elise. I want you to play her like you play your little instruments, weaving every kind of story and lie you can from her." Smoke left his mouth in thick swirls, filling the air between their faces. Mr. Saint backed away, rubbing his hand over his forehead. "This murder has shaken this household. Stephen Wayne is reconsidering our partnership now. How I will expand my empire without his funds and his projects, I have no idea. The city might fall without us. Reapers might finally overtake us all, just as the rest of the world is predicting."

Elise breathed in, the smoke singeing her nose. "Sterling can help—"

"No. Sterling has his own responsibilities to worry about," Mr. Saint grumbled.

Just the thought of her home being overrun by reapers again made Elise shudder. She could not lose anyone else to their terror—she *refused*. "I do not want the empire to fall, Father. I will get Layla to talk. Whatever it takes," Elise said, stronger this time.

Mr. Saint nodded slowly, the fire in his eyes finally settling down. "Why are you so willing, Elise?"

Elise paused, considering his words. She didn't want this at all. Just a couple weeks ago, she had been ready to spend her days in France, playing music. But things had changed. "I want Josi to be safe—"

"Don't lie," Mr. Saint said.

Elise's throat tightened. *I want control back over my life.* "I'm tired of Layla ruining everything."

A slow smile spread across Mr. Saint's face. "Understandably. When you are done uncovering this crime and collecting necessary information on the reapers, you kill her."

Elise stole a glance at her family ring. The sun never left the gold signet alone; it was almost like a taunt when the shine blinded her, reminding Elise to remember exactly where her loyalties belonged.

She stuffed her hands into her pockets and hurried along the street. The end of August neared, but the summer weather remained in full swing. Elise's curls stuck to the back of her neck, where sweat steadily formed with each passing minute she spent outside, a cool breeze being the only respite from the heat.

Finally, her destination appeared at the end of the block. At the police department, an officer led Elise straight to Layla's holding cell. The maximum-security bars, made with Saint steel, should have made Layla seem less intimidating, but the malice burning in her sharp eyes still sold her out as the most threatening thing in the room. When Elise first met her searing gaze, she felt a shift, and all those years between them, all their laughter, their happy memories, their betrayals, came rushing forward. Something unrecognizable flickered in Layla's eyes, but she continued to scowl.

Elise approached the bars and stared down at her old friend turned adversary. "Breaking into my home and threatening me wasn't enough? You had to kill three innocent people?"

Layla seemed unfazed. She lifted a brow and when she spoke, her words were cool and slow. "Did you make Daddy promise to give you money if you crack me?"

Ire flared in Elise, her skin pricking with heat. Layla seemed to sense it. Her lips pulled back into a snarl and golden light filled her eyes. "I won't talk to you."

Layla was the most stubborn person Elise ever had the displeasure of knowing. And getting her to open up was like trying to split open a rock with her fist. How Elise had managed to crack that tough exterior years ago and find exactly what made Layla tick, what made her happiest, evaded her now. And while Elise looked into the defiance set deeply in Layla's eyes, she wondered if she had gotten herself into something impossible.

"Layla," Elise said calmly.

"No," Layla said. She sat on the concrete floor of her cell. "And as long as you stand out there, and I'm in here, you will get nothing out of me."

Elise lifted a brow. "You want to be released? Talk to me."

She expected Layla to perk up at the deal, but her scowl settled deeper into her face and she turned away from Elise. "No."

Elise's throat tightened, frustration threatening to choke her. "You said you wanted to be freed."

"I'd rather rot in here than work with you on any matter that could benefit your disgusting family," Layla snapped. "Waltzing out of here on a Saint's arm would send such a *beautiful* message to my clan." Her words were dry and clipped with sarcasm.

A frustrated scream rose in Elise's throat. But she dug her heels into the ground and gritted her teeth instead. "You would not just rot in here. Someone would take you away, whether it be scientists, or government officials from another country, and you would be at their mercy until your immortal body gave out." After having gone over them with Sterling so many times before arriving, the words sounded stiff to Elise. But the faint flicker of fear in Layla's eyes told her they were working. "But let it be known, this situation is not just about my family. This is bigger than all of us."

An empty smile found Layla's lips. "Wow. I didn't know it was possible for you to think of anyone but yourself."

Elise narrowed her eyes. "If we work together, we will benefit from each other. Isn't that what your parents wanted? For reapers and humans to be united?"

Layla went still, the only movement being the newly sparked fury in her golden eyes. "*Do not* speak about my parents."

"You leave me no choice. There are people dying, and you're hissing over a broken friendship that you should've gotten over years ago."

"To *you*, it's just a broken friendship. It was easy for you. You're not the one who died." Layla's words sent chills down Elise's spine.

Elise swallowed hard. She held her stare for a long time, watching the clashing emotions Layla contended with. Then she backed away from the bars separating them and sighed. "We don't have to be friends, we don't have to like each other, hell, we don't even have to respect each other. All I'm asking is that you speak to me."

Layla pondered her words for a moment. "What do I gain?"

"Your freedom and the opportunity for you to prove your innocence with my support—if you give me the information I need," Elise said through clenched teeth. The agreement she made with her father echoed in her head, but she shut down those thoughts.

"I have no reason to trust you," Layla said.

Elise pursed her lips. "I'm willing to look into your claim that Theo was not human."

A smile spread across Layla's mouth. And even though it reached her eyes, joy was not present, but rather a sick, twisting malice that made Elise's stomach turn. "Good start," Layla nearly purred. A sizzling sound filled the air as her flesh burned when she placed her hands on the bars and bared her fangs for Elise. "Tell your father and the dumb investigators that I have all of my teeth. Whoever's tooth is in the throat of your precious Saint isn't mine. It's probably Theo's. Care to explain why Theo has a bullet wound? An innocent human shot by a steel bullet meant to kill a reaper. How odd."

Elise's expression fell into confusion. "Why would a human—"

"He wasn't human. The sooner everyone understands that, the sooner we will solve this mystery," Layla said. She pulled back and watched Elise with expectant eyes.

Elise closed her eyes for a moment, inhaling as she counted backward in her head. When she opened her eyes, she stepped closer to the bars and whispered, "I need proof and corroboration from other reapers if I'm to believe any of your claims."

Calculated malice flickered through Layla's eyes. She drew her finger over a steel bar, her damned flesh burning against the blessed metal. "I could get it for you. Just not from in here," Layla grumbled. Blood dripped between them and landed on Elise's boot.

Elise scoffed. "As if I could trust you on the other side of these bars."

Layla leaned back, her fingers slipping off the metal. "Fine. Good luck getting any of my clanmates to cooperate with you. You've been gone for so long, Harlem doesn't even recognize you as its own. The city will eat you alive, and my clan will finish whatever is left of you."

All the air in Elise's lungs went cold. Giving Layla one last stern look, she swallowed hard and looked at the officer standing guard. "Release her."

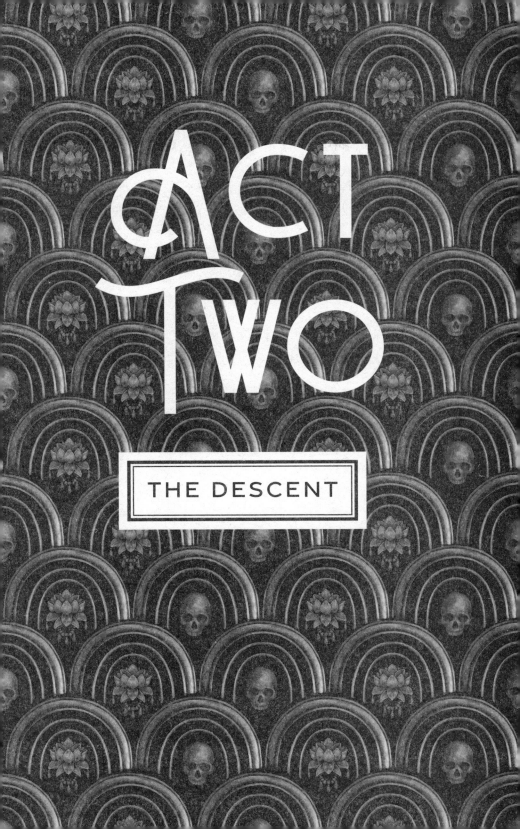

ACT TWO

THE DESCENT

12

"I S THIS REALLY NECESSARY? I'M POSITIVE A document won't prevent me from ripping your throat out if I should get so hungry." Layla ran her tongue over her enlarged canines while Elise set a contract in front of her. She glared at Layla, who only rolled her eyes. "I'm kidding. God, learn a joke, or two. You've always been so uptight."

Elise's jaw ticked as she pointed to a paragraph on the contract. "If you do such a thing, my father will remove the Hotel Clarice from Valeriya's possession and we will make sure there is no room for any reapers in Harlem. Kill me and you will have no home, no family, nothing left. And you will be locked up for the rest of your long, miserable life, claimed as free property for scientists to test on you as they please. Until the torment of your reaperhood should destroy you," Elise snapped.

Darkness passed over Layla's face, but her cold smile remained. "So personal. I admire the effort, Saint, I truly do. But I have no family. Your father made sure of that years ago," Layla mumbled. She pushed her handcuffs back on her wrists and leaned over to take a pen to the paper in front of her.

"You blame me and my father, but we are not the reapers who took your parents' lives and turned you," Elise hissed.

Layla's jaw clenched. Her hands went flat on the table while her body tensed and for a moment, Elise thought she might pounce on her. "No. But you told your father about my parents' plans to desegregate the east side of Harlem and *you* encouraged him to stop them. By whatever means necessary. You might as well have sent the reapers on us yourself. Some saint you are. A bystander to carnage does not a saint make," Layla seethed. "You killed me. You're a killer."

Elise's breath shook as she watched Layla draw out her neat signature on the dotted lines. She leaned in close enough to whisper directly into the reaper's ear. "I'd be careful how you behave around me." Elise swore she saw Layla's entire demeanor shift at her words. She felt heat roll off Layla's neck, her own body tensing as the reaper turned toward her so they were face-to-face.

Layla watched Elise, eyes glowing. "I don't know how to behave around you," she hissed. Her fangs were still out, their points digging into her lips. Blood beaded on the soft pink of her mouth. They were so close, Elise could smell the blood, feel Layla's breath.

It was as if a wicked spell had been cast, preventing her from looking away. Heat twisted in Elise's stomach and she exhaled sharply. "Layla…"

"You sound afraid, Saint. Is it because of what happened five years ago?" Leaning closer, Layla's mouth twisted into a smug curve and Elise felt something twinge in her chest. The reaper's eyes dropped first to her lips, then her throat, where Elise's pulse beat rapidly against her delicate flesh. "I will have you know, that was not personal. It was pure reaper instinct that is impossible to control when you are first turned. But…" The light in Layla's eyes flickered, and Elise's breath stilled at the cruel longing in her gaze. "Your blood has always been my favorite. Even after all these years—"

"I don't care." Elise snatched the contract up and backed away.

"Damn. Shouldn't you listen to what your partner has to say? We're in this together, are we not?" Layla leaned against the interrogation room table and held out her cuffed wrists, frowning. "These are annoying."

Elise's glare deepened. "I will listen to everything regarding the case and information surrounding this investigation. You do not need to bring up our past. We are not friends." She gave Layla the coldest look she could muster up, but Layla didn't even flinch. Elise turned and nodded to the window, where officers awaited her cue. Soon after, two men walked into the room and uncuffed Layla.

The young reaper snatched her hands back as soon as they were off. Bright red rings circled her wrists, burnt from the specialized metal meant to withstand reaper strength. The whole interrogation, Layla must have been in immense pain, yet she said nothing. Layla turned to Elise. "Well, seeing as I am a free woman and the workday is over, I will be going." She threw Elise a mocking smile on her way out of the station.

Elise swallowed a scream. Only an hour into their arrangement, and already, Layla was getting under her skin, digging up scars of their past. Already, regret plagued the decision to work together. *The Saint and the damned.* Elise feared the contract she held was no more than a litany of lies.

After nearly twenty-four hours in the interrogation chair, at the worst, Layla expected intrusive questions from her clan members. But instead, she got cold stares and snubbed attempts at conversation. The only beings who did not side-eye her were the four police officers and Saint guards standing watch outside the lair. Even Mei had a new distrust in her eyes when Layla ran into her in the hotel lobby.

The older reaper didn't even look up from the set of cards she shuffled as Layla sat in the chair across from her. "Mei—"

"I'm busy," Mei said flatly.

Layla cocked her head to one side. "Unless you're playing solitaire, which I guess is a valid excuse to be busy with, I'm sure you can speak to me. Are you playing solitaire?" Layla asked.

Mei dropped the cards and glared at Layla. "What do you want? In case you haven't noticed, everyone has been talking about you, wondering why you would do such a stupid thing to put the Harlem reapers under police scrutiny."

"Oh, that's rich coming from you," Layla spat. "You just took down an entire gang. And even worse, you ruined my bed while doing it. I didn't tell anyone about that, yet here you are, trying to make my business into a bigger problem than it actually is—"

"I'm not targeting you. I'm prioritizing my safety because the police and the Saints—the *Saints*, Layla, who regularly wipe out our kind—are watching us even closer. It's beyond just unspoken rules and mutual agreements now. They've threatened to destroy our lair." There was truth to Mei's words, but Layla had difficulty processing them. She couldn't say she wasn't at fault because she had been at the crime scene and she could not remember any of it. There was no way to extract truth from a story she didn't have.

Layla scoffed, venom spilling into her veins. "You're really freezing me out after I covered for your mess with the Diamond Dealers?"

"You were a part of that too," Mei said. Her eyes, already dark and distant, looked away.

A bitter hiss left Layla as she nodded slowly. "So you think I just snapped one night and said to hell with every moral code we have here?"

"You're a reaper. Just because you hate it does not make you any better than the things you do because of it." Mei's voice was cold and absolute. Just like the half-life full of blood and damnation Layla had been forced into since becoming a reaper.

Rage suddenly bubbled to the surface and spilled over, shaking her hands and hardening her voice. "Fuck you," Layla hissed.

"You need to get over your strange complex, Quinn," Mei said.

But Layla was already gone. She stormed out of the hotel lobby and into her bedroom.

More than anything now, Layla wanted the burden of her

reaperhood gone. She was sick of having a reputation follow her just because of what she was, rather than *who* she was.

The envy she'd felt looking at Theo's body, somehow turned human, strained her senses now. It was all she wanted, her human life back. When times were simpler, when she still had people to love and who loved her back, when she *loved her life*. To be human again, in death or in life, Layla was scared she would damn every shade of morality to return to that state.

And there was only one person she knew who had a path to that end.

Shadows shrouded the sitting room when Elise walked in. Her father stood, leaning against the fireplace mantel, unmoving even when Elise muttered a goodbye to Sterling at the door.

"Hey." Sterling grabbed her hand before she could turn away from him. "Don't be nervous. He trusts you. You are the future of this empire, and he knows it," he said softly.

Elise chewed her lip. "Right." She didn't believe him, but the words felt good to hear. She squeezed his hand as he left the room, then turned to her father, exhaling heavily. "Father."

Mr. Saint did not face her. "Yes, Elise."

"Layla signed the agreement. I'm not sure how much the police have told you, but there seem to be discrepancies—"

"Any news?" Mr. Saint interjected.

Elise blinked. "Well. Layla is certain it's not just a reaper problem—"

"I implore you, Elise, to focus on our mission as an empire. You cannot forget what reapers have done to our family. To this world." Mr. Saint finally turned away from the mantel and in his hands he had the box with Charlotte's gun. His voice went hard, "Don't tell me a few years in France has made you forget."

Tears filled Elise's eyes and she swallowed hard, but could not breathe past the lump in her throat. "Of course not—"

"Look at me," her father said sharply. Elise complied. The stark pain in his dark eyes pierced her heart and she had to look away again, settling right on the gun, the last thing she had to remember her older sister by. "You've only just stepped into this role, yet you've already become sidetracked, tempted by the reapers' contagious allure for sin…"

The memories came rushing back to her. In an instant, she was back at the 148th Street brownstone, fingers clamped around her older sister's wrist so hard, she was sure her skin would bruise. There was so much blood, Elise couldn't even see the natural color of the wood floor beneath Charlotte's body. Her slick fingers slipped over the syringe as she positioned the needle containing Mrs. Gray's antidote over her sister's limp arm.

The only thing Elise could see through her tears was the glint of Charlotte's revolver in the faint moonlight streaming through the window. Even when she stabbed the needle into her sister's flesh and prayed for a miracle, all Elise could focus on was the blood.

A gentle hand touched her cheek, and Elise jerked, trembling with fear. She blinked and stared up at her father. Satisfaction had replaced the pain in his eyes, but Elise could not stamp out the memory of her sister's screams, no matter how hard she tried to ground herself in the present. Her fingers curled around her father's hand and he held her back, thumb stroking over the pounding pulse in her wrist. "No reaper, not even ones we used to be close to, are to be trusted. Ever. Am I understood?" Mr. Saint asked gently.

Elise nodded.

"Speak up, Elise," he grated out.

"Yes, Father."

Mr. Saint released her hand, stepping back. He closed the gun case and nodded to the door. "Go now. I will see you for dinner later."

"I wish I could help you," Sterling murmured into Elise's hair. His arms tightened around her, and Elise buried her face in his chest.

"I don't trust myself with this role. I wish we could have taken it on together," Elise whispered as she pulled away.

Sterling brushed her hair back and smirked. "You give me too much credit."

Elise scoffed. "You're my father's favorite. I think he likes you more than he likes me and Josi."

"Elise, your fears are speaking nonsense again," he muttered.

Sterling reached into his holster and pulled out one of his guns. "Here." He held it out to Elise.

She gave him a confused look. "No. It's a gift from my father, you can't—" Elise remembered reading his excitement in a letter a few months ago while in her bed after collapsing from an especially long orchestra rehearsal. "You can't give it up."

"Your safety is more important, Elise. I'll take it back once this is all over," Sterling insisted. He offered her a tight smile as he pressed the revolver into her hand.

Elise nodded. She gave him a teary smile. "I'm sorry for everything, Sterling."

Sterling shook his head. "None of this is your fault."

"Layla attacked because I came back. Thalia is dead because I suggested going out that night. Now your favorite Saint sister is going to France—"

"You know Josi is my favorite? Do I really make it that obvious?" Sterling feigned shock. Elise slapped his shoulder, but she finally cracked a smile. He grabbed her hand, grinning back. "How do you think I survived without my best friend for all those years? I told myself you were safer there. And I know it will be the same for Josi. Thalia is not your fault either." His jaw tightened and he swallowed hard. "These damn reapers ruin everything. But the empire's new plans with Stephen Wayne are going to fix things, make us stronger. And you will be at the forefront of it all."

Elise knew he meant well, but his words only added pressure. He patted her arm and backed away.

"As long as I have this family, I have nothing to worry about. I believe in you, Lise," he said gently.

He might as well have shown her his heart. Elise smiled. This time it felt real.

13

FOR THE FIRST TIME EVER, ELISE ARRIVED AT THE Chelsea Piers without the intention to board a ship. Instead of her trunks, the chauffeur unloaded her little sister's luggage. Elise held Josi's hand as she looked around, apprehension crossing her soft face.

Their parents had said their goodbyes at the house; a tutor was accompanying Josi to France. Elise knew Josi was bound to break down at the departure, and she didn't want to make it worse for her sister by having her entire family crowding her at the docks. So she brought Josi herself, the tutor and guards walking a good distance behind to give them privacy.

As they approached the gangway of the ship, Josi squeezed Elise's hand and dug her heels into the ground to stop their movement. "I'm not ready," Josi whispered. The heavy salt air disturbed her hair, her curls and the pink bows that matched her dress fluttering with the breeze.

Elise set her bag down so she could kneel in front of her sister. Tears crested in her eyes, and Elise's heart cracked at the sight. "I was this nervous, too, before I went to France. But do you remember reading the letters I sent you?"

Josi nodded.

"What did I tell you about?" Elise asked.

"You had fun. You made music and met lots of friends," Josi said in a small voice.

"Yes. That's what you want, right?" Elise tried to keep her voice from wavering, but raw emotions seeped into her words.

Josi nodded again. "I want to dance."

"That's exactly what you will do. You will meet so many new friends, and you will get to spend time practicing your ballet." She wiped a tear from Josi's cheek.

"I wish you could come," Josi whimpered.

Elise held her hand and pointed to their matching Saint rings. She tried not to think about how Josi's had been clutched in Layla's hands just days earlier. "We will never really be separated," she whispered.

Josi's eyes brightened. Elise pulled her into a strong hug, breathing in the soft scent of her soap while her curls brushed her cheek. "I love you, my dove. More than anything. Even when I'm not with you." She moved her hand between them and placed it over Josi's heart. "I'm with you in here. Always."

A sob tore from Josi. "Promise?"

Elise's throat burned with the effort of holding back tears. "I promise."

Elise watched the boat until it was a speck in the distance across the huge expanse of the ocean. The tutor had promised to bring Josi to the deck to wave goodbye, but they never emerged. Now the last image Elise had of her younger sister was one of despair. In only a few minutes, miles of sea had stretched between her and her sister. Tears filled her eyes, and her throat tightened to the point of pain to keep them back. Every part of her being wanted to crumple. But the tiny shred of knowledge that she had done what she could to keep Josi safe held her together. Each step she took with Layla, no matter how damned it made her feel, would benefit Josi in the long run, keeping her far from the chaos that had killed their older sister.

A rough sigh escaped her lips before Elise turned away from the waterfront. She expected to see the new Saint chauffeur, Colm's replacement, coming to meet her; instead, Layla emerged from the crowd. She looked especially peeved, the downturn of her mouth and crease in her brow defiant. The expression sparked recognition in Elise's mind. When they had been younger and arguing about which game to play next, Layla had always managed to pull such an angry face that Elise could only laugh and give in to her demands. But now, Elise just turned and walked past her.

Layla fell into step beside Elise. She wore loose pants and a sweater, all black, with boots to match. "You'll see her again. She's not dying," Layla muttered.

Elise stopped and turned a fierce glare onto Layla. "Do not speak about her. *Ever*. Or I will ensure you do not come out of this partnership alive."

Layla's lips parted and a slight smile crossed her face. "You speak in sins more than I do, Saint."

Ignoring her quip, Elise ground her teeth together. "You owe me proof, Layla," she said.

"Proof of your sinful way of speaking? Well, I do recall—*years ago*—that time you began swearing during a game of chess—"

Elise whirled on Layla and snapped, "Proof for the murder." Her breath came out in a heated rasp of irritation and the satisfied smile from Layla only made Elise's chest feel hotter.

Layla tilted her head to one side. Sunlight stroked across the slope of her neck, illuminating her skin like honey set ablaze. She brushed a stray curl behind her ear and Elise watched her hand until it disappeared into her coat pocket. "We need to start with Theo. I'm assuming you were given his home address so we can visit—"

"He didn't live in your lair?" Elise asked, confused.

Layla shook her head. "No. In fact, I found him on a blood high and offered him solace in my lair, but he refused it." Darkness covered her eyes, but Elise could not quite decipher the emotions behind it.

She crossed her arms and straightened her back, lifting her chin. "You should have reported him if he was newly turned."

"Oh, please, Saint. I know the law protects you and your people, but reapers are not so lucky. You and the police are true monsters. Fewer people got hurt because I didn't turn Theo in," Layla muttered.

Elise gave her a sidelong glance. There was no universe in which she considered humans to be more monstrous than reapers. She had seen what Layla and the other reapers were capable of. Elise still could not get the crime scene and Thalia's lifeless body out of her mind, not to mention the near death that had taken place in her own room years ago. Nothing came close to the caliber of violence and depravity reapers created and lived by.

"Oh my God," Layla hissed. "Stop looking at me like that. You look like a scared rat."

"Stop calling me Saint."

"It's your name." Layla smirked, looking Elise up and down. "Would you rather I call you 'sweet blood'? Or 'pretty girl'?"

Overwhelming irritation wiped out every other emotion stirring in Elise. Looking away, she clenched her jaw to keep from shouting her next words. "We cannot go to Theo's house. His family is grieving—"

"Okay. Then you can go home and tell your father you're an awful investigator and an even worse heir, because there is no way you're cut out for this," Layla spat.

The pressure in her chest from the combating emotions Layla caused threatened to explode. Elise wasn't sure how she would survive this partnership. Frustration was quickly burning through all of her patience.

The sooner she got answers, the sooner she rid herself of Layla and won her father's trust. "Fine," Elise gritted out. She started to turn away, but Layla stopped, her body tensing.

"*Oh.* Theo's parents might have been his first kill…" She spoke so quietly, it must have been to herself.

Something acidic circled Elise's throat, and her stomach turned at the thought of visiting another crime scene. "You think we will walk into a bloodbath?" she asked.

A smile broke across Layla's face. And when she spoke, the bittersweet tone of her voice sent a chill down Elise's spine, "No. I'm just trying to prepare you for the worst, Saint. Because if you're going to work with me, you'll need to get used to the blood."

14

THEO SMITH'S HOME WAS AN ORDINARY ROW HOUSE with an ivy-covered fence in front and neatly kept flowers on the front stoop. Already, Elise was confused. They had come here to Brooklyn, yet the scene of the crime sat right at the edge of Harlem reaper territory. Why had a human been lurking there at all?

Elise allowed herself to consider that Layla's claim about Theo—that he had not been human when she knew him—was in the realm of possibility.

"You should stay out here," she told Layla. "His parents probably still think you're involved in the murder, and I want them to feel like they can open up to me."

Layla nodded and remained on the sidewalk. Elise climbed the front steps but turned back for a moment. She knew this area wasn't far from the neighborhood where Layla had lived with her family; she watched the reaper for any sense of acknowledgment. But there was only a sharp bitterness in Layla's eyes. Elise's own memories were rife with familiarity; when her parents would come for tea at the Quinn home and Elise would follow Layla to the attic, where they would point at the stars through the tiny round window and make wishes.

To dance the lead in *Swan Lake* in Paris had always been Layla's wish.

To perform her own original music throughout the world in front of an awe-filled audience had always been Elise's dream.

Knocking on the door to the Smith house felt strangely familiar. In Paris, visiting friends involved strolling into different neighborhoods where they lived. There were no vengeful reapers after her in Paris, making her afraid to go out on her own. But here, back at home, chauffeurs drove her everywhere or else the Saint guards brought people to the house. She should have paid attention to the moment Paris began to feel more like home than Harlem.

A young Black woman with tired eyes opened the door. It was nearly midday, but she wore a silk robe and a scarf on her head, like she had just gotten out of bed. A pang of sympathy hit Elise; Theo's mother was taking her son's death like a physical blow.

"Theo isn't home. He's not coming home. Please stop coming by, and tell his other friends to stop coming by. I can send the funeral information, but I…" Her face went slack while she stared Elise down, as if she was just now seeing her clearly. "You're not his classmate, are you? I don't recognize you."

Elise shook her head. "I'm Elise Saint. I'm here to see you, if I may please have a moment of your time."

"Saint?" Mrs. Smith's grip tightened on the door as she noticed Elise's ring. "Can you help us?"

"I just have a few questions about Theo. I'm hoping your answers will help me figure out what happened to him," Elise said.

But Mrs. Smith looked skeptical. "You look too young to... You're even younger than my daughter, Millie." She finally moved back and let Elise inside. The Saint name was well enough known throughout New York that it either roused resentment, or trust. Elise was lucky to have the latter on her side today.

"I'm sorry, I would offer you tea, but we ran out. It's the only thing I can stomach right now."

Once they were settled in the living room, Elise pulled out a notebook and pen. "When was the last time you saw Theo alive?"

A new wave of sadness seemed to crash over Mrs. Smith, her hands shaking while she wrung them together. "The day before it happened. He said he was going to stay the night with friends and that I would see him in the morning, but he never came home." Her voice trembled. "I knew I should have made him come home. These damn reapers are killing us. Our poor children can't be normal children."

"I understand how that feels." Elise swallowed hard, thinking of how just a few hours ago, Josi wept while she walked up the gangway to the ship. "That's why I'm here today."

Mrs. Smith took a deep breath before speaking again. "Theo was a very social young man. He was always with friends after school, sometimes even before school. It's strange, I feel like I hardly saw him in the days leading up to…" Mrs. Smith's voice caught. "His usual group of friends came by one day and they asked for him and I was confused because I thought he was with them. That's when I found out he was hanging around new people. I thought he had joined a gang. He was spending so much time at the Cotton Club, and he came home smelling like alcohol." She whispered the last words.

The anguish and fear in the woman's voice was almost too much for Elise to bear. She desperately wanted to stop her, but she knew she needed to hear more. "Do you know the names of the people Theo was seeing at the Cotton Club?"

"I can't be sure that he ever went in the club. You know that's not allowed. But he associated with performers and people who supplied products there, I believe. Or so I've heard from neighbors," Mrs. Smith said. "I really don't…" She trailed off, pursing her lips as her eyes filled with new tears. "I'm not sure how much longer I can go on, Miss Saint."

Elise leaned across the table and placed her hand over Mrs. Smith's shaking ones. "Thank you for taking the time to speak with me. Would you mind sharing with me the information you've gotten from the police? Autopsy results, anything—"

Mrs. Smith's frown deepened. "They have not stopped by yet. I've gone to the station, but they say they have other cases to take care of first."

A sour taste filled Elise's mouth at those words. Still, she stood, smiling gently. "I will get answers for you. I'm so sorry for your loss. I pray his soul is at peace."

Layla was leaning against the fence when Elise left the house. "How did it go?" she asked.

Elise sighed. "As well as an interrogation of a grieving mother can go." She paused on the sidewalk, thinking. "Mrs. Smith said Theo spent time outside the Cotton Club. But...why? He was a fifteen-year-old boy who probably had much better things to do." She stiffened when she felt Layla lean close to her, her shoulder brushing her arm while she looked over the notes she'd taken.

"Maybe he worked there," Layla said.

"Don't you think his mother would have known that, though?" Elise asked.

Layla sighed. "Not if it was a speakeasy."

"Right." Elise swallowed. "Mrs. Smith said the police have not been by, nor have they helped her at the station. I thought..." She bit her lower lip as it trembled. "I thought we would assist on the case, but I think we're the only ones who are invested at all."

A low noise left Layla's throat.

Elise blinked. "Excuse you."

"I said 'of course,'" Layla snapped. And despite the tough exterior she upheld, Elise saw pain darkening her eyes. "No one ever cares when it's a Black body."

Elise's mind went back to the radio report she had heard the day after the murder. "The news opinions are all about how the country's image is tainted by our growing reaper problem. Yet, there has been no call to action. Sometimes I feel like my family are the only people who care about fixing things," she muttered.

Layla raised her eyebrows. "You cannot possibly be that delusional."

"Excuse me?" Elise scoffed. "I'm delusional for believing in my family's desire to do good for our community?"

"You are delusional to believe that anyone with as much power and money as your father would ever act purely on a principle of goodness. I know you've lived in a high-society bubble your whole life, so it might be difficult to believe, but the world is not so black and white. People are more than just good or bad," Layla huffed out.

The conversation with Mrs. Smith still weighed so heavily on her that Elise did not have the energy to challenge Layla's words. But her mind hung on to them, turning them over and over while she considered her family's role in the spread of reaperhood. Everything her father did was to keep their family and Harlem safe. She had never considered the possibility of malice, or some ulterior motive behind his actions. Elise knew her father.

She snapped her notebook shut. "You are so keen on giving me every bit of information except for the proof I asked for," Elise said coolly.

Layla's eyes glimmered on Elise. "Okay, *princess*. I'll get you your proof. Let's go to the morgue and see how you do with a dead body."

The morgue was just as Elise had imagined it to be. Cold and desolate. Antiseptic burned the inside of her nose while they entered the examination room. It was as if the scent of years and years of blood and rotting flesh still lingered, even if it had been cleaned up long ago.

"Damn. I'm kind of mad I didn't get a Saint ring in the time I was a part of that cult because that thing gives you access everywhere. Imagine all the fancy clubs I could get into…" Layla said as they walked in.

Elise ignored her, reading the name tags in order to locate Theo's body. "He should be in—Layla, *wait*," she called when Layla left her side. But the reaper did not acknowledge her. Rolling her eyes, Elise approached a wall of body drawers. She made it through only two name tags before the insufferable sound of metal grinding on metal pulled her focus.

Layla peered down at a body bag in the drawer she'd opened. "I found him." Her expression seemed painfully bored for someone in the presence of a dead body. "I recognized his scent. No matter how much you scrub at them, or how much bleach you lather on them, a person's essence always remains." She unzipped the bag and inhaled.

Elise wanted to gag. She shuddered and swallowed back bile. The scent of death and decay was rather subdued, but the mixture of cleaning chemicals almost did her in.

Layla, however, was as close as she could get, peering down at Theo, her fingers resting right on his ashen skin. "I can smell the Saint members' blood in him. But there's something else…" She looked up and smiled cruelly at Elise. Then she sank her nails into Theo's throat.

Theo's blood smelled purely human. His essence, though, was of himself and four other beings. The older Saint member, Thalia, and Layla. The fourth scent was unknown.

"He fed on someone before he died," Layla said. She reached into his mouth, feeling a gap where his reaper fangs should have been. "He's missing a tooth." Layla gestured for Elise to look. Elise, hesitant at first, moved slowly into a position that allowed her to see inside his mouth.

"So he really bit them…" Elise said in a quiet voice. "Why would they hide this?"

"It's easier to blame reapers for every problem," Layla muttered.

Elise didn't react. She continued to stare at Theo, her eyes shifting from sadness to anger. It took Layla a moment to remember that Elise's friends were dead—likely at Theo's hands. Death was a common visitor in Layla's life. It became routine, a daily occurrence that she had grown numb to. She forgot most humans didn't deal with the macabre as closely as she did. They got to enjoy the beautiful parts of life while reapers had no choice but to partake of the darkest aspects of living. The parts no one wanted to talk about, or acknowledge.

But even before becoming a reaper, Layla knew death was as important and necessary to life as living was. Being a reaper just made her appreciate it more.

Layla removed her hands from Theo's mouth and zipped his body bag back up. "He might have fed on the Saints, but there is someone else he hunted that night. I can taste them." She licked the remaining drops of blood from her finger. They were stale and bitter to the taste, but they confirmed her suspicions—there was someone else involved in the crime.

Layla sensed the blood rush in Elise's cheeks. The Saint girl was uncomfortable. "You did not need to perform your own pseudo autopsy on him like that," she muttered.

Layla resisted the urge to smile. She had never seen a Saint undone like this before. "Well, this is how reapers work. I told you it would be too much for you." Her words carried a taunt.

Elise shot Layla a look over her shoulder, flat and unimpressed. Though she hadn't managed to get a rise out of her, Layla was glad to no longer be scrutinized by those terrified eyes.

Elise reached for the clipboard hanging from Theo's drawer. "This is how *people* work," Elise said calmly. But as she read over the pages, her expression changed. Finally she looked up, a realization widening her eyes. "He went to the clinic for a reaper bite just before the murder. I saw him there… He looked really scared."

Layla pressed her fingertips to her lips, thinking. "If he frequented the Cotton Club, there's a chance he got involved with some bad people…or reapers," she said.

Elise blinked. "So it's true. There *are* reapers at jazz clubs."

15

THE COTTON CLUB CAME TO LIFE AT NIGHT. LIGHTS pulsed through the windows, and music vibrated from the inside all the way out to the street. Even the passersby not keen on finding a drink, or quick entertainment, stopped to peer into the windows and see the source of the commotion. Those that craved debauchery and desired sin and mutiny entered. Authorities be damned, it was one of the few places in the city where cultures clashed.

Brown-skinned dancers lined up by the stage, swaying and bouncing to the evocative live music. Their long legs glimmered in the light, beaded skirts and flashy tops catching the eyes of the audience. Some of the girls blew kisses and the crowd hollered for more.

Now that she was seeing the club at night, Layla found the place quite fascinating. A beautiful Black girl on the street would never be treated as kindly; not even well-educated Black people in the workforce garnered much respect. But here, in the Cotton Club, where white people paid for this entertainment, whooping and clapping at the performers as if they were animals, Black people were praised.

It felt like a circus. Layla couldn't imagine how the performers felt, being scrutinized by the white gaze every night on that stage.

"Interesting," Elise murmured by her side.

Layla couldn't disagree. Since walking in with the Saint heiress, she'd been captivated, though the idea of voluntarily going to an establishment that usually forbade Black patrons made Layla's skin prickle. While Elise gave the club hostess the name of one of the club managers who had done business with her father, Layla noticed a poster in the foyer detailing the opening of a new clinic. Before she could get a closer look, the manager showed up.

"Elise Saint, daughter of my favorite business partner," greeted the white man who had been called to let them backstage. He wore a tailored suit and swirled a glass of amber liquid in his hand while he chewed a cigar. The smoke weaved between them and Layla blinked as it clouded her eyes. "If I tell your father you're here, he won't question me, will he?" the man asked Elise.

"No, Mr. Calhoun," Elise said. "He will be very appreciative that you donated your time and space to help our investigation."

"I sure hope my club is not involved in anything dirty. We're already bleeding money, and the police are on us most busy nights. One more blow might just finish this place," Calhoun muttered around his cigar. "You can talk to the dancers that aren't performing, but don't bother anyone else. If I get a single complaint from any customers, you're out of here. Got it?"

Elise nodded. "Yes, sir."

Layla hardly waited for Calhoun to be out of earshot before she began to mock Elise. "'Yes, sir. No, sir.' God, if you stooped any lower, you might end up in hell."

"You're *so lovely* to be around," Elise said, sarcasm dripping from her words. "You know it's easier to play the long game with them than to be resistant. It only makes things harder. Police have done worse to Black men for misspeaking in the South. Be grateful you have rights at all."

This, Layla could not ignore. "Excuse you? You must be brainwashed, Miss 'I have a dress for every type of occasion' and 'I'm gifted jewelry as frequently as a parent buys their child candy.' I will never be grateful for being treated like a second-class citizen, or barely human. If you want to be disrespected, that's your choice, but I refuse. It's bad enough that I can't choose how I function as a damned reaper."

Layla stepped back to distance herself from Elise. She tried not to acknowledge the resentment she had toward her reaperhood because it was like beating a dead horse. But still, it unnerved her that people like Elise were so horribly adjusted, they couldn't even acknowledge their own faults or privileges. Humanity was the one thing Layla wished she had. While being a reaper moved her further from being considered human, being Black already set her back several steps. Elise was foolish to accept the scraps they were handed. That was exactly how white people controlled minority groups: by making themselves out to be graceful saviors everyone was lucky to have.

But there was nothing lucky about being forced to assimilate just for a chance of being given rights that you already deserved in the first place. There was nothing lucky about relying on others for validation. There was nothing lucky about only being acknowledged while you were on your knees. And for white people to acquire superiority only through forcing others down to their knees made them bereft. Layla had lasted her whole life without kneeling to the white standard. She would continue to do so for as long as she existed.

Layla clamped her mouth shut, pressing her lips together so tightly, the color drained from them. She remained silent as she followed Elise around the back of the club. The bustle of the club decreased the farther they went. Once they reached a dressing room, the sounds from the busy stage almost faded completely. Layla stopped clenching her fists, her sensitive ears no longer ringing with the bumps and vibrations of the music. A relieved breath left her body and she looked around the dressing room for Giana.

She was easy to spot. The dancer with the darkest skin and the longest legs stuck out like a glistening mirror among stained glass. Rhinestones embedded in her corset bodice glinted in the light; the white fabric of her skirt stood out against her brown skin—Giana was radiant.

The dancer watched Layla in the vanity mirror. She set her makeup brush down, turning to face her. "Welcome to my humble abroad."

Layla laughed sharply. "It's *abode*. But thank you, Gigi."

"Gigi? You haven't called me that in ages. You must need something." Giana pulled her mink shrug off a stool beside her and gestured toward it. "Please sit, lovey." That hospitality of hers never got old. She was the closest thing to a sibling for Layla. Giana had been there for Layla throughout the adjustment period after turning, and Layla was glad to see her now.

Elise nudged Layla. "Who is this?"

"This is my friend, Giana Taylor. Giana, this is Elise Saint—"

"Oh, I know you, Miss Saint." Giana grinned. "Welcome home. Please tell your father that Harlem is grateful for his contributions to the Cotton Club. The neighborhood has been thriving. Your family seems to have no shortage of financial gains." Giana eyed the pearl necklace at Elise's throat, then the gold signet ring she wore.

"If her father were white," Layla remarked, "he would probably own the world. He knows how to make a profit from anything."

"Truly," Giana said. "Your Saint friend is quite—"

"She's not my friend," Layla snapped.

At the same time, Elise laughed dryly, "Oh, please."

Most people in Harlem knew of the feud between Saints and reapers, and more significantly, the spilled blood between Elise and Layla. Sometimes Layla thought that the two of them existed as an ancient legend in another life.

"Hmm." Giana lifted a brow and slipped the fur shrug over her shoulders. "What did you need? Please make this quick. I need to rehearse my routine."

Layla took the stool beside her friend. "Did you know a young man named Theo Smith? His mother said he spent a lot of time here before he died."

Giana's eyes flashed. "You knew him?"

"Hardly. I'm trying to figure out how it was that he turned, but was human when he died," Layla said.

Confusion twisted Giana's expression. "Oh, Layla, you know I don't like getting involved in other people's dramas."

"I know, Gigi, but it's not just drama; it's reaper business too," Layla said.

Elise had remained standing, her eyes wandering around the room. But now she turned to stare at Giana and went still.

Giana sighed. "Theo did stop by here a few times. But not to work. For the…" She lowered her voice. "The speakeasy. Jamie could tell you all about it. Theo had a crush on one of the dancers; oh, they were adorable," Giana said.

"Who?" Layla asked.

Elise also pressed closer, her interest piqued.

Giana paused. Her lower lip trembled as she considered her next words. "Shirley Redfield. She hasn't been here recently. I've heard she's sick." Giana breathed in deeply. "When did Theo die?"

"Two days ago."

"That's when Shirley stopped showing up for work," Giana whispered.

Layla opened her mouth to ask another question, but Elise beat her to it. "Do you know where she lives?"

16

NIGHT CLOAKED THE CITY AS THEY HEADED DOWN-
town. Elise tightened her coat against the wind, but Layla
was unbothered, her arms bare even when the temperature
dropped several degrees. The arrival of fall stood just around the
corner and Elise was glad for it.

She had been on her feet all day, trekking across the city with
Layla. Neither of them had come to any clear conclusion about
the murders. Whenever an answer felt possible to Elise, it slipped
between her fingers, remaining just out of reach.

She also could not shake the unease she'd felt when she realized
she had been standing in a room with two reapers, one of whom was
a complete stranger. "Why didn't you tell me Giana was a reaper?"
she asked Layla.

Layla continued to stare ahead. "I thought you assumed. I spend
my time with other reapers."

"I did not believe reapers could be at a jazz club. I thought they…" Elise trailed off.

This time, Layla glared at Elise. "You thought they what? Because reapers are beneath you, they cannot participate in the arts?" A bitter smile broke across Layla's face. "No, you believe that reapers are monsters who have nothing to live for, right?"

Elise looked away. She had never imagined reapers participating in any mundane activities; it seemed futile with their condition. "I do not think it's absurd to assume nonhumans would not participate in human activities—"

"We were human once. Do you think we just stopped loving what we had and wanted as humans because we turned?" Layla asked. "You really know nothing about us. That bubble you live in is far more opaque than I first believed it to be."

Elise scoffed. "Oh, please. I have done more and traveled more than you. There is no bubble—"

"*That is the bubble*," Layla snapped. "Not everyone can do as they please just like you, Saint. What do you think of the people who cannot get into your fancy jazz clubs because of their skin color?" Layla demanded.

Elise stammered, "I—I have no problem and my family frequents them just fine—"

"What about those who do not have the money and status your family has? Do they not deserve to experience the beauty and sanctity of art and music? Do you even know where it comes from?"

"Of course—"

"Then how can you say something so stupid when you just witnessed people who look just like you on that stage? They are the heart of the arts you bleed for. Shame on you for assuming otherwise," Layla muttered. She pushed forward, her strides getting faster, as if she wanted to put more distance between them.

Swallowing hard, Elise followed. She could hardly keep up and she wasn't sure she wanted to anymore. Layla's words only weighed her down further.

"Tired?" Layla asked. She was several paces ahead of Elise on the street. "You're dragging your feet."

A hot flush burned Elise's cheeks. She scowled at the back of Layla's head while she scrambled to catch up, trying to keep her footsteps light. "I spend my time composing music and practicing, not breaking and entering like you. I was not raised to have the stealth of a bandit," Elise muttered. While she bristled with irritation at Layla's comment, a small part of her remembered when they were younger; whenever Elise got tired, her entire body seemed to slump, her legs and feet especially. It bothered her mother, but Layla was always the first to notice. She would squeeze Elise's hand and rise onto her tiptoes to whisper in her ear, *"gentle steps, Lisey."* That warning would save her from getting a scolding from her mother.

Now, Layla's words were more like mockery than a gentle warning. Still, Elise picked her feet up and tried to walk in a quieter manner.

Up ahead, Layla's shoulders tensed. "In case you forgot, we were basically raised together. If I'm a bandit, then so are you."

Elise rolled her eyes. Though Layla was not wrong. They had been raised together, the Quinns and Saints building their lives in a parallel fashion since Mr. and Mrs. Saint had first arrived in New York. A fateful shared train car brought them together, and their bond only grew once they each had daughters the same age. "I'm so sorry, *Your Majesty*," Elise drew out sarcastically. "I will do my best to no longer annoy you."

"I'm not worried about you annoying me. I am, however, worried about your shuffling drawing attention to us. One day you will get me killed." Layla stopped and stared hard at Elise. "Oh, wait. You already did."

Elise's heart skipped a beat.

The smile that curved Layla's lips started that painful thrumming in Elise's chest, an electric current coursing through her. "One thing I will allow you to do is call me 'Your Majesty,'" Layla said. She leaned closer, and Elise felt her breath on her face, warm, yet threatening. "Say it again; it sounded good."

This time, Elise was certain her heart stopped. Heat bloomed in her chest, her pulse going hot while it rushed through her, as if chasing after Layla's words. For once, what held her heart was not ire, and Elise almost welcomed the thorny thrill Layla's words stirred in her. She went still, her feet fixed to the sidewalk even when Layla walked off. If she wasn't made of flesh and pure resistance, Elise might have crumpled in Layla's wake.

Layla loved getting under Elise's skin. It incited in her an exhilaration akin to the high she got from feeding. The stunned look on Elise's face lit a flame in her so bright, Layla was tempted to fan the embers and relish in whatever destruction they brought. But she knew it was reckless to further fray the already tense strings between them.

When they finally found Shirley Redfield's apartment building, Layla sensed something was wrong. The scent of decay followed them up the staircase all the way to the dancer's door. Their knocks were met with silence on the other side. Though Layla sensed no movement inside, she still held a hand up to stop Elise.

"Stay out here," she said quietly.

Elise shook her head and reached for the gun at her belt. "No. We're working together. Besides, I don't want to give you an opportunity to sweep your illegal activity under the rug."

"Really? There could be a reaper who is coming down from a blood high in there and you're worried about me double-crossing you?" Layla asked.

"Always," Elise said flatly.

Layla's lips pursed. Whatever Elise saw in her had nothing to do with Layla and everything to do with Elise proving herself to her father. Still, her stubbornness got under Layla's skin more than she cared to admit. "Fine," she said through gritted teeth. Layla tried to open the door, but Elise grabbed her wrist.

"You can't just break into people's homes!" Elise said in a low voice.

Elise's fingers on Layla's skin sent an icy shock through her. Layla released a nervous breath and wrenched her arm free. "Shirley has turned. I can smell the blood. This home is no longer for people, it's now a reaper's lair. Trust me, I know what I'm doing," she said.

Elise's jaw tightened. The hand with which she had grabbed Layla flexed by her side. She swallowed and nodded toward the door. "I don't trust you. But go ahead."

Inside the apartment was darker than the falling dusk outside. Shadows covered every surface where light was supposed to hit and the stale scent of old blood clung to the air. A quick glance at Elise's face and the noticeable scrunching of her nose told Layla she could smell it too.

Elise pulled her gun out. The silver revolver glinted against the dark, her hand holding it steady while they moved farther into the apartment.

"Do you even know how to use that?" Layla hissed. "I distinctly remember you being too afraid to kill spiders; your father trusting you with a gun was a mistake—"

Elise ground her teeth so hard, Layla could practically hear her frustration. Satisfaction curled in Layla's stomach, and the corner of her mouth ticked up into a slight smile.

Layla followed the murky scent of blood to a room in the back that had to be Shirley's bedroom. Besides the disarray and blood spots, there was no indication of anyone living in the apartment. The kitchen was spotless, no used dishes in the sink, and the living room was orderly, throw blankets folded neatly on the couch, magazines stacked in place on the coffee table. Framed photographs depicted a happy family.

"No sign of the parents," Elise said.

Layla sighed. "They're most likely dead. There's enough blood in this place to bathe in it."

"That was unnecessary," Elise mumbled.

Layla ignored her discomfort. She placed a hand on the doorknob of the bedroom door. "Last chance to take cover," Layla warned.

Elise looked pointedly at the door and lifted her gun. Her thumb traced a cross over the handle. Once, twice, then a third time. "Stop stalling."

Her muscles tensing and her senses sharpening, Layla shoved the door open. Cold air seeped out of the room, cutting straight through the atmosphere around them. Layla's eyes went to the huddled form in the corner. Shirley Redfield. Blood coated her arms up to the elbows, and she clutched her knees to her chest while she rocked back and forth among the scattered remains that Layla could only assume were her parents. Her hair was black, but Layla could see the blood matting her curls. The rank smell told her it was more than a few days old. She wondered how long this girl had been hiding, scared out of her mind.

Layla placed a hand over Elise's gun and lowered it. Surprisingly Elise gave no pushback. She actually stepped closer to Layla, expression bright with alarm and eyes wide while she watched Shirley.

"Shirley," Layla said gently.

Shirley lifted her head. Her face was ashen, lips pale despite the blood splattered across them. She opened her mouth to speak, but her body convulsed and she clamped her mouth shut.

"You dance with Giana Taylor, right?" Layla asked.

Shirley nodded. She released her knees, and the damage became more obvious. The dance costume she wore was white, but the only indication of that were small white spots near her shoulders and hips. Scarlet splashes of blood covered the rest of it, causing the jeweled feathers on the skirt to stick together.

Layla stepped slightly in front of Elise. She extended her arm, her fingers brushing over Elise's waist. The slight shudder that rolled through Elise's body almost made Layla turn around. Whatever the reaction was, Layla wanted to see it. But she gnawed on the inside of her cheek and focused on Shirley. "Can you please tell us what happened?" she asked.

"I don't remember." Shirley's voice trembled. "I was working, and Theo came to visit like he usually did. I know that day was special because the club got a delivery for new costume materials and there were posters about a new Harlem clinic being put up. And then Theo said he liked me a lot. It was like a dream." Shirley's breath caught. "I think he drank from me. But he said it would be okay and that as long as I stayed conscious, I wouldn't turn." She wiped her eyes. "I don't feel like myself anymore. I haven't left my room in I don't know how long. I don't remember much. I want my parents." Her voice broke and more tears spilled down her cheeks. "I'm afraid I hurt them."

Elise shifted behind Layla. She tried to whisper something in her ear, but Layla moved away from her and toward Shirley. This girl was so young. Layla had seen Theo in this exact same position only a few days earlier, but his life had ended in a manner so heinous and violent, Layla was determined to prevent the same thing from happening to Shirley. Even though the life thrumming through Shirley's veins was more decayed than lively now. All the hell that was bound to come for her now as a reaper... She didn't deserve it.

Shirley went to wipe her tears again, but smeared blood across her face. Layla reached forward and dried Shirley's cheeks with her sleeve. "You don't have to go through this alone; I can help you. I was in the same position as you a few years ago, and I have found my way. Do you trust me?" Layla asked. Though Layla's heart ached for the dissipating humanity barely strung as a whisper between them, she remained strong, her voice firm in the face of Shirley's fear.

Something broke in Shirley's eyes. She lifted her brown gaze to Layla's and nodded. The moment their hands met—Layla's squeezing around Shirley's—relief crashed through her. Elise had left the room already. Layla was so wrapped up in making sure Shirley got out okay, she didn't notice when the younger girl's eyes went bright, a sheen of untamed desire lighting her brown irises. She didn't realize the reaction was a direct response to Elise until Shirley lunged forward, hands outstretched and fangs bared.

Elise's gun went flying as Shirley's hands clutched her throat.

A sharp gasp left Elise, her eyes going wide while the reaper's fingers dug in.

Layla sprang up and slammed Shirley into the wall, holding Shirley's arms tight to her sides so she couldn't move. "*Shirley*. Look at me."

Shirley stopped hissing after some time and concentrated on

Layla. Her eyes were so hollow, so lost, Layla thought she was too far gone. She wanted to tell Elise to go and find safety while she took care of Shirley, whether that be putting her out of her own misery, or locking her up until she calmed down. But Layla couldn't stomach either of those options. Her fingers tightened around Shirley's wrists the more the younger girl tried to fight back.

"You're safe. *Shirley*," Layla gritted out with the effort to keep Shirley back. "We're here to help you." Shirley let out a shriek so loud the entire room seemed to shake with it. Being so close to her, Layla's ears rang, and it took more will than the strength she held Shirley back with to keep herself from retreating and covering her sensitive ears. "Shirley. Look at me."

Shirley fell silent. Her glazed-over eyes focused on Layla and her body relaxed. She whimpered, eyes finally settling back to their original brown color. "I need help."

"I know. I'm going to help you," Layla said gently. She released one of Shirley's arms and lifted her wrist to her mouth, sinking her teeth in. "Take some of my blood. It will subdue you for a bit so you aren't so volatile. I'll take you to my lair, and you can calm down there. Okay?" The longer the silence spread between them, Shirley pondering Layla's offer, blood continued to drip down her arm.

Finally, after a moment of consideration and deep breaths, Shirley nodded. She lapped up a few droplets of Layla's blood and soon after Shirley finished, the cut began to stitch itself back together. Only moments later, Shirley's eyes dulled. She no longer trembled in Layla's arms, and when she looked at Elise, Shirley remained calm. No more feral cravings controlling her from the inside out.

Layla passed a lingering look over Elise, confirming that she was safe. "We've done enough for today. Go home. I need to go with her."

Elise opened her mouth as if to protest, but nothing came out. In the time Layla had taken to calm Shirley down, she had picked her gun up. Layla saw the handle peeking out of her coat, but Elise made no move to grab it even when Shirley moved between them. She nodded reluctantly and followed them out of the apartment.

Layla couldn't be positive, but she thought she saw a hint of surprise in Elise's eyes. As if that one image she had of Layla had cracked and the light that shone through stunned her. Layla was glad to be parting ways with her for now. She was tired of being judged by a Saint.

17

SEEING LAYLA BE SO GENTLE WITH THAT NEWLY turned girl surprised Elise. She once knew Layla to be kind. As a little girl, she would save her dessert to split it with Elise and help her discard her vegetables when their parents weren't looking. But surely that Layla was dead. The last image of her before going to France had been one of blood and vengeance, with Layla's hands wrapped around Elise's throat. Layla's gold eyes, lit with a furious fire that demanded to be fed, were all that filled Elise's memories, no matter how much she tried to recall their younger days. A summoner of death and darkness—for a long time, Elise assumed that was all Layla had become.

But after seeing Layla with Shirley, Elise had other thoughts.

More than anything, Elise wanted to kick her shoes off and soak in a hot bath the second she got home. But her father beckoned her into his office and demanded that she update him on her day.

"And the reaper, has she behaved?" Mr. Saint asked once Elise finished her report.

"Layla? Yes. Talking to Theo's parents was actually her idea," Elise said.

"Hmmm…" Mr. Saint paced his study, his arms crossed while he thought. A cigarette hung out of his mouth, smoke puffing through the side of his lips while his arms remained crossed. "I'm sure she's told you more nonsense than truth," he muttered.

Elise blinked. "Maybe. But there seems to be more at stake for her."

"Elise…"

"I'm not saying she didn't commit the crime. Trust me, I'm the last person who would ever defend her," Elise said strongly. "But there are details we've come across that don't make sense. Theo Smith was human when he died, but he was a reaper before. He had a bullet from Colm's gun in his back. A Saint member would never shoot an innocent human, and Layla confirmed that he fed on Thalia and Colm as well as another young girl before he died. That girl, Shirley Redfield, is now a reaper. Layla is convinced Theo turned her."

Mr. Saint rubbed his chin, his mouth curving downward.

"But…that makes Theo's humanity at death more confusing," Elise continued. "Reapers have existed for centuries—since the first enslaved person was brought to this country—and there has never been a cure for reaperhood. This might prove that there is one."

Elise stepped closer to her father. Her eyes shone with hope, but it faltered when her father's frown deepened. "You saw Theo at the clinic when we visited. Maybe Dr. Harding has started running trials on the antidote for reaper venom. We could talk to him, or Mr. Wayne—"

"And ask what?" her father demanded, his voice sharper.

Elise flinched. "Ask if he knows anything about Theo's reaperhood?"

"You want me to implicate the man that is to be my business partner? Do you even hear yourself, Elise? I saw Theo Smith's body, and he was human. Yet you question me and want to question our allies," Mr. Saint spat. He took his cigarette from his mouth and stabbed it in the ashtray so hard, ash flew onto his desk surface.

The room seemed to close in on Elise. Her breathing grew shallow and her chest tightened, making it difficult for enough air to circulate. "Father, I...I do not intend to upset you. I only want to evaluate every piece of information we have. And Thalia... She wanted to cure reaperhood, so if there was a way, I would feel obligated to—"

"Thalia is dead," Mr. Saint said flatly.

Elise's heart skipped a beat. She dug her teeth into her lower lip as her father leaned back in his chair, glaring at her.

"Might I remind you that you were the one who insisted on becoming heir to this empire. In this empire, we kill reapers. Yet now you think they should be cured." Mr. Saint drew closer to Elise now and the fury lighting his eyes scared her. "Without credibility, you might as well be nothing to me. Should you fail at this task you've been given, what will come of you next? Back to Paris, where you will have to beg to get into that conservatory? They do not accept failures, Elise. You asked me to stay here instead of your sister. You chose to be my heir, to dedicate yourself to learning this business. Will you look me in my eye and tell me you cannot do it?" he seethed.

"No, sir." Her voice remained strong despite the tears choking her throat.

"Stop crying. Tears won't solve this crime, Elise. The empire's legacy is on the line. We have an opportunity to secure more prestige alongside Stephen Wayne; you cannot mess this up. Don't let Thalia's death have been for nothing. And most importantly, Charlotte's death. Remember, it was *you* she was protecting."

Elise blinked her tears back. "I won't."

At her words, her father finally retreated. His shoulders relaxed and he lit another cigarette. "It sounds to me like there is a bit of manipulation and misinformation coming from Layla Quinn. I thought you were more careful, Elise. More exemplary."

"I am, Father," Elise said.

His eyes cut into her. "Then prove it to me." Mr. Saint pointed to his door. Elise left, her shoulders feeling even heavier than when she had first returned home. Despite all that had happened today—seeing a dead body, watching Layla taste its blood, seeing a new reaper lair, and being attacked by that new reaper—the encounter that left her the most shaken was a conversation with her father.

And today she'd learned that reapers were hidden in places that she'd always considered to be only for humans. That meant the reapers she had seen dancing at the Savoy were *real*. Yet her father, with his gentle violence, had convinced her otherwise.

She trembled as she made her way up to her bedroom, her hands clammy and cold on the stairway railing. Elise didn't know what to make of this new revelation. Her thoughts were too scattered and she was far too tired to try and organize them. So she drew herself a bath. The water scorched her skin as she sank into the tub, but she accepted the pain. Anything to distract her from the cold resentment her father's words stirred in her.

Dear my dovey,

I miss you more than my words can express through the page. Please tell me about everything you have done since arriving in France. I am dying to hear about your studies and all the new friends you are making. How was your first ballet class?

I know you're scared. I was very scared when I first moved there too. But let me tell you a secret. You're better at making friends than I am. People like you far better than people like me. You will have no trouble making friends and meeting fun people. I promise you. If you're ever feeling lonely, just know I am there with you always. In your heart.

I love you more than anything,
Lisey

Valeriya took a long look at Shirley's trembling form and allowed her into the lair. "Another mouth to feed," Valeriya grumbled. She glanced at Layla. "This one is your responsibility." Then she was gone.

Layla let Shirley sleep in her bed that night. The young girl's eyes darted around the room, apprehensive. Layla's bedroom was nothing spectacular. Its purpose was for sleep, so it had just enough to fit a bed and a chest of drawers that had more empty space than clothes. The best part of the room was the large windows that gave view to the hustling nightlife of Harlem. On tense nights when nightmares made her feverish and spiteful, she cracked her windows to cool down, and fell asleep to the live jazz music that drifted down from the nearby clubs. After looking at the fear still etched deeply into Shirley's face, Layla made her way to the windows and opened them. A cool breeze blew in, bringing with it a soft piano ballad.

"I heard this place is haunted," Shirley whispered.

Layla laughed sharply. "Even if it was, ghosts are no threat to us."

Shirley's eyes darkened. Sometimes Layla forgot how long of an adjustment period there was between being turned and finding some sense of normalcy. So she settled on the end of the bed and sighed. "Rogue reapers ruined the Clarice in its first year of being open. Dead bodies kept turning up in hotel rooms and the owners spread rumors about the place being haunted because that's easier to get past than actual bloodthirsty reapers roaming the hallways. Still, people refused to stay here. And when the owners tried to sell, no one wanted to buy the building. Valeriya ended up taking it over many years ago. She swears the moonlight guided her here, but no one really believes that. Mei and I like to think that she was the one lurking in the walls during the hotel's working days, slitting throats and feeding on unlucky bodies at night."

Shirley frowned. "Is this supposed to make me feel better?"

"I was never good at telling stories. I just want you to feel better. Valeriya has much worse stories," Layla said.

"What exactly is she?" Shirley asked.

"She is one of the first reapers. Hundreds of years old. She could tell you all about the god-awful experiments they ran on her and her family that made her turn. I refuse to hear them because I have enough to keep me up at night already." Layla sighed, falling against her pillows.

Moonlight streaked across Shirley's face and somehow she looked even younger than before. The girl was all round cheeks and hopeful eyes. "What happened to her family?" she asked.

Though she spoke gently, the words pierced Layla's heart. She shrugged, her eyes growing distant. "She never talks about them." Layla patted the bed and waited for Shirley to sit before she continued. "You don't have to be afraid of her. Valeriya can be cold, but deep down she cares. She's the reason I'm still here."

Shirley's brows lifted. "She helped you survive reaperhood?"

"Something like that," Layla said. Her voice was so soft, it came out like a whisper. A memory flashed through her mind of a Saint gun in her hand and Valeriya's fingers closing around her wrist. The memory was soaked with Layla's tears, and thinking of it almost always brought them back. She sniffed, blinking hard. "Again, nothing to be scared of. You are one of us now, and you must understand that we respect humans here. We're not allowed to kill humans because of our agreement with the Saints now, but if Valeriya never killed humans, she would not be the reaper she is today. She would be very, very ugly," Layla said.

A gasp left Shirley. "So it's true? Reapers who don't drink human blood lose their humanity as they age?"

Layla nodded. "The true number of years that Valeriya has lived as a reaper is a holy secret."

Shirley sat up straighter. "I heard reapers have been here since the seventeenth century."

"Not enough people know that, but it's true." As Layla understood it, the reaper population began to grow in the 1800s, from just one that had survived for centuries.

"My grandparents were raised to believe reapers were myths," Shirley went on. "But then… So many came to be after the Civil War, right?"

"Right." According to some old stories, reapers came from the rot and ruin of the battlefields, but reapers had been around for far longer. Valeriya certainly had.

Shirley's voice wavered. "My mother actually wanted to leave New York because reaperhood is like an epidemic here. They're much less rampant in the countryside. But it's spreading, isn't it? Since they're getting difficult to distinguish from humans. Europe has gotten good at hiding them, but they're still there. My friend went abroad for a year and she said they only come out at night in Italy. In France, they're given a curfew." Shirley tucked her knees up to her chest, her brown eyes growing dark. "It's scary to think that just one experiment caused such worldly horrors."

A soft sigh left Layla. "It wasn't just one experiment."

Shirley's lips parted. "No?"

Silence filled the room as Layla carefully considered her next words. "I could tell you more about the early origins of reaperhood, but it's an abomination that is certain to give you nightmares."

After a brief pause, Shirley nodded. "Okay. Maybe I can hear about it later?"

Layla stood and gave Shirley a stern look. "We'll talk more tomor-row. For now, get some sleep." Layla left the room, closing the door after her. But the sound of Shirley stirring behind the door made her pause. She leaned closer to the door and heard sniffles between heavy sobs.

"I'm sorry, Mama. I'm so sorry, Daddy."

Layla's heart dropped. Just five years ago, that had been her. Grieving for the ones she lost and the life that was taken from her. Her hand fell away from the door as if she had been shocked. Then

Layla hurried down the hallway and kept going until she could no longer hear Shirley's cries.

Giana Taylor returned to the lair at dawn. Her dance costume was gone, and she now wore her fur coat over a plain blue dress and stockings. Stage makeup still painted her face, but it was slightly smudged from sweat. Layla met her in the sitting room and chose the love seat beside her, setting a glass of blood down on the side table. "Thank you for coming," she told her.

Giana pulled her coat off and laid it neatly across the back of her chair. "Of course. I figured she would want to see a familiar face."

"She's so young. I don't think she should return to work at the club."

"Most new girls there are around sixteen. Shirley is almost that age." Giana shrugged.

"Right. But the performers are getting younger and younger. The manager, Calhoun, is a predator. You've said so yourself. Shirley is already going to face new hell just by being a reaper. Her life will only get harder from here on out." Layla wished she'd had someone to fight for her at her age. Sixteen being a typical age for club girls didn't make it okay.

Giana sighed. "I understand. But she needs some part of her previous life back. It's so much harder to transition when you're uprooted with nothing to keep you grounded."

THIS RAVENOUS FATE

Contemplative silence stretched between them. Then Layla nodded. "Promise to look out for her."

Giana agreed. She looked over Layla's shoulder, and her expression softened. Layla recognized Shirley's scent and turned to see her standing in cotton pajamas, her body looking especially frail in the dawn light shining through the windows.

"Giana?" Shirley whispered.

"Hi, baby doll. How are you feeling?" Giana asked gently.

Shirley took a deep breath. When she spoke again, her voice was light, but stronger. "I feel...steadier. There isn't as much rushing in my head. And I can't sense every living being around me as closely as I could before. It was like... If I opened my mouth, the scent of blood running through people's veins just infested me. I hated it, but I also craved it. The taste gives me a sensation unlike anything I've ever experienced before." Shirley drew closer to Layla and Giana, finally settling into a seated position in front of the fireplace.

"I still don't remember anything besides running home because I was scared I would hurt the other dancers. But then my parents kept banging on my door and I was so, so hungry—" Her voice hitched and a sob rose in her throat. Layla looked away when tears spilled down her cheeks. "At first, I thought I was in this nightmare. There was blood everywhere, and everything felt fuzzy. But seeing you and Giana now is the clearest I've felt since being turned." Shirley sniffed. "Thank you for coming to me."

Giana reached across the table to squeeze Shirley's hand. "Of course. It happened to me, too, my first night in New York. I know

157

how much it means to have someone there for you." Her eyes warmed. "None of the dancers know you're a reaper, by the way. They just think you're sick. It's probably better we keep it that way."

"Can I still dance?" she asked.

Layla finally looked at her again. "Sure. If you learn to control your urges and prevent blood furies."

Shirley nodded. "That's when reapers lose control and kill anything that moves?"

Giana's lips twisted.

Layla sighed. "More or less," she muttered. "It's something that happens when reapers are in a state of starvation. Don't ignore the need to feed. Blood highs are less dangerous because they're a reaction to feeding, so you won't have as many impulses. In fact, you're slightly subdued, but you will get an adrenaline rush," Layla said. She was feeling tired herself—her muscles ached at the thought of blood, signaling the need for another feeding. Letting Shirley have her blood had only increased her hunger.

"You gave me your blood last night. What kind of properties does reaper blood contain? Yours made me feel good." Shirley's eyelashes fluttered as she looked down at her hands. A hot blush rose in Layla's cheeks. She hadn't considered the aftermath of Shirley drinking her blood; the situation needed a quick fix and that was all Layla could think of.

"Reaper blood can heal mild wounds on anyone. But for humans, it can be hypnotizing when consumed. That's why humans might be drawn to their donor for a while. Because they're weak. For reapers, it produces calming effects. That's why I gave it to you. I thought you were about to kill the Saint girl." She watched Shirley take her first sip of the blood in the glass. "And I cannot have her murdered when she's the only thing keeping me out of prison right now."

"How is that going?" Giana asked. She held a silver compact in her hand, fingers patting at the smudged liner around her eyes.

"*So well*," Layla groaned, standing up. "Giana will stay with you for now, Shirley—"

"I will?" Giana asked, looking up from her compact.

Layla ignored her and looked at Shirley. "When I come back, we can discuss the future."

"I'm already half-dead; I don't think I have a future," Shirley whispered.

The room went still. Layla looked to Giana, whose face briefly flickered with pain. But she leaned forward and gently touched Shirley's hand, then flashed an easy smile.

"Don't worry, doll. We'll take good care of you."

18

"Y OU LOOK TIRED," ELISE'S MOTHER TOLD HER. "HOW are you sleeping?"

She and her mother were the first two at the breakfast table. After last night's conversation with her father, Elise couldn't stomach more than fruit. But now she looked over at Analia Saint. In another life, Elise might have admired her mother's strength, but now she could see in her eyes the hollow darkness came from being the wife of a man like her father, from having to suppress her own emotions. Young girls were supposed to look up to their mothers and want to be just like them. But Elise had always been scared to see any part of herself in her mother.

"There are some nightmares, but I'm okay," Elise said quietly.

"I'm sorry, I don't mean to baby you, I just... I miss when you were smaller. When things were easier. I miss your sisters so much."

"I don't feel babied," Elise whispered. If her mother needed to see her as little again to keep herself together, then Elise would allow it.

"You're calm just like Charlotte," she breathed. Elise stiffened, but she softened again as her mother smiled. "Even when times are tough, you hold yourself together. And I believe that calmness will get you through this darkness, Elise." The tenderness in her mother's tone made Elise want to cry. After everything she had been through in the past few days, having a moment where someone just *loved* her felt like everything.

Elise blinked back tears. "Mama, I—"

"Not now," her mother said quickly. "Your father's coming."

"Good morning to my beautiful family." Mr. Saint wore a beaming smile, which Elise at first thought was for her and her mother. But her father had brought Mr. Wayne to join them. Her mother straightened up in her seat as Mr. Wayne took the chair across from her father. "Why, it's a pleasure for you to join us today, Stephen."

The philanthropist shared an exuberant smile with Analia Saint as he fixed his tie. Elise understood why her parents had been so charmed by him all those years ago. She supposed the combination of friendliness and money made a man especially captivating. It was strange being around him now; as a child, she had always been excused to go play with Sterling and Layla whenever he arrived for a meeting with her father.

"Elise." Mr. Wayne nodded to her.

"Mr. Wayne—" Elise's fork hit her plate as she picked it up and everyone looked at her. "I'm sorry!" she exclaimed.

"Relax," Mr. Saint said firmly.

But her father's austerity only increased her anxiety. Elise shut her mouth and went still.

Mr. Wayne clasped his hands together over his plate, smiling. "You do have a lovely family. It makes me miss mine back in Oklahoma. I'm afraid with all the ruin—it's practically just ashes now—it will never be home again."

He meant the race riots in Tulsa. They had happened not long before Elise had left for France, and the stories haunted her. She shivered, knowing much destruction could happen all because a white man assumed something vile of a Black man. None of it had involved the violence of reapers, but she'd heard they now lurked in the ruins of the neighborhood that had been burned to the ground.

"Those damned riots," Mr. Wayne said. "It's maddening to think that humans are capable of such destruction." He paused, his voice going sharp, "This is why I've been interested in politics from a young age. If I ever become mayor, you can be assured nothing like that will happen here," Mr. Wayne said. Elise noticed he hadn't touched his food. He raised his glass for the servant hovering nearby. "Whiskey, please."

"Thank God for you," Mr. Saint said. A moment of silence passed while they ate.

Mrs. Saint swallowed hard and looked at Mr. Wayne. "I'm not sure if Tobias ever told you, but we had originally planned to move to Tulsa from Texas after the war instead of Harlem. To think that could have happened to us. Such uncivilized behavior." She shook her head, eyes shining with anguish. "So many innocent people lost their lives and I fear our community will never fully heal from such a huge devastation. Those riots wiped a thriving part of Tulsa off the map. I worry about it happening here, what with this family's success being in the limelight. They turned one of the most successful Black neighborhoods into a place of carnage. A massacre."

Mr. Wayne sipped his drink. "I wouldn't call Tulsa a massacre, Analia."

Elise's mother put her fork down.

"It wasn't a slaughter," Mr. Wayne went on. "Some say three hundred died, but it was closer to thirty. The more lies we build on that day, the more likely history is to repeat itself."

Analia Saint's eyes narrowed. "Thirty casualties is far from what I heard and it was an atrocity regardless—"

"You know the newspaper loves to sensationalize these things," Mr. Wayne said quickly. He set his glass down. "Your people have been through enough. With the lab and the upcoming election, I've put my dollar in places that will change things. No more ruthless violence in these streets. But to be frank, Tobias, there is so much tension in this empire, I fear it snapping while I align myself with it."

Mr. Wayne's tone unsettled Elise. *Your people*—as if the Black community was a herd of slow-moving beings, easily swayed.

Her father's easy smile faltered. "This empire is far from collapsing, Stephen. I assure you, we have this murder investigation under control. With your contributions, we can get reaperhood contained and expand the empire."

"I feel that I must be transparent with you and say that I have received other offers from competing organizations." Mr. Wayne let out a rough sigh.

This time Mr. Saint frowned. "What do you mean? Who is our competition in the business of eliminating reapers?"

"It's quite the opposite of elimination, actually. There are some individuals who believe reapers will never be completely eradicated and that they should be used to benefit our military. They have expressed interest in Dr. Harding's research at the lab to develop reapers into weapons," Mr. Wayne said. He leaned toward Mr. Saint and continued, his voice lower. "I refused them, of course, but you have to know there are others who want to take your business right from beneath you. There are people who want to capitalize on the man-made monsters that are destroying this world."

Elise blinked, her mind spinning. Reapers had existed for centuries, but she had only ever known the universal desire to destroy them.

Analia Saint sucked in a sharp breath. "Do you mean…wars?"

Mr. Wayne nodded. "Potentially, yes. That's why I refused them. We are still recovering from the last war. I can only imagine this making other countries more wary of us. Though I understand the need for self-defense, turning reapers into weapons could be devastating."

Mr. Saint ran a finger around the rim of his glass. His frown had deepened. "The longer I live, the more people I see become death incarnate." He lifted his glass and swallowed the last of the liquor.

"We will not let that happen anymore," Mr. Wayne said.

"There is no hope with reapers," Mr. Saint said. "They've been slipping through the cracks, as they get harder to identify and people get greedier for money. Calhoun is letting reapers work at the Cotton Club. I'll have to cover the revenue they bring in if I want him to stop."

Mr. Wayne shook his head. "Dr. Harding is developing a purity testing system to prevent that. His first goal with the lab is to provide resources and accessibility to the underprivileged. People who come in and offer up their blood to be tested for reaperhood will receive free meals, free medical exams, and burial insurance. That way we ensure that people are safe from reaper infection while lessening any financial burdens. All-around good."

Elise's mind went right to Shirley. Young Shirley, who had nothing now but the club. Elise would need to warn her about returning. Her fingers picked at the edge of her napkin. "What about Thalia's antidote research?" she asked.

Mr. Saint shot her a fierce glare.

Mr. Wayne's smile wilted a bit. "We've paused on that venture since Miss Gray's untimely passing."

For a moment, Elise considered bringing up Theo Smith. But her father spoke first, "I recognize that look, my pearl. It is the exact look you gave me before you told me about the Quinns' plans to work with the Harlem reapers all those years ago."

The pain his words stirred in her was so intense, she had to look away.

Mr. Wayne looked thoughtful for a moment. He regarded Elise with a gentle pity that only made her more nervous. "Reapers corrupt everything they touch. I'm funding Dr. Harding's research on how their proximity affects humans. He believes they are spreading a poison we have yet to fully understand. But if we can find out what it is, maybe we can put a stop to it before things get worse around here."

Elise's lips parted with surprise. America had been drowning in the damnation of reapers for generations. Perhaps someone like Stephen Wayne, with his money and genuine promises, was not so bad. Maybe he could create new light in this darkened world.

"Darling," Mr. Saint addressed his wife in a soft tone. "I think today is a lovely day for you and Elise to explore the new shops. You haven't spent enough time together lately."

Elise cleared her throat. "I have to meet with Layla to continue our investigation. I'm sorry, Mother."

But Analia Saint nodded her understanding. "Next time, my love."

Elise turned back to her father, who gave her a smug, tight smile. "Good job," he said.

The gun at Elise's hip made her feel like an impostor. All Saint members carried guns, and while Elise knew she would need to do the same as her father's successor, the weight of such a deadly weapon never felt normal.

She was waiting in the alley across the street from the Hotel Clarice. Not quite on reaper territory, but not in Saint provinces either. She pulled her gun out, finger poised on the trigger just like Sterling had taught her. *Always be prepared.*

Minutes passed, and still there was no sign of Layla. Elise was beginning to wonder whether she should walk into the hotel when a shadow passed over her. She looked up, free hand blocking the sunlight from her eyes. She could have sworn someone was in the alley with her.

The silence became a deafening roar as she peered around. Finally she lowered her gun. She closed her eyes and slumped against the wall, exhaling. She traced a cross over the gun's handle once, twice, then again and again until it felt right.

Then she felt the air move beside her.

"Miss me?"

Elise scrambled away from the wall, gun raised. Layla stood facing the barrel. She had her hands on her hips and grinned despite the gun staring her down. Elise lowered her weapon and glared. "I almost shot you."

Layla said nothing, but slinked closer to Elise, who glared and stepped back until she hit the alley wall. Still, Layla closed in, moving into Elise's space, their faces now inches apart.

Elise used the last bit of space she had to shove the gun into Layla's chin, but the reaper didn't flinch. She kept smiling. Elise was aware of how close they were, how Layla bracketed her arms on either side of her, forming a cage.

The reaper's warm breath feathered against Elise's collarbone, and her heartbeat quickened. But not from fear. She stared Layla in the eye, her stare only dipping when Layla's lips parted. The contrast of the sharp fang peeking from behind her pillow-soft lips made Elise's breath stall in her chest. And she continued to watch her lips as they moved to form words.

"I don't think you did, actually," Layla said. She eyed the revolver, then dragged her gaze up Elise's face slowly, as if studying her design.

Elise finally met her eyes again and almost immediately, Layla backed off.

The instant relief of pressure nearly made her drop the gun. Elise followed Layla out of the alley, her hands a shaky mess on the handle, now slippery from her sweat. "Next time," Elise muttered.

Layla shot her a sideways glance. "Would it be so bad if you did shoot me? You could leave me to bleed out on the cold ground. You did seem to enjoy doing that the first time." Layla's tone was surprisingly light.

"I wasn't the one..." Elise's jaw tightened. She stared ahead, already counting down the minutes until she could be alone again. "I would never leave you to die on your own. In fact..." The words came to her in a heated rush. "I've been dreaming of what it would be like to squeeze your heart in my hands. I want to feel your last beat of life seep between my fingers."

Layla stopped walking then. Her dark eyes roamed over Elise's stony expression and the corner of her mouth twitched. "You might be more reaper than me."

Elise chose to ignore that insult. They continued down the street, Layla following closely behind her long strides with shorter strides of her own. Her mind raced as she tried to remember what she'd meant to tell Layla, back before that little game in the alley took place.

Finally it came to her. "Stephen Wayne joined my family at breakfast this morning—"

"I'm bored, Saint—"

"*Listen*," Elise snapped. "Wayne's philanthropy is about eradicating reapers and he's working with my father to clear reaperhood through the Cotton Club. He plans to fund the study of reapers in the lab too."

Layla crossed her arms, frowning. "What does that mean for our investigation?"

Elise swallowed. "I just thought you should know. For Shirley and Giana. It won't be safe for them there."

Layla shook her head. "They're already there."

Jamie Kelly sat in his usual spot at the Cotton Club entrance, holding a pen in his teeth and a stack of papers in his hands. He looked up and grinned when Layla called his name. Something about the curl of his blond hair against his forehead and the way his eyes brightened relaxed Layla. She knew she was letting her guard down around him these days. Maybe too much. Still, she smiled back. Better to play the role of a friend and get what she needed than cause trouble.

"Morning. Didn't get everything you needed last time you were here, Quinn?" Jamie stood and made his way toward her and Elise, pulling the pen from his mouth.

Layla sighed, a little too tired to engage in the tease. With Jamie staring her down and Elise staring pretentiously at anything that moved, Layla needed to get to the point. "I need to see Giana and Shirley."

"And Calhoun. The manager," Elise inputted sharply.

Layla exhaled, closing her eyes. "And Calhoun."

Jamie lifted a brow. "You think I have control over who sees him? I'm just here because he needs liquor. If you want to talk to him, you'll owe me something."

Frustration seeped into Layla. "The last time I did a favor for you, I ended up as the most wanted person in the city."

Elise scoffed at the same time Jamie laughed. "Please," Elise muttered.

Layla glared at Jamie. "Don't say it."

But Jamie, of course, did. "You're not a person, you're a reaper. But if you want something from me, then I'm going to ask for something from you. We all have responsibilities. I have a son to feed," he said.

Layla blinked. "You have a child?"

Jamie looked away for a moment, then back at her. "I do. Why are you surprised?"

Several questions filled her mind, but before she could ask anything, Elise smacked her arm.

Layla shot her a glare, then turned back to Jamie. "Right, fine. What do you need from me?"

Jamie's eyes shifted for a moment before leaning in close. "I don't need anything *from* you. I need *you*."

This unsettled Layla. But she had no other choice. Right as she was opening her mouth to agree to his conditions, Elise spoke up, "That's not how business transactions work."

Jamie gave Elise a side-eyed look. "Sweetheart, respectfully, unless you're part of a gang, stay out of our business."

"Don't call me 'sweetheart,' you criminal," Elise snarled.

"Shut up, both of you," Layla snapped.

Elise glared at Jamie. "I would mind how you speak to me, or I'll have the Saint—"

Quick as a whip, Jamie aimed his gun at Elise. Layla darted forward between him and Elise. "Watch yourself," she seethed. Her fangs had sprung free and they dug into her lips hard enough to draw blood.

Jamie's eyes widened a bit to see her reaperhood on full display. But he kept his gun raised, gaze sharp on Elise. "You brought a damn Saint here? It's almost like you're looking for bad attention," Jamie said in a low voice. "The Saints are the ones who rat us out to police; they've sacked as many of my men as they've killed your clanmates. You're on their side now?"

"I don't pick sides. Everything I do is for myself." A cold satisfaction filled her chest when he flinched at those words. "You didn't think we were friends, did you?"

"I certainly thought you hated the Saints," Jamie muttered.

He finally lowered his gun, but Layla's eyes continued to glow and she kept her fangs on display for him. "If anyone kills her, it will be me. Don't even try it," she hissed.

Jamie lifted his hands in deference. "Fine." He nodded to the back room and sighed. "Calhoun won't be in for a few minutes, but you should probably wait out the time in there so no one sees you. Especially don't let anyone see *her*," he spat while pointing to Elise. "We've got enough tension in the club without a Saint spawn lurking around."

Elise gave him a nasty look.

"What about Giana and Shirley—" Layla started.

"Not here. Not my problem either," Jamie huffed. "Go look for them if you want, but I already did you a favor." He walked off.

Layla could only glare after him. Her nerves began to cool once she and Elise were alone in one of the backstage rooms of the club, where they'd hoped to find the two dancers. Being around humans was never easy. Their blood seemed to tease her at every chance it got, its scent haunting her, the sound of it rushing through veins amplified with every conversation.

As a reaper, getting upset was an easy thing to do, but a tough situation to come back from. Layla couldn't remember the number of times she had failed her impulse training. Valeriya had gotten her rats to start out with for feeding because there were so many in the city and *"if you kill one, no one will know; if you kill one hundred, the city will probably start to thank you."* Layla ended up killing close to one hundred rats while Valeriya tested her. It was bad for every new reaper—nearly impossible most times. Every time Layla trained under voluntary starvation, she imagined the rat's tangy blood seeping between her teeth and their tiny bones cracking with the slightest pressure from her jaw. Her whole life, Layla had been warned against crime and taught that murder was the worst thing a person could do. She believed killing was an act of defiance so great, there was no coming back from it.

But since becoming a reaper, that idea had dissipated almost immediately.

Killing was easy. It was resisting the temptation that felt impossible.

Layla pricked the tip of her thumb with her fang and swallowed a few drops of her own blood. It was nowhere near as effective as drinking from another reaper would have been, but it helped to ground her. And that was all she could ask for right now.

"Layla—" Elise's hand on her shoulder felt like an electric current.

Layla snatched herself away from Elise and scowled at her. "Don't you know not to touch a reaper when they're on the edge?" It came out as more of a hostile demand than a question. Layla was glad when Elise shrank back and lowered her hand. Her hunger was so palpable at this point, she could imagine the urges forcing her hand. A swift grab of the Saint's wrist and Layla could tug her down and have her mouth at her throat. The blood would be sweet, just as the Saint heiress smelled, but it would be wrong—beyond that. Layla's fangs poked into her gums and she groaned slightly. She touched a

Saint and she would be dead. But the *thrill*… Her fangs pierced her gums, spilling her own blood into her mouth.

"I just had a thought," Elise began slowly. Her dark eyes clouded over with something unrecognizable. "Maybe we should keep an eye on the club from both sides, human and reaper. It will be easy since my father is involved here. And Mr. Wayne is getting involved so there could be an opportunity to ask him about the lab."

"Are you going to tell your father about the reapers that work here?" Layla breathed weakly. Her limbs felt heavy, muscles exhausted from working without being sufficiently fed. She swallowed hard, hot breath sticking in her throat.

Elise's lips twitched. "No, I…I wouldn't do that to Shirley."

Layla held her stare, but Elise looked away. "If your father works with the club, why does Jamie not trust the Saints?"

"I don't think my father has made his investment in the club public knowledge. It doesn't exactly look good to work for a place like this. But it makes a lot of money for the community. Though he does hate gangsters," Elise said.

"But he uses them for buying liquor, too, I'm guessing. The dichotomy of wanting to live and wanting to be respected. It never ends here." A sour taste filled Layla's mouth. Money. Power. Notability. Why did anyone do anything these days if not to gain something, even if it meant isolating yourself and damning your morals? Layla could almost see herself in their mirror of sins. She ground her teeth in frustration.

Layla leaned against the wall and carefully slid down into a sitting position. Her heart was still racing, each beat sending a jolt through her body. The thought of blood consumed her. When she closed her eyes, it was all she saw; when she inhaled, it was all she smelled. And when Elise opened her mouth, it was all Layla could do to not—

Her eyes flew open. Elise stood over her, watching her with curious eyes, her hands on her hips. "You look feral."

Layla's fangs had emerged again and they dug into her lips. "I'm hungry," Layla muttered. All she could smell was Elise and the blood rushing through her veins. Today she had come too close. And when Layla could smell blood through flesh, she knew she had gone too long without feeding.

Elise didn't back away. A flash of fear lit her eyes for an instant, but then she was kneeling in front of Layla, her brown irises warm in the soft light. "You should probably go home, right? I should worry about you tearing my throat out. What really happens when a reaper does not feed on enough human blood? Do they truly turn into a demon with no recollection of their human past?"

Layla groaned. Now her focus was on Elise's throat, her pulse humming against her delicate skin. Should Layla sink her fangs into Elise's jugular, blood would explode into her mouth like water from a fountain. The thought made saliva pool in her mouth. Layla looked away, urging herself to concentrate on something else. "Stop."

"I know you're bound by a Saint agreement to leave humans alone. But surely you slip up occasionally. Animal blood cannot be that satisfactory," Elise said. She cocked her head to one side, a tiny smile forming on her lips.

"Sure it can," Layla muttered.

Elise lifted a brow. "Perhaps you are already transitioning from reaper to demon," she said. Feigned fascination coated her words, and it took a considerable effort for Layla to not lunge forward and rip out her vocal cords just to shut her up. "Oh my God, you're so upset." Elise almost laughed.

A sharp breath left Layla's chest. "I'm *so* close to tearing into your throat," she muttered. Her eyes dipped to the soft curve of Elise's throat leading to her collarbones. The dress she wore had a scooped neckline and in this moment, Layla both damned it and thanked it. Being close to the Saint was torture, having a sensory overload of every part of her, the suppleness of her skin, the sweetness of her blood, and not being able to indulge in any of it. What she would give to run her tongue along her throat just to feel her pulse quicken—to know if she felt that same thrill.

Elise's lips parted. Her eyes traveled over Layla's face, hesitating on the blood smeared across her lips. "I don't like how you look at me," she murmured.

Elise finally moved back. But she kept poking at Layla with her words while she paced the room, eyes roaming over the rehearsal piano, the dusty furniture, and the cloudy mirrors. "What's it like when you hunt? Is there a certain body part you like best? An organ that contains the most nutrients? The easiest way to get the most blood?"

Layla shifted uncomfortably. "I thought this made you squeamish."

"It does." Elise turned an icy look on to Layla, her eyes lighting up when she saw Layla's discomfort. "But it's worth it if I get to make *you* squirm for once."

"How cruel. You should just put me out of my misery now," Layla sneered. She sucked on her finger again, drawing more blood into her mouth. A cool sensation settled over her body, and she sighed, tipping her head back against the wall. "By the way, it takes *years* for reapers to reach their final form of damnation. But the first stage is forgetting human memories."

Elise paused for a moment, watching Layla with careful eyes. "Have you started to forget yet?"

Layla remained quiet. She hated thinking about this. What she was destined to become. Even if it took years, or centuries, she did not want it. To forget all the things that made her happy, forget her family, her friends, her history, everything that made her human— there would be no joy, no purpose in such a life. Her hands tightened into fists, and she grumbled.

Elise took the hint and continued to move around the room. "It's been a while since we came back here, no? You don't think this is some sort of ambush, do you?"

Layla closed her eyes. "I'm not currently thinking at all, actually."

The room fell silent for a few minutes. For once, impatient thoughts didn't immediately rush to crowd Layla's mind. She sat in the quiet, breath steady against the ebb and flow of hunger still coursing through her body. Then, the notes of a faintly familiar song found their way into her head. Layla opened her eyes.

Elise sat at the piano, fingers poised gracefully over the keys in front of her. She paid Layla no mind while she played a song from memory, each note hit flawlessly and without hesitation.

Realization struck Layla. She waited until Elise finished playing before asking, "Is that 'Josi's Melody'?"

Elise looked down at the piano keys, stretching her fingers. "Yes."

"Is that what you played for your school audition?" Layla asked.

Elise finally looked at Layla. "No. It just happens to be my favorite original piece." There was no rancor in her tone, but her words were guarded. "I know this piece by heart because *Josi* is my heart. It's easy to do anything when you love someone. Even if it's the hardest choice you've ever made."

An entire minute had passed and the thought of feeding didn't cross Layla's mind once. The side of Elise she was seeing now captured her attention as easily as freshly drawn blood. She sat up. "Is that why you stepped up as the heir? You're doing this for Josi?"

Elise would have answered but for the sudden commotion that rumbled through the empty club. They were both on their feet in a moment, Elise with her gun in hand, and sprinted down the hall to the door.

Out in the lounge, two club bouncers gripped Shirley's wrists and were trying to drag her out. She dug her heels in, tears streaming down her face while she cried out. "I'll do it! I'm sorry, I'll do it!" Shirley cried.

Giana stood between two other men, her face drawn. She mouthed a single word to Layla: *help*.

As Layla moved toward Shirley, two more men, who Layla came to realize were not Cotton Club employees but gangsters, pointed their guns at her.

"What is going on?"

"None of you should be in here unless you've got a contract. This one here owes us lab tests to prove her humanity," one of the men holding Shirley snarled.

"Since when has that been required?" Layla demanded.

"Since we've had dancers dropping like flies because of reaper-hood," the man snapped.

Shirley whimpered, looking impossibly small between the two gangsters holding her with tight grasps.

Layla glared at the gangsters. "Let her go. She's not yours," Layla snapped. She didn't stop the hunger that surged through her this time. Feral desire glowed in her eyes and she knew the gangsters saw it when they hesitated. It was enough for Shirley to break free, sprinting right to Layla's side.

"We're going," Layla said strongly. She tried to turn away and leave with Elise and Shirley, but more gangsters swarmed the room. Jamie was among them, eyes wild. Layla turned her him. "Jamie. Please—"

"You need to listen to them," he warned.

"Layla." Shirley let out a hurried whisper.

Layla didn't have time to reassure the younger girl now. Elise was already posted beside her with her gun raised and Giana was still trapped by the two gangsters. "Whatever Giana taught you about control, forget it now. I want you to kill these men."

"*What?*" Shirley hissed, eyes wide.

"You heard me." Layla turned to Elise. "Shoot. *Now.*"

Elise hesitated. Layla should have known a human would falter under such circumstances. She grabbed the gun and fired it at the closest man. The bullet ripped through his thigh and Shirley launched herself onto the bleeding man. Her fangs tore at his throat, sending a spray of blood across the room.

Layla had been hoping to get out in the midst of the chaos. But the gangsters raised their guns again and trained them on her and Elise. When several more dancers emerged from a backstage door, Layla braced for their screams. But their faces showed no panic.

Confused, Layla watched until she saw the glazed-over look in the dancers' eyes and her body tensed with realization. The scent of spoiled blood overwhelmed her senses. Rogue reapers. They were under what seemed to be a blood high, but their movements were more controlled. She threw herself between Shirley and the new dancers swarming the room. Shirley hissed at her, bloody spittle flying from her mouth.

Layla's fangs sprung out on impulse, but she ignored the hunger gnawing at her and shoved Shirley toward the door. "Get out. Now."

"Layla." Elise's voice rang out over the commotion.

In her rush to get Shirley out of the door, Layla couldn't place Elise. She finally spotted her backed against a wall, eyes wide on the scene around her. Two of the gangsters had been attacked by Shirley, and more were being taken down by Giana and the rogue dancers who by far now outnumbered the gang members.

The remaining gangsters still in the fray trained their guns at Giana and the rogues. They hadn't fired yet; without Saint bullets, they had to choose their shots more carefully. It was then that Layla realized Elise had no weapon. Her silver revolver was still clutched in Layla's hand. Blood slicked over the handle, but Layla tightened her grip on it, then slid it across the floor to Elise.

Elise picked it up and aimed at the gangster in front of her. Before she could shoot, a dancer pounced on him. More dancers rushed right past her toward some other prey, but Layla was too focused on Elise to notice who it was. Until she heard Shirley scream.

Two dancers had gotten to Shirley, and their hands were digging into her chest. Nails tore through fabric and flesh, separating ribs until they cracked beneath the force of their voracity. Layla's breath stopped. She could only watch, too far away to reach, as Shirley collapsed. Her mouth fell open in a horrified shriek, blood erupting from her chest and throat. Layla scrambled to stand, but she slipped on the gangsters' blood and was forced to crawl. But Shirley was already gone. By the time the dancers broke away from her, her eyes were lifeless and trained on nothing.

Giana was the last to back away from Shirley. Layla's heart skipped at the sight of her friend. She sat up, blood sliding between her fingers as she gasped. Not an ounce of recognition flashed through Giana's unfocused eyes while she looked at Layla. A memory tore through Layla's mind of the night Theo had attacked her. Only pure, undiluted rage crossed her expression, like it controlled her from the inside out.

"Giana," Layla called. "This isn't you."

But Giana didn't hear her. She lunged for Layla, arms outstretched and fangs bared. Layla braced herself to meet her with the same intensity, but they never collided.

The sound of a gun going off snapped them apart. Layla stared down in horror at the blood blooming across Giana's chest. The older girl's eyes finally seemed to focus, as if the pain brought her back to her senses. She looked at Layla, her face reflecting a hollow recognition that twisted Layla's heart. "I'm sorry," Giana whispered. Then she crashed to the floor.

One of the afflicted dancers tore her fangs from an unlucky gangster's throat and dropped him to approach Giana's body. Layla shoved the gangster's corpse toward her, successfully tripping her and stalling her on the blood-slick floor. As she looked around, she noticed Jamie standing by, smoking gun in his hand. He glared. "You owe me." Then he rushed out of the club.

Layla was so lost in her shock, she failed to realize that the rest of the room had gone silent. Bodies littered the floor, leaving only Elise and Layla standing. She crawled over to Giana's fallen form. Her hands were reaching for her, shaking, when Elise's voice turned her around. "Layla..."

She touched her back and Layla flinched. "*Don't touch me*," Layla seethed. Red covered her vision, her hunger-induced rage turning her blind to Elise's reaction and everything around her. Layla pried a piece of bloody flesh from the chest of a nearby dead gangster and stumbled out of the club and into the alley.

Her chest was wound so tight, she worried it would snap at the slightest nudge. The blood in her fists grew less appetizing the farther it strayed from its original body. Layla craved something fresh and warm. Something *living*. Nothing besides blood would calm the heat that ravaged her. And the longer she stood there, trying to breathe, the more dangerous it became for herself and those around her.

Or the only one around her.

Elise stood, her figure dark against the pale light at the end of the alley.

On instinct, Layla ran at her and slammed her into the alley wall. Elise's breath left her body. The sweet scent of her blood was so close to Layla now, thriving and pulsing beneath her paper-thin skin. Layla traced a finger down her throat, feeling the beat of her pulse. Her fangs snapped out once again, ready to sink them into the weeping flesh in front of her.

19

ELISE HAD ALMOST LET HER. SHE FROZE AS LAYLA dropped her bloody arm to her side and closed the distance between them. Then the scent of blood was rushing Elise's senses and she wrapped a gloved hand around Layla's wrist, directing her to the dripping flesh still clutched in her fist. She watched as Layla drank the gangster's heart dry. Layla crouched, spine curved, while she sank her teeth into the heart over and over. Watching Layla pull the thing from the dead gangster's chest had been chilling, but that heart had saved Elise's life. As Elise watched Layla lick the remaining blood from her hands, a part of her wondered if this whole arrangement had been a mistake.

Finally, when the heart was no more than a shriveled-up hunk of muscle, Layla stood. She dropped the scraps of her meal onto the ground and wiped blood from her face. It smudged around her mouth and fangs, making her look wild. A satisfied glint lit her eyes, the brown sparking with life for once.

While Layla watched her intently, Elise still felt the press of her fingers against her neck. A few minutes ago, her fangs had been snapping out, eyes glazed over with the intention of drinking straight from her. And Elise almost let it happen. The split second she had between shoving the heart into her mouth and watching Layla's frenzy, Elise considered letting Layla *sink her teeth into her.* Layla had always had this captivating energy about her. It was what drew Elise to her in the first place. That vibrant, burning passion she held for life. Elise saw it when they played together, when Layla danced to Elise's music; she even saw it when they fought as little girls. It seemed that no matter how much reaperhood had changed her, the essence of Layla remained.

She looked down at Layla now, mouth twisted with scorn. "You almost bit me."

Layla crossed her arms over her chest and looked up at Elise. "You almost *let* me bite you. I would have loved to taste you. If your blood smells that good, it must taste heavenly."

The words sent a chill up Elise's spine. Suddenly, making eye contact with Layla became very hard, and she had to look away. "You're obscene."

"You can't even look me in the eye when you accuse me," Layla spat. Her voice spiraled around Elise, her tone weighted with possibility. Elise couldn't help but wonder if reaper voices contained special properties, meant to allure listeners. She snapped her gaze to Layla's and her heart skipped a beat at the tease in her eyes. "Tell me, Saint. There's no one listening, no one watching. You don't need to keep this act up."

Elise's breath caught. "It's not an act."

"Are you sure about that? You came after me despite me being ready to kill," Layla hissed. She stepped up, her face so close to Elise, her nose almost brushed her throat. Elise went still. To allow someone at her neck like this was risky. But Elise didn't care. For once, letting go of her responsibilities felt good, no matter the danger. "I remember little you ripping her stockings the second her mother left the room, and swapping her sheet music when the tutor wasn't looking. You put on an act for everyone including yourself. But I see right through it. *I see you*," Layla whispered.

The pounding in her chest intensified at Layla's words, her proximity only aggravating the tension. Layla's fingertips pressed into Elise's sternum. When her palm laid flat against her racing heartbeat, Elise gripped her wrist. "Human blood makes you deranged. You see *nothing*," she snapped.

Beneath her fingers, Elise felt Layla's pulse quicken. Despite the chaos and the urgency of the club, Layla had still managed to distance herself from Elise when she was halfway to succumbing to her monstrous urges. Even now, with carnage following in their wake, Layla held her gaze as if Elise was the only thing in the world. With a gangster's blood on her tongue, the reaper still drank in Elise's presence.

The harsh sound of bells clanging pulled Elise's focus. Police cars ground to a halt in front of the club, officers and Saint members swarming the scene. A few drew close to the alley and even turned their attention toward where Elise and Layla stood.

Layla, with her lips and chin still stained with blood, tried to move away from Elise, but Elise acted quickly, cornering her and shoving her back into the wall.

"Look at me," Elise demanded.

Layla's eyes flicked to hers. A crooked smile split her bloodred lips. The light in her eyes told Elise that more than just bloodlust filled her veins. "You want a taste, Saint?" she asked. Bloodstained fangs flashed up at Elise, and she shuddered, her hand trembling on the wall by Layla's head.

"Police," Elise breathed. "If they see your feast, we'll both be in trouble."

"Me more than you." Layla's smile slipped as her eyes moved to something beyond the alley. Then suddenly she lunged forward, one hand grabbing Elise's waist, while the other seized the back of her neck.

Elise yelped. But Layla breathed into her throat. "Shhh…"

Elise went still. The rush of armed officers passed behind them, but all Elise could focus on was the sharp scent of blood and piercing apprehension that seeped between them. Layla's face pressed against her throat, the blood on her cheek and chin smearing on Elise's skin. It felt raw—nearly animalistic. She did not despise it. Instead, Elise's fingers gathered in the fabric of Layla's shirt and she clenched it into her fist. Her own blood felt electric, her skin burning with a vicious craving. But Elise's devotion was to an opposing fate. And for this touch, she would burn.

As soon as the passing officers were gone, their commotion

faded to the scene across the street, Elise tore herself away from Layla. The world spun and her legs trembled. The current between them fell quiet, nothing more than a cold tension replacing it.

"I'm going home," she said, trying to keep her voice steady. "We'll meet up again tomorrow."

Layla's pupils were dilated and her breath shook while her hands clenched by her sides. "Sure, Saint."

Elise walked all the way home and did not let go of the fact that she had survived touching Layla Quinn again.

At the Saint estate, guards and associates gathered outside Mr. Saint's office, discussing the news of the Cotton Club attack. Elise knew that her father's office would be full of policemen and associates, so she slipped upstairs to her room. She needed to talk to her father but wanted to wait until they were alone. She hadn't bargained on Sterling waiting in the upstairs hallway for her.

"Thank God you're back." He enveloped her in a tight hug, then pulled back just enough to get a good look at her. "Are you hurt?"

"No, Sterling, I'm fine." But she wasn't sure.

"You don't look it." He pulled a handkerchief from his pocket then wiped it over her cheek. It came away bloody. Elise's eyes widened and pins prickled all over her body at the sight. Never mind the bloodbath she had just witnessed; a layer of grime covered her and she suddenly felt like she was suffocating.

Elise swallowed a breath. "Sterling, it's bad. It's so bad."

"Let me help you." Sterling touched her hand, but Elise shrugged away from him.

Nothing made sense to Elise now. An hour ago, she had been stuck between debauchery and peace, almost ready for Layla to sink her teeth into her. She wanted to feel something other than responsibility, she wanted to act without the worry of whether she was being perfect.

"Something happened at the Cotton Club," Elise muttered.

"I know—"

"It was my fault. I need to apologize to Father—"

"Elise, relax for a moment."

But she couldn't.

The itchy feeling all over her body intensified while she looked down at her ruined clothes, caked with debris and blood. "No. I need to fix this—" Elise choked on her own words as she backed away into her bedroom, where she began to pull off her filthy clothes.

"Elise—" Sterling tried to follow her in, but she ran into the bathroom and closed the door on him. Elise took out Sterling's gun and removed the remaining bullets. She laid out the five bullets on the counter, her breathing going shaky when she realized one was slightly farther away from the others. Her finger pushed it closer in line, then traced a cross over the handle of the gun seven times, exhaling when she finished. But still, the tension remained. Threats surrounded Harlem, and Elise's skin itched—her chest twisted at the thought of not being able to control them. One wrong move, one misstep, and chaos would unfold.

She paced the bathroom, opening and snapping the revolver closed seven times. Even on the seventh movement, her body didn't feel settled. Her scalp buzzed, and her chest felt so tight, breathing became difficult. Elise turned, preparing to count her steps in sevens and restart the ritual with the gun, but the moment she opened the chamber, the bullets slipped out, scattering across the floor. A new wave of panic crashed over her, and Elise's breath stopped altogether while she watched the rounds roll to a halt around her.

Sterling banged on the door again. "Elise, I will break this door down. Please, just let me help you."

Elise paused. She could handle this on her own. Her father expected her to anyway. But any error would be her fault and the city would be in ruins soon if she was not careful. She needed more than just security in her numbers and rituals.

Elise draped her robe over her body and opened the door.

Sterling stood in the doorway, his brow creased with worry. He noticed the bullets on the floor and the incessant twitching of Elise's hands. "Sit," he said firmly, pushing her into her vanity seat.

Her reflection in the mirror was a haunting image she refused to face. Instead, she watched Sterling sit before her and take her hands into his. It had been ages since she had had a compulsive episode this bad. And Elise hated the frenzied state they left her in almost as much as she hated people seeing her in it.

"I'm okay," Elise whimpered.

"Is your number still seven?" he asked.

Just the mention of it had Elise counting in her head again. But Sterling's hand tightened on her and he shook his head, cursing under his breath. The longer Elise forced her attention to him, the quieter the numbers became in her own mind.

"Just talk me through what you're feeling. What else happened at the club?" Sterling asked.

Elise didn't want to tell him about the close brush she had had with Layla. She certainly didn't want to tell him about how she had considered letting Layla bite her. Sterling had more anger toward Layla than Elise might have herself. He had been the one to pull Layla off Elise five years ago, and he was the first one to tend to Elise's wounds. The fear that shook his hands and darkened his eyes that night never quite left him. Elise still saw echoes of it when she looked at him now, especially with Layla back in their lives.

"I underestimated the responsibility involved in being the heir," Elise said quietly. "When I was in France, my biggest worry was whether my music was good enough. Now, I come home and there are reapers coming for my throat—none of them quite as aggressively as my father..." she trailed off when Sterling's expression hardened. Already, Elise was regretting having shared so much. Sterling's tentative suspicion created a sinking feeling in her chest.

Elise tried to steady her voice, but her nerves remained evident in her trembling hands. "How do you deal with him?"

Sterling pressed his palms over her knuckles, willing them to still. "I'm used to it. Besides, the pressure of Mr. Saint demanding perfection cannot be worse than having no one at all. Being a part of a family involves making sacrifices. I'm willing to do whatever if it means I get to stay here."

Guilt began to set in. She was foolish to take her family's presence for granted. Especially in front of Sterling. The Saints were all he had. Elise took a deep breath. "I don't feel like I'm doing anything right. Ever. My father picks up on that. Sometimes… I feel like he doesn't even like me."

The room seemed to still as those words spilled out of her. Elise broke their eye contact and looked down at her lap. Then Sterling's hands were cupping her face and he was tilting her gaze back up to his. The heat from his palms spread through her cheeks, soothing the cold tracks the tears had left and warming the emptiness in her chest. "That is not possible, Elise. You are the loveliest person I know. Your father would be a fool to not love you. Your father is not a fool, is he?" Sterling asked.

A tender smile appeared on Elise's lips. "No. He isn't."

"It's difficult to not love you. Impossible, actually." Sterling pulled her into his chest.

Warmth spread through Elise. "Are you working tonight?" she asked.

Sterling shook his head. "No. I'm all yours."

Later, Elise sat in her favorite spot in the library balcony, Sterling beside her. They shared a box of chocolate-covered strawberries while half-listening to her father and Stephen Wayne talking below.

The library loft had been a kind of hideout over the years. Elise remembered climbing the ladder with Layla, where they would pick random books for each other and take turns trying to pronounce the longest words they could find. It never lasted too long because the dust between the pages would irritate Layla's allergies, and before they even made it through a full chapter, she would be sneezing and rubbing her eyes until they were red.

Elise bit back a smile as she sucked a spot of chocolate off her finger. "How much do you know about Stephen Wayne?" she asked, keeping her voice low.

Sterling shrugged. "Nothing besides the glorified opinions Thalia had of him. I think there's more to him than he lets on. Most politicians these days put on a show they know people will love, but it's never truly real," Sterling said. The corner of his lips twitched. "Also, he's *so cocky*."

Laughing softly, Elise nudged him with her shoulder. "You don't like him, do you?"

"I mean, what does he want with us so badly? Everything we have he could get himself. He reminds me of my mother's brother." Sterling grimaced. "Of course I can never say that around your father, but the fact still stands."

Elise covered his hand with hers. "You never mention your uncle. Do you want to talk about it now?"

Sterling's shoulders tensed. His hand curled into a fist beneath hers and he looked away. "That bastard is not my uncle," he muttered.

And with that, the conversation ended. Elise understood. He had become an orphan in the most horrific way possible and still lived with a lineage that went back to the violently intolerant South, where he had watched his father die.

Elise leaned back on her hands, letting the muffled conversation from below wash over her. While she watched her father and Mr. Wayne clink their glasses together and talk over some whiskey, the unsettling sensation piqued in her.

"I'm terribly sorry about the mess at the club," she heard her father say. "I will be sure to get to the bottom of it."

Elise's shoulders tensed, but she reached for another strawberry.

"I miss helping Josi write letters to you up here," Sterling said. "You know we made a goal to get through all the books on this shelf by the end of the year." He ran his finger over the lowest shelf behind him.

The thought of Josi and her best friend spending time together in their favorite spot made Elise's heart warm. She sat back, her lips lifting at the corners. "So you're the reason she was including Voltaire quotes in her letters to me while I was in France. I was wondering how her handwriting improved so quickly." Elise laughed.

"The quotes were her idea. I simply helped her write them," Sterling said, smiling.

She pulled a book from the shelf and cracked it open. "Let's continue the tradition, then. I haven't gotten a letter from her yet."

"She's probably busy having fun. Not everyone can be a dullard like you, spending all their free time perfecting their craft," Sterling said.

Elise smacked him with the book.

20

"IT DOESN'T MAKE ANY SENSE," LAYLA SAID UNDER HER breath.

The lights of the morgue glared down on the two bodies before her, turning their ashen brown skin a sickly shade of dark green. Even though the blood in the bodies had gone putrid, and the stench burned her nose, the main thought in her mind was how her friends, who had been reapers just twenty-four hours ago, were now human.

Elise stood over her, arms crossed. "It never does," she sighed.

Layla pulled Giana's mouth open, checking once again for the enlarged canines that indicated reaperhood. Those same teeth that had been bared for her a day ago, glistening with fresh blood, were gone. A normal set of human canines sat in her mouth, as if the extra reaper teeth had never existed.

"Have there ever been instances of reapers turning human in death? Maybe there are ancient cases—"

"No," Layla said. Her tone was stern, but without malice. She had entertained this question herself many times. But every reaper understood that their fate as a reaper was final. Until now. Nothing made sense anymore. Layla pulled her hand out of Giana's mouth and got to her feet. "There have always been people and reapers looking into cures. We've never been lucky enough to find one," she said.

Elise merely raised a brow. She had always been a master at hiding her true self; Layla hated it. Once, she had loved being the one person Elise allowed in to see the real her. Now she resented ever having been that open with her at all. She knew all of Layla, as much as Layla hated to admit it. Years ago, that had been a thing Layla treasured, but Elise had burned their abundance to ashes.

What Layla once loved could kill her as easily as blood passed through a vein. Swift, fluid, and without a conscious thought. It intrigued Layla as much as it infuriated her.

Elise still watched Layla, doubt twisting her features. Layla rolled her eyes. "I'm sure you have plenty of books in that fancy library of yours to consult if you want to. I won't be participating in that research."

"Because of your allergies?" Elise asked.

The question caught Layla off guard. She blinked several times, confused. "No?"

"Oh. Well, I just thought…you know, because when we would sit in the—" Elise stumbled over her words so badly, it actually pained Layla to watch.

"I know," Layla whispered. Tempted to keep that glimpse of the real Elise shining through her tough exterior, Layla hesitated in interrupting her. But the little relieved sigh Elise let out when Layla stopped her made the corner of her mouth tick up. "I no longer have allergies since becoming a reaper. I have no afflictions, actually," Layla said.

A tight smile spread across Elise's face. "Well. No afflictions except for...you know."

Cold resentment froze Layla's amusement. "Shut up." She zipped the body bags and pushed the drawers back into the wall. "So we've found ourselves back at square one with this stupid investigation. The newspapers failed to report on two dead Black girls, despite the crimes being at a popular club. It's clear no one will believe a damn thing I have to say. So why don't you announce to your father that it was not only reapers attacking the club, but also humans," Layla said dryly.

Elise followed her out of the morgue and into the hallway. She remained quiet for so long, Layla started to get irritated. She turned, waving a hand in front of Elise's blank expression. "Hello? Partner? Do you have any suggestions?"

Elise smacked Layla's hand away and glared. "I do. You could be more cordial."

"No," Layla snapped back. "My friend has died. *Again*. My clan and I could be next. If not dead, then arrested under suspicion of attacking humans. I'm not kneeling to your petty demands when we have more pressing issues to figure out."

Elise pursed her lips, sighing. "How is your memory?" she asked.

"You're really going to mock me right now? I'm not losing my humanity as we speak—"

"But what if you were?" Elise countered.

Layla's shone with anger. "Excuse you?"

"I'm not trying to mock you, Layla," Elise said quickly. "I know you said you could not remember anything the night of the murders, but consider when reapers experience memory loss. It doesn't happen unless they experience blood fury. Back in the club, Giana looked at you like she didn't know you. Like her memory of you was gone."

A heavy breath rattled through Layla. Her face had gone ashen as Elise spoke, jaw clenched so tightly, it ached. "Something came over her. And I think the same thing came over Theo the night of the murders," she murmured. "It could not have been a blood fury. I know for a fact Giana had fed."

"If not a blood fury, then what?" Elise asked. "And what about those other dancers? Why did the club have so many reapers hiding out, just waiting to attack?"

A sour taste filled Layla's mouth and her throat went dry. Her mind flashed back to the attack. Then, things had been too hectic to question anything, but now, as Layla mulled over the memory of the other dancers tearing into Shirley, questions arose. They had gone right for Shirley, despite the gangsters hemorrhaging blood all around them and they had reeked of rancid blood—as if they themselves were rotting from the inside out. Layla's heart sank. She looked up at Elise, whose brows were bunched in thought. "I don't think those dancers were reapers. They were something else."

"Maybe this is what Dr. Harding meant about a poison spreading," Elise mumbled. She ran her hands through her hair, dividing dark curls between her fingers and twisting the ends until they sprung back into place.

Layla watched the Saint heiress pace back and forth between the fountain and her, where she sat on a bench in a private park. A park she had not visited in years since the Saints owned it. Layla glanced up at the iron gate surrounding the small garden and the plaque that held the park's name, CHARLOTTE'S SANCTUARY.

Elise stopped short. "The clinic," she said.

"What?" Layla asked, only half-interested. She could not stop looking at the carefully arranged flowers. Roses, lilies, hydrangeas, chrysanthemums—every blossom one could imagine. She wondered if any of these plants had outlasted her welcome in the Saint estate.

"The Harding lab and clinic. Are you paying attention?" Elise demanded.

Layla blinked up at her. "No."

"Classic," Elise huffed. She crossed her arms and sat beside Layla. "Dr. Harding is researching the long-term effects of reaperhood and whether prolonged proximity with reapers can cause infection."

"I think we would have noticed that already," Layla said flatly.

"We just have. Those dancers were infected. If not by reapers, then by something else. We need to figure out what. The lab must have answers. If not him, then Mr. Wayne," Elise said.

At this, Layla's full attention returned, and she frowned at Elise. "You want to consult the white man?" There was truth to Elise's words; Layla could not doubt that. But a prickling sensation formed in her chest at the thought of the rest of the Saint family involving themselves in reaper business even more than they already did. "Reaperhood started with a white man and a laboratory, so if a poison is coming from anywhere, it must be them."

Elise gaped. "They might know something worthwhile. Why do you think you're so much better than them? Than this—"

"Why do you think you aren't?" Layla demanded. "You're so ready to kiss the ground your father and his empire slaves walk on. Have you ever considered that maybe they do not have all the right answers? You don't even know this doctor, or Stephen Wayne. Why are you so willing to trust him? Just because your father—"

"Yes, because of my father. I trust who he trusts," Elise said firmly. "Mr. Wayne has helped many businesses and contributed to Harlem's economy. He helps people. It's what he does," Elise insisted.

But apprehension cracked her visage of certainty, and Layla sensed her doubt. She spoke slowly, "I don't know what this man has told you, but you must know that we will always give them more than they could ever give us," Layla said. "They'll do whatever it takes to keep themselves on top and keep us beneath their feet. If you want to consult Stephen Wayne, fine, but we treat him like the suspect he is."

"*No*," Elise seethed. Her breathing quickened and then she was back on her feet, pacing again. "I cannot treat him as an enemy. I've already messed up at the club and I have not solved the murder. My father expects me to *fix* things. If I don't, he won't…he won't…" Elise trailed off.

The distress in Elise's voice caught Layla off guard. "He won't what?" she asked as she leaned forward.

Elise's throat bobbed. She turned back to Layla, shaking her head. "Nothing."

The determination and desolation in Elise's eyes were not bound to vanish any time soon. Layla knew it would be easier to go along with Elise rather than fight her. The more she got to know this new Elise, the more it felt like a long ice path stretching across a frozen river. Slow and steady steps would get her to where she needed to go, but stalling and succumbing to her hot temper would only send her crashing into an icy abyss.

Layla nodded. "Fine. We'll consult Stephen Wayne. As allies."

Relief seemed to soften Elise's edges. Even her voice was gentler when she spoke. "He is endorsing the new mayoral candidate. I will be able to attend some rallies to learn more about him. As for you, it would be best to track down the Cotton Club dancers—"

"You mean the ones from the club we destroyed two days ago? That will be tough if not impossible," Layla said.

"Oh, please. You've never shied away from a challenge before."

Elise cocked her head to the side and offered her a sharp smile. The look she gave Layla was made of pure virulence. How Elise got her eyes to look so picturesque, the essence of fatal attraction that only a siren could conjure up, Layla would never know. But she fell victim to it every time.

Layla's skin buzzed. She had to tear her eyes away and watch the flowers *again* to concentrate. But the pounding of Elise's blood, the glow in her eyes followed Layla's thoughts. "Meet up again in a week?" she muttered.

"Of course." In a flurry of gray skirts and luscious curls, Elise was gone. But her sweet scent of intrigue and betrayal lingered.

Elise gave herself to the beautifully demonic score she played on her grand piano that evening. Her fingers brushed the keys in shallow strokes over the bridge of the song, breathing life into the notes that projected hope. But as soon as the chorus came, her fingers struck down upon the keys as if she was striking death's gong. Notes smashed together like stormy waves against the shore, crashing into a haunting crescendo. The song ended as softly as it began, but with notes filling only an echo of the hope the song's first verse offered. It was as if a love letter had been written, detailing one's affection in great detail, only to be sent to a grave.

When she finished, all that Elise could picture in her mind was that grave. Frozen over, too barren to grow new life.

She never understood why such a melancholic piece was so popular to play at weddings, or considered to be joyful at all. Anyone who sat down and really listened to the song would understand the push and pull of the notes, and the pitting sadness they evoked.

Elise closed the piano. Her eyes caught on Sterling's reflection in the shine of the fallboard. "How was it?" she asked, turning away from the piano.

"Beautiful, as always," Sterling said. He pulled his hands from his pockets and sat on the stool beside her. "I'm no musical genius, but that song sounds very complicated. I can never tell if it's supposed to be sad, or happy."

"You don't have to be a musical genius to understand music. I think this song is about happiness, sadness, and everything in between. That's the beauty of music. Even if you're not trying to decipher it, it calls out to you. It demands perception," Elise said wistfully. She was still caught up in the last few notes of the song. Most music haunted her for hours after playing, but she knew today was especially different because of the specific song she played. It was a piece she played whenever her nerves were too fragile to talk through. Whenever she couldn't sit still, or relax, her fingers found the keys. They seemed to work through everything for her, even if it was just for a bit.

Sterling nudged his knee into hers. "How are you feeling today?"

He was warm against her thigh, but Elise didn't welcome the comfort like she normally did. Today, she craved the company of music more than anything, or anyone else. "Okay."

"Just okay?" Sterling asked.

"Just okay," she confirmed. "I suppose that's not too bad, considering the circumstances."

Sterling let out a gentle laugh. He was undeniably charming when his guard was down. For once, his soft curls were not completely slicked back; some bent around his ears and one particularly loose piece of hair flopped over his forehead. As children, a day would never pass without Layla teasing Sterling about his hair being too long and him needing a haircut. Elise was the only one to smooth his hair out of his face without a scolding word. Now, he kept his hair slicked back while working *for a more professional look*, something she imagined him saying when he sent her a letter with a picture of his new hairstyle attached.

Elise brushed the hair off his forehead. He caught her hand when she was done and clasped it between his palms. "Please be careful, Elise. I mean it." The sudden serious tone he took on surprised her.

She wanted to pull her hand back, stop this vulnerable moment from happening before they were in too deep, but it was too late. "Sterling…"

The anguish in his eyes cut the words right from her throat. "I always hoped for you to come back from France—for you to be unchanged, and for you to still be my best friend. I'm an awful friend for hoping you wouldn't find anyone you loved more than me while you were away. I couldn't stand the thought of you sharing your deepest secrets with anyone but me; I still can't. I know it makes me selfish, but I've lost everyone. I won't lose you too."

For a moment, Elise was speechless. She could watch him, silently willing the tears cresting in his eyes to not fall because if he descended into despair, then she would follow quickly after him and Elise wasn't sure she could handle that. "You won't," Elise whispered. She stood and drew him into her arms. Even standing while he sat, she was barely taller than him. His head fit against her chest, forehead resting right over her sternum.

Aside from Elise and her family, Sterling had no one. When he was just four years old, he had seen his father being lynched. In the Deep South, interracial relationships were inconceivable, much less tolerated. His mother was shunned for being a white woman who associated with a Black man, and when she gave birth to Sterling, who represented the very thing white people feared—whiteness tainted by otherness—their entire family became a target. The uncle had led the lynching of his own sister's husband. She tried to escape the South and find peace up north, but the grief her heart carried for the loss of her husband proved to be too much for her. Sterling was an orphan by the time he was eight years old.

Elise still remembered the day her father brought Mrs. Walker and Sterling into their house for a job opportunity. The overbearing sadness in Mrs. Walker's eyes bore into Elise and to this day, she still saw it in her darkest moments with Sterling. It had almost scared her off from playing with him then. But Layla had feared nothing. At just six years old, she threw their toys down and went right up to Sterling with her hand outstretched.

"I'm Layla. This is my best friend, Elise. Do you want to be our friend?" Layla demanded.

Sterling had raised his brows, curious. Elise couldn't blame him; Layla was incredibly vociferous as a child and that could be intimidating. They might not have been friends if their parents hadn't put them together as infants. Separation was never an option. They grew up closer than roots spiraling across a neighboring tree's trunk.

Now, inhaling the familiar scent of Sterling, guilt crushed her heart.

"Some part of me is more jealous than scared of you working with Layla now," he muttered.

Elise's throat went dry. "There is nothing to be jealous of." Her own words felt like a lie. She had grown to crave the heart-pounding thrill Layla caused in her.

She was a fool who didn't even understand her own feelings. Elise desperately hoped that wouldn't make fools of them all.

21

WASHINGTON SQUARE PARK WAS CROWDED WITH people waving flyers for the mayoral candidate, Hugh Arendale, in the late September air. Elise had never been to a political rally before, but she had an idea that this one would be particularly flashy. Just like Stephen Wayne. She wondered how much of this display he had personally funded.

Mr. Wayne moved through the crowd right behind Mr. Arendale with a bright smile on his face, though his security scowled every time someone got too close to them. The man was like a puppeteer, never straying too far from the strings he chased after.

His smile stretched even wider when he approached the Saints and stopped Mr. Arendale to greet them. "Sir, you are lucky to be graced with such wonderful people."

Mr. Arendale lowered his cigar and his gaze passed over Elise slowly at first, then stopped short when he got to Sterling. "Thank you for being here."

Sterling offered his hand for Mr. Arendale to shake. "Pleasure to be here, sir," he said with a gentle smile.

Mr. Arendale clamped his mouth over his cigar then gripped Sterling's hand hard with both of his own. "Pleasure to have you, son." Happiness lit his eyes as he beamed before moving over to kiss Analia Saint's cheek.

Elise shared a look with Sterling. "Well, if you ever see yourself in politics, you know who to call."

"And be a part of this country's corruption? Absolutely not," Sterling muttered.

Had her life not been firmly rooted to the ground she currently stood on, Elise would have agreed. It felt impossible to imagine this place without spite. Once they stood among the crowd, watching Mr. Arendale take the stage, Elise whispered back, "He wants to fix racism. Is it possible for a country built on the backs of others to ever consider those others as human? As more than tools to be used and discarded until we're needed again? The chances of a country conceived out of bigotry reconciling with justice…"

Sterling shook his head. "Never."

"I want a brighter future for everyone." Mr. Arendale's voice rang out. He stood on the dais in the middle of the square, eyes gleaming with ambition. "No one should live beneath the feet of others. As mayor, delivering equality to everyone will be my priority." Mr. Arendale raised his fist in the air. Several shouts rang out from the crowd.

"No more gangsters!"

"Eliminate all reapers!"

Elise anticipated fear from these individuals, but their angry voices seared through her.

Her father pressed into her side then, his knuckles brushing the back of her wrist. "Listen closely, Elise."

Elise looked out over the overly white crowd that appeared before the mayoral candidate. Some were Greenwich Village art types—people whose eyes never focused on one thing in sight. People who walked right from their projects to join the rally with paint still on their faces and flour still dashed on their clothing. Elise could imagine them passing around papers detailing their wishes for new legislation in the park during the evenings. Here, art and radicalism mixed, creating an environment of stifling want.

"Imagine ripping away the tiny shreds of hope all these people still manage to hold. You don't want that to dissipate, do you, Elise?" her father asked.

The crowd roared as Mr. Arendale continued to speak, but it was merely a murmur in Elise's ears. She could only focus on her father and the severity in his tone. "No, Father," she said strongly.

"Then why was one of Harlem's most prosperous businesses shut down after your visit? Another reaper attack left in your wake and all you've created is more paranoia," Mr. Saint hissed.

Elise took a deep breath. Her heart pounded so hard, she felt it in her ears, her temples, her arms. She wanted to leave; have this conversation in private, without the increased pressure of the crowd around them. All she could do was sweat while her father picked out every anxiety in her until she was more fear than person. She glanced up as Mr. Arendale said something that made the crowd laugh. "You will be happy to know that Layla and I have made a plan that involves Mr. Wayne. He is bound to lead us in the right direction."

"So you are going behind my back. Stephen is a very busy man, Elise. We are here to support him, not distract him," her father said coolly.

"I thought you would be happy to know." Elise swallowed.

Her father's expression turned cold. His mouth twitched, as if to keep back an aggravated smile, and he locked his jaw while he stared down at Elise. "Happy?" A shadow passed over his eyes and Elise's heart stopped. "If you are vying for my happiness rather than your success, Elise, then you have already failed. The success of performers relies on applause and pride. But you are no longer a performer. You are a Saint." He leaned closer to her when Analia Saint glanced over, concerned. "Do you think I accept awards when I eliminate reapers? No. Do not fall victim to the false god that is pride. *Do better.*"

In a split second, that mask of honed anger was gone. Mr. Saint leaned back, his relaxed smile returned. Elise dug her teeth into her bottom lip and willed her trembling body to still.

The rally carried on while Elise felt like the world was slipping from beneath her feet. Mr. Arendale spoke so smoothly, without a single doubt attached to his words. Elise could not imagine having that level of confidence. To speak, knowing everyone listened, to act, knowing those who watched were judging not his appearance, but the content of his character. To exist as the sole owner of his freedom.

"The Negro community is just as influential as ours. And we must unite if we want to see proper change," Mr. Arendale exclaimed.

Mr. Saint applauded with the crowd and his smile stretched even wider. Elise swallowed past a lump in her throat.

Elise could not brush away her fears; not when one of them stood right beside her. She thought of Layla in the garden the other week, her eyes filled with concern. Even if she had not shown it, Elise had felt it. And yet Elise had not been able to answer Layla's question, about what Elise feared with her father. *He won't what?* the reaper had asked.

He won't trust me, he won't see my worth, he won't love me. And then what good am I? What purpose do I serve?

The back of her eyes burned. Elise pressed her hands into her face, breathing hard. She was a fool. For how could she make him happy—how could she make anyone happy, or proud, when she could not even satisfy herself?

A gentle hand rubbed her shoulder, then Sterling's voice was in her ear. "Just a few more minutes. It's painfully boring here, I know."

Elise wanted to cry. She wasn't bored, she was exhausted. No one around her had seen that but Layla. *A reaper had seen right into her.*

She lowered her hands and stared ahead, right into the setting sun.

For so long, Elise assumed reapers bereft. They were stretched beyond their life expectancies, forced to contend with parts of their life that they would never get back, and denied the privilege of even experiencing a natural death. Reapers lived without the breath of life, eternal sinners trapped in agony.

They lived for no one but themselves.

Elise would never know what that was like.

Something burrowed in the back of Layla's mind. It bothered her so much, she eventually had to tear out the hair tie that held up her bun, letting her long curls bounce freely across her back so her head stopped throbbing. Not much relief came from the change, but she pushed a curl back from her face and continued perusing through Valeriya's various books, looking for anything at all about reapers turning back into humans.

Layla dropped the five-hundred-page book on medical evolution. It hit the desk so hard, the wood creaked and dust billowed up around the room. The only thing these books were good for was collecting dust and potentially being a deadly weapon. Layla lifted her brow, considering.

"What are you looking for?" Mei's voice turned Layla around.

Mei leaned against the door, hip popped out and arms crossed. Her black hair was plated beautifully and the red qipao she wore was so striking on her, Layla's breath nearly caught in her throat at the sight. She swallowed. "Nothing."

"Really? That is the only thing you could come up with?" Mei walked into the room and shut the door behind her, the ruined lock dangling against the wood. "I see you broke the lock. Valeriya told me to tell you to stay out of her study while she's away. The entire clan is whispering about you."

Layla rolled her eyes. "Of course. 'Reapers stick together'?" she scoffed. "We should rethink that."

Mei sighed and went silent for a long moment. Her lips pursed, brows going flat as she watched Layla. "Are you finished?"

"Why are you suddenly wanting to interact with me again? Has my case gone stale enough that it's now appealing, rather than dis-turbing?" Annoyed, Layla couldn't help the bitterness that soured her tone. "I'm busy, Mei. Go bother someone else."

"So, you *are* looking for something." Mei placed her hand over the massive book sitting on the desk between them. "Whatever it is, it can wait. And it should wait. The entire clan is on your ass about working for a Saint. Word got out about the Cotton Club incident and how you are at the center of it."

Layla gaped. "I am not—"

"The papers have reported on the incident. The *papers* are what people believe. *You* are in danger," Mei said through gritted teeth.

Layla huffed out a breath. "First of all, I am not working *for* a Saint. I am working *with* a Saint. I would never stoop so low, and I am highly offended that you think I would—"

Mei sighed. "Layla—"

"Second of all, I don't exactly have a choice here," Layla snapped.

Mei's biting expression fell into confusion. "What are you talking about?"

"I was offered immunity to solve the crime *with* the Saint heir." She gestured to the books surrounding them. "Believe it or not, research is heavily involved in solving crime. Anyone could have asked me what was going on, but no. For such bloodthirsty menaces to the world, these reapers are pretty cowardly."

Mei snorted. "It's not cowardice. It's leverage. It's easier to stay away from a bomb that will inevitably explode. But we will remain in the ashes to sift for the valuables left behind. No one cares about what you're *doing*, Layla; that's my whole point. They care about the precedent you're setting."

As logical as Mei's words were, Layla couldn't bring herself to latch on to them with any sincerity. "I don't care, Mei. And as far as I'm concerned, we are not friends. So whatever 'word of advice' you have for me, you can keep to yourself," Layla said coldly.

She expected pushback from Mei. But the determination that seemed to always be aflame in her eyes was damp around the edges, duller than usual. Mei sank away from the desk and walked to the door. Her hand rested on the handle while she turned to look back at Layla. "You're relying on a Saint's word. You of all people should know their word is as good as shit. Remember the ones who have been there for you since you became damned. It was not the Saints. And it never will be." Mei left, slamming the door behind her.

Her words echoed in Layla's mind until the dust, stirred from the slammed door, filled her throat as she inhaled. After a violent fit of coughing, Layla gave up. She reached for one of the stationery sets on the desk, intending to write her mentor a note, but paused when she saw the name scrawled across every envelope in the set: *Sena*.

Layla's heart stopped. These were the letters her mentor wrote endlessly. She was tempted to look, craving a glimpse into Valeriya's life. But Layla snatched her hand back, remembering whose study she stood in and the grace she had been offered. She would not spoil that trust to satisfy her own curiosities. With one last glance at the stack of letters, Layla left the room, her mind spinning and her throat burning.

22

LAYLA WAS STILL COUGHING OUT BITS OF DUST WHEN she went out to the street outside the Clarice. For the first time since becoming a reaper, she considered ripping her own throat out to relieve the irritation, but that would only—

"I thought you said your allergies were gone?" Elise's voice startled the remnants of dust right from Layla's system. She turned to see her waiting on the sidewalk.

"Why are you here?" Layla demanded.

"What a beautiful welcome," she said sarcastically.

Layla ignored her tone. "You said we were meeting in a few days. I haven't found anything yet."

Elise shrugged. "Fine."

Something was off. Elise seemed less rigid than usual, her shoulders relaxed into a gentle curve rather than the harsh edges they typically formed. And there was a softer presence in her eyes. For once, her body didn't bend to bear the weight of her responsibilities, her jaw was not clenched so tightly.

Layla sighed. "I'm assuming you have information to share, otherwise you wouldn't be here—"

"Can I not just *be* here?" Elise quipped.

Layla shook her head. "No. You cannot. This is quite literally not your territory. So unless you have anything new to share with me, you should go. Reapers would love to watch a Saint fall," she said icily.

Elise didn't move. Her eyes remained trained on Layla, wavering with something undecipherable. After a few long seconds, she let out a huff of air and looked away. "Nothing substantial to report back on the mayoral rally."

"Of course not," Layla muttered.

Elise shot her a stern look. At once, the cold Saint Layla recognized had returned. The searing familiarity almost warmed her. "I'm sure the labs are where the important information is, anyway. How is the research going for you?"

"It's not going," Layla said. She thought back to just a few minutes ago when Mei had interrupted her study search and given her a warning. It seemed that nothing Layla did was right, no matter which direction she went in; work with the Saints to clear the reaper name, or ignore the Saints and go to prison for the rest of her long, grueling life. Layla cleared her throat and lifted her head, not wanting Elise to see her dejection. "My clanmates are on my case. My clan leader also hates me right now."

A soft chuckle broke from Elise. "All of New York hates you.

Layla Quinn, reaper under suspicion of murderous rampage." Elise dramatized a reading of a popular newspaper headline. She thumbed at her lower lip, thinking, while Layla glowered at her. "You're not going to deny it?"

Layla swallowed past the hard lump in her throat. "There's no point. They believe what they want to believe." The breeze picked up around them, and Layla had to claw her hair out of the way when it blew into her face.

Elise was still watching her, quiet. Finally, she spoke, voice lowered, "I don't listen to them and their accusations of you being the murderer. I believe *you*."

Layla's heart stopped. She searched Elise's eyes for any sign she was lying. But all she saw was an affirming warmth aflame within.

"*Why?*" Layla whispered.

Just a few weeks ago, Elise had Layla sign a contract to ensure no double-crossing would occur during their investigation because her word was not good enough on its own. Layla wanted to feel confused. But she felt her heart tumbling headfirst into a pit of comfort—a sensation she had not felt in ages.

The feeling was almost foreign. Layla wondered if this was what it felt like when a still heart began to beat again. When a devout person, who kneeled for years in prayer, finally heard a whisper from their god. Elise was not Layla's god, nor was she adrenaline to start her heart. But the visceral reaction those three words unlocked in her was a phenomenon akin to what Layla might have attributed to divine recognition.

I believe you.

Elise didn't answer Layla's "why?" Layla was glad she didn't. To put conditions on a feeling as fleeting as this one would crush it.

I believe you.

All earlier misery had been chased away by those three words. Her mind echoed them over and over, Mei's threats long forgotten.

I believe you.

When Elise turned to leave, Layla let her face crack, like a stone, weatherworn and finally facing the sun, into a genuine smile.

The downtown lights were already beginning to glimmer along the skyline as Elise settled onto her piano seat in her music room. She set her fingers on the starting keys and sighed.

Layla crossed her mind once. Then she became an all-consuming thought. Elise wasn't sure what her impromptu visit to Layla was supposed to accomplish. All she knew was that the clawing feeling in her chest she always associated with Layla did not occur when she saw her this time.

At first Elise figured it was because Layla looked different.

Her hair was down. Even before Elise left for France, Layla always wore her hair up to keep it out of her face while she danced. Today, her hair was down. A wild, soft crown that framed her sharp face. Where Elise remembered gentle curves, there were now rough edges. She had anticipated feeling the sting of those edges during this visit, but there was nothing. Nothing but a subtle throb of the new emotion now gnawing at her chest, making it ache.

Maybe Elise had visited Layla to ensure that her hatred for the girl who had upended her life was still intact. The hate was still there, but it was nowhere as near to her heart as it used to be.

Elise's fingers slammed down on the piano keys, and the song screeched out of its deep, harrowing tone. She cursed, rubbing her eyes with the back of her knuckles.

Everywhere she turned, trying to find a new thread to bring her out of her confusion, Layla was there, blocking her. For once, the consistency of her brain irked her. Instead of finding one problem, there were thousands, and they were all tied to Layla Quinn.

She recalled a sweeter memory now, where Layla stood behind Elise at the piano, her fingers tangling in her curls. It was a soothing gesture; something Layla just knew how to do to help Elise release some tension while practicing a particularly difficult piece. When Elise had finished playing, she tugged Layla's arm further around her shoulders and sighed.

"You're going to be so famous one day, leading the orchestra at the fancy conservatory in Paris," Layla insisted.

Elise had laughed at the then-fanciful hope. "Sure. But only if you dance at the fancy ballet school nearby."

Layla released her then and Elise felt an immense loss until she slid onto the bench beside her, sitting so close, their thighs pressed together. "Well, of course. You're my best friend. I don't want to do life without you."

A smile lit Elise's face while Layla looked up at her. In that moment, Elise wanted to risk everything for Layla to truly understand the depth of her feelings. It was just one look, but it made Elise's world move. She felt it in the following silence and saw it despite the room's dim lighting.

Now, Elise pushed against the tender knots dotting her brain, but they only tightened. Her mind, forbidden to cave, made a prison for Elise's own feelings. She inhaled. On her exhale, Elise began to play. This time, she leaned into the newly raised emotions. Grace poured into her mind like warmed honey. Slowly, the tangles unraveled. Her mind mapped itself out before her, music painting a vivid backdrop of her feelings.

Each note was a gentle awakening from a long slumber. Her fingers stretched and curled with the music, inviting the swell of vulnerability to fill her previously hollow crevices. In this room, music was the sole eye of her perception, the window cracked just enough to let her glimpse at the delicate dissection of her heart and mind.

The song carried Elise like a breath of fresh air back into her body. She finished it, fingers trembling slightly against the damp keys as the final notes faded around her. Tears coated her cheeks. Her mind felt gloriously cleared with no more blocks forcing her to look inward.

Layla was gone from her thoughts, her only presence existing in the now silent song.

Elise closed the piano.

When Elise was younger, her father had a habit of drinking black coffee at midnight. Now, she glowered at her father's closed door as the maid, Helen, knocked on it, holding a steaming mug of the stuff. Elise could smell it the second it started brewing. The scent filled the house, curling around every corner and diving into every crevice it could find. Elise wrinkled her nose.

She sat up in the sitting room across from his study, moving pieces across a chessboard while she listened for him to come out. An hour had already passed, during which Sterling had bade her goodnight.

The study door finally cracked open.

"Please take it up to my bedroom, Helen. Thank you."

The knight piece fell from Elise's hand while she looked up. Helen hurried down the hall with the coffee in her hands. Then Mr. Saint emerged. Elise righted the chess piece and straightened up in her seat. "Father," she said solemnly.

Her father chuckled. "Allow me to be the first victim of this new defense you're working out." He pointed to the chessboard and sat in the chair opposite hers.

"Are you sure? You aren't tired?" Elise asked.

"Elise," he said flatly. She noticed the least expected emotion residing in his eyes: guilt. "Give me a chance. You've been waiting up all night for me. I should be taking more time to spend with you, and I'm sorry I haven't. Work has just been so busy."

Elise nodded quickly. "I understand, Father. That's why I assumed you would want to go to bed. Not play chess. I'm not even good." She laughed, and it was soft enough to make him smile.

"I love watching you learn," her father said. "All right, then. I'm black. You're white."

It was nearly three o'clock in the morning by the time her father went to bed and Elise could sneak into his study. He beat her badly in two games, which Elise had not minded at first. But then he went into critiques, telling her how sloppy her defenses were and how it could all be a grand metaphor for her job as heiress.

"You lack self-awareness, my pearl. I don't want you to get hurt because you assume those around you are playing this game of life as safely as you are." His voice had been so soft as he spoke, like a proper father giving her advice and guiding her into an important stage of her life.

Then he had taken her queen.

Elise closed the study door behind her and turned to face the massive room. She caught the whiff of roses first, a sickeningly sweet scent that overwhelmed her senses.

She started at her father's desk, rummaging through drawers, shifting papers about. Most of the letters she found that were addressed to Mr. Wayne were already sealed. There was no way for her to open them without making it obvious they had been tampered with. Elise set those aside and continued to search the room. By the fireplace sat two plush armchairs. A crystal glass half full of red wine rested on one of the chair's side tables, a worn notebook planner on the other.

Elise picked it up and flipped to the most recent pages:

DELIVERY WITH VEX
VENUE MAINTENANCE
SUIT FITTING

She ran her fingers over the rough pen marks of her father's handwriting. He must have been upset; the gouges of the pen nearly ripped the page. Almost every page was full, details scrawled even in the margins. Until she found a mostly blank page for the first of October.

All it said was 'BUSY,' with an X crossed over the whole page.

Elise shut the planner and put it back where she found it. Whatever her father was planning was big enough to warrant plans weeks in advance. Yet Mr. Saint, the man who carefully ensured timeliness and organization, had not told his family a single thing.

23

MEI POKED HER HEAD INTO LAYLA'S ROOM EARLY one morning. "Layla—"

"No," Layla said flatly. She dragged the tip of a dagger across her fingertip, watching her blood bead, then admiring the quick seal of her skin.

Mei huffed from the doorway. "You don't even know what I'm going to ask for."

"I don't care. You can show yourself out," Layla muttered. She relaxed when she heard the door close behind Mei.

"Layla." An icy voice made Layla's blood freeze in her veins. Valeriya stood in the doorway, her sour expression cutting into Layla. "Next time, when your clan member calls for you, you answer. I have done the same for you for many years. It would be a slight against me if you did not return the gesture in my clan," Valeriya said sharply.

Layla dropped the knife onto her lap and sat up. She tried to pull a neutral expression, but could not hide her discomfort. "My apologies, Valeriya. Mei and I are not on the best terms right now," Layla said quietly.

"You need to fix that. Both of you." Valeriya nodded to Mei, who swiftly left the room, closing the door behind her. The entire atmosphere seemed to shift whenever Valeriya entered a room. One glance at her told any person that she was just an ordinary woman—beautiful, with her smooth brown skin and dark green eyes, but still ordinary. Any reaper could tell she was an immortal soul with the face of a timeless beauty. Layla sensed her subtle heartbeat now, blood pooling like a calm creek in her veins. Her eyes held centuries of experience in them and they had always drawn Layla in. Years spent living in the States, not yet united, terrorizing the weakhearted men at night. The ones who threatened their wives would end up on a stake several yards from the forest line, their chests gaping and heartless. Rumors surrounded Valeriya like snakes on a vine. The one Layla knew to be true was that she kept the hearts of all of her victims. Carnage and gloom forever in her crimson wake.

Nothing promised violence like Valeriya's calculating gaze. She stood before Layla now, hands clasped behind her, shoulders squared and eyes tense while she watched Layla's face.

"When you came to me as a child, you were bloody and aimless and without family." Valeriya was only just beginning, but already, Layla's heart ached. One mention of her family threatened to crack open the vault of feelings she kept locked away.

An unpredictable bomb, a true reaper.

Valeriya's voice hardened as she continued, "You were alone, Layla, and the youngest reaper I had met since testing first began. I don't understand why you would spend all this time building stability for yourself if you're just going to throw it away. And for a worse than bad reason, you've thrown away your life to help the Saints. *The Saints*, Layla. The same people who got you into this mess in the first place."

Irritation seeped into Layla. She clenched her fists so hard, her nails nearly tore the blankets on her bed. "The Saints offered me more of a choice than you have in these trying times—"

"Really." Valeriya's frame went rigid, and the green of her eyes turned so dark they looked almost black. "You speak to me as if I did not let you in off the street five years ago, as if I did not sing you to sleep when nightmares shook your body and you couldn't stop screaming that girl's name and calling for your parents. Your dead parents. *Dead*. Because of the Saints. Not me, not Mei, not any of the reapers—"

"*It was reapers who killed my parents!*" Layla screamed. She couldn't hold her rage back anymore. She was done trying. The vault burst at the locks, hinges flying off rusted metal, and her emotions came pouring out of her. "I watched them tear into my mother's chest while she screamed. I watched them rip out my father's throat while he cried for my mother. If the Saints called the reapers onto my parents, then that's their doing, but the reapers took the bait. They took my parents from me, they took my whole life from me. Don't tell me who killed my parents because you weren't there to see it. I saw all of it. I remember *every second*. And I will not allow anyone to tell me how to grieve the life that I should be living." Layla's voice quavered with every emotion she had let fester and tear at her for the past few years. Her soul rose into her throat, desperate for a way to stop the hurting that consumed her from the inside out, and for a moment, she thought she might lunge for Valeriya. She imagined her fangs and nails tearing at Valeriya's perfect polished skin until she bled as red as Layla felt on the inside.

But Layla braced herself. She planted her feet against the floor and let her fangs sink into her gums instead. The familiar tang of her blood filled her mouth and Layla let out a soft sigh as a coolness soothed her fiery nerves.

"It was a betrayal, nonetheless." Valeriya, the ever-cold pillar of strength and ancient history, did not flinch. A small shadow of darkness unfurled in her eyes, but she merely lifted her hand and opened the door to leave. She stopped in the doorway, still facing Layla. "Remember how the result of their orders tormented you so badly, you wound up standing on the edge of the Clarice's roof. Months after your deadly attack and you were ready to die again. Ma fille, you've come so far from that night you tried to take your own life with the Saint bullet. I would hate for anything to happen to you." She left without giving Layla a chance to respond.

My daughter. My girl.

That old nickname gave Layla pause. It had been ages since her mentor had called her that—the first time the words slipped out of Valeriya's mouth, they seemed to startle her. They almost never came out again. Until now. Layla felt Valeriya's honesty; the vulnerability alone made her nerves relax and her thoughts slow down. This was her home now. And she had to fight to keep it.

A droplet of blood dribbled down her chin and splashed onto her bedsheets. The tiniest splotch of ruby bloomed across the white cotton, instantly jerking Layla back to memories of similar imagery.

Mei in her bed, choking on others' blood while Layla tried to coax her into a fitful sleep. Weeks before then, Layla pinning Mei's wrists to the headboard while she lapped at the fresh blood falling from the puncture marks on Mei's throat. Years before then, Layla on top of Elise in her previously picturesque bedroom, then wrecked by Elise's blood.

And lastly, days before the attack, when Layla had sat, hand in hand with Elise, watching the sunset while Elise played the notes of her favorite song with one hand.

Layla marveled at that image now, just as much as she had marveled then. How Elise played so elegantly with only one hand, seeming to put as much concentration into the notes as she put into stroking Layla's knuckles along with the music. The song was perfect, the sunset was marvelous, but the only thing Layla could focus on was how lovely her best friend looked in the light and how beautiful she made her feel.

A flame had come alive in her that day, years ago at the piano. How brightly her embers burned for Elise then, Layla wondered if the reapers that claimed her life had fully extinguished them.

❀

"Don't look her in the eye. Don't speak to her. Don't even breathe at her," Elise said sharply. A fire raged in the fireplace beside her, which only made it harder to shove tight leather gloves onto her increasingly sweaty hands.

Sterling watched her with parted lips. "How does one breathe at someone?" he asked.

Elise rolled her eyes. "I've seen you do it before. Or heard it, actually. It's awfully loud."

"Okay, Lise." Sterling paced the sitting room, one hand on the gun in his chest holster. "So if I cannot look at, speak to, or breathe at Layla Quinn, then what exactly are you bringing me along for?" he wondered out loud.

"Sterling." Elise stopped messing with her gloves and looked at him. Her brow flattened into a frustrated line. "I need you as my damage control. Also, it's probably better that I have an alibi tonight."

Sterling stopped his pacing in front of her and rolled his sleeves up past his elbows. His hands rested on his hips, forearms flexing while he watched her. "Are you planning on committing a crime? That's something I should definitely know beforehand—"

"No crime. Just chaos." Elise flashed him a sharp smile, then pulled him out of the room.

Autumn finally began to settle throughout New York. The day was unusually cold with fog seeping in over the coast, blurring the peaks of the downtown buildings together. Perched on a railing looking over the sea, Layla awaited her rendezvous. She wore a light coat, though she didn't need it. Her body quickly adjusted to external environments due to her reaperhood, but sometimes it felt nice to act normal. Blending in with the rest of New York, who had been excited to pull out their heavier clothes for the arrival of cooler weather, felt grounding after the whirlwind of her past few days.

"Hey, kid."

Layla turned to face Jamie. The last time she had seen him, she had threatened him and blood had spilled. Today he looked like his normal self. Blond hair slicked back, blue eyes so pale they seemed gray in the cloudy weather. Layla searched his face for any lingering resentment from the Cotton Club incident, but he appeared perfectly stoic.

"Vex. Thank you for meeting me," Layla said.

Jamie leaned against the railing. Even though Layla sat on the railing, he still had several inches over her. When he shifted, she saw the glint of a silver revolver in his belt. "It's not a great day to watch for the skyline, is it?" Jamie asked. He glanced over the sea, the crashing waves the only noise between them while Layla thought.

"You owe me money, Quinn. Either that, or blood," Jamie muttered fiercely.

Layla's jaw tightened, irritation making her body tense up. "I'm not responsible for the bloodbath at the Cotton Club. Those dancers were already infected—"

"If it weren't for your meddling, there would have been no incident, and I would still have a speakeasy to run," Jamie snapped.

Layla glowered. "Open another one. You are a man with fair skin and corrupt police on your side. If they wanted to catch you, they would have already. There is no limit to what you can do. Do not blame me for your lapses in judgment. You're weak and stupid. That's not my fault," Layla hissed.

The air between them went still as heat rolled off Jamie's body. He glared at Layla and tightly gripped the railing. "I cannot lose my income, Quinn."

"Is that why you're supplying for Tobias Saint on the low?" Layla asked. She knew the answer already, thanks to the Saint heiress, but she liked seeing Jamie tense up.

Jamie sighed. He moved closer to Layla. "What are you trading for these secrets, Quinn?"

"Nothing. But it's nice to have the upper hand on your gang so I have something to fall back on should my clan go under. After all, you shot Giana," Layla breathed. "And I wondered why you had Saint bullets."

A true smile broke across Jamie's face. He leaned forward and a few strands of hair fell into his eyes while he chuckled. For the first time since knowing him, Layla noticed a dimple that creased his right cheek. "You could say I have a little arrangement with Mr. Saint. And you *wish* you could take my gang."

"Don't try me." Layla hopped off the railing. Jamie was so tall, she had to tip her head back to meet his eyes. "The fog isn't that thick, Jamie. I saw the cargo coming in. I know you're only here because you're expecting a delivery. I need to know what it's for."

Jamie lifted his brow. "For such a small girl, you make mighty big requests." He ran his hand over his head, fluffing his hair. "You already know, shortcake."

"I'm not that small," Layla grumbled. "What does Tobias need this alcohol for?"

Smiling, Jamie rested his elbow on her head. Layla glared up at him, but he didn't stop. "You're very tiny. I wonder what it would be like to—"

Layla flung his arm from her head and, twisting it behind his back, threw him against the railing. Jamie's face went slack with surprise. He tried to break free and grab his gun, but Layla's hold on him was too tight. Even though he had at least ninety pounds on her and stood an entire foot taller than her, Jamie was no match for Layla's reaper strength. She bared her fangs at him now and saw the reflection of the rage-induced golden sheen over her eyes in his. "Still tiny?" Layla hissed.

Despite the fresh panic seeping into his expression, Jamie still had the audacity to smile at her. "Yes. Tiny, but strong." His smile widened when she wrenched his arm further behind him. "I like this side of you, Quinn. Pull me harder and see what happens," he snarled.

Layla focused on the pulsing artery in his throat. The temptation to drink from him and shut him up was strong. But her sanity had an even tighter grip on her. Layla let him go and backed away. "You're all the same," she spat.

Goddamn gangsters always put violence above everything else. They were attracted to danger like it was a conquest.

"Hey now, don't get all sour on me." Jamie straightened up, rubbing his wrenched shoulder. "Might I remind you that you're the one who destroyed my—*shit*," he cursed.

When Layla looked up, she realized why. Elise walked toward them, a tall and unfamiliar young man beside her.

"Jesus, Quinn, is this some kind of ambush?" Jamie went to reach for his gun, but Layla already had a hand around his wrist.

"Remember what I said last time?" she asked under her breath. "I'm the only one who kills her. She's *my* Saint."

For once, Elise didn't have a snarky comeback. She stared at Layla, lips parted slightly. Layla dropped her gaze and studied the other parts of Elise. She was not wearing one of her signature expensive dresses, but was instead dressed in pants.

"You two are off to a wonderful start, I see." Elise crossed her arms and stared up at Jamie, who still gripped his gun in a tight fist while he glowered at her. "My apologies. We're a bit late because I had to remind Sterling of proper reaper and gang etiquette." Elise gave the man beside her a quick smile.

Layla couldn't believe her eyes. The last time she had seen Sterling, he had still been so childlike, his eyes bright, face round, essence overall soft with youth. But now, not only was he several inches taller than he had been at fourteen, but he was rough cut, all previously soft curves hard with experience.

"Etiquette?" Layla asked, still focused on Sterling.

"He's used to killing trespassing reapers on sight," Elise said.

Layla had never gotten as close to Sterling as Elise did. She was always more fascinated by Elise, the bond between Sterling and Elise one she had never experienced. They were a proper family, like brother and sister.

"Jamie is Vex," Layla said.

Jamie wrenched his arm free from her grasp and glared. "Wow. Thank you for selling out my alias—"

"Cut the act, Vex. We know you're supplying for my father. Just tell us what for. This doesn't have to be a hard game," Elise said. She stepped closer to Jamie, whose glare seemed to sear more.

"Why not just ask your father?" Jamie spat out.

"Hell, I never thought of that," Elise snapped. "He's intentionally keeping it a secret. If I ask my father, he will feel targeted and know that someone sold him out. And that is good for no one. Especially the people who work for him. So if you want to keep your job and if you want your gang to take you more seriously, then *answer my damn questions.*" Elise's voice hardened at the end of her words.

Jamie, who stood several inches taller than her and had the usual external fear factor a deadly gangster carried, looked small in the face of Elise's fury. She glared up at him with eyes burning so intensely, Layla nearly felt the tingle of her them on her own face. Seeing the way Jamie's expression went slack at her demeanor added to Layla's satisfaction.

This was a man who stared death in the face more often than not and constantly had reapers nipping at his heels. Jamie hardly ever flinched when Layla's fangs came out and blood sprayed. But Elise had made him shrink with her purely mortal malice.

Layla almost smiled.

Jamie's shoulders went slack as he sighed. "We're supplying alcohol for your father. He's hosting a fundraising ball with Stephen Wayne next weekend." His expression hardened. "I wonder why he didn't tell you. He normally throws himself at every opportunity to flaunt his *perfect family.*"

Elise's lip curled. "Something you would know nothing about." She didn't stay to watch the light die in his eyes as she finally backed away from him. Her words transcended cruelty. They weren't even directed at Layla, but she felt them split open a raw part of her that she fought to keep protected; the reminder that her family was gone forever. Even Sterling flinched by Elise's side.

Layla stilled; her previous awe at the Saint's aggression suddenly vanished. Her malice instead matched the hand her family had had in the death of Layla's own parents. She was struck by the much-needed reminder that Elise was not on her side. Everything she did was to benefit her family, whose sole goal was the destruction of Layla's existence and reaperhood as a whole.

"We need to be at this event," Elise said.

Layla shot an icy look at Jamie, who still looked shaken by the Saint heiress's cruelty. He nodded. "I can get you in. It's a masquerade ball, so it will be easy to go unnoticed."

Sterling glared as he watched Layla. He touched Elise's arm. "Not a word of this to your father."

"Of course not. Layla—" Elise began, but Layla was already withdrawing.

"Send me a message. I'm leaving," Layla muttered. She started walking away, but stopped, turning to Elise. Confusion muddled her pretty brown eyes as they lifted to Layla. "There is no such thing as reaper etiquette, by the way. It's the same as all other etiquette rules; just be a decent person." Layla turned and left.

"Was that how things were supposed to go?" Sterling asked.

Elise ignored him. Layla was long gone now, Jamie, too, but Elise continued to hear their final exchange repeated in her head. *Just be a decent person.*

Never in her life would Elise imagine a reaper telling her this. She certainly hadn't considered that she had said something wrong until she saw dejection darken everyone's faces, Sterling's and Layla's included.

"Jamie said we need masks for the party," Elise said quickly. She was a Saint. They prided themselves on purity, on good graces, on proper etiquette. Her father taught her since she was a little girl what would be acceptable as a young Black girl, and what wouldn't. Elise had suffered too many cruel words from her father's bitter disappointment to not have gotten something out of his treatment. "Let's get some now." She did not want to go home.

Their walk into the city was mostly quiet. Then Elise broke the silence. "I'm sorry."

Sterling looked perplexed. "Why?"

"I've dragged you into this. And I said something so callous about family—"

"We all say things we don't mean, Elise. Thank you for apologizing, but it's fine," Sterling said quietly.

Elise stopped walking. Someone bumped into her from behind and she let Sterling pull her to the side of the street so they didn't interrupt the flow of traffic. "It's not fine. I'm supposed to be your friend. I hurt your feelings, Sterling, I saw your face. And I know you hate going behind my father's back because your job means a lot to you, so you don't have to come to this fundraiser if you don't want to—in fact, you can forget all about today." Elise exhaled. Her head throbbed and her eyes burned. She wanted more than anything to sit and be alone, to pick her mind apart until it fell silent. But there was no time. "I can't do this anymore—"

"No," he said roughly, "you're right. You were unnecessarily vicious back there. But in the face of a gangster who causes more cruelty every day and your old friend, who tried to kill you, I don't care. What I care about is you accepting defeat before you've even begun. Your father expects a lot from you, Elise, and I know it's difficult, but at least it's something. Some people have nothing. Do not let your family and your legacy slip away from you so easily." Sterling's voice broke and Elise had to look away when tears filled his eyes. "There is nothing selfish about wanting the best for someone else. I think that whole idea is a myth. Because even if you're doing it for yourself, you're still helping someone else."

He paused and his eyes glazed over as he began to slip into his past, rummaging through his most treasured memories. "My father married my mother out of love. I used to think that was what got him killed. His courage and his devotion to her. But I realized it was not his fault at all. It was this world and its backward beliefs. He was caught in the cross fire of a country trying its hardest to destroy itself. If anything, it's made me realize that this world was not built for us. Even the most natural things that come to us—love, anger, fear— those things are sacred to us. We cannot take them for granted. They are what makes us human, what others try to deprive us of. Don't ever let that part of you slip, Elise. This world killed my mother just as it killed my father. Even though he died with a noose around his neck and she died with her blood drained by her own volition, the same world killed them."

Elise sniffed. "Sterling…"

"It's okay. We will be fine," Sterling said. "You are the strongest person I know. You've been to hell and back, yet you're still fighting. That alone is worth notable recognition."

Elise wanted to cry. But she didn't want to create a new situation. So she nodded and forced a smile. "Thank you, Sterling." It was always thanks to him. Because of him, she still lived, because of him, she was still a human, rather than a reaper, because of him, she still had something to live for. Elise glanced over his shoulder and spotted a boutique just a few feet away. "Do you think they have masks there?"

Sterling looked over. "Sure. Shall we go?"

"Yes. I'll meet you there in a bit. I just need to make a quick call."

Elise waited until he was in the store before she slumped against the alley wall. Her chest felt heavy, like it was on the verge of caving in on itself. Elise clutched her hand over the tightening spot on her chest and turned to face the alley. Heavy breaths tore from her body as she fought to lessen the pain, but it only worsened. She buried her face in her hands and bit the heel of her palm to keep from screaming.

The situation she had thrown herself into was far too much for her to take on herself. The only way she knew his proper validation would be bestowed on her was if she handed the city to her father on a silver platter dripping with reaper blood. But Elise played with the piano, not with guns. *This was not her.*

She wanted comfort, but she didn't want to explain her complicated web of feelings. She didn't want anyone to know she was not okay. The burden was her own to bear.

Elise had no choice but to be brave. Feeling made her vulnerable. And in a country where strength was expected of her, and anger made her a target, it was best for her to wipe her tears and keep going. No matter how hard fighting got.

So, drying her face, Elise stood up and left the alley.

24

THE HOTEL CLARICE FELT COLDER THAN USUAL. Layla's heart shuddered at the empty atmosphere and frigid glances she got from her clan members as she walked into the massive foyer.

A semicircle formed around the center of the room where Valeriya sat waiting. "Join us, Layla," Valeriya said. She quickly glanced in front of her. On the table sat a crystal glass still full of blood and a notebook. Her eyes found Layla's. "Have you decided where your loyalties lie? With us, or with the Saints?" Valeriya asked.

Reapers started murmuring around her.

Layla gaped. "Of course I'm loyal to this clan. This is my home. You—" Her voice broke and she swallowed, willing herself to sound strong. "You are the closest I've ever had to a family since I lost mine." Layla sniffed. "People say reapers are heartless, but this clan has stuck together through the hardest times, and that proves just how much we care for each other. I think we have more hearts than the entire Saint empire."

Valeriya lifted the cup to her lips and passed Layla a cold look. It pierced through Layla, her body tensing. Valeriya nodded. "I know that. But your loyalty remains unknown." She gestured to the clan members around them, who all murmured agreements under their breath. "Sit."

Layla listened. She sat in one of the free seats, somewhat farther away from everyone else. Valeriya continued the meeting as if there had been no interruption. "We've recently lost two of our own. Both times, Layla, you have been at the center of the crime. And now you are running around with a Saint—"

"I'm bound by an agreement with the Saints. We reasonably believe Theo Smith killed those Saint members that night as a reaper. The problem is that he was not just a reaper. He became something worse. Close to demonic. And in death, he was human once more. So were Giana and Shirley," Layla said.

Valeriya sucked her teeth as the entire room burst into commotion. Mei shot Layla a bewildered look from across the room. "I have lived for hundreds of years and never seen such a thing," Valeriya drawled.

"I was at the scene of both crimes and I saw such a thing," Layla seethed.

Mei spoke over the shocked murmuring around them. "How does this involve the Saints?" she asked.

Layla swallowed as she remembered the sallow skin and empty

eyes that stared up at her under the harsh morgue lights. "They are partnered with the mayoral candidate, Stephen Wayne, and are supporting his clinic."

Someone's voice rang up from the back of the room. "They are working on a cure for reaperhood?"

"If it's only a cure in death, I'm not sure it can be called a cure," someone else muttered.

Layla almost shouted her next words. "Nothing is positive yet. Only that the murder was not just a reaper attack. Knowing that there is a potential cure out there… It's what we've all wanted. I aim to find out more about it. This could be the beginning of something new, where violence is not the answer and peace is promised," she said softly as the clamor settled down.

Valeriya cleared her throat. "There is no cure for reaperhood. Whatever you've found, it's not to be trusted. Especially not if it comes from the Saints. They want to get rid of us. Not fix us. You will not ruin the order I have created for us in Harlem." She stood, her skirts billowing around her in a graceful wave of black and purple silks. "Meeting adjourned."

Layla's heart dropped. She pushed her way through her clan members to catch up with Valeriya, who was already halfway up the grand staircase. "Valeriya—"

"Save it, Quinn. You will not get my vote of confidence for inciting chaos," Valeriya said coldly.

Not thinking, Layla grabbed her mentor's elbow. Valeriya stopped on the landing and turned to face Layla. Her eyes flared with fury, the dark green replaced by a luminescent neon green. Layla did not shy away. Valeriya might have been older than her by centuries, and she might have been taller than her and bigger than her, but Layla had all of those same abilities that she had. Increased speed, increased senses, faster reflexes. She never thought she would need to face off with Valeriya, but should things ever come down to it, Layla trusted her instincts to be a fair match against hers.

"I know you don't trust the Saints, but you can trust me," Layla said.

"Oh, please. They practically raised you. They know how to manipulate you and use you against us." Valeriya's voice came out in a cold hiss.

"They did not raise me. My mother and father raised me as a human. Then you raised me as a reaper. Not the Saints. With them I associate nothing but bitter, painful memories and blood that won't stop spilling. There is nothing any Saint could do to make me leave your side," Layla said strongly. "I want this cure. I truly believe one exists and I will find it. Even if I have to suffer through a bit of Saint torture. I won't force this cure onto anyone, but let me at least make it an option."

For a moment, Valeriya was quiet. But her eyes went back to their normal dark green shade the longer she thought and began to soften her stance. Finally, she exhaled. "You have already spread this nonsense throughout my clan; at this point, they will be expecting something. But you don't have my blessing. Because if anything happens to this clan, it will not be on me, it will be on you. Think of it like this." Valeriya closed her fingers around Layla's wrist. Her nails dug in so hard that Layla felt her skin break beneath the pressure, blood already dripping out while Valeriya spoke. "This is your new family. It's up to you whether you can save them a second time around or not."

By the time the weight of her words sunk in, Valeriya was gone. Layla was left standing on the landing, wrist stinging and heart aching.

Wear a mask that covers your whole face. Bring a date. The goal is to blend in.

Layla ran Elise's message in her head over and over. Despite Layla not being excited for a night of loud music, drunken people yelling, and being forced into close proximity with Elise, she welcomed the upcoming gala as a much-needed distraction from the tension surrounding her in the clan.

She flung a simple black dress onto her bed and glared at it. The nicest piece of clothing she owned, and it was so plain. Not a single sparkle, or an ounce of fringe adorned the poor thing. Elise would probably have a heart attack if Layla wore it to the gala. She could almost picture the aghast look on the Saint's face.

"What is that? I told you to wear a dress, not a rag!"

Layla laughed to herself. She pulled the dress from its hanger and stepped into it anyway. It still fit nicely after all these years. Valeriya had gifted her the dress just a few days after her fifteenth birthday. She claimed she was tired of seeing Layla in the same sad clothes every day, but the dress was plainer than the beautifully stitched coat she had taken from Elise's room the night after she turned. And upon closer inspection, Layla realized this dress was quite vintage. For someone who prided herself on being well off and had a wonderfully indulgent closet, a used dress was an odd gift from Valeriya. If she wasn't wearing a new silk gown with a fancy coat and some glimmering jewelry, she was not herself.

Layla wondered if the dress she gifted her had belonged to someone Valeriya once knew. But she couldn't recall Valeriya being close to anyone in the few years she had known her. It was strange; for a woman of so many centuries, she didn't seem to know that many individuals other than her Harlem reapers.

Or maybe she just kept her acquaintances secret.

Sighing, Layla moved to pull off the dress. But fraying threads tangled in the fabric, catching when she tried to yank it past her shoulders. Layla groaned and stuck her leg on her bed, reaching back to try and peel the dress off. But to no avail. She knew she probably looked deranged, her body twisting to get the dress off—

"Do you need help?" A gentle voice tinged with amusement wafted over from her bedroom doorway.

Layla's foot slipped from her bed and she righted herself immediately. Of course, the fabric picked this moment to slide down just enough to make the front part of her dress slouch in the most unflattering way. Layla pressed the material against her chest, her cheeks burning as Mei stepped into the room. "I don't need help," she muttered fiercely.

Mei ignored the obvious lie. She moved in front of Layla and looked down at her with curious eyes. "You never wear this dress." Mei brushed a gentle finger over the sloping fabric on Layla's chest. "May I?" she asked.

"Fine." Layla nodded. The heat in Layla's cheeks flared at the tenderness in Mei's tone. She remembered then how it had felt to be with Mei in the darkest points of the night, her legs fitted around Mei's hips, Mei's lips moving softly over her throat. Layla wasn't sure why it started in the first place. A mutual attraction was the only thing she could come up with. But neither of them loved each other. Once upon a time, years ago, she thought she might have felt it burn in her heart for someone, but those flames had long since died. Perhaps they were never to return.

Now, Layla stared straight ahead at the wall while Mei went behind her and gently began working the zipper from its trap in the fabric. Soft fingers slid on the nape of Layla's neck. The strokes were so gentle and light, Layla felt herself leaning into Mei the slightest bit just to deepen the contact. Such tenderness had not always existed between them.

The first time the attraction between them spiraled into something more, both of their lips had been coated in blood from a recent feed. Mei had done the job of luring a stupid gangster into an empty alley, then Layla had struck. She looked up at Mei over the gangster's gaping chest, blood seeping from her mouth and down her

chin. Human blood always made Layla feel glorious. But this kill...
The adrenaline that came with the blood had unlocked all of Layla's
inhibitions. So when Mei settled beside her and began to drink her
fill, Layla leaned closer to her.

They fed until they were full, physically. But on the walk back to
the lair, Layla took one look at Mei and noted the sudden brightness
of her dark eyes that teemed with hunger. It called to the heated desire
that blazed in Layla's chest. Moonlight slanted over Mei's pale cheekbones, and Layla thought the blood in the curve of her full lips looked
so sublime, she would die to taste any part of her. They both stopped
mid path. And as Mei reached for her, Layla met her in the middle.

Blood slipped between their lips while they kissed, devouring
each other as if they were the last meal they would have. Night swallowed them. For the first time in years, Layla felt something other
than emptiness and pain. Mei pushed Layla against a nearby wall
and together they spiraled into a frenzied ecstasy.

By the time they emerged from their heated tryst, Layla couldn't
tell if it was the blood that was making her deliciously dizzy, or if
it was the taste of Mei. She never forgot the intoxicating sweetness
that lingered on her lips, coupled with the way her body had found
euphoria just with Mei.

Whatever it was, Layla didn't question it. She merely licked the
last of her sinner's meal from her lips and followed Mei back to the
Hotel Clarice.

They didn't talk about what they had done in the alley for a few
days. But it happened again. And again. And again. Mostly in Layla's

bed, sometimes after a successful hunt in the middle of an empty park at night.

Layla didn't realize how much she missed another's touch until she felt Mei at her throat now, her fingers gently working the threads out of their tangled mess on her dress. "Mei," Layla whispered.

Mei's fingers fluttered, as if surprised to hear Layla speaking. "Yes."

"I'm sorry," Layla said.

"For what?" Mei asked.

Layla hadn't prepared to answer that question. She had assumed Mei would just accept the apology and they would move on and continue tolerating each other just like they had after each kiss, no matter how violently it began. She sighed and turned to face Mei.

"I'm sorry for being selfish. I'm sorry for taking my anger out on you. You don't deserve that. You've had a rough couple of weeks—"

"We all have," Mei said strongly. "We have had a rough couple of years. I've wasted so much money on phone calls and trips across the state. And for what? Any family would have taken one look at me and rejected me anyway."

Layla didn't have to ask to know Mei was talking about their reaperhood and how it had negatively affected them both in ways they couldn't always be open about. She thought about the phone books in Mei's room and how when they had first become friends a couple years ago, Mei had an entire portion of her day blocked out just to pore over residents with her last name, wondering if any of her family members had finally come from China. It had been years since Mei left them as a teenager to find a life in New York, but that loneliness continued to chase her. Layla lowered her eyes and swallowed past the painful lump in her throat.

Mei sighed. "I don't hate you for working with the Saint girl. It's hard to let go of your past, especially when it's so violently ripped away from you. But I hope you know that whatever she says, it's not sincere. You've been through enough with her. Work with her now, but promise me you will always come back home."

The tightness in her chest increased when Layla looked up and saw the conflicting emotions in Mei's eyes. "I already know I cannot trust her, Mei," Layla said.

Mei shrugged. A tiny smile played at her lips. "I know you know that. But the Saints are master manipulators. It's made worse since they've got pretty faces to match their pretty lies."

Layla's stomach flipped. She scoffed. She wasn't sure if it was because of Mei's comment, or if it was the sudden intrusion of Elise in her thoughts. But her body loosened up, the weight of today's damage already lifting off her bit by bit. "Saint girl isn't that pretty." Layla rolled her eyes.

"No?" Mei asked. Her tone went up a notch as she took on a mocking voice. "I've seen her. Though I suppose if she wasn't so evil, she would be much prettier."

Layla snorted. "I think evilness gives *reapers* an edge. Not people."

"Are you saying what I think you're saying?" Mei asked, her smile widening.

"What do you think I'm saying?" Layla lifted a brow.

Mei trailed her fingers down Layla's arms and Layla swore her blood swirled with her bare touch. "You think I'm pretty."

"Hmmm…" Layla didn't look away, but her face went hot as she nodded. "The first time I kissed you was right after we killed a man."

Mei tapped a finger against Layla's lips. "You're wrong."

"No, I'm not—"

She silenced Layla with a soft kiss that made all of Layla's previously protesting thoughts melt away. When she pulled away, Layla's body moved toward her, wanting more of that intoxicating warmth. "*I* kissed *you*," Mei whispered.

Layla's fangs snapped out and she hissed an irreverent sigh. "Shut up." Then she pushed Mei, sending them both tumbling into her bed.

25

B EAUTIFUL." STERLING VOICED WHAT ELISE WAS too shy to say about herself.

Her father was long gone, already having left for the gala, while her mother had gone to the theater. Elise had to act like she was perfectly fine staying home alone, insisting that Sterling was out working all night. Now she stood in front of the massive mirror in her bedroom and gaped at the dress crushing her body. It was a beautiful gown, she did love it. It was just *so much*. At first glance, it seemed like a perfectly reasonable dress; it was a pearlescent white with a skirt that hung down to her ankles. Layers of silk and split lace made up the skirt, weighing it down with each step she took. The sleeves were sheer with tiny rhinestone details, making her arms look shimmery under the light.

She glanced at Sterling in the mirror. "Dashing." Her eyes roamed over the fitted black suit he wore. His hair was styled closely to his head, brown curls popping in all the right places. One curl hung over his forehead and when he smiled, a dimple creased in his cheek, making him the perfect poster of a charming, clean-cut gentleman.

Sterling knew he was a looker, but he never let it lead him astray. No matter how many beautiful girls told him how attractive he was, he remained focused on what was right in front of him, working on having the best footing in his job. For as long as Elise had known him, she had not known him to date. He took girls out here and there, but they never stuck around for more than a few nights. Thalia was the only person Elise had seen him so close to. And now she was gone.

"I always imagined you would take Thalia to a ball like this," Elise said quietly.

Sterling's smile waned and for a moment, Elise thought he would change the subject. But he shrugged and spoke up, "I always wanted to. But she was busy with her research. I miss her. So much." He rubbed a hand over his forehead, groaning.

Part of Elise wanted to unpack those residual feelings. But he was already moving away from her. "Promise me you will come to me when you need to talk," she said.

"If you think I'll disappear again and wind up in some alley, you are mistaken. I am completely healed now," Sterling said in a tightly amused voice.

Elise laughed. "Right."

Sterling grinned, but she saw the inescapable sadness in his eyes, and she knew it would consume him if she continued to bring up the past. "Tonight, we don't have to be ourselves. We can be the most outrageous socialites New York has ever seen," Elise said.

The light sprung back into his eyes. Elise hoped it would stay for a while.

Sterling handed her the masquerade mask they had bought earlier that week. Elise's was ornate, made of a gold so pale, it looked white in the dark, but the instant the light hit it, the gold came out in brilliant hues. Long, crystal designs spiraled from the edges of the mask. They weighed it down a bit, but it was something Elise was willing to deal with as long as it kept her identity secret.

"I can be the angel." The mask completely covered Elise's face; she looked like a stunning socialite, ready to mingle and perhaps donate a few hundred dollars to a less-than-stellar cause. She pulled a pair of satin gloves onto her hands, then pushed a large pearl ring onto her ring finger. "And you can be the devil." Elise tapped her fingers together as Sterling pulled his mask on.

His was silver with sequined accents and black feathers on the edges. He looked different with his curls defined and done loosely rather than flattened completely down like he usually wore them. Even without the mask, Elise hardly recognized him. But with it on, she thought she would need to keep her arm on him the entire time to not lose him that night at the party.

Sterling watched them in the mirror. "The perfect unholy pair."

The plain black dress from before was "not acceptable for a high-society party," according to Mei. The dress ended up wrinkled on her bedroom floor, anyway. All Layla had needed help with was styling the dress. The next thing she knew, she was writhing beneath Mei in the bed, her dress discarded.

Layla had sat up later, hair messy and lips swollen, then her eyes widened on the dress. "Mei…"

"You should really throw that rag away," Mei had muttered sleepily into her pillow.

"No, this is an emergency—I'm supposed to be somewhere in an hour!" Layla nearly shouted.

Mei finally sat up, yawning. "Borrow one of my dresses. I stole most from Valeriya, so they will probably fit your needs."

Layla crossed her arms. "We aren't even close to the same size, or style."

"I thought this was an *emergency?*" Mei asked, brows raised. She glared at Layla's sparse drawers. "You certainly cannot wear any of *that*."

Layla pursed her lips. "Fine. But I won't wear something shiny, or sparkly—"

"That's half of my closet, Quinn." Mei smirked, pushing past her. "I'll bring you something I've been dying to see on you."

The dress that Mei had been dying to see on Layla was something Layla would have preferred to die before rather than wear. But no matter how uncomfortable Layla felt in such a flashy dress, she could not deny that it looked stunning.

As if the bright red fabric wasn't enough, Mei insisted that Layla wear satin gloves that matched and a silver hair comb that nestled in her curls. She felt ridiculous in the red skirt and corset bodice. But it fit her body so well, Layla couldn't stop smoothing her hands over her hips and enjoying the way they curved beneath her palms. She wondered if this was the delight Mei felt when she touched her. Layla's face heated at the thought, but another part of her fluttered with delicate joy.

It had been so long since Layla let herself take pleasure in the small things that brought a smile to her face. This time, she allowed herself the happiness. Maybe this time she was doing well. Maybe this time the happiness was deserved.

Mei's hands trailed over Layla's waist and across her hip bone while she leaned in to whisper. "Don't ruin my dress."

Layla rolled her eyes. She pulled away and reached for the red mask on her nightstand. "Help me with this?" Layla asked.

Mei tied the red mask into place on Layla's head, and when Layla finally got a good look in the mirror, her stomach clenched. She looked like a completely different person. Of course there were holes for her eyes, but the mask mostly hid the reaper sheen that covered her eyes. Layla would have to be careful to not smile too wide in order to keep her reaper teeth hidden, but other than that, she looked positively human.

She wasn't sure if it was because she didn't look like herself, but Layla felt as if she was stepping into a new part of her life. Her curls fell past her ribs, the silver comb keeping them out of her face while she moved.

"You look like you'll need a chaperone tonight," Mei murmured. She stared hard at Layla's reflection in the mirror.

Layla snorted and turned to face her friend. "I have a chaperone. He has killed just as many people as you, if not more. I think I'll be fine."

Mei stopped short. "Layla, I swear to God if it's—"

"Don't worry about it." Layla blew a mocking kiss to Mei as she left the room.

Elise's mouth went dry when she saw Layla. The noise of the party in the ivy-ridden mansion just a few yards away died down and her mind filled with one thing: *Layla*. Her lips parted to say something, but no words came out. She was completely wrapped up in Layla's presence and she wasn't even close enough to hear whatever words Layla was muttering to her partner.

The red dress was one thing and the glittering mask was a complete other thing, but the energy that radiated from Layla was everything. Elise could not even properly see her face, but she would have recognized that sharp stance and threatening aura from a mile away. Having lived in New York and France all of her life, Elise had beheld many exquisite things in her life and been witness to incredibly beautiful experiences. But Layla Quinn in a dress that served her devotion for subtle violence topped every last one.

"Ah, we meet again."

It wasn't until he spoke that Elise recognized the tall man dressed in a nice suit who stood beside Layla. Even in the low light illuminating the gravel driveway they stood in, she could see the glimmer of defiance in his blue eyes.

The realization knocked every ounce of heated affection she had just felt toward Layla out of her system. "You *cannot* be serious," Elise hissed.

Layla and Jamie Kelly stood before her with devious smiles on their faces. They looked like an odd match. Jamie was well over six feet, his posture relaxed with his hands in his pockets, while Layla's height barely passed five feet and her shoulders were as rigid as her jaw was sharp.

"Is there a problem?" Layla asked.

Elise tried to step toward her, but Sterling gripped her arm, holding her in place. "You brought a gangster to a political fundraiser?" she hissed.

Layla glanced up at Jamie, whose grin widened. She looked back at Elise. "Sure. What are they going to do? Kill me?" Layla flashed her fangs, and something hot buzzed up Elise's spine at the sight.

For a moment, Elise went completely speechless. Her eyes lingered on Layla, trying to dissect the pretty package this devil had come in. The red dress no longer held a powerful spark over her; the moment Layla opened her mouth, her damn attitude ruined any impassioned feelings.

"The funny thing is your father invited me, Saint. I supplied for most of this party. He might be more crooked than you realize," Jamie said in a humor-filled voice. He draped an arm across Layla's shoulders and even with the mask covering most of her face, Elise saw irritation pass over her expression. But she didn't shake Jamie off.

A bitter taste filled Elise's mouth just watching them. She turned in to Sterling's arms and ground out, "Let's go inside."

The inside of the mansion was just as bright and festive as Layla imagined it would be. The ballroom held most of the party, where people danced and mingled, but Layla saw guests hanging on the nearby spiral staircase and sneaking through the various doors around the massive house. It was rumored to be owned by a millionaire who didn't even live there, only used it for galas and lent it out to members of high society. The room opened up into a kaleidoscope of color and chaos. Brilliant lanterns hung down from the tall ceilings or were strung along the railing of the grand staircase that led to the main party floor. Tinsel and festoons streamed from everywhere. Layla had only been inside for a few minutes, but already, a piece of shiny foil from the decor clung to her jaw. The entire atmosphere was a warm, golden glow of excitement that had people downing drinks until their eyes shone with the light of the stars, but the most alluring part of the party was the music.

Some danced, drinks in hand; socialites gossiped behind feathered fans, eyes alight with the thrill of exchanging expensive secrets. Heiresses shrugged in lengthy fur coats while they waved diamond-clad hands in each other's faces and compared the sizes of the fortunes they were destined to inherit. Governors stood by gangsters, ashes from their cigars dusting into their liquor. Smiles were shared and euphoria spread like smoke through the crowd. A proud trumpeter stood on the stage in the center of the room. His vocalists moved around him, skirts glimmering under the lights, voices booming and glorious while they led the band in summertime music.

Layla almost forgot she was there to do a job when the band began to play. So badly, she wanted to lift her skirt and spin around and around until the room became a wild blur of dazzling colors. It had been ages since she was surrounded by such soulful music.

Jamie put his hand on her back. "I'm getting us drinks. So we blend in," he said loudly over the music and winked.

"I'll come." Anything to put distance between her and the Saint heiress.

Out in the courtyard, Layla had done her best to hide her visceral reaction to seeing Elise done up and dressed to rival the exquisiteness of the moon. There were a thousand lights taking up the sky tonight, and Layla was convinced they all shined for Elise. She couldn't believe how instantly her senses had picked up on Elise's presence. Even before turning the corner, she'd smelled her blood. Layla had made sure to feed so as not to have any mishaps tonight, but Elise was overpowering, like a deafening roar that buzzed all the way through her body.

Layla's teeth sank into her cheeks. Her fangs pierced the soft flesh until blood spilled into her mouth. The calming effect was immediate, but not nearly enough to subdue the tension that Elise roused in Layla.

While waiting for Jamie to pour their drinks, Layla found herself watching Elise on the dance floor. Her arms were around Sterling's shoulders, his hands on her hips, and they swayed to the patient beats of the music. Each time Sterling said something that made Elise smile, a bitterness rose in her throat. That used to be Layla, sharing jokes and being spoken to in hushed voices and teasing tones. That used to be Layla, who had a pretty girl smiling at her jokes and telling her that she loved her more than the moon loved the stars.

That used to be Layla, who was Elise's best friend. The hollow pang of loss rang through her again. Layla was beginning to think it would never go away.

How long could she live with pain chasing her everywhere she went? How long could she outrun it for?

"A drink for my lady." Jamie pressed a cool glass filled with a clear liquid into her hand.

Layla took one sip and sighed. The liquor went down roughly, but she welcomed the burn. Any distraction to keep her from circling the same Elise-shaped thoughts. "Not a single bit of irony has escaped me at the fact that we are at a political fundraiser to which gangsters were invited and alcohol is being served. There is truly no grace in this world."

"Politicians claim to hate us because we break their laws, but they hire us to break their laws. They are so dumb." He chuckled. "We're just doing our jobs. And we have them wrapped around our fingers. Alcohol is a powerful drug, and everyone here is crooked because of it." Jamie raised his glass.

Layla lifted a brow, thinking of just how cruel white people could be to Black people just *existing*. "Among other things."

"Everyone here is crooked. No matter how rich and powerful," Jamie said.

"The more money, the less morals," Layla muttered.

"Imagine the number of writers who came just to spin a story out of the corruption they find here," Jamie said. His eyes flitted around the room and Layla followed him, spotting a young Black woman with a dark hat and full lips wearing a smile by the bar. Her silver pen hovered over a blank page. "There's one," Jamie muttered. He sipped slowly on what Layla assumed was a whiskey, by the way the dark liquid sloshed around in his glass. "I thought you were supposed to be here for a purpose. Why is the Saint girl canoodling and dancing?"

Layla resisted the urge to look back at Elise. She continued to stare hard at Jamie while she spoke. "It's not so simple. How *normal* would it look if we were just marching between a crowd of dancing people while we searched high and low for anything suspicious?" Layla asked.

It wasn't a question that warranted an actual answer, but Jamie, being the insufferable man he was, answered it anyway. "I have been to parties where it is completely normal for couples to end up on the floor." He looked around, face alight with wonder. "Clearly, this party is not one of those."

"I don't know, Jamie. Maybe you should get on the floor and find out," Layla teased.

Jamie leaned down so he was eye to eye with her. "Only if you do it with me—"

"No. None of that." Elise Saint suddenly emerged to interrupt them. She fanned herself with her gloved hands, though her cheeks only shined with her perfectly applied makeup. Layla's eyes roamed over the Saint heiress. Even her sweat made her look luminous, like a heavenly body. She was a true Saint, through and through. "You two need to be listening in to as many conversations as possible," Elise said. She gave a quick wave to the bartender and he brought out two vodka shots. "Sterling." Elise handed one to her friend. They tipped their glasses together, then swallowed the shots at once. Sterling did not flinch, but Elise began fanning herself again while her eyes watered after she swallowed the vodka. "Okay. That should be good." She tried to smile, but Layla saw her lips tremble.

She held her hand out, intending to touch Elise, as if she could absorb her anxiety for her. But right before they made contact, Layla dropped her hand. Instead, her fingers trailed over the thick fabric of Elise's dress. And as if she could feel the heat of the Saint heiress through the silk, she clenched her hand into a fist, locking the dress in her grasp. Layla let out a breathy sigh. Elise was so focused on Sterling, she did not notice, but Layla's head felt light, her mind dizzy with exhilaration from being so close to her. The sweet scent of her warm blood and gentle perfume only intoxicated her further. Layla

263

inhaled, the fabric slipping through her fingers as Elise moved back onto the dance floor with Sterling.

Jamie sneered after them. "I have never in my life seen a more miserable person," he said.

Something about his mocking tone being directed at a wounded Elise made irritation flare in Layla. "*Shut up*," she snapped.

The look in Elise's eyes while she swallowed the shot, the tremor in her hands while she fanned herself, made Layla's chest ache. Those episodes of deep dread and panic had never fully left Elise as a child. She remembered Elise telling her about how being around a lot of people tended to stress her out. Layla would offer her her hand to squeeze whenever she got overwhelmed, and she never complained, even if it felt like there was a boulder crushing her fingers.

"You're like my rock," Elise had said one night after a huge party her dad had thrown to celebrate the city's reduced reaper population.

Layla looked at the purple marks on her hand from Elise's grip. She wanted to show Elise and laugh about it, maybe say something along the lines of "I'm almost positive *you* are the rock in this relationship, not me." But the fresh apprehension in Elise's eyes stopped her.

"I take that back. You're more like my wrap, or my medicine. When I'm around too many people, or when the world gets to be too much, I feel like an open wound. But you…" Elise's breath quivered. "You are like a bandage that holds me together."

Layla had smiled back. The moonlight flickering in from the

window illuminated Elise's face at the perfect moment so her joy was on full display.

As much as she hated to admit it, it killed Layla that Elise had no way to grab for that relief tonight. Sterling might have been her friend, but Layla knew Elise was harder to crack open than a diamond. And she didn't see him walking about with bruises on his hands from Elise's anxious grip.

Layla didn't even realize she was stepping toward Elise until Jamie grabbed her elbow. "This way," he barked, pulling her into the throng of drunk, dancing people. "Careful of your mask. Make sure it doesn't fall off."

Into the crowd they went. People enveloped Layla from every angle and she immediately became overwhelmed with all the sweaty bodies and pitched singing pressing around her. If it was this crippling for Layla, she couldn't begin to imagine how stressful it must have been for Elise. Layla rose onto her tiptoes, trying to see past the people around her to find Elise.

But to no avail.

She settled back on her heels and began turning back to Jamie when a strong hand clamped around her wrist. On instinct, her fangs sprang free and she snatched herself away.

Sterling stared down at her, his face stricken white with fear. "I can't find Elise," he stammered.

Jamie curled his lip. "Tough luck, buddy, you lost your date already—"

Layla did not stay to hear the rest of his snide comments. She closed her eyes and let the ambush of the ballroom's overwhelming activity on her senses melt away. Unseeing and unfeeling, she focused on finding Elise. Her scent emerged, faint and frightened amid the roaring atmosphere. But it was enough for Layla.

"Stay here," she gritted out before plunging into the crowd.

Elise felt like she was wrapped in thorns. The party had faded away for her and now she crouched in a wardrobe, darkness closing in around her from all sides, conjured up by her battered mind. No matter how hard she pressed her hands to her ears, her sister's piercing screams tore through the wooden box she sat in. Her hands shook so hard, her vision blurred behind them. The sounds of tearing flesh and wet growls from the reapers beyond the wardrobe flooded the air. In the darkness, Elise's imagination brought forth images of them ripping into Charlotte's throat, greedily tugging her between them until her limbs tore from their sockets. Blood seeped into the wardrobe until Elise sat in a pool of it. The metallic scent clogged her throat and nose, twisting her stomach into painful knots. A scream burst into her chest, and Elise shoved her hand over her mouth to stifle it. She clamped down on her fingers until she drew blood, her breath coming out in rough pants, the scarlet rivulets bubbling around her lips.

"Saint—"

Something grabbed her ankle, and Elise kicked out on instinct.

Her foot narrowly missed the reaper's face, but she struck again, aiming for the bright golden eyes that stared down at her.

"It's me," Layla's voice cut right through her panic.

Elise pulled her hands from her face and stared at the reaper before her. Layla was on her knees, one hand wrapped around her ankle. Their dresses pooled around them; crimson met white in a striking display of defiance. For the first time in years, Layla held on to Elise, and Elise did not flinch away from her.

"I thought…I couldn't…" Elise inhaled shakily, her hands trembling. Even reaching for her usual ritualistic counting didn't help; her mind was too fractured to focus on anything but her misery. "The clothes and the loud voices, they were too much… I was back in the closet, and I heard my sister—" A sob cut her off and she dropped her face to her hands.

Layla's fingers tightened around her ankle. It was nothing menacing, but rather a gentle, reassuring squeeze. Her voice was quiet as she spoke, "I know."

An overwhelming sadness crushed Elise's heart. A night of celebration with music and cheer had turned into one of terror because of her own somber past. What should have been happy memories had been forged into weapons that threatened her own mind at the slightest trigger.

Elise pressed her fingertips to her lips and looked up at Layla. "I'm sorry." No matter how shaky her body, no matter how distressed her nerves, Elise was angered by her own fear. Years later, and still no rest came to her soul. She should have been better.

After a few more agonizing moments of silence and deep breathing, Elise pulled herself to her feet. Layla finally released her, though her eyes remained pinned to Elise's hands, where her fingertips continued to touch the face of her ring in counts of seven, over and over. Elise didn't realize she was murmuring the numbers under her breath until Layla's hand reached forward, as if to halt her movements. Concern brightened the reaper's eyes and she shifted closer, hand outstretched. "We can wait—"

"We have to go," Elise said sharply. She wiped the last of her tears away and, forcing a smile onto her face, left the alcove to rush back into the crowd.

As Layla stood near the dance floor with Jamie, her mind remained stuck on the Saint heiress. She had followed the scent of her blood to find the girl nearly drowning in her own panic. The sensation of her rushing pulse still fluttered beneath her fingers while she tried to focus on the party around her.

"Listen." Jamie grabbed her by the hips and pulled her body flush against his. Her cheek pressed to his chest, and when he whispered, his breath brushed her hair. "The couple next to us is talking about Stephen Wayne."

With the music and singing overpowering her senses, Layla only caught bits and pieces of the conversation.

"He's unveiling something big..."

"There's no such thing as a cure…"

"If anyone can do it, it's Stephen…"

Layla's blood went cold. If people were beginning to conspire about a cure, then maybe it did really exist. She had to tell Elise—

A sharp whistle suddenly cut through the air, bringing the rowdy room to a more tolerable hum of excited energy. Layla stopped dancing with Jamie and looked up to find the source of the whistle.

On a balcony above everyone else stood Tobias Saint and Stephen Wayne. They both had lifted their masks so their faces were visible to the entire room. Layla couldn't resist the urge to look around for Elise again.

But still, no luck. She turned back to face the balcony, her breath heavy while she waited for their words.

"I have had many people ask me why I spend so much time with this fine gentleman," Mr. Saint began. He clapped his hand over Stephen Wayne's shoulder and beamed at him like he was seeing a lifelong friend for the first time in ages. "Besides the fact that he is a wonderful friend and person, he is also just brilliant. Stephen Wayne matches the intensity at which I aspire to eliminate reapers from our world. So many of us have been affected by their deadly touches and we are here to prevent that lethality from spreading any longer."

Uneasy prickles traveled over Layla's skin. From the constant horrors she saw most days, blood leaking from her fingers and flesh stuck beneath her nails and between her teeth, she understood people's loathing toward reapers. Layla believed she had enough hate for herself to fill this entire room. But that didn't make the sting of their anger hurt any less. They only deepened the wounds she already made herself, encouraging her to slice deeper and with more fervor the next time she engaged in penitence for her soul.

Stephen Wayne stepped forward. His blond hair shone under the bright lights, his eyes glimmering with an emotion that appeared a bit too sinister to be pure excitement. "It's true. My donations have funded research toward a solution to this reaper problem. While Tobias has been brilliant in leading reaper executions, my dear friend Dr. Harding created a way to take fewer lives while simultaneously improving hundreds of lives." He gestured to an older man with thin white hair and sunken black eyes who stood at the base of the staircase leading into the room. Instead of waving, the old man glowered, as if he was miserable to be there.

Stephen Wayne merely continued, his tone jovial as ever, "Reapers have existed for centuries, never able to be tamed. We can kill as many reapers as we want, but they will only keep coming. They have spread to other countries, and that has made our international relations unstable. Our country is not as great as it once was. I am of the belief that the only way to completely end something is to fix it. Or in this case, to cure it."

Layla's breath stilled in her chest. She gripped Jamie's arm so hard, he snatched himself away from her. But she didn't care; she could only focus on Stephen Wayne.

"With funding from my foundation and the Saints, as well as Dr. Harding's research, we vow to cure reaperhood once and for all," he exclaimed. The crowd burst into a troubled, but excited commotion.

Layla's heart swelled, her eyes flashing like jewels in an accusing light. A smile broke across her face and for the first time since becoming a reaper, she felt pure, delicious hope.

26

ELISE WATCHED LAYLA GO RIGID AT STEPHEN Wayne's announcement. She couldn't believe it. A cure was a cruel thing to hang over the heads of reapers and humans. Humans, who lived in fear of being turned over to hell by reaper attacks, and reapers, who lived long enough to feel the wrath of hell's burn, never knowing true relief.

"Wow," Sterling murmured.

Elise pulled him closer to her. "He told me he was taking a break from this because of Thalia's death."

"I guess that break is over," Sterling said.

People around them whooped and raised their glasses into the air to celebrate Stephen Wayne. Champagne slicked the floor, confetti sticking to the bottom of Elise's shoes while she turned to survey the crowd. They had gotten drunk on liquor, then were lulled by his words that could only have been deceptive at best. Elise knew a leader's public image thrived on rhetoric; whether their message was true didn't matter. What mattered was how convincing it was. His message reeked as strongly as the spilled alcohol around them.

There is no cure for reaperhood.

"We have a problem." Jamie's voice turned Elise to him. His cheeks were slightly flushed, from the drinks, the stress, or both. He ran a hand over his blond hair and grimaced. "I can't find Layla."

"*What?*" Elise snapped. She glared. "You imbecile, good-for-nothing—"

"I'd watch how you speak to me, Saint scum," Jamie hissed.

Elise whirled to respond, but Sterling stepped between them, hand drawing his gun from his shoulder holster. "Don't even look at her."

"Or what?"

Elise didn't hear anything after that because she slipped into the crowd. Maybe she should have cared that her best friend was close to a scrap with a gangster, but all she could think about was Layla. Her hands shook as she maneuvered through the revelers, trying to find the reaper. She didn't realize how stressed she was until she resorted to digging her nails into her palms as a means for distraction.

Crescent moon cuts stung along her hands now and she flexed her fingers, the burn keeping her focused in the quickly enclosing crowd. Why, she wondered, did she get so destructive when she had trouble processing her feelings?

Finally, a relieved breath broke from Elise when she spotted Layla a few feet ahead of her. Even with the mask covering her face, Elise could see the awe that marked Layla's expression.

"I say we give them a demonstration of your cure, Stephen." A gasp rippled through the crowd. Dr. Harding was making his way down the grand staircase, hand in hand with a beautiful young woman. She wore a delicate pink gown that covered most of her body, but Elise noticed the golden sheen in her eyes that indicated her reaperhood. Her movements seemed far too graceful and fluid to be human, and the devastating smoothness of her skin made her reaperhood even more obvious.

Stephen Wayne's eyes widened on Dr. Harding. "Dr. Harding, there's no need for a demo—"

"Nellie has been a reaper for a few years now. I believe it's been four years, hasn't it, Nellie?" Dr. Harding asked roughly. He looked distinctly out of place in his white lab coat against the backdrop of glittering jewels and heavy gowns.

The young reaper nodded. Nellie's carefully styled curls came loose with her vigorous nodding, but she still looked glamorous.

Dr. Harding let go of her hand and pulled a long syringe from his coat pocket. Nellie's eyes glimmered at the sight, and when she opened her mouth, her fangs became more pronounced. Chills ran over Elise's body while she watched the reaper's visceral reaction to what had to be the cure. She looked the way most reapers looked when they were starved and sensed a feeding nearby. Her eyes went from a faded brown to almost black in an instant.

"With just a simple injection, I will set her free." Dr. Harding gently lifted Nellie's chin so they were eye to eye. "Will you allow me the pleasure of making you human again, darling?" he asked in the softest voice.

Bright-eyed and grinning, Nellie nodded again. "Yes, sir."

Dr. Harding gave her one final smile, then he sank the needle into her neck. The crowd went silent. The soft shuffling of nervous feet and anxious whispers were the few sounds heard in the silence. Elise held her breath as Nellie went stiff. For a long moment, she made no movements, then she suddenly looked up, her back straightening and throat flexing beneath the light.

Her eyes faded from their glowing state to a normal, muted brown. When she smiled, her enlarged canines were gone. Nellie touched her face and laughed. It sounded a bit maniacal, but if the tears and the ecstatic smile were any indication, she was beyond happy. She was *human.*

"Doctor!" Nellie cried. Tears flowed down her cheeks as she threw her arms around Dr. Harding.

"My pleasure, Nellie. Please." He pulled away and gestured to the crowd. "Allow me to present the new you to everyone."

Nellie spun around, arms extended. A circle opened up around her while the crowd looked on in awe. It was mesmerizing to witness such a fresh, pure joy, all for a Black woman.

Elise turned to regard the crowd's reaction, but was startled to see Layla moving through the crowd toward Nellie. Her hands stretched out, as if reaching for a highly desired object. The crowd was too engrossed in Nellie's joy to notice Layla, but she was all Elise could focus on. She began to push her way through the crowd after her.

Then pained cries tore through the air. Nellie's laughter was no longer lovely, but it instead pierced Elise's ears, shrieking as it left her body.

The crowd began to shift with unease.

Layla drew close to Nellie, watching her with wide eyes, hands twitching by her sides.

Suddenly Nellie noticed Layla, and her lips curled into a wicked taunt.

"*Kin,*" she rasped. And in that instant even though she had just been turned human, she sounded far from it. Nellie reached out toward Layla, her fingers extending to touch her.

At that same moment, a gunshot thundered through the room. Cries rose from the crowd, followed by a cracking sound that filled the air. Elise looked up in time to see the massive chandelier over the grand staircase swaying as if it had been disturbed. Another crack resounded, and then the chandelier was breaking away from the ceiling. The chains holding it together snapped.

As if propelled by a spirit, Elise tore through the scattering crowd to Layla and threw herself into her.

Then the chandelier came crashing down.

27

LAYLA HIT THE FLOOR HARD AS CHAOS EXPLODED throughout the room. Glass shattered, screams rang out, blood stained the air. But all she could focus on was the beautiful, worried face staring down at her. Elise was fully on top of her, her knees planted on either side of Layla's hips. Feet stampeded around them, but Elise was gripping her shoulders hard, shouting, "Layla, Layla, Layla—"

Layla couldn't figure out why Elise chanted her name like a devout person crying out during worship. Her lips moved to form a word, but then the lights winked out around them.

The room was thrown into darkness and for a split second, silence suffocated them all. A small flicker of the shattered chandelier persisted and someone screamed. The cord still stretched from above and a few bulbs had sparked back to life, giving light to the mangled and bloodied body within it.

Nellie was strung up like a puppet, her mouth gaping while blood spilled over her lips, arms and legs bent into awkward angles amid the shattered crystals. Blood splashed over the iridescent gems and when the light caught the stained decor, it flashed scarlet against the floor.

"No one touch her! The remaining electricity will hurt you!" Dr. Harding warned nearby. But most people were scattering anyway, taking wide steps to avoid the shattered glass and growing pool of blood.

Something warm dripped onto Layla's cheek. She switched her gaze back to Elise and noticed the blood dripping from her eyebrow.

"Layla—"

"Shut up, *shut up*," Layla hissed and went still.

Elise's mask was gone. It must have fallen in her rush to get Layla out of the way of the chandelier, but however she lost it didn't matter. What mattered was how close Layla could hear Tobias Saint's voice calling out to keep everyone calm while his daughter, who was not supposed to be there at all, straddled a reaper.

People moved quickly around them, some slowing to witness the grotesque chandelier coffin, others running to get away from the blood and destruction. The music had stopped. Elise and Layla were only a couple feet from the catastrophe. Layla felt glass beneath her body and cracks stretched across the marble floor as people continued to stampede around the chandelier. But no one offered her or Elise a hand.

"Please, everyone, exit through the front doors to safety,"

Tobias Saint called out nearby. His voice sounded even closer than before.

Layla pushed her hips up to flip the two of them over. With a gasp, Elise fell onto her back. Layla tore off a part of her skirt, then pressed the fabric to Elise's bloody face. Elise protested when Layla pulled her to her feet.

"I can't see!" Elise snapped.

"You're bleeding everywhere. Shut up so I can get us out of here without you being seen," Layla murmured into her hair. If it wasn't for the heavy scent of Elise's blood filling her nose and mouth, she might have gotten closer to whisper in her ear. But it was too risky. Elise's blood was already seeping through the cloth, staining Layla's hand. Layla pushed forward hastily, steering Elise clear of any panicked people.

Elise stepped on her feet, which Layla knew was on purpose because how in the world could she be stepping backward while they were moving forward—

"Sure. Let me trust the reaper, who is triggered by blood, to guide me into an area with no one around. No one to witness a murder—"

Layla pushed Elise into an alcove just beyond the roaring ballroom and backed away. Her nose burned at the scent of blood, her chest tightening with the need to feed. Only human blood made her want to feed beyond satiety. Elise's sweet blood, of course, was no exception.

"Keep talking and I might actually murder you," Layla snapped.

Elise opened her mouth, but no words came out. She pursed

her lips, then brought a hand up to her forehead. When she saw the amount of blood that came away on her fingers, she trembled slightly. "Father always told me eyebrows bleed a lot..." Elise locked her jaw. "Never mind that—"

"I cannot *never mind* the fact that your blood is spilling at a rapid rate," Layla muttered. She tossed a scrap of her dress at Elise. "Apply pressure."

For once, Elise listened. She took the fabric and pressed it onto her forehead. This time when she spoke, her voice was more level, calmer. But Layla could still hear the fear behind her carefully picked words. "That went badly."

Layla laughed sharply.

"Before the chandelier fell... Didn't Nellie seem strange to you?" Elise asked.

Layla had only focused on the untamable curiosity that had sprung in her when Nellie turned human. It was as if someone had put a mirror up to Layla's dreams: a pained reaper turned human, who finally felt the grace of joy in her grasp once again.

Yet, there had been a moment of cruelty between them when Nellie had turned a scowl full of malice toward Layla. It had shocked her, but Layla almost did not want to acknowledge it, much less believe it.

She shook her head. "She looked human."

Elise narrowed her eyes. "You didn't notice a single thing off about that woman?" she asked again. "Really? I thought reapers prided themselves on having advanced senses. Even I noticed that woman was deranged—"

"Does it matter? She's dead. Would it kill you to not be right about something for once?" Layla nearly shouted.

Elise finally fell silent. After a few moments, she spoke in a quiet voice. "The purpose of an investigation is to ask questions and search for answers. Even when you meet a dead end."

"Emphasis on the dead." Jamie appeared behind them, Sterling's arm slung around his shoulders.

"Oh my God!" Elise cried. She ran for her friend, abandoning Layla's dress fabric. Sterling had his hand pressed to his middle, where a bright spot of blood was quickly spreading across his shirt-front. "What happened?"

Sterling lifted his head and grimaced. "I don't know if you noticed, but a giant chandelier made of glass fell and shattered all over the place."

Jamie dropped Sterling against the wall. "Someone shot the chandelier down."

Elise blinked. "But who—"

"Probably a gangster. They always carry," Sterling grunted as he slid into a sitting position against the wall, blood falling more rapidly from his middle.

"By that logic, I'm sure it could have been a Saint," Jamie snapped.

A tight smile broke across Sterling's face. "I heard Mr. Wayne calling for the police out there. He thinks it was a scorned ex-partner of that Nellie lady. Probably still a gangster—" He coughed roughly and Elise kneeled before him, her hands pressed to her mouth.

"*Enough*," Elise hissed. "You're bleeding everywhere, for the love of God!"

Layla glared at the mess before her. Already, her body was tensing again. The new blood only further scrambled her senses. "You all know better than to bring fresh blood to a reaper," she muttered.

Elise, whose eyes shone with panic and hands shook violently, scowled up at Layla. "Is that a threat?"

"Only if you want it to be." Sighing, Layla kneeled by Elise and Sterling. Jamie leaned against the wall and Elise prodded uselessly at the glass shard in his stomach. "Move," Layla demanded, slapping Elise's hand away.

Elise let out a hot breath. "Don't you dare touch him."

"I can fix him. I'm the one with healing properties in my blood, remember?" Layla said. She was getting tired. Tired of fighting the natural urge to sip on the blood swarming her senses, and tired of trying to convince someone who actively fought against being convinced. If Elise told her "no" one more time, Layla was going to walk off, leaving her to deal with the mess.

Elise's teeth chewed on her lower lip. She shared a worried look with Sterling. "I'm not sure…"

Sterling nodded. "Respectfully, Elise, You have no idea what you're doing. You're actually making it worse. Let her try." He let his head fall back against the wall behind him. "Don't tell your father about this."

"Oh, *please*," Elise laughed, but there was no effort behind her derision. "I don't dream of being reprimanded any time soon." The silent admission in her voice told Layla she no longer protested her offer for help, but she glanced at her once more to confirm. At Elise's subtle nod, Layla lifted her wrist to her mouth.

Her fangs snapped out and everyone startled.

"No, no, no—"

"*What the hell?*"

"*God*, Layla!"

All three of them stared at Layla with gaping mouths. Elise looked a little ashen. Layla lowered her wrist and scowled. She pointed at Jamie first. "You have seen much worse than a reaper biting themselves; you've done worse yourself." Then she pointed at Sterling. "You kill reapers, so, disrespectfully, I don't want to hear any complaints when I am trying to save your life." Lastly, she looked at Elise. "*You*. I'm not sure what you were expecting when I said my blood has healing properties. How do you think I get it to Sterling, by osmosis?" Layla knew she probably should have been gentler; fear glinted in their eyes and she was only making things worse. But her exhaustion continued to grow and the constant fight against her own urges was starting to drive her mad.

Sterling grumbled, "I think I'll be okay." He breathed hard and tried to sit up, but only got so far before he winced and slid back down the wall.

"I'm okay with leaving you to test your fate. I know how long it takes a human to bleed out. Trust me." She bared her fangs and Sterling's face paled.

Jamie clicked his tongue. "I think it's safe to say no one here trusts you, Layla."

"In about three seconds, I will leave all of you to deal with this on your own," Layla threatened. She raised her fingers as if to count down, but Elise smacked her hand away.

"Do it," she demanded. "Please, just help him."

This time, Layla didn't hesitate while she tore her wrist open. Blood spilled from her artery directly onto Sterling's wound. In only a few seconds, his mangled skin began to knit itself back together. Layla couldn't stay to watch the whole process. Already, her head was getting light and her throat was dry despite her own blood filling her mouth.

Layla looked up at Elise, a significant stream of blood still seeping from her eyebrow. "Do you want me to do you next?" Layla asked. Blood coated her lips and dripped from her mouth, but she figured it was worth an offer while her wrist still hung open between them.

"No," Elise said, her face twisting with disgust. "I will heal just fine on my own."

The alcove fell silent. Layla's breath shook while her wound closed. Her blood ran hot through her veins and they pulsed, already craving and needing more blood to fill her. If she didn't get a feeding soon, she might turn this entire room red.

Layla stumbled to her feet. "I need to go." She barely managed to get the words out through her gritted teeth.

"Layla—" Elise's voice followed Layla outside, but she did not stop for her. She did not stop until she was far enough down the street that the sounds of ambulances and panicked people did not muddle her thoughts. Blood still swept over all of her senses; it was so overwhelming, the saliva in her mouth started to taste like blood, feel like blood—

Layla slumped in a quiet gangway between two buildings, breathing hard. The party was so far behind her now, the nearby streets sat mostly empty. It would be a challenge to get a hunt in. Hard because there was hardly anyone around to hunt. Easy because there was no one around to witness her kill. Layla shook her head. She had taken one human down already this month; to kill another would only draw more attention to her clan.

Blood welled in her mouth, dripping over her lips. Layla hissed. Her fangs were beyond her control now. They had never sunk back into place after bleeding all over Sterling. Her lips tore beneath their pointed ends, scabbing over after a few moments, then tearing again with each breath she took.

Brisk footsteps sounded down the sidewalk nearby. Before she could even formulate a plan, Layla found herself getting into position to strike. She backed herself against the alley wall, eyes trained on the small patch of sidewalk illuminated by the streetlights. The second the pedestrian brushed into the light, Layla struck, hands grabbing the person's dress to slam them into the alley wall, fangs bared while she hissed.

Her scent pervaded Layla's senses before her eyes registered who she had gotten ahold of. Layla backed off immediately. "Shit, Saint, I almost killed you," Layla snapped. "Why are you alone?"

Elise brushed her ruffled dress off while she scowled at Layla. "I made Sterling stay at the mansion to rest. I think Jamie left." Then she pointed an accusatory finger at Layla. "*I knew it*. You were planning on killing a person. This is why you cannot be trusted."

A venomous laugh spilled from Layla. "Yes, I was going to kill a person. That's why I ran away from the perfectly positioned feast in the ballroom, where there was already a bloodbath in place. Because the hungry intend to run from their meals, right?"

"Don't do that," Elise said roughly. She fiddled with the front of her dress, hands shaking slightly. Layla almost felt bad. Either she was genuinely stunned from being attacked in the alley, or she was still shaken up from the ballroom crowd.

Layla studied Elise. "Maybe I just wanted to kill *you*," she said coldly.

A shadow passed over Elise's face, but she remained quiet.

"Is that how I get you to shut up now? I threaten your life?" Layla tried taking in a heavy breath, but the scent of Elise's blood twisted her brain and split her focus. She ran a hand over her hair, sighing. "You need to go. I'm sure your father will be home soon and then he'll wonder where you are. Also, I'm not sure if you noticed, but I'm in desperate need of a feeding—"

"That's exactly why I cannot leave." Elise stepped closer to Layla.

The blood in her veins heated at the proximity of the sweet-smelling Saint and her blood. Layla had to step back. "Why?" she demanded, trying not to inhale too deeply.

"I cannot risk you killing someone else tonight. My father's reputation is on the line after this disastrous event, and another life does not need to be lost," Elise said. She sounded sincere, but her face remained stony.

Layla's jaw clenched. "I'm not your responsibility." She tried to walk away, but Elise grabbed her wrist. Layla whirled on her, teeth bared and eyes burning with rage. "Do you have a death wish, Saint?"

Elise did not flinch in the face of Layla's fury. "You are my responsibility. I'm the reason you're here. I'm the reason you're starving now. I don't want to bring another burden onto my father and our family name—*please.*"

The slight tremor in her voice made Layla's anger waver. She glanced into Elise's eyes and finally saw a seed of desperation ingrained with hopelessness and defeat. Was she finally starting to blame herself for getting Layla turned? Elise's words carried a guilt that went deeper than just the catastrophic events of tonight. The feeling of her fingers around her wrist did not burn, but instead ushered a welcome warmth into Layla's skin. Layla pulled her arm back. This time, Elise let her go. The defeat in her expression deepened until Layla felt as if she was almost swallowed whole by it. "What do you want me to do? Wait for you to bring me a blood meal? Because I cannot promise I will—"

"Drink from me," Elise said.

Every fiber of Layla's being froze. She stared at Elise so hard, if looks could kill, the Saint heiress would be deep in hell now. For a moment Layla thought she was dreaming. The words could not have possibly come from the Saint heiress, successor of New York's most notorious reaper hunter. Those words could not have come from someone who claimed to hate Layla as much as she hated any little thing being out of place in her perfect life.

Layla blinked, still not quite breathing. "What?"

"You heard me. I know you heard me, with that powerful reaper hearing and all." Elise reached for the front of her dress and pulled it open so more of her neck was exposed. The air between them stilled. Layla's breathing quickened, and her body ignited with heat as she imagined sinking her teeth into that perfect flesh... *Elise was giving her access to her throat.*

Layla's fangs pierced her gums again, driving home that painful reminder that she needed to eat. Still, Layla shook her head. "No. Absolutely not."

Elise's lips twisted, unpleased. "Don't be ridiculous. No one has to know. And you'll be full. And there will be one less dead person tonight. It's a win for us all."

"I could kill you," Layla said quietly.

Finally, a falter crossed Elise's expression. "*You're* telling *me* that?" Her tone came across snarkier and more confident than the worried crease in her brow made her look. She bit her lip. "I know just one bite won't kill me, nor will it turn me. If you're desirable enough, I'll probably think about you for a few days after—or, at least until my blood has cycled through your venom. But I'll ultimately be fine..." She seemed to be reciting the first known rules of reaperhood to herself to soothe her own nerves.

Layla nodded. "You'll be fine."

Elise let out a shaky breath. She pushed her hair behind her shoulders and lifted her chin so her throat was even more vulnerable. "Okay. I'm ready."

"Are you sure?" Layla asked. "I mean… Are you sure you trust me?"

"Are you really asking me that when I've just bared my throat for you?" Elise demanded.

Layla blinked. A tiny smile pulled at her lips and she nodded to her dress. "That wasn't necessary, by the way. I can drink from your wrist just fine."

The color in Elise's cheeks darkened as realization crossed her features. And while she nodded, she did not move out of position with her neck bared for Layla. "Drinking from my throat will be faster. Hurry up before your food gets cold." She laughed nervously.

Layla's face broke into a true smile. "Shut up." She gently gripped the back of Elise's head, her hand curving over her nape, fingers just brushing her curls. Elise let out a soft gasp of surprise. Normally when Layla was hungry, she dug into her food with the intensity of a half-starved beast. If it was anyone but Elise, blood would be spraying by now, drenching the alley walls and staining her clothes. The body would be half-drained in a few minutes and Layla's stomach full, heart alight with euphoria.

But this was Elise. For that reason alone, Layla was soft. She was careful. She did not rip her fangs through her flesh. But she let her lips graze Elise's throat first, testing the tenderness and giving her a chance to back out and understand what was happening before Layla made her final move. The kiss of Elise's skin against her lips made Layla's stomach flutter. Elise let out another soft sigh and Layla closed her eyes, drowning in the sound. The Saint heiress stroked her hand up the small of Layla's back. And it was at that wordless admission that Layla let herself go.

She sank her fangs into Elise's throat.

In all eighteen years of her life, whether living or damned, Layla had never felt this good. It suddenly made sense to her then, with Elise's blood flowing into her mouth at a steady rate, filling her hollow parts and smoothing her jagged edges, when people claimed everything was better when done with heart. If feeding on strangers struck Layla with sublime light, then feeding on Elise struck her with divine radiance. It was as if Elise was made up of stars and the dust between the planets. In her, Layla was certain she would find the whole universe.

Though the alley was dark, night cascading around them, enveloping them in shadows, Layla felt imbued with light. The only kind of light that one found in a perilous search. The only kind of light that bloomed in the palm of a chosen being. Layla had chosen Elise and Elise bloomed for her, vulnerable light, sweet blood and all.

If it weren't for Elise's fingers digging into Layla's back and scratching up her shoulder blades, Layla might have completely lost herself in her. She pulled back suddenly. Her fingers, once tangled in Elise's hair, loosened, and she dropped her hands to Elise's shoulder. They still stood impossibly close. So close, they shared breath. Layla saw the tired flutter of Elise's eyelashes against her cheeks, the bright sheen covering her brown eyes that indicated a euphoria only a reaper's venom could give. Layla's thumb ran over Elise's collarbone, then she traced over the base of her neck, feeling for the reassuring steady, strong beat of her pulse.

Layla exhaled. "I didn't take too much?" she asked.

Elise blinked several times, then finally met her eyes. "No."

"You're okay?" Layla demanded. Her voice grew shaky, already experiencing the effects of pure human blood on her damned reaper body. A small droplet of blood beaded from the puncture wounds in Elise's throat. Some spilled onto the pearls layered on her neck, a dash of scarlet tainting the glowing white gems. Without thinking, Layla leaned forward to lick it from her skin. The warmth of Elise beneath Layla's tongue coupled with the sensation of her fresh blood nearly drove Layla into a new frenzy. And if she didn't know Elise to be the daughter of the most-revered reaper hunter, she would have believed the sound she let out was one of pleasure, rather than fear.

"Yes." Elise nodded slowly. Her gaze was locked on Layla's lips, her eyes glowing with a fuzzy desire.

"Saint—" Layla parted her lips to speak, but Elise had already lifted her hand to cradle Layla's jaw. A stunned gasped left Layla as Elise's thumb pressed into her lower lip, swiping at a drop of blood. The heat of her mortal flesh nearly stung against Layla's cool skin and she yearned for more, leaning into her touch. Unable to think of anything but Elise and her softness pressing against her, Layla opened her lips further and sucked the tip of Elise's thumb into her mouth. Her blood, her essence, was a sweet sanctity on Layla's tongue. She held Elise's gaze while she lapped the last of the blood from her fingertip. And when she pulled away, she watched light flash in Elise's eyes, her lashes fluttering. Before Layla had time to process what had just happened, the Saint heiress was rocking into her. Her gloved hand hit the wall, catching herself right as her body crashed into Layla's. Instinctively, Layla slung her arms around Elise's waist to steady her. No matter how good it felt to give in to that heat and feel Elise's softness against her, Layla pushed her feelings aside for more important matters. "Dizzy?" Layla asked.

A delicate laugh broke from Elise. She pulled back just enough to look Layla in the eye. "I'm sorry."

Layla couldn't stop herself from grabbing Elise's chin. Her fingers were gentle on her jaw, but she felt the Saint girl's body tense up, her eyes tracing over Layla's features as if collecting prized memories along her face. The way Elise looked at her… She wished she could tell the Saint heiress to return the kindness to herself. *Look at you*, she wanted to whisper. But her lips merely pursed and she dropped her hand.

It wasn't until Elise stepped away from Layla did she release her. Layla hadn't even realized she was still clutching her waist, fingers digging into her back. It felt so natural, she had barely noticed—

"I can walk you home—"

"No." Elise adjusted her dress so she was properly covered, then she began fussing with her hair, trying to hide the bite mark. "Sterling is waiting for me at the mansion. I told him I was just debriefing with you…" She glanced at Layla, eyes still shining with ecstasy. "This stays between us."

Biting her lip, Layla nodded. "Of course." She watched Elise hurry to the end of the alleyway. Then, muttering under her breath, she smiled and laughed softly. "Goddamn Saint."

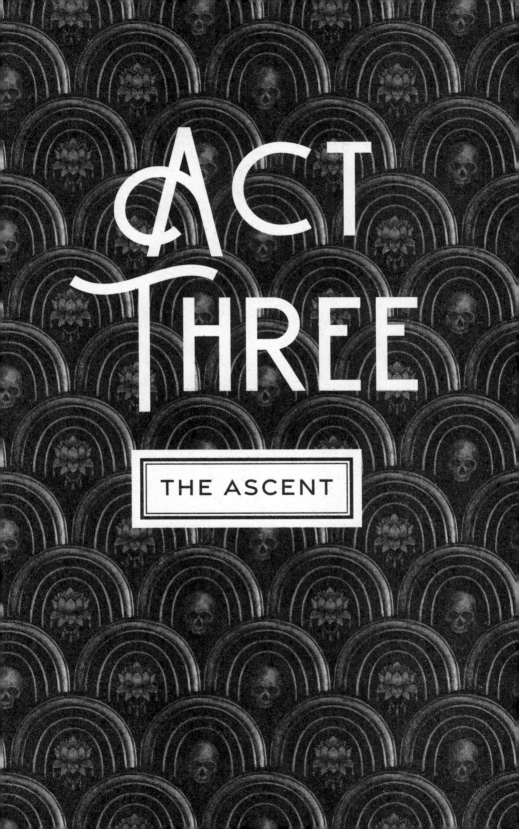

ACT THREE

THE ASCENT

28

"OW. I'M GOING TO TELL MY GRANDCHILDREN I fought a reaper off for this scar." Sterling eyed the newly healed skin stretching over his taut stomach in the mirror. Elise could hardly concentrate on getting her shoes off, much less whatever nonsense her friend was spewing. All she could think about was the intoxicating sensation of Layla's lips on her throat and then her thumb, her fingers gentle but firm on her waist. Goose bumps rose across her flesh, and her blood seemed to ignite with heat.

She wanted more.

"What?" Elise asked. Her slipper finally came off her foot, and she had to grab her chair to balance herself. An hour later and she was still feeling the entrancing effects of Layla's venom. Her body was heated, already slick with sweat from trying to fight the urges swarming her mind. She had pinned her hair back on the walk back home, but even getting extra cool air on the back of her neck couldn't stop her internal temperature from rising.

All because of Layla.

Elise threw her slipper into her closet.

Sterling shot her a strange look. "Is everything all right? Elise, you look feverish—"

"I think I'm coming down with something," she mumbled, gathering her skirts to try and pull her dress off. "You should go before my father comes back. I told him you were working—"

"Elise, darling!" Her father's voice rang up from downstairs and both Elise and Sterling froze in their respective positions in her bedroom.

Sterling's eyes widened as heavy footsteps sounded up the hallway. "What is wrong with him?" he whispered loudly.

"I think he's drunk. You need to hide—give me that." Elise snatched Sterling's shirt from his hands and started shoving him behind her bed. Of course, his massive size did not allow for proper stuffing beneath the bed, so his best chance at going unseen was standing, rigid, behind Elise's headboard. She sincerely hoped the night's alcohol had worn off in Sterling.

With her father only steps away from her bedroom, Elise threw herself into her bed and covered up her messy dress with her blankets. Her door cracked open right as her head found her pillow. "Oh!" She laughed weakly at her father while he walked into her room. "Father, I wasn't expecting you home so soon."

Mr. Saint returned her smile. His was lopsided and his eyes were a bit unfocused. *Drunk.* Just as Elise had thought. He leaned heavily against her bed, his hand coming up to stroke her face. "Elise, I—" Mr. Saint frowned. "Heavens above, my pearl, you're burning up. I will have your mother fetch you some tea—"

"Oh, no, Father, I'm okay," she insisted, but he was already shaking his head.

"Nonsense. I must make sure you're all right." Her father sighed. He looked down at his hands and his shoulders slumped. "I fear I am a horrendous father," he said in a low voice.

Elise's lips parted. She wanted to sit up and comfort her father, but the risk of the covers falling back and exposing her evening dress attire was too great. "Do not say that. That is so far from the truth. I'm okay. You are such a hard worker and I know you do it all for us."

His head lifted then, eyes misty. "Charlotte…" he said in a sad voice.

Elise blinked. "Father?"

"She was a wonderful sister; wanted to protect you even before you were born. Sometimes I fear that's all we're family for. Protectors of each other, never able to step back and appreciate the joy in between dangers." Her father ducked his head.

Elise wasn't sure what to say. She swallowed and took her father's hand into her own. "You've done an incredible job protecting us, Father. I wish you did not worry so much." Despite only being under the stifling covers for a few minutes, her flesh burned, dying for some cool air. "You're too hard on yourself."

Mr. Saint patted her hand, and his smile returned as he stood. "I will have the tea sent to you shortly. Maybe you should take a cold bath. I'm getting concerned, Elise. If you weren't dark, I think you would be turning into a tomato right about now."

A stifled laughter shook the bed. Elise, knowing it was Sterling, forced a dry laugh from her throat. "You kill me, Father." She playfully smacked his arm.

Mr. Saint laughed a full, genuine laugh. Finally, after a swift kiss to her forehead, he left her room.

Elise didn't allow herself to sigh until she heard his footsteps descending the stairs. She was about to throw her blanket off when her mother walked right into her bedroom. "Elise, my love, how are you doing?" Analia Saint asked, taking her husband's previous seat beside Elise's bed.

"I'm all right, Mother. I'm just a bit tired," Elise assured her.

Analia Saint did not look convinced. Elise knew the sweat beading on her brow and her increasingly heavy breathing only worsened her mother's doubt. "Let me get you a cool compress." Analia Saint left for Elise's bathroom. Elise stared at the ceiling, trying to calm her breathing while her mother soaked a cloth with cold water.

"Sterling," she whispered.

"Yes." His voice was strained.

"How are you doing?" Elise asked.

A pause. Then, "I've been better."

Elise's mother returned to her bedside with a damp cloth in her hand. She pressed it to Elise's forehead. The coolness soaked into her skin, spreading an ample amount of relief through her body.

But only for a few moments. Then Elise was back to resisting the urge to twitch beneath her blanket of heat. "I put some lavender and chamomile oil on the cloth, so it should help you sleep." She leaned in and gently brushed her lips over Elise's cheek. "Try to rest tonight, love, okay?"

Elise nodded. "I will, Mother. Thank you." She reached for her mother's hand as she stood to go. "I love you."

Then Elise's bedroom door swung open again. Her father walked in, teacup in hand. "A family affair, how wonderful!" he cheered. "It turns out we are all out of tea. So I brought you hot lemon water with honey. I heard that it works wonders against illness."

Mrs. Saint nodded. "Yes, darling, it does." She patted his chest, smiling. "We should let her get some rest now."

Mr. Saint murmured his agreement, leaning in to kiss her. Elise's eyes widened as he attempted to set the steaming cup down on the nightstand while still focused on his wife. He missed. Horribly. The teacup shattered on the floor, hot water spilling across the floor-boards behind her bed.

Elise covered her face as Sterling let out a pained stream of expletives. He darted from behind her bed, limping on reddened feet. With his bloody shirt and his attempt at hiding, Elise knew her parents would get the wrong idea. She sat up, the blankets falling back to reveal her dress. "Father, I—"

Mr. Saint held his hand up. His eyes were trained on Sterling, who was still hobbling to the bathroom. "I'm going to assume that Sterling left work early to take care of you since you've been sick.

Because he would never abandon his post." His voice was grave. Even though inebriation still gleamed in his eyes, Mr. Saint managed to remain completely severe.

Mrs. Saint had a hand clamped over her mouth. Tobias Saint gripped her arm with gentle fingers and pulled her into his side. "Elise, I will speak with you about this when you are well." He looked to the bathroom, where Sterling was sticking one of his feet into the sink. "Sterling, I want you in my office in five minutes."

"Yes, sir," Sterling called.

Mr. Saint gave her a final stern look, then pulled her mother out of the room with him. Elise threw her covers back and shot out of bed. She went right to the bathroom, but Sterling had already emerged, feet damp, and covered in painful, red splotches. "Sterling…" she started. "I'm sorry. I didn't think—"

"No, you didn't. You certainly did not think." Sterling yanked at his shirt. He cursed when he remembered the bloodstain on the front and grabbed one of Elise's robes to cover himself with. It stretched across his broad shoulders in an unflattering way, and the fur-lined collar stuck up behind his head. Elise almost laughed at the sight. But she could only bite her lip, stifling the smile that threatened to crack her face. Sterling's anger seemed to increase with each heated word. "This is your family; you're allowed to mess up. This is my job. I was invited here. I cannot screw this up." He glared at her when she couldn't keep in a small giggle. "Really, Elise?"

Elise clamped her mouth shut. She ran after him, grabbing his arm as he tried to leave. "Are you really upset?" she asked.

Sterling's eyes dropped to her throat and they sharpened. Then he scowled. "I cannot believe you."

"What—"

"*You let a reaper bite you?*" Sterling hissed.

Her hand flew to the spot where Layla had sunk her fangs. "I swear it's not… Sterling, please listen—"

"Look where that got me tonight. I might be fired." His voice shook.

Elise released his arm. "He would never. You're a Saint lieutenant. You're like his son—"

"You don't get it. That's exactly why I'm upset. You take all this family stuff for granted. Not all of us can be reckless with the ones we love," Sterling snapped.

The well of hurt in his eyes pierced Elise's heart. Not a moment passed where Sterling did not think of his biological family; Elise knew that. She had never stopped to consider how that made him connect with her family, or how it made him twice as afraid to lose them. Still, his words picked at a soreness in her soul. Thinking of Josi, of Charlotte, and even of Layla, who had all had something taken from them, and how Elise gave herself to the Saint empire to give them a sense of normalcy and justice.

Sterling's words echoed through Elise again. *Not all of us can be reckless with the ones we love.* Her chest tightened and she glared at her friend. "What is that supposed to mean?" Elise demanded.

"You know exactly what it means," Sterling said. He left her then, cold words still hanging in the air.

Elise sank onto her bed, shoulders slumped and exhaustion burning her eyes. Her throat constricted to the point of pain with the effort to keep her tears at bay.

The worst part was that Elise knew Sterling was right.

Layla knew better than to believe she could sneak into the lair, but she did it anyway. Her feet were soundless on the floor all the way to her room, but when she opened her bedroom door, the light clicked on and there was Mei, waiting.

Her pretty face twisted into an expression of pure horror. "*Layla, oh my God, my dress!*" she nearly shrieked.

Her piercing voice hurt Layla's ears, but she knew she deserved it. Layla had promised to take care of this dress; Mei had trusted her with it. Now it hung on her body in tatters, blood covering the delicate fabric. Layla fixed her face with a sharp glare and stepped out of the dress. As beautiful as it looked on her, even in ruins, she was tired of lugging the thing around. And it smelling like Elise's blood, which still ravaged, or rather, bewitched her system, did not make wearing it any easier.

"We're even now," Layla said. She pointed to her mattress, still ruined from Mei's accident a few weeks ago. "Actually, I would say you still owe me because what is a dress compared to a mattress, but I'm feeling generous tonight."

Mei stood. The initial shock was gone from her face and had

been replaced with cold annoyance. "You are such an ass. Sometimes you can be really selfish, you know."

Layla gave her a dry smile. "Then I guess that makes me a real reaper." She collapsed onto her bed, half expecting Mei to join her, though she did not desire another presence. Despite the human blood running through her system, the day's events beat out the adrenaline with exhaust.

Sighing, Mei scooped up her dress and headed out of the room. She stopped by the door. "You reek, by the way," Mei said flatly.

"Do I?" Layla asked, disinterested. She knew she smelled like blood, but there was no way Mei would know whose it was. And as long as her and Elise's tryst remained secret, Layla did not care what Mei thought about her nightly activities.

"There better not be another dead body on the news tomorrow. Or the whole clan will have your ass." Mei shut the door behind her.

Layla closed her eyes, exhaling. Alone, she didn't stop her mind from slipping to the Saint heiress. She wondered if Elise thought of her too. She knew her venom created urges that heightened a reaper's appeal, forcing the infected to yearn for another bite. Layla wondered if the feeding had left a mark on Elise in other ways besides physical.

She turned her face into her pillow, forcing herself to breathe in Mei's scent and cover any thoughts of Elise. It worked for only a few moments. Then Elise came slipping back into her mind. She always did.

Layla wanted more than just a bite.

She drifted off to sleep with the Saint heiress controlling her thoughts, her essence running through her body. Veins open, heart racing, Layla tumbled headfirst into a pit of vulnerability that only ended with her limbs loosening and heart softening. Elise Saint was a bittersweet entity of destruction and healing against which nothing could be done. Layla was fully stuck with her. She was completely full of Elise. And it scared her.

29

LISE WOKE UP WINCING. SHARP, PINCHING PAIN traveled through her body as she got ready for the day. Every muscle ached, stiffness locking her joints together with each movement. She could not tell if it was from the chaos of last night's events, or if it had to do with Layla's venom still circulating in her body. Elise wanted to blame the latter. But even while her muscles creaked and groaned in pain, agony screaming down her nerves, she craved the feeling of Layla's fangs in her again and the steady eye contact between them—

"Elise?" Her mother asked.

Elise glanced down. Lost in thought, she had poured her apple juice over her cup and spilled it all over the table. She set the pitcher down, cheeks flaring with an embarrassed heat. "Apologies. I got distracted." Elise began mopping up the mess with her napkins.

"I'll say," her mother muttered. She went back to staring over the

Sunday newspaper, eyebrows knitted together. "You certainly seem better today. No longer ill, though a little absent-minded."

"Mother..." Elise sighed.

"I am so glad I chose to go to the theater last night instead of the fundraiser. The papers are already talking about what a disaster it was. The police are searching for the gunman, who is allegedly Nellie's ex. The incident has people requesting another formal demonstration of the cure and they've called your father and Mr. Wayne 'rich idiots who should act with their money and nothing else.' Now your father is upset. I swear to God, if I have to hear one more time about this being a *stain* on his perfect record, I might..." Analia Saint set the newspaper down and sighed. "He was right to not tell you about this event."

Elise blinked. "Why? Because I would have made things worse? Because I cause him stress?"

Mrs. Saint's lips pursed, and her eyes went dark with disappointment. "Well, no. I would have been worried if you were there last night." She reached for Elise's hand. "Are you sure you're all right? You can tell me anything, Elise. I wish you would. You've always been so attached to your father. I feel like an outsider when it comes to you two—"

"Excuse me." Elise pushed away from the table and started for the door at the end of the dining room. She could not be the one to spill the sordid secrets of this house. She would not be the one to cause problems again.

Analia Saint gasped. "Elise Claire Saint, you return to this table right now. I am speaking to you!"

Elise ignored her mother's orders. A sinking feeling had broken open in her chest at the first mention of her father and Sterling. Elise felt like her world went sideways. She could not understand how her mother remained oblivious to the searing pressure her father loved her with. It was not at all pretty, and nothing to be envious of. Elise wasn't sure how long it would be like this, her nerves flaring with panic whenever her family made inquiries. There was no hope for her as an heir if her nerves could not handle the responsibilities. And even though Elise knew how her dark thoughts liked to lie to her and ruin her, she still clung on to the small idea that Layla's venom had her in an inescapable clutch; she was not her faults.

But none of it felt real. A lie was a lie, no matter how convincing it became, no matter how much it comforted the soul it spoke to. Elise's only reassurance crumbled. Her hands trembled by her sides and she longed for the comfort of piano keys while her heart raced, searching for a tune to synchronize with.

But instead of going up to her music room to play out her emotions, Elise grabbed her coat and left the house. She went to the one constant in her life—the place that roused in her cursed complexities and feelings that hurt so much, she confused them for pleasure. Elise Saint walked straight into the heart of Harlem reaper territory for Layla Quinn.

Elise felt reaper eyes on her while she approached the Hotel Clarice. She regretted having left so early and impulsively now. She did not have a weapon on her, and no one knew where she was. Should the reapers decide to strike, her life was forfeit.

"Bold of you to show up here." A soft feminine voice sounded in the courtyard around Elise. She turned to see a young woman approaching. The shadows shrouding the hotel seemed to cling to her as she crept forward. Her red lips spread into a smile that looked more sinister than friendly. "Are you looking for your little reaper friend?"

Shivers spread up Elise's spine at the reaper's taunting tone. "I need to speak to Layla Quinn."

The woman stopped suddenly, her nose flaring and the corners of her lips turning down as if she smelled something foul. "She's not here. I suggest you leave. Most reapers here crave Saint blood. And I won't stop them when they come for you."

"Then my father would destroy your entire clan. I might die, but the city will feel the echoes of my death after I go. And I'm not sure you and your little reaper friends could handle that," Elise said coldly.

It had been the wrong thing to say. The woman bared her fangs and sprinted toward Elise. Bracing herself against the inevitable blow, Elise raised her arms.

But the impact never came. Instead, a figure darted in front of Elise and, with a swift swipe of her arm, slammed the reaper down.

"Back off, Mei. You know she's with me," Layla snapped, shooting the woman a poisonous glare.

Goose bumps spread down Elise's arms as she stepped closer to Layla, eyes shifting between her and Mei.

Mei scrambled to her feet. Her eyes had gone almost black and her fangs dug into her lower lip so hard, blood began to leak down her chin. "She's on our territory. As far as I'm concerned, she's fair game—"

"She's not fair game, she's *mine*," Layla seethed. She stepped in front of Elise, her hand clamping over Elise's hip to move her farther back. "You touch her, I kill you."

Heat jolted through Elise at those words. She almost smiled.

Mei's lip curled in a sneer. "I *knew* it. I knew I recognized her scent."

Layla went still. Her body tensed, and Elise's expression shifted when she heard Mei's accusation.

"*You drank from a Saint.*" Mei's voice shook. With hysteria, anger, or disbelief, Elise couldn't tell.

"You don't know the situation," Layla grumbled.

Mei scowled. "Then tell me. Because it sure as hell doesn't look like you've been trying to kill her." Elise's throat tightened as Mei's gaze traveled over her. "You finally fell victim to Saint manipulation, is that it? You're choosing her over me? Choosing a Saint over your clan?"

Layla narrowed her eyes, but she said nothing.

"You are an idiot. Fuck reaper-human boundaries, you've desecrated Saint property. Valeriya will banish you if she finds out. And she will annul every agreement we've ever had with the Saints. No one in this clan will trust you. All this time you've been trying to reject your reaperhood, but you are the worst of us all. You want a cure, but all you've gotten yourself is a death wish," Mei spat. Her shoulders trembled with rage as she retreated to the hotel.

Elise crossed her arms as Layla turned to her. Her face was still drawn, darkened by the heated exchange between her and Mei. But when she spoke, her voice was steady. "You should not have come here—"

"I can take care of myself," Elise said roughly.

"Is that why you showed up with no weapons and smelling like I marked you?" Layla laughed dryly. "I thought you were smart, but you're clueless. Or is it my venom that has you acting like a damn fool?"

Both. Elise wanted to say. Her brain was twisted and her thoughts were as complex as her feelings all because of Layla and this stupid ordeal she had gotten herself into. Elise clenched her jaw and shot back, "You're one to talk. I saw how you looked at Nellie last night. You almost exposed yourself as a reaper just to get to her."

Layla's lips twitched, but she said nothing.

"Valeriya doesn't have to know. About the bite, I mean," Elise said softly.

Something flickered in Layla's eyes. "If Mei knows, then Valeriya certainly does too. Her senses are far stronger than any other reaper's I know."

Frustration bit through Elise as she ground her teeth.

Finally, Layla's gaze snapped back to Elise. "Why are you really here, Saint?" she demanded.

Elise sighed, defeated. "You want a cure. By now, the whole city knows about Dr. Harding's research and Mr. Wayne's plans, and soon enough the whole country will, if not the whole world. Yet no one has ever seen a cured reaper survive. There's been a pattern between Theo and the dancers being infected and them all having gone to the clinic and the Cotton Club at some point. Mr. Wayne is the common name beneath all of this. You were right earlier when you said we shouldn't trust him. Ever since Mr. Wayne became involved, things have gone wrong. He doesn't want to help reapers, or even people. He's probably funding illegal trials and I think Theo was his first victim," Elise said.

"Well, his trials are working. Nellie became human—" Layla started. But Elise didn't let her finish.

"She *died*. And no one, not the papers, not even Mr. Wayne seems to care—"

"What about your father?" Layla challenged.

Elise blinked. "What about him?"

"Why can't you see any wrong in your father's actions?" Layla asked, voice trembling with wild anger.

Elise blanched and stammered, "*What?* I'm talking about Mr. Wayne—"

"Your father is still involved in this too. Just admit it. Your father isn't perfect. He isn't some flawless person that makes everything better just because of who he is."

"He's my father—"

"You sure do love saying that. As if that proves anything. Did he even react to the chandelier falling? Tell me—did he seem distressed at all that his party got someone killed? Or was he just upset that his image was tainted?" Layla demanded.

Her father had been drunk last night. But he didn't seem upset because of the party. His focus had been almost entirely on Elise. Which she had to admit was unlike him, especially when it came to the empire.

If the empire was a tangible thing in her mind, one brick might have crumbled while she considered Layla's words. The foundation of the empire would crack and cleave while Layla poked holes in its image. Elise didn't like the direction this conversation was going in.

"It wasn't his fault, Layla. He knows what he's doing, he always does. He hates reapers more than anyone—"

"Exactly," Layla snapped. "He wants them gone. He doesn't want to cure the monsters that killed his child."

Elise stopped breathing at the mention of Charlotte.

"At least Stephen Wayne wants to fix things. There is not an ounce of goodness in your father. I know that's how you see me, so you should see it in him too." Layla swallowed. "I know what it's like to be blinded by vengeance and to only want the blood of the ones who hurt you. There is no room for hope, or anything light. Your father doesn't love…" Layla paused, her eyes flashing while Elise flinched. "If you're going to accuse Stephen Wayne, then accuse your father, as well. Tobias Saint doesn't care about anything besides his empire and what it stands for."

Silence filled the space between them. For a long moment, Elise only watched Layla, her eyes searching her expression. She stumbled through her next words as she shifted the topic, "You want the cure so badly, you are willing to ignore the terrible things Mr. Wayne might be doing to get it?"

"I'm a reaper, Saint. You already know what I want. The whole world does," Layla breathed.

Months ago, Elise might have agreed; she might have answered with "carnage," because that was what rogue reapers wanted. But Layla was not a rogue reaper. Elise stepped closer to Layla. "Why are you changing your mind so suddenly? I told you I believed you were innocent."

A defeated sigh left Layla. "Maybe you shouldn't have." She lowered her gaze, fingers clenching into fists against her sides. "I don't want to do this with you anymore. It's clear our endgames are nowhere near aligned," she muttered.

Elise's heart fell. "Layla, wait—" Layla started to walk away, but Elise caught up with her, grabbing her sleeve. "We're close. I can...I know we are...please—"

But Layla was already shaking her head. "I don't know why I ever assumed this would work. We don't work. And if our past is any indication of how we will end up, then I would rather not go through this again."

Layla's voice was soft, and she spoke without malice. But it cut straight into Elise's heart. Elise stood and watched Layla walk away until she disappeared into an alleyway. Then she was all alone.

30

DINNER FELT MORE LIKE A WAKE THAN A FAMILY meal. It did not help that Stephen Wayne was there once again, this time having brought Dr. Harding along. The philanthropist's presence felt like an icy wedge driven between the family members. Elise glared at him across the table every chance she got when he was not looking, though her mother caught her a few times and nudged her beneath the table.

"This cure is already the talk of the town. Not all good talk, but I'm sure the chandelier incident will blow over soon enough." Tobias Saint raised his wineglass to Dr. Harding. The doctor nodded, but did not lift his own glass. Elise's father toasted Mr. Wayne instead.

Elise stabbed at her food, and her fork clinked the plate so hard, everyone turned to look at her. Mr. Saint cleared his throat. "Elise, if you want, you may be excused," he said.

"I don't want that, Father," Elise said flatly.

Her father's lips pursed. He turned back to Mr. Wayne. "How will we get the reapers to trust us to administer the cure to them?"

Mr. Wayne leaned back in his chair, expression relaxed. "Easy. We promise to propose official legislation to Mr. Arendale that protects all reapers and considers them part human beings in the eyes of the law rather than beasts."

The room went still. Elise watched her father's expression. The slight twitch of his eye told her he was just as displeased hearing this news from Mr. Wayne now as he was hearing it from Layla's parents five years ago. And that had just been a written agreement between the empire and the Harlem reaper clan. Though Mr. Saint had eventually come around to making that agreement, it took him two years after the Quinns' deaths to do it.

"Is that even possible? Just forcing the Harlem reapers into an agreement with the empire felt like pulling teeth. And they did that to avoid certain death." Tobias Saint spoke calmly, though his hands fisted around his silverware.

"Mr. Arendale has already agreed to the new law if he becomes mayor. I believe it would incentivize reapers to behave better. My hope is that rogue reapers will follow suit as well. They will be allowed to apply for jobs and housing without hiding anything— this will allow us to keep track of every reaper in New York. To have the most powerful clan initiate this gesture will do everyone well," Mr. Wayne said.

Stephen Wayne's gray eyes twinkled while he spoke. Elise had trouble trusting his motives beyond his public persona. "The next demonstration of the cure should take place at the Hotel Clarice. We already have a decent bond with the Harlem reapers from supporting their economy through the Cotton Club. But I will need the Saints' approval to ensure that things go smoothly. There is little that they will be able to resist in the face of a cure—"

"About that," Elise interrupted.

Both of her parents shot her stern looks. "*Elise.*"

She shrugged. "I have a question."

Mr. Wayne shared a gentle look with her. "Go ahead, Elise."

Elise took a deep breath. "How did you find this cure?" she asked.

"Testing," Dr. Harding said, it like it was the most obvious thing in the world. But to Elise, it was an empty response.

"Testing on who?" she nearly demanded. "Did you give a dose to Theo Smith?"

"*Elise,*" her father said sharply. He turned a softer look onto Dr. Harding. "My apologies. She has been unwell recently."

Dr. Harding raised his hand in dismissal. "Nonsense. I enjoy an intellectual conversation with the youth." He nodded at Elise. "Carry on."

"Who did you run tests on?" Elise asked.

Dr. Harding just shrugged. "Science is wonderfully complex. I wouldn't expect you to understand it."

"I went to the best schools in New York and Paris. Try me," Elise said flatly. She leveled her gaze with his.

The doctor took another sip of his drink. He set his glass down and moved into the chair next to Elise. He was suddenly so close,

Elise felt a bit uncomfortable, but she continued to make eye contact so as not to let his overwhelming presence defeat her. "We do have a little secret, actually. It was all my idea, and even Stephen doesn't know about it."

Mr. Wayne's jaw dropped slightly. "I beg your pardon?"

Elise swallowed. Her heart pounded so hard, she wondered if everyone could hear it. "Sure."

"Your father has raised you well," Dr. Harding said, in a tone that made Elise uneasy.

Mr. Saint cleared his throat. "If you're going to thank me, make sure you thank my beautiful wife as well. She's done more than I ever have when it comes to raising our girls. Analia is the reason why Elise is so talented. It was her idea to get her piano lessons. In fact… Elise, darling, don't you have some practice to get done?"

Elise decided she would not take the hint. Besides, she was too drained to play anything well at all.

"I'm enjoying my conversation with Dr. Harding, Father; piano can wait." Elise nodded to the doctor. "I know my parents are wonderful. Tell me. What's your secret?"

"I take the bodies of the reapers your empire kills and my scientists study them," Dr. Harding replied. "Reaper venom has become like a drug abroad, and people all over the world pay high prices for it. Moreover, I get a new offer every month from someone who would like to collaborate with me to create the next great race of human beings. I'm half inclined to accept them."

Chills covered Elise's arms as her insides turned to ice.

"A cure would surely conflict with this business, though," the doctor went on. "So I must make the more morally sound decision. It's quite a divergence from the scientists who first created this mess and left us to deal with the consequences. So, to fix what they left behind, you can understand that sometimes, we must make decisions that are not the most ethical?"

Elise began, "As a practitioner of medicine, you are expected to heal—"

"And heal I do." Dr. Harding nodded and picked up the knife at his place setting. He ran his thumb over the blade, a cold smile forming on his lips. "You would not last one day in the madness that is this line of work."

Elise regretted not leaving the table. She felt impossibly uncomfortable now, her body caving in on itself the longer Dr. Harding watched her. It was a relief when someone else finally spoke.

"I'm desperate to discuss this again later, Dr. Harding. But for now, Elise, I would love it if you helped me with the Harlem reapers," Stephen Wayne said. "You already seem so close to Layla Quinn. If you've got her on your side, the rest of the clan is sure to follow. Those bastards who killed Thalia are still out there, but perhaps if we all work together, we can stop them."

Elise turned and saw the whole table watching her with anticipation. The promise to kill Layla at the end of the investigation still stood. The promise that she would figure out who was responsible for the crime that rocked their community still stood.

The burdens piled on top of her were sure to crush her soon.

Elise sighed and gave Stephen Wayne a brief nod. "I would be honored to help."

"You sound stiff."

Elise's fingers slipped on the piano keys at the sound of her father's voice. She lowered the fallboard and turned to face him as he walked into the music room. Though she hadn't wanted to practice, Elise had not been able to stop fidgeting once she returned to her room after dinner. Playing basic scales helped clear her head, but when her father walked in, she went rigid once more.

"You never told me what you played for your conservatory audition." Mr. Saint slid onto the seat beside her. Elise could smell his cologne; she hated having anyone this close to her while she played. Except for one person, at least. And that was different. It was always different when it came to Layla.

"It's very personal to me," Elise said quietly.

Her father ran his finger over the glossy piano board. "So personal that you couldn't tell the person who paid for your lessons and your instruments?" he asked. His tone was mild, but the words conveyed every ounce of displeasure he had with her. Elise swallowed and remained quiet.

"Have you ever played it for me?" he asked.

"No."

His knuckles rapped against the piano board so hard, Elise flinched.

"My pearl, what is this about?"

She finally looked up. "It's bad luck to share audition details before the decision is made."

"That's understandable." A wry smile split her father's lips. For a moment, Elise thought she had convinced him. But he reached into his jacket pocket and pulled out a mask. It was the mask Elise had worn and lost at the fundraiser. Then he revealed a letter: the one she had written to decline her acceptance at the Paris Conservatory.

Elise's mouth went dry.

"It is an understandable excuse for a superstitious musician. But you're not superstitious." Her father leaned closer to her. "You're just a liar."

A tight knot formed in Elise's chest, pain increasing with each racing heartbeat, and she looked away, trying to focus on her breathing. But her father continued speaking. "Sterling told me about your recent activities. When did you become a liar, Elise? You had me place all my faith in you, and now you're no better than the demons I trusted you to beat."

Tears welled in her eyes as she swallowed past the painful lump in her throat. Already, she was too scared to move, to think, to breathe. Elise could only sit there and listen, hoping his searing words would be enough for him.

"I am very disappointed in you. This is why I couldn't tell you about the fundraiser. You ruin things. You have made almost no progress on this case. You made me look like an imbecile in front of Mr. Wayne and Dr. Harding today. Stephen might say you're an intelligent, kind, sophisticated young lady, but do you think he believes any of that? Of course not. It makes me wonder what else you've been up to with that Quinn girl behind my back." Tobias Saint's voice was steady and calm. Waiting for his explosion was always the worst part of any conflict with him. Elise hated tiptoeing around her words, not knowing what would set him off. He stood and she moved away off the bench, trying to put distance between them.

"*Fuck*, Elise." Her father shoved the piano hard. It slammed the wall behind it and the room shook. Next, he kicked the bench, sending it into the wall. Wood splintered, the perfect glossy finish damaged beyond repair. It creaked and groaned like a wounded creature.

Elise whimpered. Tears finally broke past Elise's defenses. Her lips trembled, and she tried to turn away, but her father gripped her chin, forcing her to look at him. "Don't you know that I've put all of my faith into you continuing my empire's legacy? Charlotte's legacy? You might as well have killed her. You owe us something more than piano and your useless tears. Yet here you are, crying when it gets too hard. Your weak self wrongfully takes up Charlotte's space. Are you a failure, or are you going to be a Saint?"

"I'm a Saint," Elise whispered.

Her father sighed and dropped her chin. "Unless I ask you to perform, you are not allowed to play anymore. You're not good enough anyway, seeing as how the Paris Conservatory doesn't miss you. I might reconsider if you bring the Harlem reapers to their knees for their crimes against this city. But if you really cannot do this, please tell me. I will send you back to France and have Josi come home.

She's always been a much better listener than you. I'd rather have her around, even if she's too young to contribute to the business now. At least she's worth something."

"No, please," Elise cried.

His scowl deepened at the sight of her tears. "Since you're already working with Quinn, I want you to present the cure to the reapers with Stephen. I want that girl eating right out of the palm of your hand when you turn your gun on her." Mr. Saint stood, smoothing the wrinkles in his suit. He smiled at her. The anger suddenly vanished from his face, and the smile replaced it all with light. "Saints show no mercy. Make me proud."

As soon as the door shut behind him, Elise folded into herself and sobbed.

31

WITH THE ELECTION COMING UP, TOBIAS SAINT spent more time with Mr. Wayne, away from the mansion. Elise could still feel her father's fingers digging into her jaw, could hear the piano hitting the wall. Most of all, she couldn't stop thinking about Josi at the receiving end of his anger. If there was any motivation to keep Elise going, it was imagining her little sister crying just as she had after their father had torn her down.

In the week after that episode, Elise wrote letters to Josi daily. It wasn't until her mother came into her room that she realized how obsessive it had become.

"Oh heavens, Elise…" Analia Saint's eyes roamed over the piles of letters. "You miss her so much." She bit back a sob. "I miss her too."

Elise wanted to tell her it wasn't as simple as missing her sister. But she knew her mother wouldn't understand. "I do," Elise whispered.

❁

Elise's anxiety crested when her father requested that she perform for his dinner party. The night he came to her room to tell her, Elise, shaking, had looked up from her desk. "I thought I wasn't allowed to play."

Tobias Saint's expression hardened. "You do what I ask, Elise. You should be able to play a piece you know as well as your heart without much practice, right?"

"Yes, Father." Elise nodded.

"Wonderful." He left her room then and Elise had caved in on herself. For so long, she had assumed that through the pain of working herself to be good enough, she would eventually find healing in her father's pride. But there was no redemption. His expectations had become her torture.

Now, as Elise settled her fingers over the piano keys, her father's crowd of onlookers on one side and the fireplace raging on the other side, she felt the most uncertain she'd ever had about her own playing.

It persisted throughout the entire song. Sharp, beating pulses of pain stabbing into her heart with each short breath, as if something inhumane was cleaving the fatigued flesh of her muscles. She didn't feel the usual relief that swept through her when she finished a performance. Even when the crowd clapped for her and murmured their praise, Elise continued to sweat, her dress heavy and cold against her clammy skin. More dread seeped into her already aching and anxious chest. She could only take a shaky bow before thanking them and dismissing herself.

Back in her room, Elise cried. Not for her messy, misled

performance, but for the lost comfort. No longer could she find herself in music and use it to unravel her tense, tangled emotions. Her father had taken even that away from her.

Layla never thought she would find herself living with a gangster, and even though it was temporary, she was disgusted with herself for crawling to Jamie Kelly with no other options.

His blue eyes had lit up with amusement, scorching her with embarrassment when she had shown up at the club needing a place to stay. She thought she would rather take her chances living with a clan that wanted to rip her limb from limb than deal with Jamie's mockery. But then Jamie had straightened up and stopped laughing and invited her to his apartment.

One week later, Layla was only just beginning to settle in.

"What is a four-letter word for the tamed beasts humans now love?" Jamie asked. He glared down at the newspaper crossword puzzle, a steaming mug of coffee beside him.

Layla glanced up from the newspaper—the part with actual news on it that Jamie did not bother with—and scrunched her nose in thought. "Dogs. Obviously," she said.

The newsprint should have ripped with the intensity of Jamie's scribbles. He shot her a dirty look. "Don't say 'obviously' like that. You had to think about it for a moment."

"And yet you were stuck on a question like that? I'm not even human, and I got it before you." Layla leaned over the arm of the couch to see the crossword before Jamie pulled it out of sight. "You've only got four!" she exclaimed. "You started an hour ago! It's taken you this long to guess *dogs*?" Layla threw herself back against the couch cushions and laughed.

Jamie snapped the paper out so it lay flat on the table in front of him. "Are you calling me dumb? Because that's quite a rude thing to call someone who has offered you their home."

Sighing, Layla sat up. "You said it, not me. And have I not shown you how grateful I am just by being pleasant to you?"

"No," Jamie said flatly. "I will have you know that there is no time limit on genius. Intelligence is not quantified. It's about the quality of the thoughts that cross the mind."

Layla grinned. "Jamie… Intelligence *is* quantified. What do you think IQ tests are?"

Jamie slid one last foul look at Layla, then he crumpled the cross-word in his fists and dropped it onto the floor. "I'm leaving. I'll be gone for a while since I have work. Don't touch anything. And don't forget to feed Hen."

Hen, or Hendricks, Jamie's hateful gray cat, was even less tolerable than Jamie. Layla wasn't sure how it was possible. Such a feat probably should have been applauded, but she was almost positive that Hendricks would try to claw her eyes out if she went near him—even to praise him.

"How am I supposed to feed Hendricks if I can't touch any-thing?" Layla asked.

Jamie waved her off while he walked out the door. "Figure it out, or he will eat you."

Layla sighed. The gray cat perched in a patch of sunlight on the kitchen floor. He looked at the door after his owner, green eyes wide with longing.

"He's coming back," Layla said quietly.

No matter how gently she spoke to the cat, he still seemed to sense that she raised hell.

Hendricks whipped his head in her direction and hissed, his teeth bared. Layla covered her mouth. "Do I look that ridiculous?" Her own fangs prodded against her lower lip, and she lifted her brow in curiosity.

Stretching across the sofa to the side table, she flipped the phonograph on and gently lowered the needle onto the record that Jamie had left on. It sputtered to life, saxophone and a melancholy voice belting a gentle blues song. She settled against the couch in silent solidarity with the feline that was most likely plotting her murder.

The door opened just a few minutes later. Layla didn't look up. "Back so soon?"

"Don't be rude." The familiar voice spiked Layla's heart rate. The music stopped with a rough screech of the needle. Layla set the newspaper down. Mei was dressed in all black, hair done up in a tight chignon against the back of her head. Under her coat her pale legs were long and graceful, skin bravely bared in the fast-approaching autumn weather. Next to her stood Jamie, his expression weary. Mei scowled and took her hand off the phonograph.

Jamie rubbed his head, and some of his blond hair fell into his eyes. "So, she showed up. She also threatened me, which I will be holding against *you*, Layla, since I'm not even sure how she knew where I lived. So now she's your problem. Goodbye." He slammed the door on his way out.

The room seemed to close in, darkening with each stride Mei took toward Layla. "So here's where you've been hiding all this time," she said. Her eyes roamed over the sitting room and kitchen as she sat beside Layla on the couch. "I thought you would have found solace with the Saints."

"I told you, my loyalty is to the Harlem reapers." Venom dripped from her words.

Mei did not flinch. She brushed one of her wispy bangs out of her eyes and spoke calmly, "Is that why you came home reeking of that Saint girl? She trusted you enough to let you at her throat."

"So I've gotten her to drop her guards. But mine are still well intact," Layla mumbled. She wasn't sure it was something she wanted to boast about. Getting so close to Elise over the past few weeks had made her feel something besides despair and dread for the first time in a long time. She couldn't force the gently blooming hope away. So Layla had done what she could to force the Saint heiress away instead.

"Very well." Those two words were more than confirmation from Mei. They were an admission. "Valeriya needs you back. The Saints and Stephen Wayne have made requests for a summit between them and our clan. Valeriya needs assurance they are not going to set us up."

Layla almost laughed. "For once, me working with the Saint girl is not a dirty thing? I am to be used for this reassurance, then discarded, correct?" Layla spat.

"Nonsense," Mei said. She sighed, her shoulders loosening and her expression softening; it was a gesture that Layla recognized as honesty. "You know how hard it is to find trust in people once you've turned, Layla. It's easier to push everyone away than it is to let them in. I couldn't help myself when I saw you with her. No one could. We are all asking ourselves how the girl who lost her life and her family at the hands of Saints has returned to the Saints."

It felt as if a spear had gone through Layla's heart. She looked away, willing herself to not crack under the pressure Mei was applying.

"It's all out of necessity." Layla lifted her gaze back to Mei's. "I will speak with the Saint heiress and make sure it's not a setup."

"Do I have your word?" Mei asked. Layla held her hand out and Mei shook it. A small smile formed on her glossy red lips and she stood up. "Once we have confirmation, you will be allowed back home."

Layla almost mentioned not wanting to go back, but Mei was already on her way out. So she just nodded her agreement and absorbed the silence that followed Mei's departure.

Part of her tried to be happy she'd been invited to come back home. But Layla wondered if she could truly call a place home if there were conditions for belonging there.

She took a can of tuna from the cabinet and plopped a serving of the fish into a saucer. The raw, putrid stench stung the inside of her nose even when she covered it. "Hendricks, this is my last straw." The small gray cat trotted into the room and appeared to be in a much better mood now; he didn't hiss at her when she approached him with the food. His tail even swished against the linoleum while he watched her with patient green eyes.

"Wow." Layla set the saucer down in front of him. "Good boy—"

His claws swiped across her hand. Layla snatched herself away, cradling her hand as the cat calmly bent to eat his food.

"No. *That* was my last straw." Layla shook her hand out, hissing as the burning pain faded. She reached for the empty tuna can and dropped it into the kitchen trash bin. "Because of that, you don't get to lick the can. There go your tuna juices." Layla crept cautiously around the feeding cat and found her place back on the couch. But not before she picked up the crossword puzzle Jamie had crumpled up earlier. As she leaned back into the cushions, she smoothed out the paper, already eyeing some obvious answers on the page. A smile crept across her face at the thought of Jamie scratching his head over the puzzle. *How could such a notoriously vicious gangster be so slow at these things?* Layla laughed, but it was soft with affection.

In just a few minutes, Layla finished the crossword.

She purposefully did not answer the last few words correctly, filling the blocks in instead with her own message to Jamie:

Thank you for letting me stay.

32

ELISE SHOVED HER HANDS INTO HER COAT POCKETS and walked down the front steps of the Saint estate. October introduced a crisp breeze into the air. The season reminded her of France in the little things such as the autumn leaves, the trench coats people began to wear as the temperature dropped, the jazz floating out of busy cafés. She missed the freedom of being abroad. Not just in the sense of being away from her parents and their rules. In Paris, Elise could walk onto a bus and sit wherever she wanted. She did not have to enter the downtown hotels from the back entrances, nor was she prohibited from entering nightclubs.

Elise never saw a Black musician or singer in France walk off the stage with the empty look in their eyes that so often followed the performances of Black artists here. She was almost glad to think she would never experience that, now that she was her father's successor instead of a pianist. But almost was not enough.

"Saint."

Elise stopped short. Layla Quinn stood at the estate front gates. She leaned against the iron curves, arms crossed while she watched Elise approach her.

"How did you get in here?" Elise asked, slightly awed.

Layla shrugged. "Your escort let me in."

Elise's heart stopped, realizing who she meant. "Did Sterling speak to you?"

"He might have grumbled," Layla shrugged.

A sad sigh left Elise. "He hasn't spoken to me in days."

"Oh, forget him." Layla pushed off the gate and straightened up, her toned arms catching the bold evening light while she stretched.

Elise couldn't help but stare. Everything about Layla was lithe and smooth. Her skin seemed to glow a radiant golden even when the sun didn't beam directly onto it, her eyes luminous amber pools at any tame moment. It was when she became hostile that the amber lit up into a fiery, almost white gold. Against Elise's own precautions, she couldn't help but long for that intensity. To be on the other end of those eyes while Layla was feeling particularly charged up and volatile... Elise wanted her devouring attention. She could only imagine how it would be to feel those eyes on her while her fangs sank into her throat—

Layla cleared her throat. Elise blinked, her cheeks growing warm while Layla watched her with suspicious eyes. "Saint?" she asked.

Elise nodded quickly. "Fine. I'm fine." She pushed past Layla and the gates. If she was going to have such sinful thoughts, she might as well have waited until she was off Saint property. Elise was surprised she and Layla didn't go up in flames while they stood there together.

"Why did you come? I thought you were done with me," Elise asked once they were on a public street.

Layla didn't look at her. She watched the sky while they walked, only occasionally glancing down to see where she was going. "I would like to know whether the treaty your father and Stephen Wayne have proposed is real."

Elise let out a dry laugh. "I think you know. Last time we spoke, you seemed to know my father better than me."

Layla stopped walking and regarded her with suspicion. "Saint. Be serious."

"I *am* serious," Elise said sharply.

The two of them watched each other, Layla's face contemplative and perplexed, while Elise's twisted with irritation. Layla broke the silence first. "What happened?" she demanded.

"*Nothing*," Elise insisted. "I can't help you, Layla. My father hardly lets me in anymore. We're not…" She swallowed hard as tears crested in her eyes. "We're not as close since I've screwed everything up. I'm sorry, I can't help you. I can't help anyone," she muttered.

Layla pursed her lips. Silence fell between them while Elise wiped her eyes, and as she started back down the street, Layla spoke up. "Your father is wrong, Saint."

"You've said that a hundred times—"

"No, I mean…" Layla sighed. "There should be no conditions on the love he gives you. He's wrong for that."

Elise blinked, her breath faltering. "I know that. But that doesn't change the fact that I know nothing of what he's planning besides wanting to deliver your clan a cure."

Layla's eyes widened. "*What—*"

"This cure is not a perfect fix—"

"It's no small thing. Most of us have been tortured for years by our reaperhood. A cure would change everything for us," Layla said quickly.

Elise sighed. "*Layla.* I understand this is important to you, but I implore you to reconsider trusting it. This cure has come at too convenient of a time." Her voice trembled and Layla looked at her strangely, eyebrows creased. Elise began to spiral again. Her chest grew tight and hot despite the cool air pressing around her.

Layla's expression hardened. "That's how I know you don't understand. You're asking us to wait for options and to consider alternatives, but we have none. Reapers have never had a choice. To ask me—me, of all people—to wait and examine my other options is bullshit. And you know it." Layla pressed closer to Elise now and that familiar rage glazed over her eyes. "I have never had a choice. *Ever.*"

A cold silence seeped between them. Layla's eyes settled back to their usual color and she backed off, though Elise remained tense. "I just ask that you be more cautious. My father is involved in this, too, and I know you hate him. You would be eating out of the palm of his hand if you took the cure from him and Mr. Wayne," she said quietly.

Layla was quiet for a moment. Her expression softened while she thought, fingers tapping on her forearms, which were still firmly crossed over her chest. "He knows better than to offer his hand to a reaper. But if you're so concerned, why won't you tell me what changed your mind?"

Elise hesitated. Then she whispered, "Come with me."

"I must say, Elise, I am surprised to see you approach me without your father. And, my apologies, but Dr. Harding is too busy to join us today. I hope you understand." Stephen Wayne's cool voice swept over the empty hallway while he led them through the lab. Layla watched Elise pull her coat tighter around her, as if blocking out an invisible breeze. Discomfort looked rather odd on the Saint heiress.

"He prefers it when I take on more independence," Elise said softly.

Mr. Wayne stopped in front of a door, his hand resting on the lock while he glanced at Layla. "And Miss Quinn. You are quite far from your territory."

Layla laughed dryly. "Not far enough."

Elise nodded toward the door. "Is that where you keep reapers you're running experiments on?" she asked.

Something dark flashed over his eyes. "No reapers are kept on this floor since we have patients frequenting the clinic." He pushed the door open. A large room opened up before them, with gleaming white walls and examination tables. The white-coated staff tended to patients, taking blood and recording observations. All of the patients, Layla noticed, were Black.

She and Elise watched the doctors and nurses with both hope and apprehension. Hundreds of years ago, Black and brown people had been studied under microscopes. They were prodded, drugged, bled, and tortured until they became the very monsters that Stephen Wayne claimed he now wanted to rid the world of.

Layla turned to Stephen Wayne. "What are you doing here?" she asked.

"Purity tests." He led them to a cot where a young Black girl sat having her arm examined by a nurse. "This is Clara. She used to dance at the Cotton Club. As I'm sure you are aware, there were reapers there. She was sick from what my scientists determined to be reaper venom, spread through close proximity to other reapers. But now she is better. Isn't that right, Clara?" Stephen Wayne asked.

Clara gave the girls a shy smile and nodded. "I thought I would turn, but Dr. Harding was able to reverse the effects. I'm very lucky."

Elise let out a slow breath. "Wow."

A sharp whip of envy tore through Layla. Biting her lip, she looked away.

"It would have been nice to have such a resource when you were younger, Quinn, I'm sure. But now you have the opportunity to help others," Stephen Wayne said.

Layla shook her head. "My clan are already all turned. How would an antidote help them? They're too far gone." She felt Elise's stare boring into her as they talked. The Saint heiress, for once, was silent.

Stephen Wayne nodded. "Follow me."

They followed him down another hallway, then up a flight of stairs. The scent of rot and ruin began to penetrate the air, and Layla wrinkled her nose. Neither Elise nor Stephen Wayne seemed to comprehend that they might have been walking straight toward death.

"As we were working on the cure, we developed something essential." Mr. Wayne gestured to a lab technician standing by an observation window, and the man began to pull the blinds back, revealing a dark examination room. For a moment, there was only silence. Then a low growl sounded from the room, and every cell in Layla's body froze.

Elise gasped, "*Oh my God.*"

What looked like an ancient reaper lay strapped to the examination table. Their skin sagged in gray and purple creases against their body, their hands stretching into long talons that were black under the low lighting. Even the eyes looked empty, though an intense yellow burned around the pupils each time the reaper blinked and peeled back their lids.

"Horrifying, isn't it?" Stephen Wayne muttered. "I know it's hard to believe, but this gentleman was a normal human once just like you and me, Elise. He was turned only twenty years ago, but could not stomach the thought of killing and draining humans, so he didn't. And here he is now. Decrepit, demonic, diseased."

The breath stalled in Layla's chest. She could not believe what she saw. She had only seen this type of reaper in pictures. They might as well have been legends, because no reaper would deny human blood for long enough to become this.

"Hell," Layla whispered.

"Indeed," Mr. Wayne said. "Your own clan leader forbids you from killing humans now, so what is there to stop you from becoming *this*?" He pointed to the reaper once more, and again, Layla's heart stopped. "Dr. Harding has already cured humans from reaper venom, and he's developed an antidote to keep you closer to your humanity and prevent you from becoming this demon." Stephen Wayne tapped on the window. The reaper looked up and growled again, spit flying from his mouth. His eyes shifted from the pale yellow to an enraged red. "Poor thing has lost every part of his human past. He doesn't even remember his own name," Stephen Wayne said.

Everything hit Layla at once. The white lights hovering above them glowed so bright, a haze covered her surroundings and it took effort just to keep her eyes focused on the people in front of her. Elise spoke, but the words did not reach Layla's ears. All she heard was roaring as blood rushed into her head and panic ensued. She stumbled back, and things shifted into perspective just long enough for her to hear Elise.

"Layla?"

But Layla was already gone.

The thought of blood consumed Layla. It didn't help that the Cotton Club still reeked of old blood from the crime scene and sneaking into the closed-down establishment for a bit of peace and quiet to calm down had been a *choice*. But certainly better than staying in the lab while she had a breakdown about her inevitable fate. In front of a Saint, nonetheless.

She twisted an old Saint bullet from the attack in her hands. The steel burned her fingers, but the pain distracted her from her frightening thoughts of the reaper at the lab. The rancid stench of the old blood did keep her from feeling especially feral. But it only helped for a few long minutes before the scent of a blood so sweet Layla would recognize it anywhere filled the dressing room where she hid.

"Saint," Layla muttered. She came out from beneath a dressing room table and saw the Saint heiress standing in the middle of the room. Her cheeks looked warm and dark with blood, her curls messy, no doubt from running through the city after Layla.

"Considering how deadly you are, I was surprised to see you break down like that at the lab." Elise smoothed her hands over her windswept hair and took a step toward Layla. "I didn't think you were afraid of anything. But that reaper certainly—"

"Why are you here, Saint?" Layla gritted out.

Elise pursed her lips. "We're partners. I cannot do this without you. And this place is probably full of important evidence we should go through."

Something warm crossed through Layla and she almost forgot about her fears having nearly overcome her earlier. Fighting back a smile, she asked, "Does the blood not bother you?"

"What blood?" Elise placed her hands on her hips, frowning.

"The crime scene here has been cleaned rather thoroughly…" She gasped. "You can *still* smell it?" She brushed a stray curl behind her ear and looked away, lips pursing.

Layla caught her scent. "Yes. And I can smell you too."

"What do you smell on me?" Elise breathed, vaguely stiff.

All four immediate notes of her perfume, specifically. Gardenia, vanilla, coconut, and sage. There might have been a hint of bergamot too. But beneath all of those luxurious scents, Layla could sense Elise. And it wasn't just the essence of her skin and the natural scent she gave off. But Layla also sensed the warmth that radiated from her and whatever emotion tainted her aura in that moment. Right now it was unease, coupled with a bit of unbridled excitement.

The corner of Layla's lips ticked up into a faint smile. Oh how she loved bringing the Saint girl to the edge, forcing her to reach out for stability, inevitably afraid, but helplessly, hopelessly engaged and eager.

Thrill sprung up between both of them.

At the quickening of Elise's pulse, Layla's smile widened. And when Elise finally turned back to look at her, expectancy heavy in her eyes, she saw the glow of her heated blood in the curve of her ears, outlined gently by the sun filtering through the windows.

Layla wanted to reach out and touch her ear, feeling the softness of humanity beneath her fingertips. "I can smell your blood too," Layla muttered.

The heat in Elise's cheeks went cool. As much as Layla deigned to feel that human fire, she wasn't sure she could bear the loss of its warmth when she had to draw away.

Her mind switched instinctively back to the topic of the cure, which made her tear away from Elise. "The blood in this room is rancid. Someone here was infected." She crossed the room, expecting Elise to follow her. But the Saint girl did not budge. "Saint?"

Elise looked up at her and swallowed. Something shifted in her eyes and for a moment, Layla thought she might back down. Nothing could have prepared Layla for what actually came out of Elise's mouth.

"Did you like my blood?" she asked.

The question caught Layla so off guard, she choked on her own air. Layla, blinking and inhaling past the lump in her throat, nearly shouted at Elise. "*What?*"

Elise's face brightened a bit at Layla's tone. "Was my blood good?"

"Why do you want to know?" Layla asked. "If this is about feeding your superiority complex, I'm going to tell you it was disgusting."

Shock crossed Elise's features. The second a smile began to curve her lips, Layla knew she had made herself too obvious. She was practically transparent at this point, begging for Elise to see right through her and notice how her heart beat for the chance to cycle Elise's blood through her body again. "My blood was disgusting?" Elise asked, unconvinced.

"So disgusting. It was actually unbelievable," Layla said strongly. It was a lie. She wanted to wonder if Elise could see through it, but she feared that thinking about it too hard would give her away.

343

"You would never want to taste it again, would you?" Elise asked.

"No. Never. Not a day goes by where I don't think about how wrong you felt on my tongue and how you poisoned my mouth." If blood could intoxicate, drinking from Elise probably would have bewitched Layla. And in moments like these, when her veins closed up and breathing became hard because her senses felt so overwhelmed by her immediate surroundings, Layla wondered if she really had been bewitched by this Saint heiress.

It was like she transcended body and soul. Just as she tasted, like the dust between planets coated Layla's tongue, Elise Saint contained the whole universe in her when Layla felt her.

Layla wondered why Elise couldn't see that in herself.

Elise shrugged. "Fine. Next time, I'll let you starve." And just like that, the conversation was over. Elise turned and finally began to examine her part of the room. "Do you believe Stephen Wayne? Do you really think humans are being poisoned just by being close to reapers?" she asked.

"Sure, why not. The dancers here were sick. We saw them and the way they attacked Giana and Shirley. Theo spent time here as well and got sick and attacked your friend. It makes sense," Layla said.

"But what about me? I'm not sick."

Layla paused. "Sure, but you *are* different."

"Are you saying you've corrupted me?" Elise demanded.

"You're certainly becoming a little heathen when you're around me." Layla smirked. Heat bloomed across the Saint heiress's face and satisfaction swept through Layla at the sight.

"Everything I do around you is of my own volition. And as you've pointed out, I happen to have a lot of that because of my status. I take none of it for granted when I'm around you."

Layla hissed, "Ouch."

"I didn't mean it like that—" Elise sighed.

"Then how did you mean it?" Layla challenged.

A pause. And then, "I don't hate the time that we spend together. In fact, I look forward to it," Elise whispered.

Layla's breath caught. Elise stepped closer to her and her heart pounded so hard, her chest began to ache. "I've been awful to you," Layla murmured.

"I was worse." Elise's voice was breathy as she spoke. She reached forward, her hand brushing Layla's as she took the bullet. Instinctively, Layla curled her fingers around Elise's. It was as if a match had been struck up and then refused to burn out. Layla had no idea when her desire for Elise's blood had turned into a desire for Elise. But it carved into her now, her heart throbbing while she held Elise's hand and looked into her eyes. She wasn't sure why she ever tried to resist the Saint heiress. Her ice was desperately drawn to her heat. And the burn felt good, no matter how severe.

Elise cleared her throat, and Layla dropped her hand. She stood back as she watched the Saint heiress walk to the main performance hall, bullet clutched firmly in her grasp.

The most dangerous part of the Cotton Club might have been the stage. The wooden floor had a layer of dust so thick, one swipe of Layla's fingers on the edge turned her fingertips gray.

She knew how hard it was to dance on wood; Layla couldn't imagine having to do it in dim lights, and a tightly packed, hot environment such as the Cotton Club. And while the stage must have been cleaned frequently, no amount of water or rosin helped make it any less slippery. The dancers were at the mercy of the stage each night.

"Wow." Elise's voice echoed around the room. Her eyes crossed over every surface, every corner, her expression dimming as she took in the performance area. Murals on the ceiling were so faded, it was nearly impossible to make out the designs. Still, the room encompassed a feeling of general unease, one that Layla almost felt reverberating from Elise just by taking one look at the tight lines of her lips and jaw. Her hands remained close to her sides, as if she was afraid of touching anything in the room. But despite the obvious disgust in her eyes, she spoke with awe. "This is eerie," Elise muttered.

"Agreed," Layla said. Without thinking, Layla hauled herself onto the stage. The soles of her boots were slippery on the wood. But she could still imagine herself turning on this floor, over and over, her glittering skirts billowing around her like a cloud of magic. Once upon a time, it had been her dream to travel the world, dancing across stages of every country she could visit in a lifetime. But reaperhood had cut that dream short and quickly turned her life into a waking nightmare.

Now, Layla wasn't sure she could do more than a couple fouettés or pirouettes even though, five years ago, she had been able to do thirty-two fouettés and ten consecutive pirouettes. Her flexibility remained intact even after years without training, probably due to some gross mutation that occurred in reaperhood—flexibility wasn't a unique feat among the damned.

"Why didn't you ever dance here like Giana and Shirley?" Elise asked.

Layla faced the Saint heiress. She didn't have an explanation beyond the fact that it was risky to be around humans constantly as a reaper. When she was younger and didn't know how to control her urges as well, dancing among other humans was out of the question. By the time she matured and could stand to be around fresh blood without snapping, Layla had assumed her dream had passed her by.

A small animosity grew between her and Giana whenever she saw her in costume, ready to dance. But Layla did not want to risk it. She looked away, shoulders relaxing as she exhaled. "It didn't feel right," Layla said. "But I know you've been keeping up with your playing. The Saint princess is destined to tour the world playing the grand piano." A bit of bitterness seeped into her tone. She couldn't control the fraying of her patience when it came to talking about anything regarding her past. They had shared a childhood and music and dance tutor growing up, but only one of them got to see their dreams blossom. Elise consumed her past and so did Layla's broken dream of dancing abroad.

Elise fell quiet. Layla didn't face her, so she couldn't see what she was doing, but moments later, she heard Elise moving around the room. The sound of wood sliding into place and a seat being taken came next. Then the soft notes of a familiar song filled the room.

If it was possible for a damned heart to start again and ascend to the heavens, then Layla's might have in that moment. She did not face Elise, afraid for her to see the bareness of her face, the raw emotions she conveyed. But Layla fisted her hands when they began to shake. And, as if spurred on by some natural, uncontrollable force inside, Layla began to hum along to the song.

Flashes of her poring over the handwritten sheet music for hours slammed into her mind. Layla closed her eyes, and it was as if her eyelids were wallpapered over with the image of Elise playing. She had never heard Elise play the song, but Layla had learned it. As a dancer, she was required to study music and recognize notes. Layla knew the tune of the song by heart. She could have asked someone else to play it while she choreographed a dance to it, but she had wanted it to be a surprise for Elise and she had only ever wanted to hear the song from Elise; no one else.

The final measures of the song were slow and melancholy, the edges of the notes lifting to offer the sweetest bit of joy in such a tender moment. In Layla's mind, it was the perfect depiction of the gentle beats of love. Just barely concrete, but so overwhelmingly there, it was impossible to not be thoroughly and utterly wrecked by it.

When Layla finally turned to face Elise, she noticed the tears cresting in her eyes. And in only a moment, Layla's eyes were growing damp as well. She had finally heard Elise play her song. After five years.

Elise swallowed. "Does that sound like the music of a prodigy, destined for the Paris Conservatory?" Elise asked in a voice so small, Layla waited in pain to hear it break. "Because I'm no expert. But I know I'm certainly unfit to be granted such a coveted position."

Layla's lips parted. "It was perfect." She didn't stop the awe that seeped into her tone.

Elise's eyes flickered up to hers, as if checking for any sign of a lie. "You couldn't possibly know that."

Layla knew the song from top to bottom; she knew Elise's playing and musical tendencies like she knew the back of her hand. She knew how Elise chewed on her lip while passing through a particularly difficult part of the music, she knew how Elise's fingers tensed up when she wanted to play, but couldn't, and she knew how lost she got in the music when she fell in love with the notes and they fell madly in love with her back. Because how could anyone not love Elise Saint?

A painful lump rose in Layla's throat then. "You didn't finish the song."

Elise narrowed her eyes at Layla. "How do you know—" Her face went ashen. "You..."

The lump twisted and Layla's chest constricted as she came to a full realization. Elise had played that song because she thought no one knew it. She thought she could get away with making mistakes because no one would be able to call her out on them. But Layla knew that song. And even if she had stumbled over a few notes here and there, it was perfect because it was Elise. Every note, composed from her brain, by her heart. It was so wonderfully, maddeningly Elise. And she had mapped her heart out so precariously in this song, she had not wanted to show it to anyone.

"How do you know it, *Layla*?" Elise stood then. The tears in her eyes were no longer that of an overwhelmed, exhausted young girl, but they were angry, storm-filled clouds, threatening to burst at the slightest provocation. "Tell me."

"Layla's Night." Layla whispered the title of the piece, as if it were a spell that could break either one of them if spoken too roughly. "You wrote it for me. I found the sheet music years ago and choreographed a dance to it to surprise you before I turned..." *The song has haunted me for years.*

Elise scoffed. "I didn't write it *for* you." The dismissal in her tone might have cleaved Layla's heart in half. But when she spoke again, her voice was softer, although still heavily on guard. "I wrote it *about* you. There's a difference."

Layla's eyelids fluttered. The difference was lost on her. As far as Layla was concerned, Elise Saint had poured her heart out into a composition about Layla, meant for Layla, centered on Layla. She looked Elise right in the eye, past all the self-doubt and the hatred and the dark depths of her disdain. "It was perfect."

"You're a liar and a thief," Elise seethed.

The words stung. Layla's hand twitched by her side and, looking down, she saw Elise's fingers clenched into tight fists. They glimmered in the faint light, as if she held a flickering ember against her palm. But minutes later, as Layla left the room, wiping the dust from her fingertips, she realized it was just crushed glass.

Another illusion beneath all the dust.

33

DOCUMENTS IN HAND, ELISE BURST INTO HER father's study. She had run all the way home from the Cotton Club in a torrential downpour that had not deterred her one bit. After her argument with Layla, she had torn through the club's management office until she had calmed down. Eventually she'd found records that showed a connection between one of the gangs and Dr. Harding's lab. So when her father glanced up at her from his desk with an irritated scowl, she did not hold back.

"Do you know what was going on in the Cotton Club?" Elise asked, breathing hard while she slammed the now-damp contract on her father's desk.

He glared at her sopping form. "Heavens above, Elise, you are making a mess."

"And you might be making an even bigger mess by working with someone who is distributing reaper venom to criminals," Elise said strongly.

Mr. Saint snatched the pages from her. He studied them for a long moment, jaw tight while his eyes moved back and forth. Finally, he set the papers down and his glare deepened. "This arrangement is old. And the Diamond Dealers are dead."

"But this indicates that Dr. Harding lied about turning down the offers to sell reaper venom—"

"Sometimes bending the truth is necessary—"

"You're not listening to me."

"I always listen—"

"Dr. Harding's medical license was revoked!" Elise screamed. She breathed hard as her father stared at her with startled eyes. "He's practicing illegally." Moments passed, and when he still did not speak, she continued, voice shaky and quiet. "You shut out Thalia's mother for creating a failed cure. You should cut off Dr. Harding for lying about his medical certification."

Mr. Saint moved slowly through the room, going to sit at his desk while he looked at his watch.

"Father—" Elise started.

"That's enough, Elise. You're dismissed. We can talk later," he said sternly.

Elise's shoulders slumped. She stared in bewilderment at her father, but he was unmoved. Swallowing down her frustration, Elise stormed out of the room and slammed the door after herself.

The glass shards dug into her flesh as Layla scrubbed at her hands in Jamie's kitchen sink. She started to get aggravated when her skin began to peel and tiny glass flakes still clung to her fingertips.

"You're running up my water bill," Jamie huffed as he emerged from his bedroom. Hendricks trotted after him, nose high in the air, tail swishing with what Layla knew was malice.

Layla turned the water off and faced Jamie. He looked tired, blond hair damp from a shower, eyes a bit glazed over. But still, he scowled at Layla and the water she had splashed on the counter. "You're a menace." He slumped onto the couch and picked up the crossword puzzle Layla had left there earlier. The scowl slowly melted away as he read her thank-you message. A small smile graced his lips and even though Layla hated that surge of warm softness that flooded her because it meant she was cracking beneath his whims, she was glad to have a distraction from her complex feelings surrounding Elise.

Layla would have rather spent hours scrubbing her hands in the sink until they were raw as long as it meant she did not need to confront her feelings for the Saint heiress. But there she was, hands wet and raw, specks of blood and glass still stuck to her, and Elise still on her mind.

"Why do you look so peeved? I thought you had some kind of breakthrough," Jamie asked.

Layla moved toward the couch. She gingerly sat on the only available cushion that just happened to be beside a sleeping Hendricks. He lifted his head as she sank onto the seat, green eyes narrowing on her. Layla shot him a quick glare, then focused back on Jamie. "Not quite. The Saint heiress and I ran into a problem at the club."

Jamie's eyes widened with curiosity. "What? More gangsters? Most of my guys don't have stable homes; they are probably just staying there until they find a place."

Layla shook her head. "No…" She realized now just how stupid it would sound if she mentioned getting sidetracked because of the tension that had risen between her and Elise. But frankly, who was Jamie to judge her when he thought *Vex* was a good name for a gangster? She sighed. "The problem is the Saint girl. And me. We just don't work well together."

"Obviously. But that can't be it." Jamie folded the crossword puzzle and turned to her. "I think you hold yourself back a lot. I don't understand that. What are you afraid of? You've already lost everything."

His words hurt. Layla looked away for a moment, throat burning with unshed tears. She forced her emotions back down and swallowed before she looked at him again. "I know I should work past everything to get to the bottom of this so I can get the cure, but you have no idea what it's like to have to constantly be around the ghost of the most traumatic moment of your life. When I'm around her, it's like pouring alcohol on an open wound."

"Ah, but you open yourself up to be healed eventually. It's all part of the process," Jamie said gently. He stroked a hand down Hendrick's back, and the damn cat purred. His eyes closed, head craning back, purrs traveling through his body and to the couch, where Layla felt them vibrating through her cushion.

She bit into her bottom lip. "I don't want to talk about this anymore. Tell me about the Cotton Club. Do you really think it's bound to reopen?"

Jamie snorted. "Doubtful. The owner is not even in the city."

Layla frowned. "No?"

"He was so upset about the incident with the reapers and the dancers, he had to fly off to Europe to spend time with his other, more successful, less liable club." Jamie laughed softly. "His words, not mine. He's really pissed off Stephen Wayne, actually."

"Why Stephen?"

"They're in business together. Why do you think Wayne had posters for his lab all over the club? He approached me to be a product supplier for Calhoun initially, but I was already too busy with the speakeasy. So Stephen went with the Diamond Dealers." Jamie gaped. "And now they're dead. Thank God I listened to my gut."

Layla paused, thoughts spinning in her mind. "Do you try the liquor that you get?"

Jamie almost laughed. "To make sure it's good? Hell no. These people are so desperate for a fix, they would drink bleach."

"What if it was? I mean, there's been so much death surrounding the Cotton Club, you never stopped to think something was off with your supply? The Saint heiress told me Stephen might have enemies—"

Jamie's eyes darkened and his expression fell. "Are you accusing me of something, Quinn?"

"No. But maybe someone used you as a cover to hide their own illegal activities. And that same person probably killed Theo Smith and those Saints." Layla sighed. "It's only a matter of time before more people die."

Jamie stared at her for a while. "Your mind always goes to violence. You are so violent. All the time. Does it ever get tiring?"

"No."

Hendricks let out a low meow. Jamie grinned. "I know, she's crazy."

"Says the man talking to a cat. Who you call your 'son.'" Layla teased. She could still remember the shock of finding out that Jamie's "son" was not a human child. Layla had laughed on the couch for five minutes straight when she first met Hendricks—before he made an enemy out of her. She was glad for the break in tension now, a welcome relief from the day's stressors. Tenderly, Layla reached a hand out to pet Hendricks, but Jamie shook his head.

"Let him smell you first," he said.

So Layla did. Or she tried. Her hand hovered in front of Hendricks's face for one second before his eyes shot open. But to Layla's surprise, he did not hiss. He lapped at her fingers with his tongue for a few moments, no aggression in sight. Layla huffed. "Wow, Hendricks, you *can* be nice—"

Hendricks, as if turned on by a switch, suddenly lunged for her hand. Yowling, he clamped down on her fingers and drew blood. Layla snatched her hand back right as Jamie pulled Hendricks onto his lap.

"Never again," Layla muttered, rubbing her blood off onto her pants.

Jamie stared. "I have never seen him so angry before. That was beyond anger; it was pure warfare."

Layla only rolled her eyes and left the room.

Elise's father called her to his study hours after her initial confrontation. She stepped into the room cautiously, her eyes landing on her father behind his desk.

Mr. Saint said nothing, just watched her settle in front of him.

His silence frightened her and Elise scrambled to say something before he exploded, "Father, I want to apologize—"

But he lifted his hand and gestured to the door, which swung open. In stepped Mr. Wayne and Dr. Harding. The latter looked exhausted as usual, dark purple smudges beneath his sunk-in eyes. He slumped a bit after Mr. Wayne, whose bright smile dimmed when he noticed the room's waning atmosphere. "Has our meeting been moved?" he asked.

Mr. Saint shook his head. "No. You're right on time. It's been brought to my attention, though, that Dr. Harding here is no real doctor," he said darkly.

Elise felt the storm of her father's wrath starting to close around the room. She pressed herself against the wall, lips tight.

Stephen Wayne glanced down at his colleague, astounded. "What is he talking about?"

Dr. Harding's eyes darkened. "There is something terrible

spreading among reapers and humans, and I only wanted a chance to stop it before they could destroy our city—"

"You're not a real doctor?" Stephen Wayne demanded.

"Listen to me. The poison is still out there—"

"I think the only poison is you." Mr. Saint gestured to the door and two Saint members walked in, immediately restraining the doctor between them.

"No. Wait! *You don't understand…*" The rest of Dr. Harding's words trailed off as the Saint members dragged him from the room.

Silence cloaked Tobias Saint's office. Elise stepped away from the wall and faced him, guilt already flooding her upon seeing the sudden exhaustion etched into her father's face.

"We will not go public with this. It would only humiliate us further," Mr. Saint said.

Mr. Wayne nodded. "Of course. My deepest apologies, Tobias. He had me completely fooled."

"He used a fake identity," Elise whispered.

Mr. Saint stood, sticking a cigar into his mouth. He cleared his throat. "No more mistakes. We must move forward. Do you stand with this empire, Elise?"

Tightness constricted her chest and her breathing faltered, but Elise remained tall, her jaw clenched to keep her panic from exploding. "I do."

Sighing, her father tore his gaze away from her.

"Perfect." Mr. Wayne clasped his hands together. "Elise, I need you tomorrow. We will still deliver the cure to the Harlem clan, and

Layla will be our first subject to demonstrate to the rest of the reapers that our cure is perfectly safe. There's bound to be mistrust. But if you offer a bargain first, there will be significantly less tension." He raised an eyebrow, expectant. "Are you with me, Elise?"

Elise shared a look with her father, who only gave her a firm nod. She looked back at Mr. Wayne and reached forward to shake his hand. "I'm with you."

34

A MIRACLE WAS TAKING PLACE IN JAMIE'S TINY apartment just past midnight. Layla, being the bigger person, had gotten over Hendricks's early assault on her. So when Jamie retired for the night and Hendricks did not follow him to his bed, Layla remained on the couch with him. Her blood had barely dried in his fur and he now sat so close to her, his fur brushed her leg whenever he breathed deeply in his sleep.

Now, Hendricks twisted onto his back, belly exposed, fully snuggling against Layla's leg. Layla stiffened at first. Then when he started to purr, she relaxed. *Okay.* She thought, setting her book down so her hands were free. *Let's settle this right now.*

The second Layla moved into place to pet him, Hendricks's eyes flew open. They focused on her, the green luminescent in the moonlight coming through the window beside the couch. But he did not move away from her, nor did he hiss.

She reached down to let him sniff her hand. He gave her one sniff. And then the unthinkable happened. Hendricks rubbed his face against her knuckles. He wriggled on the couch to get closer to her, his purrs increasing.

Excitement spread through Layla like a drug. She grinned while Hendricks continued to purr and she returned his affection with gentle pets on his head and scratches behind his ears. Layla laughed to herself. This stupid little cat was the cause of the most joy she had experienced in weeks.

She opened her mouth to say something to the cat, and was interrupted by glass shattering. Hendricks leapt to his feet and hissed, beelining for Jamie's bedroom. Layla stood, alarmed. She immediately noticed the rock on the rug among the scattered glass and the hole in the window.

Layla stepped over the glass and looked outside, expecting to scold a neighborhood kid for breaking windows. Shock stole her intended insults right from her mouth when she saw Elise Saint standing below the window, in a golden circle of streetlight.

"Can you please come down here?" she called.

"Are you insane?" Layla shrieked. "Why didn't you knock like a normal person?"

Elise glared up at her. "Funny how I ask you that constantly, yet you don't know the answer all of a sudden. Get down here."

"You're so demanding," Layla hissed.

"Should I throw another rock?" Elise taunted her.

"Give me a minute." Layla backed away from the window and

winced when she saw Jamie emerging from his bedroom, his eyes on the glass covering the floor. "What the hell happened?" Jamie asked.

Layla stuffed her feet into her shoes and grumbled. "Some idiot threw a rock through your window. Don't worry, she'll pay for it." Layla pushed past a perplexed Jamie. She stormed down the stairs so fast, she realized she had no idea what to say to Elise when she came face-to-face with her in the courtyard.

Rain plastered Elise's curls to her head and her cheeks were wet, eyes red. She was breathing hard, but when she spoke, her voice was level. "Thank you. Can we please talk?"

Layla crossed her arms. "This couldn't wait until tomorrow?"

"No. Because tomorrow is when everything changes, and I need your help to make sure it doesn't." Elise pulled a paper from her coat and thrust it toward Layla. "I think Stephen Wayne is responsible for the reaper incident at the Cotton Club. He used gangsters to distribute his products to Calhoun and they died. Theo and the dancers followed soon after. He's been selling reaper venom and now he's trying to cover his tracks."

"Stephen Wayne didn't kill the Dealers. Mei did," Layla said quietly. She took the papers, but didn't look at them. She remained focused on the Saint heiress and just how undone she looked. It wasn't just the rain and her soaked clothes; there was a frayed look in her eyes, like she was on the verge of falling into the great unknown. "Why are you here?" Layla asked. She was sure Elise would bring up that day at the Cotton Club.

"Stephen Wayne is coming to your lair tomorrow to offer your clan a cure for reaperhood," Elise said instead. "I don't think you should take it."

The mix of disappointment and hope Elise's words stirred in Layla was the most confusing thing she might have ever experienced. Disappointment from Elise not acknowledging the pain that she had caused her the other day, hope aligned with her desire to be cured—Layla wasn't sure what she should have clung on to more.

Her instinct chose for her. "You can't help yourself, can you? I've had everything taken from me because of you and now you want more," Layla said coldly. "Why are you still so hell-bent on trying to ruin everything for me? Was it not enough when I had to watch my parents die? And then when you left me alone to be preyed on by reapers?" Layla's voice shook so hard she had to stop to take a breath and steady herself. Even after that, her emotions remained unstable. She stepped forward, coming out of the shelter of the building and into the downpour of rain. "Do you have any idea how cruel this is? Making me relive this all over again? You weren't just my best friend, Saint, you were my best person, my best everything. And you threw that away for what? To impress your father?"

"No," Elise ground out. Her lips were pale. Layla couldn't tell if it was from the cold, or her nerves, but she told herself she didn't care; she couldn't. Not while she was so close to getting what she wanted, with Elise being the only thing that stood in her way.

"Bullshit," Layla snapped. "Everything you do is for him. You're so blinded by your need to please him that you can't see how sick and twisted he is. I told you in confidence about my parents' plan to meet with Valeriya to finally have some peace in Harlem, and you violated that trust. Your father watched me bleed out after the rogue reapers left and he cruelly let me know that you were the one who told him about my parents' plans. He said it was *you* who begged him to find a way to stop my parents. And he spread the lie that my parents were going to eliminate Valeriya's clan. He had the reapers kill them because he cannot stand not being in control. And you had to tell him my family's secret because you cannot stand not being Tobias's pride and joy. You can't see how he hurts everyone, including you. Why do you break yourself for him every day? Why did you kill me for him?" Layla demanded.

She was crying now. Tears rushed down her cheeks like a river funneling through a crack in a dam. She couldn't stop the hurt coursing through her no matter how much she willed her heart to seal itself up. As intensely as she felt the rain pouring down her neck and into her shoes, she felt her heart breaking open again. Layla choked on her sobs when Elise said nothing. "You can't even answer me? Five years after you left me to die, you won't even give me the satisfaction of telling me why?"

Elise's expression hardened then, as if Layla had struck a chord. "You know why," she declared.

"No. I don't," Layla said through gritted teeth.

"I wrote it in every goddamn note I put in the song I composed for you. Which I know you stole. By the way," Elise said.

Layla scoffed. Her throat burned from her tears, but she raised her voice anyway. "You want to talk about music right now? Really?" she nearly shouted.

"Yes. Because it's the only way I know how to express myself anymore," Elise yelled back. She stepped toward Layla until they were close enough that she could see the rising haze of ire covering her eyes. "You know what? You are right. I *am* blinded by my father. I did make a lot of mistakes in the past because of him. His fear after Charlotte died took over my life. It's why I told him to stop your parents because I didn't want them hurt by reapers too. He controlled a lot of me and my decisions, but the one thing he didn't control were my feelings for you."

Elise's voice broke as she continued. "I forced myself to hate you for so long. I tried to hate myself, thinking because you're such an integral part of me, maybe I should start picking myself apart piece by piece to get you out of my system. But nothing worked. I went halfway around the world and I still felt you in me. I felt you under all of my pain and I told myself it was better to hurt than to feel for you because my father sent me letters every day, cursing your name. I lost you. I couldn't lose him too." Elise sniffed.

Layla was unconvinced. The emotion in Elise's voice was raw, but that didn't change the fact that her own hard edges and the emptiness in her soul were because of her. She deepened her glare. "How dare you talk about loss. You had everything—you still do. Yet somehow, you have managed to pin this on me. How in the world are your feelings toward me my fault—"

"*Because I fell in love with you!*" Elise exploded.

Layla went still. If it was possible for time to stop, it would have in this moment. The rain seemed to fall more slowly around them, the air dropping several degrees. Layla willed herself to look away from the bright pain in Elise's eyes, not wanting to fall into them, fall into her, but she couldn't.

Elise wept. "I didn't mean to hurt you. I was worried for you when your parents wanted to work with the reapers. I thought my father would convince them not to—he told me he would keep you safe. He lied to me. I didn't want you to die." Her voice broke and her sobs intensified. "Do you have any idea how hard it is to continue on with life when the person you love tried to kill you, but you *still* love them? You tried to rip my heart from my chest, but you've already had my heart; it's always been yours—"

"Shut up," Layla whispered. Her voice sounded unlike her own. She wasn't even sure if she was still existing. Her body was numb to the rain, numb to the cold, numb to Elise's storm of emotions.

"Don't tell me to shut up. I've been sick without you for years. I'm going to say whatever the hell I want—" Elise tried to step toward Layla, but Layla backed away, stumbling a bit. Elise's expression fell. "Layla—"

"Stop talking, Saint." They were the only words Layla could get out before she started running.

35

AYLA RAN SO FAST, RAIN MISTED AROUND HER. Her feet slipped on the soaked ground, but she kept going, not stopping until she made it to her destination. A place she hadn't been in years, the empty clearing shocked her enough to vanish Elise from Layla's mind, even if it was just for a few moments.

Layla considered this part of Central Park forbidden. She refused to return to the place where she had died, the place where she watched her parents die. She couldn't believe how much of it looked the same—the hill sloping down to the Harlem Meer, a river that mirrored Layla's greatest nightmare right back at her. She still remembered her hand clutching the snow while life trickled out of her, her parents' blood staining the brilliant white a scarlet so deep, she wondered if it had soaked all the way through to the earth beneath the ice. The moon's reflection on the water shone back at her, and when Layla opened her eyes one last time, she saw herself, bloody and battered.

Reaper venom already had a hold on her system then, and even through the shimmering reflection she could see the blackness spreading across her eyes while the venom changed her body.

Now, Layla collapsed onto the ground, breathing so hard, her ribs ached. Her fingers dug into the damp earth, and she released a shattering scream. Everything rose to the surface at that moment. Years of unresolved trauma, the feelings she had buried since being betrayed, the grief for her parents and her own lost life that she had never fully processed.

This had been the first place Layla had thought to come to because if there was anything that could snap her out of that damned Saint's cyclic manipulation, it was the place that shifted her entire existence. But now, Layla feared she was just breaking herself over and over. And just like five years ago, there was no help on the horizon.

Layla dropped her face into her hands and wept.

36

EVEN IN THE SOFT LIGHT OF EARLY MORNING, SHAD-
ows still seemed to encroach on every corner and edge of the
Harlem territory. As expected, several reapers were waiting
to intercept the Saints before they even made it to the front door of
the Clarice.

Mr. Wayne held his hands up. "We are here for Layla Quinn. She
has an agreement with Elise Saint," he said coolly.

Even just hearing her name made a painful shudder pass through
Elise. It was over. In an attempt to get Layla to see the truth, Elise had
done the one thing she promised herself she would never do. But
confessing her forbidden love for her old friend had destroyed her
instead. Every part of her felt like a shard of broken glass. Only the
sadness that echoed through her gave her any semblance of comfort
because of its familiarity.

She swallowed hard and stared ahead. The reapers standing in front of them were not familiar to her, but they nodded along with Mr. Wayne's words. One of them beamed, his fangs peeking out. "Come inside."

Everything in Elise screamed at her to turn back, to not follow the reapers into their lair, but her feet moved her forward and she walked inside with her father and Sterling by her side. They had been together all morning, but Sterling had yet to speak to her. He would barely even look at her. Elise tried not to let this get to her, but her heart hurt at the thought of being near her best friend, but still far from him.

Once the darkness cleared in the hotel foyer, Elise's eyes found her first.

Layla stood directly in her line of sight, but she refused to even look at her. Elise wanted to snap at her, she wanted to force her eyes onto her—she would let the reapers attack her if it meant Layla would pay her any attention at all. But she was stuck, a hopelessly yearning soul with nothing to pour her affection into.

"As I'm sure you all are aware, Elise Saint has worked with Layla Quinn for some time to uncover the darkness that's spreading through this city," Mr. Wayne began. At the mention of their names, Layla finally stirred, her gaze flickering once to Elise. But then she was focusing on Mr. Wayne again. Elise felt her heart wrench. "I am hopeful that their partnership has shown you all that we can coexist peacefully. And I have come to demonstrate the first part of my plan to unite us as a community." Mr. Wayne reached into his pocket and pulled out a vial of dark purple fluid. "This is a cure for reaperhood."

The entire room began to murmur. Reapers shifted, whispering to each other with wide eyes, some more doubtful than others. Many looked to Layla, who remained stone-faced and scowling while they whispered about her.

"Layla." Mr. Wayne looked right at her. "If you would do the honors of being the first to receive the dose—"

"No," Elise said sharply.

Mr. Wayne gave her a strange look. "Elise—"

"I said no." She glared up at him until he actually backed down. Mr. Wayne muttered something beneath his breath, but before Elise could try to decipher his words, another reaper was stepping forward.

"I'll do it. I'll go first." It was Mei. She tried to move closer, but Layla stopped her, gripping her wrist so hard, Mei grimaced. "What?"

Layla loosened her hold on her and whispered something inaudible. Mei shot her a dirty look. She yanked her arm free and closed the distance between her and Mr. Wayne. "I'm ready."

A satisfied smile spread across Mr. Wayne's face. "This is certainly not the outcome I was expecting. But it's a great first step, nonetheless." His eyes shifted between Layla and Mei. "One at a time, then. It's not recommended that another reaper watches the procedure. The sudden surge of fresh human blood might trigger—"

"I can control myself," Layla said roughly. She stepped closer to Mei. "I'm staying with her."

Mr. Wayne nodded. "At your risk, I suppose. We will do it upstairs."

Elise's skin prickled at his calculating tone. She wanted to say something else, but Mr. Saint curved his hand over her shoulder. "I want you to wait outside with Sterling," he ordered.

"But, Father—"

His fingers dug into her shoulder so hard, all she could do was bite her lip to stifle her wince. "Now, Elise," he snapped.

Layla's eyes slid to Elise very briefly. But before Elise could even register it, she was turning and heading out of the hotel. Sterling trailed behind her. Various thoughts crashed through her mind while they waited. The image of her father and Mr. Wayne closing in on the clan would not leave her mind, no matter how many other feelings arose in her. It was already a lot to process the instinctual feeling to protect a reaper who hated her and it was even more to process the instinctual feeling that her own father posed a threat.

Elise looked up, watching as growing storm clouds stamped out the light.

37

LAYLA COULDN'T TELL IF MEI LOOKED PALE BECAUSE of the unflattering hotel lights or her nerves. She sat on a velvet chair in an empty room upstairs, legs swinging back and forth. In the few minutes that they had been waiting for Stephen Wayne and Tobias Saint to ready the cure after leaving the rest of their clan in the lobby, none of them had said much.

Mei let out a shaky breath, and she pulled her knees up to her chest. "I don't know why I'm so nervous. I've dreamed of this for years." She sighed sadly. "That and seeing my family again were the only two things I ever wanted."

A gentle warmth filled Layla's heart. But it was quickly dashed by the overwhelming apprehension she had been feeling in deciding to trust the Saints. She stood, moving closer to Mei. "You'll be okay."

"Do you really believe that?" Mei asked. When her voice trembled, Layla couldn't take it. She lifted her wrist to her mouth and sank her teeth into her vein. Layla offered her blood to Mei, who took it without hesitation. She drank until she no longer trembled, Layla's blood granting her soothing effects immediately.

Layla sighed as Mei released her and leaned her face into Layla's palm. Her eyes glazed over with a subdued look, dull and unfocused while she exhaled. After a few moments, Mei finally looked up at Layla, eyes slightly teary. "Thank you for being mine when I had no one else," she whispered.

Something in Layla's chest squeezed. She stroked her thumb over Mei's cheek. "Of course."

Finally, the men returned; Stephen Wayne carried with him a syringe and vial of the cure. Layla moved back to give them some space, but Mei kept a firm grasp on her hand.

Tobias Saint stared down at their intertwined hands with the ghost of a smile gracing his lips. "Imagine if you were afraid of needles. That would be rather ironic," he said, chuckling.

Layla's hand tightened around Mei's, and she glared at the white man while he plunged the needle into the vial.

"How odd that your clan leader is not here to witness such a momentous occasion," Tobias Saint said softly.

Layla averted her eyes. Mei shrugged. No one knew where Valeriya was. She had left without a word before Layla returned.

Mr. Wayne gestured to Mei with his free hand. "I will need to inject you in the throat. If you do not mind moving your hair back."

Mei trembled. She pulled her hand back from Layla and moved her hair behind her shoulder so her neck was exposed.

Cool air hit Layla's hand and she closed her fist around emptiness.

Watching Mei bare herself to this man stirred more than just discomfort. Chills covered her own neck and she began to wonder whether Elise had been right—if Layla had been wrong to be so trusting of something that had to be beyond her wildest dreams.

"Wait," Layla said quickly. Everyone looked up at her with expectant eyes. She swallowed, lips pursing. "Will it hurt her?"

Stephen Wayne lifted a brow. "As much as it hurt when she first turned." Without another hesitation, he sank the needle into Mei's throat. Layla watched, waiting to sense any immediate change in her clanmate. But besides the slight twitch of her eyes and sharp intake of breath, Mei wasn't yet showing a reaction to the shot. Stephen Wayne moved away from her and faced Tobias Saint, mouth opening like he wanted to say something. But then another Saint member stepped into the foyer.

"Sir. You have a call outside. Both of you are needed," he said to the men.

Mr. Wayne nodded. "The cure will take a few minutes to start working," he announced to the room.

Mr. Saint stole a final glance at Layla, then followed Stephen Wayne out of the room.

Layla dropped her hand to Mei's shoulder and said gently, "How are you feeling?"

Mei shrugged. "I feel fine…I feel…normal." She sounded disappointed. "What if this is all just a hoax?" she asked.

"Then we expose the Saints and Stephen Wayne for being dirty liars and bring their empire down," Layla muttered fiercely.

An amused laugh bubbled out of Mei and a tentative smile returned to her face. "I've always loved your ambition." Layla was about to return the smile, but Mei stopped suddenly, her hand going to her chest while she gasped.

"What is it?" Layla demanded as Mei slipped from the chair and crumpled to the floor. She was paler now, her face so white, she looked translucent. Her veins bulged blue beneath her skin and her eyes bled. Mei gasped for air, fingers clawing at her throat.

"*Mei*—" Layla tried to steady Mei's writhing, but the girl was too far gone. She let her go and sank her teeth into her wrist, determined to shove her blood down Mei's throat if she needed to. But by the time Layla reached forward to open Mei's mouth, Mei had gone still. Blood dripped down Layla's hand, but she ignored it, leaning closer to Mei as she assessed her.

Mei heaved a deep breath and sat up so fast, she almost knocked Layla over. She felt her face, which had brightened, her paleness diminished. A rosy color painted her cheeks, and her eyes no longer contained the unnatural reaper glow. "Oh my God," Mei whispered. Her body convulsed and for a moment, Layla thought she would start panicking again. But she didn't. Mei laughed with delight. Wonder pierced her tone as she beheld her brand-new liveliness, examining her hands first, then feeling her face again, and when she gave Layla a full smile, Layla finally saw the depths of her humanity. No enlarged fangs sat in her mouth. Layla even sensed the steady rush of a normal human pulse. She had seen this before. Her heart jolted with the memory of Nellie, that unlucky reaper turned human who had died beneath the weight of the chandelier so many nights ago.

"It worked," Mei gasped. She erupted into joyful laughter as she stood up. "Layla, *it worked!*" Mei pulled her into a tight hug. The glorious humanity was overpowering, but Layla accepted her embrace, burying her face in Mei's neck while she cried. The scent of her human blood stuck in her throat, making Layla's eyes sting with tears of envy and her muscles tense with restraint. She rubbed the other girl's back and held her until her tears stopped. "I never thought I would feel this way ever again." Mei pulled back, wiping at her eyes.

A twinge of jealousy struck Layla. For so long, she had dreamed of waking up in her human body, but never once had she believed it was possible. Until now. Layla squeezed Mei's hand and smiled tightly. "You're glowing." She pushed Mei toward the mirror by the double doors so she could look at herself.

"Wow." Mei cupped her chin. Her smile never wavered while she took in her new human features.

Layla watched her for a moment. Envy bit at her so hard, she clenched her jaw to keep a neutral face and swallowed past the bitter taste in her mouth. "Too bad Valeriya isn't here to see this," she muttered.

Mei shuddered. At first Layla thought it was because of the mention of their absent clan leader. But then she saw Mei frowning at her own reflection. A bright red drop of blood trickled from her nose. Without thinking, Layla reached forward and wiped the blood from her friend's face. The scent was one thing, but the feeling of the fresh human blood on her own skin made Layla's nerves spark with fire. She trembled slightly, her hands growing blurry while her cravings rose to the surface and crowded her vision with the urge to devour blood.

"*Layla.*" Mei's voice was sharp.

"Mei…" Layla said slowly. Something was wrong. A new scent filled the air, souring all of Mei's beautiful humanity from before. Now, an acrid scent of decay arose and it spilled from Mei. Layla's fangs emerged and her shoulders went rigid. With each breath, her consciousness slipped further and further away from her. Black and red spots covered her vision and blood rushed in her ears until Mei was barely a shadow before her, her voice a futile echo of terror.

Then she pitched forward and fell into an abyss of darkness.

38

THE SCENT OF FRESH BLOOD GREETED LAYLA WHEN she woke up. She sat up, head pounding, and opened her eyes. It was as if a massacre had unfolded in the lair. Blood coated every wall and even splattered on the ceiling. Layla tried to stand, but she slipped, her hands covered in blood, her body surrounded by a large puddle of it.

The blood was not what shocked Layla. She had woken up to bloodbaths countless times before she got a handle on her reaper-hood when she was younger. What drew unease across her skin like a serrated blade was the body lying beside her.

Her friend. Dead.

Mei stared up at the ceiling with glassy eyes. Blood poured over her shirtfront and skirt, still dripping from the gaping wound in her throat. Even in death, Layla could smell the humanity on her.

The last thing she remembered was Mei's nose bleeding right

after the cure had begun to work. Everything went fuzzy after that, memories showing up in her mind as nameless blood-soaked screams and cries for help. Layla couldn't believe that anything had gone this wrong. Even though she could taste the metallic tang of blood in her mouth and felt the torn, bloody flesh beneath her nails.

She pulled her knees up to her chest and tried to steady her shallow breathing as the blood pooling around her soaked into her pants. No matter how hard she tried to convince herself that it could not have been her, the blame continued to wear her name.

The door opened and Mr. Saint and Mr. Wayne entered the room. Neither of them looked shocked to see the blood everywhere. They took in the soaked walls, noses wrinkling at the stench.

One more slip and she might end up killing them too. Then what would happen to the treaty? It would go unwritten, the cure would be revoked, and Layla would have ruined countless lives for her clan mates and reapers beyond.

Stephen Wayne let out a low whistle while he approached Layla in her mess of blood. "Oh, Miss Quinn…"

A scoff left Mr. Saint's mouth and he came to stand beside his colleague, a satisfied smirk on his face. "Look what you've done, Layla. Just as Theo Smith's death is on you, so is your friend's. Mr. Wayne tried to warn you, but your arrogance clouded your judgment. You've never had control over your reaper instincts, and no reaper ever will. Now you can live with this shame," he snapped.

Layla finally looked up at them. Her body trembled and when

she spoke, her voice was small. "No. I want the cure. I can't…I can't live like this anymore," she whispered.

Layla waited for him to shake his head and refuse to help her. She had spent so long in the shadow of death, waiting for life to crush her and finally force her to choose the latter option because a reaper had nowhere to go but to hell in the end, but now, the person she least expected to, was offering her a hand up. Now, Layla might have had a chance at life. And she had no one to thank but the very man who had ruined her in the first place.

Nothing about reaperhood was natural, or right. She would have to be a fool to refuse a chance at restarting her life. So when Stephen Wayne reached for her, she took his hand and let him pull her to her feet.

A storm had broken out over New York. The darkest clouds loomed above the Saint territory and hung lower than the ones encroaching on the rest of the city. Even over the hotel, the sky remained relatively clear, though a thick mist had begun to form around Elise and Sterling—who still refused to speak to her.

"Sterling. Please talk to me," Elise said.

He turned by the doors to the hotel, but didn't face her. "Your father says you are not to be trusted."

Elise blinked. "Pardon me—"

Finally, Sterling turned around. Shadows covered his eyes and he met her gaze with only cool resentment. "He believes you're headed down the wrong path. I'm afraid of the choices you'll make, and I won't go down this path with you." He faced the door again.

Her heart might have broken in half, but Elise refused to give him the satisfaction of knowing that his words hit her exactly where he intended to hurt her. She pursed her lips and was thankful when the door swung open and Mr. Wayne and her father emerged.

"I'm afraid there's been an incident," Mr. Saint said. He pushed the door open wider, revealing Layla, who sat, soaked in blood, in the entryway.

"*What the hell*," Elise almost shrieked when she saw Layla. Blood covered so much of her body, Elise couldn't even remember the original color of her clothes. She stepped in front of Layla and reached for her, but her father slapped her hands away.

"Do not touch her," he said firmly.

Elise didn't even look at him. Her attention remained, alarmed and concerned, on Layla, who couldn't seem to focus on her. Her brown eyes were glazed over and she stared right through Elise. "What did you do to her?" She looked past Layla and down the hallway, expecting to see Mei, but it was empty. "Where is Mei?" Elise demanded. She glared at her father.

"Your darling reaper friend killed her," her father said strongly. He pushed Elise back so hard, she stumbled. "Do not try to defend her. I know where your loyalties lie now. I was a fool to believe you would ever do anything good for this family. You've never gotten over whatever infatuation you have for her and all that she represents."

Air seared Elise's chest and throat as she struggled to breathe. "No." Her eyes flickered down to Layla, hoping and begging for some sign of that usual fire she had in her. But the young reaper's eyes remained dull and lifeless, as if her flame had been snuffed out. Elise looked to her father once more. "You're the one in the wrong. You have been wrong for years. You just cannot stand it when anyone challenges you. So when Genevieve and Daniel Quinn suggested working with the reapers all those years ago, you snapped. You're not interested in relinquishing power and sharing anything. You're built on lies. Just like this *cure*." Elise pushed her hands into her father's chest. He hardly shifted under her shove.

Her father's hand gripped her wrist. He leaned so close to her, she felt his breath on her face when he hissed, "You know *nothing*. If you knew what was good for you, you would shut up and do as I say."

Elise yanked her arm free. "I've been doing what you said since I was born. I refuse to listen anymore," she snapped.

Something lethal lit her father's eyes. For a moment, true fear struck Elise, and she almost considered backing off. He was a terrible father and a liar, but he was still one of the most powerful men in New York, and Elise was nothing compared to him. Mr. Saint gripped her chin hard. "You promised me. You kill the Quinn girl. You are still to do that. And, fine, you no longer have to listen to me after that. I remove you as my heir. Sterling will replace you." He released her so aggressively, Elise hit the wall as she fell back.

"Sir?" Sterling asked.

"You heard me," Mr. Saint barked. He gave Elise one final dirty look, then gripped Layla's arm and pushed her into the hotel. Weeks ago, had her father done this to her, Elise might have cried until she could no longer breathe. But now, she stood against the wall, trembling with a rage she wasn't sure was possible until now, after seeing him drag Layla away from her.

Mr. Wayne, who had hardly moved since the altercation began, thrust his open hand toward Elise. In it was a vial. "You made me a promise, Elise."

39

THE SYRINGE FELT STRANGELY LIGHT IN ELISE'S hand. Standing in the middle of the Hotel Clarice foyer, Layla seated in a chair in front of her, Elise tightened her grip on the syringe. Her father watched from a balcony above the room, Sterling and Mr. Wayne by his side. Some of Layla's clan members looked on from a few yards back, murmurs few and far between. Elise had no doubt that the substance in the syringe was not a cure. Per her father's agreement and strict guidelines, she was to kill Layla, not make her human. Even on the off chance that it could be a true cure, Elise had already decided that she no longer trusted a word out of her father's mouth. It hurt more than anything now to see Sterling still standing by his side, staring at her with disappointment deep in his eyes.

Elise pursed her lips. She dropped her gaze to the slope of Layla's neck. One puncture of this needle and maybe everything would be over. But Elise knew better than to take her father at his word. She had done so years ago, thinking he would end the growing reaper problem that Layla was trying to fix with her parents. But he had only assured her with hidden lies and hollow promises.

"Someone please hold her down," Elise said quietly. "I won't be able to if she struggles."

Sterling descended the staircase and placed his hands on Layla's shoulders, pushing her down into the seat. Elise waited, wanting Layla to stir, to show any sign of her usual self. But she remained quiet and unmoving.

Tears brimming in her eyes, Elise positioned the needle in place at the edge of Layla's neck. "Layla," she whispered. "I'm sorry. For everything, I'm so sorry."

Then she pushed the needle in.

Elise hesitated with her thumb on the plunger. She took a deep breath and yanked the needle from Layla's skin, shoving it into Sterling's hand. Elise plunged the drug into him.

Sterling pulled away from them with a shriek, tearing the needle from his skin.

Layla finally blinked as blood pooled in the juncture between her neck and collarbone. She looked up, confused. Sterling stumbled away and roared as the needle clattered to the floor. Harlem reapers braced themselves, fangs emerging while Sterling approached them.

Elise clamped her hand over Layla's wound and stepped in front of her.

Then Sterling lost control. With his eyes red as blood and his veins bulging, he tore around the room, knocking chairs over and shrieking. Elise covered her own mouth as she watched reapers throw themselves at her best friend. But even as they clawed at him, hissing and snarling like frenzied beasts, Sterling threw them off. To Elise's horror, his nails had grown into the size of monstrous claws, and they pierced the reapers' flesh, leaving deep scratches behind.

Something dug into Elise's arm and she jumped at first seeing Layla on her feet, fingers clamped around her wrist. "We need to go," Layla hissed. Her clanmates scrambled, some running for the door, others facing the scene in frozen shock. Mr. Saint and Mr. Wayne went unnoticed by the unfolding frenzy, still watching from above. Elise noticed a slight smile on Mr. Wayne's face, and she recoiled at the sight.

Elise headed for the door, but Sterling stumbled closer as one of Layla's clanmates charged him, blocking the exit. Layla tugged her back and quickly found an alcove beneath the grand staircase, away from the chaos. She shoved Elise in first, pressing her body into the remaining space while they watched the carnage unfold.

One clan member tried to help his fallen comrade at Sterling's feet, but he was no match for this newly evolved Sterling. It was as if all humanity had been sucked from him. His cheekbones protruded beneath sagging, hollowed-out skin and his eyes bled red, as if every vein in his skull had burst and coated his eyeballs in the scarlet substance. He stepped toward the reaper charging him and, with one swipe of his clawed hands, sent him slamming against the wall. The reaper's shirt fell off in bloody tatters where he was hit.

But only moments after going down, the reaper's eyes flew open, scarlet just like Sterling's. His hands extended into claws as well, and he released a deafening growl, purely demonic and deranged. Then he turned on his own clanmates.

One by one, they each began to turn. Elise watched in horror as reapers tore through each other. But only minutes into the destruction, they jerked upright and, with their claws still clinging to dripping flesh, crashed to the floor. The rampage ended almost as soon as it began, leaving nothing but blood and bodies littering the foyer. Sterling was the only one left standing, his chest heaving as he stepped over the fallen reapers, finally calming down.

In that moment, something whistled through the air and Sterling jerked back, having been shot with something.

"*Sterling.*" Mr. Wayne's voice rang out around the room. He turned to Mr. Saint, lowering his own gun. "The antidote will start working in a bit. Just give him a few more moments. In the meantime, he can search for the girls while he's still craving blood." Mr. Wayne grumbled and looked around the room. "I intended for Layla to do all the destruction. But it seems your daughter has more of a brain than we anticipated. Wherever the hell she is."

Elise whimpered and Layla clamped a hand over her mouth.

Mr. Saint was eerily quiet. "This is no cure, Stephen."

"I know. But this is something better. I knew you would never approve if I told you, so I had to show you. I can explain everything back at the house, I promise," Mr. Wayne said.

Mr. Saint said nothing. He just gave one more look around the room, scowling, before leaving.

Just as Mr. Wayne had said, in a few moments, Sterling collapsed, breathing into his humanity once more.

"I want you to find them," Mr. Wayne commanded.

Sterling let out a grunt as he stumbled out of the hotel with her father and Mr. Wayne, his body still twitching with the effects of the poison.

Even after they were gone, Layla kept Elise in the alcove until they were sure no one was coming back. Minutes passed, then, finally, Layla released Elise and they stepped out of the alcove.

"It's them," Elise muttered shakily. "Dr. Harding mentioned a poison spreading, and it's Stephen Wayne spreading it. My father…" She gasped. "Maybe this could explain the dancers at the Cotton Club incident? And Theo too. Close contact seems to spread the poison."

"But Theo scratched me and I didn't turn. It could be spreading the way it usually does: Sterling's blood must have gotten into my clanmates when he attacked them. And if the poison works on humans, too, then he's not only targeting reapers. He's turning them into weapons. Everyone is in danger," Layla breathed.

She walked through the lobby, looking over the fallen reapers. With each body she passed, her face grew more and more ashen. After examining all of them, Mei included, Layla straightened up. Her expression fell blank, but her voice came out raw and conveyed a deep hurt. "The mutations from the poison are gone. They're all human now. How cruel." She let out a weak sob.

Elise took a shaky breath. "I'm sorry, Layla. I'm really sorry." Her voice broke. "I'm sorry—" But Layla suddenly rushed toward her. She threw herself at Elise, wrapping her arms around her in a tight embrace. Shock stole Elise's breath. It took her a moment to hug Layla back, but when she did, for the first time in forever, everything felt right.

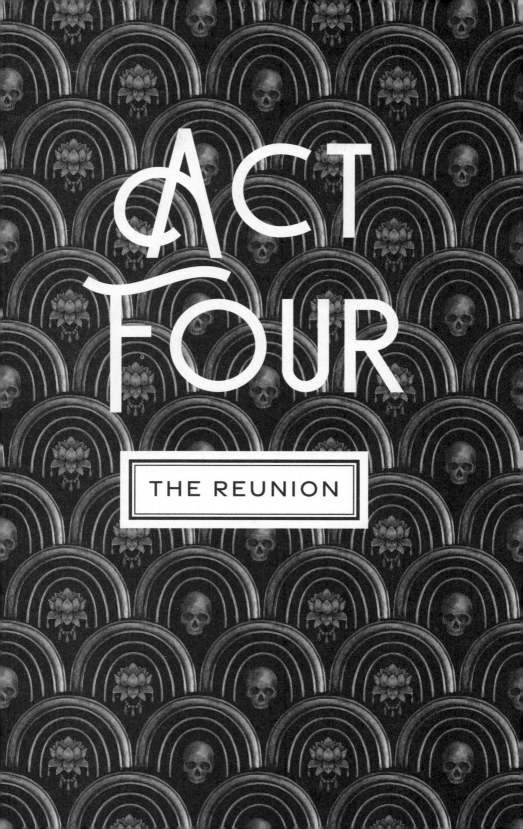

ACT FOUR

THE REUNION

4O

I AM NOT RUNNING A HOTEL HERE. I'M GOING TO START charging rent if you keep bringing more people into my apartment," Jamie grumbled. He slapped a pillow onto the couch and stalked out of the living room. Hendricks stared up at Elise from the rug, his tail swishing in satisfaction behind him.

Elise gripped the end of Layla's borrowed shirt. She was not particularly fond of cats, and the way this one stared up at her was starting to make her feel stranger than she had felt when Layla proposed they stay with a gangster for the night.

"I have no idea where Valeriya is, and Sterling is still out there looking for you. You need to hide. It's just until we figure out what to do," Layla had insisted as they hurried out of the Clarice and into the storm outside.

Elise had stopped in the downpour, rain pounding against her head so hard, she was certain she had heard Layla wrong. "Are you insane? It could take days to figure out what to do next! You want me to sleep in the same apartment as a criminal?"

Lightning struck, and thunder shook the area around them. Layla grinned at the fear that dashed across Elise's face. "If you want to stay out in this storm, or return to your father, be my guest."

Elise had never run harder after Layla. But when Jamie had opened his door for them, Layla had hesitated.

"I need to find Dr. Harding. He can give us more information." Layla touched Elise's cheek, her eyes fierce. "Do not leave this apartment and do not open the door for anyone." Then, before Elise could protest, Layla was gone.

Now, Elise stared down at this gray cat, who had not stopped following her around since she arrived.

"Layla thinks he's evil," Jamie said. He nudged Hendricks with his foot and he hissed, then finally trotted out of the room.

"No wonder he likes me, then," Elise muttered. She hugged her arms around her chest and sat on the couch. She had not been expected to sleep anywhere but a four-poster bed since France, when she went out with friends on weekends and fell asleep wherever there was an available spot.

"The world is full of sin. I'm more surprised when people aren't evil. You'll be just fine," Jamie called as he walked down the hall to his room.

Elise took one more look at the couch, then got up and crept to the first door in the hallway. Layla's room. The tension in her body eased up as if Layla was beside her right then, gentle hands of assurance guiding her to the bed. When she laid down, Elise pressed her face into the pillow and smiled. It still smelled faintly of Layla.

The lab was something of a haunted spectacle at night. Shadows stretched across the linoleum floors, the white tiles dim and gray in the faint moonlight that filtered through the windows. Layla crept through the clinic first, which felt unnervingly dead at this hour. She made her way to the back rooms, where she hoped to find offices and did.

Layla pushed the door labeled "Dr. Harding" open, then threw herself against the wood as a bullet rushed past her.

"Oh, Christ!" Dr. Harding ducked behind his desk, gun still pointed toward Layla. "I thought you were Stephen!" he whimpered. "Please don't kill me. I swear, I didn't want to do any of this. He made me!"

Layla lifted her hands, coming away from the door. Luckily for her, the man only had regular lead bullets loaded into the gun. "I'm not here to hurt you. I just need some information about this poison you mentioned to the Saints. Stephen Wayne gave my friend a cure, and she ended up dead. I still don't remember what exactly happened."

Dr. Harding seemed to relax a bit. He lowered the gun and sat up so his face was no longer blocked by the desk. "Small contact with the drug will cause amnesia. Your friend might have killed herself to save you. I've seen it happen in trials. When a reaper is given the cure and is unable to destroy someone near them, they destroy themselves instead. The drug creates an insatiable urge to kill."

Elise thought back to Theo and Mei, who had been infected and still somehow stopped themselves from hurting her.

Dr. Harding continued, "Stephen Wayne is working on controlling the reaper venom market. He was going broke and figured this would be his big chance to make his money back. He probably went to other scientists first, who refused his ideas because they are so destructive. But I guess my failure caught his eye. My license was revoked after I ran a trial on a reaperhood cure without proper permission and my cure turned them into worse monsters. I want to cure reapers. I want to *help* them. It was never my intention to turn them worse, or kill them. But Stephen told me I made something wonderful. It was my mistake believing him. But by the time I realized his intentions to make weapons out of reapers, he had already begun poisoning me with reaper venom. It made me bone tired and obedient. I swear, I wanted to do good." Dr. Harding dropped his head.

Layla narrowed her eyes. She vaguely remembered how strangely he had behaved at the fundraiser. "How do I know you're telling the truth?"

The doctor moved back behind his desk and pulled open the door to a cabinet where a row of vials sat. "These are actual antidotes that might have the ability to be turned into true cures. Thalia Gray was working on these, developing them from her mother's work.

They should have been given to Mrs. Gray," Dr. Harding said sadly. "I confiscated them because I knew Stephen would get upset if he saw her working on them, but I believe he already had suspicions…"

Understanding weighed heavily on Layla's shoulders. She crossed her arms, her glare deepening. "So what are you going to do now?"

"I want to stop Stephen Wayne. I tried to expose him the night of the fundraiser by exposing the real effects of the drug, but the chandelier…I think that was his doing. To stop my demonstration." Dr. Harding shook his head. "He is planning on presenting these weapons to Hugh Arendale at a rally at the Alhambra tonight. It could be great for Arendale's platform; people are afraid after the war and they want to make sure they're protected. The deadlier weapons we have, the safer people will feel. There are many variations of these developing drugs, but none of them are ready. I believe Stephen Wayne originally saw hope in a cure, but grew impatient when so many tests failed. He turned to the darker route of using the monsters to his advantage. Now everyone is in danger." Dr. Harding shut the door. "Too many people in power choose evil. Stephen wants glory even if it's in creating destruction. One might say humans are innately malevolent—look at history. It's not made by great men and great minds, but rather selfish motivations. Great minds can come up with valuable things, but also unfathomable destruction. But regardless, there is always an option. Always a choice to do good. I want to stop him before it's too late."

Layla nodded, an idea already popping into her mind. "Can you explain how this poison works?"

The Saint mansion rose up in front of Elise. Just a few more steps, and she would be able to face her family again. It had not been her idea; Layla had been the one to insist that she go home and apologize to get back into her father's good graces.

"We need you in that house, Saint. It's the only way we can keep close tabs on him," Layla had said earlier that morning.

Elise's throat went tight then. "I'm not even positive my father will let me back in the house."

"Tell him your behavior was completely out of your control because I entranced you with my reaper venom." Layla leaned against the kitchen counter, her arms crossed. She had been out all night, and when Elise found her in the living room this morning, she had resisted the urge to fall into her arms like a love-cursed muse. "Saint, I've got your back. If your father tries anything, I will be right there—"

"No. You have to stay away. He will have you killed," Elise said quickly.

Layla's eyes went soft. "I'll be fine—"

"Promise me you won't show up. No matter what," Elise had commanded.

Now she stopped in front of the gates to the Saint estate, her hands up as Saint guards pointed their guns at her. Despite the time she had spent there since coming home, she still didn't recognize any faces. It seemed the empire was growing and training new members every day. Her home started to feel less like one and more like a business the longer time passed.

"I'm here to apologize. Please just tell my father. I'm not here to cause chaos," Elise insisted.

The Saint guard who was nearest her scoffed. But before he could speak, Sterling's voice rang out from the now-open front door. "Let her in."

Elise pushed past the guards and stepped into the house. It felt empty, mostly because her mother did not come sweeping in with a hug and stern words. "Where's my mother?" Elise asked.

"She's busy." Instead of Sterling, it was her father who spoke. He stood outside his study, the door shut firmly behind him, his hands shoved into his pockets. "Care to explain yourself, Elise?"

Guilt dampened Elise's eyes and she looked down. "Layla made me act for her. You were right. She has corrupted me with her venom." She looked up, forcing tears into her eyes. "I didn't mean any of it. I'm sorry for the destruction I've caused."

Her father's stony expression did not change. "Go clean yourself up. Then we will continue this conversation." He looked at Sterling, nodding slightly. "Get her Stephen's antidote—whatever you have left of the one he gave you," Tobias Saint grumbled as he left the room, Sterling following after him.

Smiling to herself, Elise slipped upstairs to her room. She changed out of Layla's borrowed clothes and into a formal dress, making sure to hide Layla's shirt and pants beneath her mattress.

"I want my gun back." Sterling's voice turned her around. He set a vial on the nightstand—Stephen Wayne's antidote.

Elise winced. "I lost it. I'm sorry."

Sterling stared down at her with a strong jaw and steady amber eyes. He pointed to the antidote. "Take that. Don't come down until you do." His voice strained.

Elise's heart fell as she watched him leave her room. Minutes ticked by, the vial glinting in the evening sun. She swept it into her pocket and headed into the hallway.

The second the elevator doors closed, Elise could not hold back anymore. She doubled over, sobs pouring out of her. Was this all she would amount to in her life? Walking away from one person she loved just so she could take a risk on someone who could barely look at her because it felt like it was the right thing to do?

Elise gripped the elevator railing and breathed hard, trying to calm the torrential downpour of tears. Moments passed as she steadied her breathing. By the time the weight on her chest lifted and the pain alleviated the slightest bit, the elevator reached the main floor.

Elise reached forward to open the door, but a hurried whisper stopped her. "*Wait*." She looked up to see Layla peeking through the escape hatch at the top of the elevator.

"*Christ*, Layla. What are you doing here—I told you not to come!" Elise exclaimed, stunned. Her tears had not yet dried and she was already fighting back laughter at the sight of Layla dropping headfirst out of the elevator ceiling.

Layla stopped mid-descent, her legs hooked over the ledge. She threw Elise a nasty look. "Don't look so surprised. You didn't notice, so obviously it's a great hiding spot. And like I said, I. Will. Be. Fine." Layla gritted out. "Did they hurt you?"

Elise shook her head and removed the vial of antidote from her pocket. "Sterling gave me an antidote. They must believe you've infected me."

"Good." Layla nodded. Then she grabbed Elise's sleeve and pulled her closer. "Give me your blood," she demanded.

"Okay." Elise began to unbutton the top of her dress, but Layla grabbed her wrist, stopping her.

She gaped. "Are you not going to ask me why?"

Elise shrugged. "I trust you," she said. Once she was unbuttoned, she stared at Layla, who had gone still in her upside-down position. "How will you drink from me like that? Won't it be hard to swallow?"

"You underestimate me." Flashing a wicked grin, Layla reached forward and sank her fangs into Elise's throat.

Elise certainly did underestimate Layla. Not her skill, but the effect she would have on her. Layla's teeth in her neck, reaper venom numbing the pain and rousing every pleasure center in her body, made Elise's skin tingle and eyelids flutter. Warmth rushed through her and she felt light, on the verge of floating. Elise rocked forward, her hand coming up to steady herself against the elevator wall. Layla's hand fisted in her dress, and Elise closed her eyes, a soft moan leaving her throat. The slight pain in her neck from the bite dissolved into a pleasure so great, her stomach clenched and knees went weak. The heat in her body increased until she was nearly panting, her hand tightening around the elevator railing so hard, her fingers went numb. In this moment, Elise was convinced heaven existed and that she had found it with Layla. She almost opened her mouth to say so, but she wasn't sure she would be able to get any words out among all of her bliss.

Then, in a split second, the intensity rushed away and faded to an aching pulse in the pit of her stomach. Elise opened her eyes to see Layla staring up at her. Her eyes glowed gold and Elise's blood stained her lips. She ran her tongue over the blood, her mouth curving into a satisfied smile. "Look at you," Layla murmured wistfully.

Elise still felt like she was on fire. A new craving arose for that heavenly pain. The blush that heated her face when she remembered just how vocally and physically she had reacted to Layla's bite only made it worse. She nodded, buttoning the front of her dress. "Holy hell, Layla."

Layla nodded slowly. If Elise didn't know any better, she would think the fire in her glowing eyes was more than just an instinctual reaction to her human blood. "If he tries anything against you, he will know you're under the influence of my venom." Layla tugged on Elise's dress when she didn't say anything. "Hey, Saint?"

Elise looked back at her. She tried to keep her breathing steady, but failed. "Yes?" she barely managed to grit out.

"We're so close. Don't go to pieces now," Layla whispered fiercely.

Elise wanted to shake Layla and tell her that was impossible. It was impossible not to fall apart when it came to her. But she just nodded. "I'm good." And when Layla retreated back up on top of the elevator, Elise still felt her bite, lingering like a drawn-out kiss against her pulse, her life force forever altered by Layla Quinn.

Back in her father's study, Elise felt like she was suffocating. She stood before her father's desk, staring right into his eyes while Mr. Wayne stood beside him and Sterling leaned against the far wall. He watched Elise with doubtful eyes, his gun fully visible on his hip.

The pressure of their attention on her made her chest ache, and her breath became shallower with each second. Layla's venom only heightened her agitation, her skin prickling and heart yearning to be near her and only her.

"How do I know I can trust you again?" her father demanded.

Elise bit her lip. "I never wanted any of this to happen. I just wanted to figure out who killed Thalia and get rid of Layla. But she outsmarted me at every turn."

Her father frowned. His eyes were red and his fingers shook as he lifted a glass of wine to his mouth. "You're not quite apologetic enough. You need to understand that your actions have consequences. Right now, you are no longer my heir. That role has gone to Sterling. He's proven his loyalty to me time and time again. The only time he fumbled was when he was with you. It seems that you are the poison in this empire, Elise."

Though his words stung, a weight lifted from her shoulders at the knowledge that she was no longer his heir. As long as she had freed Josi from her father's clutches, as far as Elise was concerned, she had done exactly what she had set out to do and she had gotten what she wanted.

The sound of the front door opening split their attention and shouting sounded in the hallway outside. Elise turned right in time to see the door fling open, several Saint guards scrambling to speak at once. "Sir, apologies, she threatened to kill him—"

Then Layla Quinn shoved her way between them, Dr. Harding in tow. She held a gun to his head—Sterling's gun.

Sterling raised his remaining gun when he saw her. "Release him—"

"No, I think we can have a civil conversation first," Layla snapped.

Mr. Wayne held his hands up, panic slipping through his haughty mask. "What is this about?"

Layla nodded to Dr. Harding. "Go ahead. Explain yourself."

Dr. Harding stumbled through his words, detailing the things he had told Layla the previous night. Even though Elise had heard everything from Layla this morning, the devastation in his voice still shocked her. She couldn't understand how anyone could have the desire to create such desolation.

Mr. Wayne rolled his eyes and turned to Elise's father. "This is bullshit. She could not tell the truth if her life depended on it. I had nothing to do with Dr. Harding's malpractice. I did not know about it until Elise told us."

Mr. Saint's eyes darted from the doctor to Mr. Wayne. His expression looked less stern than before and almost gaunt now. He breathed hard and shook his head. "Dr. Harding, you've committed many atrocities since we endorsed your practice. This will only look terrible for our reputations."

Layla snarled. "So what will it be? Prison? Or I could just kill him and you won't have to worry about your reputation—"

Stephen Wayne shook his head. "Now, wait a minute. He is still my friend. Nothing has to happen to him."

Mr. Saint looked at Mr. Wayne oddly. "Are you defending him?"

Layla's eyes sparked and she grinned.

Mr. Wayne waved his hand around, as if he could physically dismiss the accusations. "No, but we need him. We all do," he hissed.

Elise's brows drew together in confusion. She glanced down at the wineglasses on the desk, only then noticing that there was an extra one. "Who else is here?"

As if on cue, the door leading to the sitting room opened, and in stepped Valeriya.

Behind her, Josephine Saint.

Elise's heart stopped when she saw her little sister. She froze, her pulse skipping several beats. Josi was supposed to be in France— Elise had seen her off at the pier.

Elise's breath stilled as her chest constricted with realization. Josi had never gotten on that boat. The whole trip had been a lie.

She tried to go toward her, but Layla held her back, her eyes wide and body bristling. "Don't touch her. She's infected."

"It's true. She's starting to really enjoy my venom," Valeriya said. She held her hand out and Josi took it.

Josephine cocked her head to the side and gazed at her sister. "You look sad, Lisey." The girl seemed distant, her eyes glassy and unfocused. Elise almost couldn't recognize her. The whole thing felt disturbing—like a mirror held up to all the atrocities and fears Elise had witnessed over the past few weeks.

All air left Elise's lungs. She strained against Layla's grasp and screamed at her father and Mr. Wayne, "*What did you do?*"

"She's not turned. Not yet. But she's developed a very strong bond to Valeriya. I suppose separating them will be difficult." Mr. Saint regarded Valeriya almost wistfully. Something clicked for Elise as she noticed his bloodshot eyes and unsteady frame.

"You too. You're infected too," Elise whimpered. Poison was seeping through her family at an alarming rate.

Her father turned back to her. "I can give you one more chance, Elise, to prove your loyalty to this family. Hand over the Quinn girl and the doctor. You need him to fix Josephine anyway. You have no choice."

"No," Layla said sharply. "You always have a choice."

But Elise did not. Each inhalation felt like knives to her chest. She let out a sob as she looked at Josi again. Her sister was in even worse danger than before, and Elise had no idea where her mother was. She did not want to make one more wrong decision that led to disastrous consequences. She was done.

In the end, Saint steel and reaper blood was all it took to rein them in. Sterling handcuffed a stunned Layla and dragged her out of the room.

"We will go to the Alhambra, where Mr. Arendale is awaiting us before he departs on his final tour ahead of the mayoral election. I expect excellent behavior. For now, the Quinn girl is mine. The perfect specimen," Mr. Wayne had announced.

Now, Elise sat in the back of the car, Josi between her and Valeriya, while Layla was shoved into another car with Sterling and several other Saint guards. Her father and Mr. Wayne headed the entire party in their own car with Dr. Harding.

Despite her anger and defeat, Elise did not cry. She stared ahead, trying not to look at her sister's new, crass appearance. Josi sat like a statue in her seat, unmoving and eyes locked on the distance. She seemed to be in a trance. The sight of her made Elise's stomach turn, but more than anything, she felt guilty Josi had been involved in all of this.

Valeriya gave her a smug smile. "To be fair, this was not your father's idea. He thought an alliance with me would help him figure out a way to turn you and Layla against each other. He despises how well you work with her. But he never even noticed that I slipped my own blood into his wine. That was Stephen's idea. He wants your empire gone. What he does not know is that I want reapers gone and his work might just be the beginning of that." She stroked her hand over Josi's hair. "Now there's just one more Saint to infect before the entire empire comes crumbling down."

"You'd work against your own kind?" Elise breathed.

"You don't understand what it's like to live so long with so much stacked against you. Life as a reaper is closer to hell on earth. It's time for it to end."

Elise said nothing for the rest of the car ride. She was the only one instructed to get out of the car when they arrived at the theater. With a painfully tight grip on her arm, a Saint guard led her to the middle of the ballroom floor. Any other day, Elise might have marveled at the grandeur of the building around her. If she closed her eyes, she could almost hear the music of some of the greatest performers still echoing within the walls. But now, all she could do was stare warily at the glossy floors beneath her and the chandeliers that hung overhead. Above her sat Mr. Wayne and Mr. Saint, who were sharing a glass of dark liquor with the mayoral candidate. It was truly a spectacle to see now—three men, with enough money to shut down a wildly popular theater for a few hours just so they could witness something sinister unfold.

Sterling arrived with Layla in tow, shoving her beside Elise. Dr. Harding followed closely, and when he caught Stephen Wayne's eye up above, he glared.

"What do you have for me, gentlemen?" Mr. Arendale asked. He was a heavyset man, with wide shoulders and a torso stiff like a tree trunk. His saggy forehead puckered when he saw the blood trickling down Layla's wrists from the cuffs she wore. "Something better than this, I hope?"

Mr. Wayne nodded, smiling. "My partner here has come up with what could be a weapon to change our world. Any war that occurred would be in our hands."

Layla breathed so hard, Elise half expected to see steam coming from her nose. She scowled right at her, the vitriol in her eyes nearly as palpable as the blood that dripped from her hands.

"Consider me intrigued," Mr. Arendale said.

Elise barely paid attention to the activity around her. She was too focused on Layla. So when a Saint associate moved behind her and Layla's eyes darted up, she could only stare. Until Layla barreled into her, tackling her to the ground.

She gasped, pushing at Layla's shoulders. And as Layla sat up, rolling off her, Elise saw the needle and syringe poking out of her neck. Her heart dropped. "No," she whispered. "No, no, no, no, no—"

"Run," Layla rasped. She looked at Elise, blood already spilling over the whites of her eyes. "Run. And don't look back."

Elise hesitated. She watched as Layla's hands braced against the ground, massive talons tearing from her fingers and sinking into the floor. It wasn't until she looked up again, eyes bloodshot and fangs dripping blood, that Elise did as she was told.

She ran.

41

TWO MINUTES. THAT WAS ALL LAYLA HAD BEFORE
the poison would stop her heart. She felt lighter with her
body under the influence of such a powerful drug and the
way everyone stared at her like she was the world's greatest horror,
only spurred her on. Heavy rage crashed over her and she grabbed
the closest person to her.

Dr. Harding cried out in her clutches. Layla snarled. Even as Tobias
Saint, Stephen Wayne, and the mayoral candidate watched her with a
sick sense of hunger in their eyes. They wanted a monster. So she would
be one. Until every last one of them was red with each other's blood.

Layla wrapped her chains around Dr. Harding's throat and
pulled. Saint bullets rained against her back, but the poison in her
newly enforced body prevented them from sinking in. The chains
dug into Dr. Harding's skin, tugging until his flesh tore open, tendons
and muscles splitting to reveal his vertebrae. She yanked the chains

further, cracking his bones apart and pulling his head from his body. When it tumbled to the ground, Layla turned, blood drenching her front, and pulled her arms apart, snapping the Saint metal. Cuffs still encircled her wrists, but the chains between them were gone, rendering her completely free.

Beyond Stephen Wayne and Tobias Saint, all Layla saw was crimson. They thought they were safe on the balcony, but she would become their nightmare soon enough, once the Saint members scattered about the ballroom floor were destroyed. They tried to step in front of her, but she blew right past them. Blood sprayed as her talons tore into them, their organs spilling through the split flesh. It was an entirely new sensation for Layla: she did not crave blood as much as she just craved death. She truly felt invincible, death incarnate.

Other reapers would not be able to resist so much spilled blood, however. The moment the thought cracked into her mind, Layla sensed movement outside the windows and doors of the theater. Rogue reapers appeared, fangs already bared and bodies braced for a fight as soon as the rest of the armed Saints noticed them. Their arrival had most of the other Saints distracted. Layla knew now was her chance if she was to get to Tobias Saint and Stephen Wayne. They were already beginning to squirm in their seats. Security approached the mayoral candidate now, rushing him out of her line of vision. But the spark of intrigue in his eyes told Layla he was intent on making the wrong choice. Just like Mr. Wayne and Mr. Saint.

She took one step toward them and stopped, her heart thundering in her chest. When she looked down, the talons were already sinking away, her own hands returning to her. That buzz of strength she was getting used to ebbed, leaving her with a sense of dread and immediate panic. Everything in her body seemed to slow. Her vision swam and Layla's eyes rolled back as she began to collapse.

But someone caught her.

That familiar sweet scent of gardenia and vanilla filled her nose and Layla clutched Elise, knowing if she had to die, she could do so happily in her arms.

"*Wake up.* You hardheaded beast—I told you not to come," Elise snapped.

Layla would have laughed if she had the strength. But she could barely muster up a whimper when she felt a pinch in her neck. A rush of adrenaline and relief flooded her body and Layla pulled back to see Elise standing before her with an empty syringe. The antidote Sterling had given her earlier. "You...?"

"We don't have time. They're getting away," Elise said, panicked.

They both turned to see rogue reapers surrounding the entrance Stephen Wayne and Tobias Saint were running toward. Layla sneered, "No, they aren't." By now the Saints were greatly outnumbered by the reapers. As Layla approached the crowd of her bloodthirsty allies, she wondered if Elise had anything to do with this. She had told her to run and not only had she come back, but there had been an entire flood of reapers in her wake. Even just opening the doors would have allowed for the blood to seep into the air outside. Perhaps it was just the bloodshed that called the reapers to the scene. Or maybe the Saint girl had more misdeed in her than Layla previously thought.

"Stay here," Layla commanded before bolting toward the Saint patriarch and his philanthropist partner. The rogue reapers stopped when they saw her, hissing and baring their fangs as Tobias Saint turned a gun on her.

"Do not touch the Saint girl. You can go. I will handle them," she said to the reapers.

Mr. Saint watched as the rogue reapers backed away, disappearing into the slowly growing fog that crept through the city. Stephen Wayne noticed his distraction and shoved his shoulder into the Saint patriarch, catching the gun when Tobias Saint dropped it.

"We can talk about this, Miss Quinn," Stephen Wayne breathed. His blond hair was messy, a few strands covering his forehead, which glinted with nervous sweat. "I will be close with the mayor of this city. I can offer you immunity. I can offer you anything you want."

"Really?" Layla asked. She crossed her arms and smirked. "Will you offer me your death?"

Stephen Wayne paled. He swallowed hard, and his gun arm actually trembled. Of course it did; he stared an agent of hell right in the eye. Blood covered Layla, and her eyes glinted with a wild need for violence. She thanked her reaperhood then, for putting this man in his place, even if it was just for a moment.

"I will give you the actual cure," Stephen Wayne said quickly.

Layla nodded, but she didn't believe him. "Bullshit." She tilted her head to the side and glared. "I'm half-dead, you imbecile. I'm not an idiot."

A confident rage exploded across Stephen Wayne's face. "Fully dead now—"

The gun went off, but Layla didn't flinch. The bullet flew past her as Tobias Saint kicked Stephen Wayne's ankle, throwing him off-balance. The gun slid across the hardwood and out of sight. Both men were suddenly on the floor, tearing at each other. Tobias Saint threw the first punch. "Asshole. I put everything on the line for you, and this is how you repay me?" He pounded into Stephen Wayne's face so hard, the man's skin went from pale to bloody in mere moments.

Layla grabbed a handful of Tobias Saint's coat and pulled him off Stephen Wayne. She threw him onto his back, her knee pressing into his sternum until he gasped for breath. "You should have known better than to trust *him*," Layla hissed. "I don't feel sorry for you at all. *Idiot.*"

Mr. Saint's jaw tightened, but the fear in his eyes overrode every ounce of confidence he tried to boast. "I'm not the villain," he gritted out.

"You are." Layla backhanded him so hard, blood flew from his mouth. "You owe your daughter an apology," she spat.

Confusion muddled his features for a moment. Then that stupid, vile smile returned. And Layla knew this man was a true monster, inside and out. When he looked at Elise, he didn't see his child. Layla recognized that spiteful look in his eyes; she saw it every time she looked in the mirror. The Saint patriarch had no daughter; to him, Elise represented the amalgamation of his own faults. Nothing Elise did would ever be good enough to him because he had already failed himself. The thought made Layla so angry, she was sure her blood boiled in her veins. How dare he damage a soul as untainted and innocent as Elise's. How dare he *ruin* her—

Blood gurgled out of Tobias Saint's mouth as he laughed. Layla looked down, realizing then that her hands were crushing his throat. She pressed her fingers deeper into his neck, but the air shifted behind her, drawing her attention away from him.

"Let him go." Sterling's stern voice turned her around. He stood several feet away, but his gun pointed straight for her heart.

Layla laughed roughly. She would entertain him. For now. She released Mr. Saint and turned to Sterling. "You would rather protect this man than your own friend?" Layla asked.

Sterling's eyes shifted. He tightened his grip on the gun and stepped closer to her. "You know what it's like to lose family. I would never risk it again. Not if I could stop it."

"There is no risk, Sterling," Layla said. "You've already lost them." Her fangs sprung free right as his gun went off. But before the bullet found her, something slammed Layla's body to the floor. She winced, her head spinning from the scent of Elise and blood. *So much blood.*

The Saint heiress lay on the ground a few feet away, her hand pressed against her chest. Sterling lowered his gun, a horrified look on his face as he realized just where his bullet had ended up.

Elise's blood filled Layla's nose—it filled every part of Layla. She sat up, rolling Elise onto her back. The wound was in the center of her chest, right beside her heart—if it had not grazed her on entrance.

Layla cursed. Sterling moved to tend to Tobias Saint, and Layla thought she saw pain flash in his eyes while he hesitated between the Saint patriarch and Elise, but she hardly noticed. Layla was too focused on the light quickly leaving Elise's eyes.

"*Why?*" Layla shrieked. "*Why, why, why would you do that?*" She ripped Elise's dress open.

Elise whimpered, her body shaking with pain. "Layla, I'm sorry—"

"Stop talking. You're not dying," Layla said hurriedly. All Layla could think about was Elise. Her blood, her pain, her shallow breathing. Ignoring the gnawing desire she had for Elise's blood felt impossible, but she did it anyway. The one thing keeping Layla focused, preventing her collapse, was the slowing heartbeat right beneath her fingertips. Layla shoved the fingers of one hand into Elise's mouth and with the other scrambled around her chest for the wound. Pearls, slippery and wet, tangled her up. Layla tore those free and reached into her gaping chest wound. Elise clamped down around Layla's fingers, screaming so hard, Layla couldn't even feel the pain of her teeth digging into her fingers.

Once she found the bullet, she pulled her hands back and dropped it onto the floor. Blood poured freely from Elise's chest. Her eyes rolled back and her head lolled to the side. Layla gripped her chin. "Saint—" she said, frantic. Elise had not bitten her fingers hard enough to draw blood. Layla cursed. She lifted her wrist to her mouth and tore it open with her teeth. Blood spilled onto Elise's wound. But her split skin wasn't closing fast enough.

Layla felt drained after only a few moments. Soon, she would join Elise in death if a miracle didn't make itself out of her blood. Layla drew closer to Elise, tears welling in her eyes. She touched her face, pulling her back to her. "Come on." Her voice broke. "Elise."

Her muscles ached. Blood loss had Layla feeling both empty and weighed down at once, but she sat up straighter and clasped her hands over Elise's newly scarred skin. She put every last bit of her strength into chest compressions. Blood pooled around them both, soaking the pearls and the glass that had rained onto the floor. Layla cursed the tears that continued to fall from her eyes, knowing they only drained her further. *Tears won't save her*, Layla thought fiercely.

"*Elise*," Layla said again, her voice stronger than before. "*Please*, Lisey."

A faint pulse grew stronger with each passing compression. Though blood rushed in her ears so loudly, Layla couldn't tell if she was actually helping. She gazed at Elise through eyes bleary with exhaust and nearly collapsed when she saw her cheeks warming up and her eyelids fluttering with life.

Elise coughed then, gasping for breath. Layla stopped the compressions and cupped her cheek. "Elise," she pleaded frantically. The reveal of Elise's now bright eyes electrified Layla's heart. She tried to pull Elise into her arms, but her body gave out, and she fell on top of her. Layla pressed her face into Elise's neck and cried.

42

ROGUE REAPERS DRAGGED LAYLA AWAY FROM THE scene the moment police and ambulances showed up. *You cannot be here. Not while you're starving and covered in blood.* So she went back to Harlem reaper territory and hunted, then waited by Saint territory until dawn. The moment she saw Elise's bedroom light flicker on, Layla climbed the vines leading to her window and tumbled into her room.

Elise had changed out of her bloody, torn dress, and now she sat at her window seat in a pristine, white nightgown. Layla underestimated just how much she would react to seeing Elise alive and well when only an hour ago, she had been dying in her arms. When Elise looked at her from her seat, eyes bright with recent tears, Layla went to her, arms outstretched. Despite having just fed, her knees gave out when she felt Elise's warm, human body against her own. The life thrumming through her veins beat right against her own damned heart and Layla hugged her tighter. They were almost on top of each other, their legs tangled on the cushioned window seat while Elise stroked her fingers over Layla's back.

"Thank you," Elise whispered. She placed her hand over her chest, where new scars covered her heart.

"Are you…" Layla pulled back and studied the scars. "I've never used so much of my blood to bring someone back from the brink of death. If it has any effects—"

Elise covered Layla's hand with her own and smiled. "I feel fine. Human, if that's what you're asking. The rogue reapers sensed your bite on me and I think that's why they showed up for us even when your plans went south."

Layla's mouth twisted as she remembered the carnage she had awoken. Her eyes dropped to the scars on Elise's chest, this time lingering on the older ones from her attack years ago. "I was a monster."

Elise touched her chin and lifted Layla's gaze to hers. "You were my salvation. You saved me." The glint of fresh tears on Elise's cheeks cleaved Layla's heart. But she understood it was better to process her emotions now. To hold them in and keep them against her heart would only turn it cold. Layla could attest to that. For the first time in ages, she felt warmth now and it was all because of Elise. And this Saint girl had no idea.

"It was instinct. Though I cannot believe you jumped in front of a bullet for me," Layla said softly.

A smile broke across Elise's beautiful face. "It was instinct," she said gently. "How are you feeling?"

Layla moved closer to Elise, her hand coming up to wipe her tears. "Better now. Better than I have in years."

Elise nodded. "Good." She reached forward to touch Layla's jaw. "I wish we didn't have five years of hate between us."

Layla laughed. "It builds character."

A soft sigh escaped Elise's lips. "Right."

"We can start over," Layla offered.

To Layla's surprise, Elise shook her head. "No. If you have never felt better than you do now, then I like where we are."

The faintest tear in Layla's heart mended at the whispered assurance in Elise's voice. And in that moment, Layla tumbled hopelessly back into every emotion she had left behind for the five years they had been distanced from each other. New hopes sprung up around her and she welcomed those, her heart stretching to accommodate every part of her that wanted to love Elise Saint.

She had never felt so full. So right.

"You're my best everything," Layla whispered.

Smiling, Elise blinked more tears away. She touched Layla's cheek, her hand warm and perfectly placed. And when her eyes dipped to her mouth, Layla's heart leapt in her chest. "Saint," she whispered.

"Say my name," Elise murmured.

A smile broke across Layla's face. "Elise. My Elise."

Light spilled in from the window as Elise closed the distance between them. Her lips brushed Layla's gently at first, tentatively, then as she drew more confidence from the answering stroke of Layla's hand down her arm, Elise kissed her with more fervor. Layla was peacefully unprepared for the way kissing Elise Saint would make her feel. Warmth blossomed in her chest and unfurled in every aching, cold part of her body. Where she hurt, the sensation of Elise mended. The gentle pull of Elise was the only source of heat. And for once, Layla embraced it. She let Elise in. Once she opened up, there was no stopping. Elise poured into her in waves, with each stroke of her tongue and each whispered word against Layla's lips. They were so fully each other's by now, should they pull apart, Layla knew Elise would be imprinted in her like a tattoo on her heart. There was no escaping her feelings now. Elise had set Layla on fire. And Layla welcomed the burn.

By the time they pulled apart for air, Layla was on Elise's lap. Layla's hands tangled in Elise's hair, and Elise's lips moved down to Layla's neck. Already, Layla was wanting more of Elise, and they had not even separated.

Elise glanced up at her, eyes heavy with bliss. "You're my best everything too."

Layla opened her mouth to respond, but the bedroom door flew open, and Analia Saint walked in. "Oh!" Elise's mother covered her mouth with her hands. Layla stilled as Elise stiffened beneath her. But when Analia Saint dropped her hands, she was smiling. "I never thought I would live to see the day you two made up. I always thought you had the best friendship." She paused with her hand on the doorknob. "I came to check on you, Elise, but you're clearly fine. Let me know if you two need anything." Mrs. Saint was gone another second later.

Layla shared a look with Elise. Then they both burst into a fit of laughter.

"I cannot tell if it's denial, or pure ignorance," Elise managed to get out between laughs.

"It must be denial. It's the only way she can carry on right now," Layla breathed, still trying to tame her amusement.

"My father sent her across town because he knew what would happen today. At least he saved her." Elise wiped at her eyes and moved away from Layla. Missing her, Layla followed her while she crossed the room to put on her slippers and robe. "I should check on her. I need to tell her that Josi is gone." Elise's voice broke.

Layla nodded. There had been no sign of Josi, even back at her lair. No one had seen Valeriya escape with her earlier. "I'll go back to the lair. There are bound to be questions anyway."

Elise waited at the door, one hand resting on the frame. "I wish you could stay. I want things to go back to the way we were before. When we were together all the time. I'm sorry for everything I've done to make this worse. And for what my father has done."

The memory of blood spilling from Tobias Saint's lips surfaced in Layla's mind, and her heart thundered at the thought of him refusing to apologize for everything he had done that hurt Elise. Layla came forward and took Elise's hand in hers. "Don't apologize for your father. He doesn't deserve any part of you."

Elise's jaw tightened. She looked like she wanted to cry again and that broke something in Layla. "I'm tired of crying. I just want this whole situation to be over. I'm not anticipating a happy ending. I just want an ending."

Layla's thumb stroked over Elise's knuckles. "You deserve a happy ending."

"I cannot believe any of this. I thought we... I thought your father wanted things to get better. Now he's lying in a hospital bed, and our youngest is nowhere to be found. I won't sleep tonight. Not while the police are out looking for her." Mrs. Saint shook her head and pressed a handkerchief to the edge of her eye. Elise sat on top of a mound of pillows at the foot of her bed. It felt empty now without her father to take up at least half of it.

Elise's mother lowered her hand and stroked a curl behind Elise's ear. "How could I not have known how much pain you were in? It's like I... *let* him do this to you." Her voice trembled as her eyes filled with more tears.

"I don't think there is anything you could have done, Mother," Elise spoke softly. "You know how Father is. I'm just glad you and Josi are all right. Stephen almost ruined us today, and to think Josi was almost here to witness all of this..."

A sob tore from Mrs. Saint then, and Elise tensed as her mother broke down. "I'm your mother. You should not be worrying about me. I'm supposed to be the strong one."

Elise moved closer and rested her head on her mother's shoulder. "Neither of us *need* to be strong. It's okay to just be."

Mrs. Saint sniffed. "This is how my own mother taught me to survive. Listen to my husband, always keep moving, never slow down enough to let me realize my pain, or ask for help because I would fall apart otherwise. But I see the damage that has caused now and I want you to know, Elise..." She moved back so she could look her daughter in the eye. "I am always here for you and I do not want you to carry your pain alone."

With those words, the pressure of the past few weeks began to drop from Elise's shoulders. She thought then of Layla and how she had no one to go home to, no one to assure her.

"Mother," Elise said quietly. "It's not your fault."

Her mother's brow creased. "He is not the man I married. Josi was so little, still sleeping in our room after the incident with the Quinns. Your father was having a hard time letting her out of his sight. I'd never seen him so scared. He...he never seemed like the person to intentionally hurt anyone, much less a child." Analia Saint dabbed at her eyes. Her voice broke as she continued. "He said it was an accident and that he only wanted the reapers to refuse the treaty, not kill the Quinns. He certainly did not think Layla would have been involved."

Tears filled Elise's eyes, and her mouth went dry. "Mama, I think he lied. He might have been honest about wanting to protect us, but his means to do so were just as sinister as his fear of losing us was intense."

Analia Saint touched her fingertips to her lips. Her eyes were shiny, and her hand shook. "I always thought it was admirable how much he cared for us, but I can see now how suffocating and dangerous it's become. Particularly for you." She cupped Elise's cheek. "I'm so sorry, baby."

Elise broke down. And when her mother pulled her in for an embrace, she finally felt at home.

A familiar face met Layla at the entrance of the Hotel Clarice when she returned that night. Valeriya stood by the door, arms crossed while she blew out smoke from her cigarette.

"You've made a mess of my clan, Layla," Valeriya drawled.

Layla's jaw ticked. "You were gone for weeks. I assumed you didn't care about us."

"There's no one left to care for. You made sure of that." Valeriya stubbed out her cigarette and approached Layla. Despite having just finished a smoke, she smelled of crushed roses and powder. The sweetness drew Layla in like a moth to a flame, memories of comfort associated with that scent.

"Where is Josephine Saint?" Layla demanded.

The older reaper sighed. "You're not here for her."

"You worked with Stephen and Tobias behind my back—"

Valeriya shook her head. "But you said we could trust them, remember? I only did as you asked." She pulled something out of her pocket and it wasn't until the wind picked up and the white fabric spread that Layla realized Valeriya held Josi's ribbon between her fingers. "I know I'm selfish. I no longer want this life. Josephine reminds me of my own daughter. Innocent and undeserving of the inevitable cruelty of this world. I only wished to protect her when her father approached me with a deal. How depraved this world has made us...eradicating reaperhood is the only chance for her. For everyone else." Valeriya crushed the ribbon in her hand and glared at Layla. "I would have made you my heir. But you never know when to quit."

Layla's heart lurched. "Valeriya, I'm sorry—"

"No, you are not." Valeriya's next words emerged as a low snarl. "I gave you everything I could not give my own child, and you still turned away from me."

Goose bumps rose on Layla's body. "I want to make things up to you. The Saints are done. And with Elise and her mother on our side, perhaps we can settle this mutiny."

At this, Valeriya laughed. "You cannot possibly think any of this will end well. It has been only a few weeks and you're already so infatuated with that Saint girl, you're willing to put everything on the line for her—"

Layla glared. "It's not just about her. A eugenicist wants to turn us into weapons and destroy the world. Stephen Wayne poisoned us; he turned Giana and Shirley and Mei into monsters and wanted to use science to justify violence against us. He stole a young woman's research to benefit his philanthropy, then he killed her. His power is built on nothing but lies and manipulation. Elise Saint *helped* us. She did that on her own. Her father had no hand in that."

"You're sick with love, and that's all it is: an illness. It will pass. She is a Saint, Layla. I know you're not dumb enough to believe she will ever truly be on your side. For heaven's sake, the Saint patriarch was willing to hurt his own daughters to get ahead. In centuries of living, I have never seen a human change," Valeriya snapped.

Her words flipped in Layla's mind for a moment. She knew there was no simplicity in the choices they made surrounding the Saints, nor would there be any simplicity in the consequences that arose with those decisions.

"I'm not dumb. Maybe I'm a slow learner, but I learn. And you might have hundreds of years of knowledge and experience on me, but you were the one who hid while your reapers put their lives on the line to prevent a poison from being administered to our entire community. I made things happen. You did nothing."

Anger rose around Valeriya so strongly, Layla felt it bristle between them. But she did not lash out. She looked back down at her fists and said in a soft voice, "When you live as long as me, life becomes less precious and second chances less feasible. Until you have been sold like cattle, bound to a surgical table, forced to ingest contaminants, and stripped of everything but your name, you will not speak of my sacrifices for our race. My body was host to countless abuses. I was made to hold the plagues that the white men brought to this country so they could figure out how to cure them. I was made to suffer the consequences of their ignorance. Do not tell me I did nothing when I was held down and injected over and over, forced to hear my daughter scream for me while they filled her with another experimental cure. Even when my body was chained down, I did not do nothing. I fed her opium until her heart stopped so she would no longer need to suffer. And even then I said her name so the last thing she heard was my voice. How dare you condemn me. *You know nothing.* So do what you want. But do not expect my sympathy, or my mercy when the Saint stabs you in the back."

Layla's breath stuck in her throat. The pain in her mentor's fixed stare was so sharp, Layla felt her own eyes burning with tears. "Valeriya. I won't accept the destruction of this relationship on my end. If you don't want to help me, that's fine, but if you need me, I will be here for you. Because I still appreciate you for what you've done for me." Layla didn't wait to hear Valeriya's response. She left with a decision made.

43

N THE WEEK FOLLOWING THE SAINT MASSACRE, ALL Elise could do was read Josi's old letters over and over.

Elise blinked back tears at the thought of her little sister lost and afraid.

"Why do you torture yourself like this?" Layla asked. She leaned against Elise's desk, flipping the envelope in her restless fingers.

"I can't help it. My mother is busy running the house with my father in the hospital, so I have nothing to do but mope," Elise said. The Saint estate felt especially empty with far fewer associates milling around. And with Sterling having moved out, the distance between Elise and him only grew every day, no matter how much she hoped for him to come to his senses and see her side.

Layla laid a gentle hand on her arm. Elise was grateful to have her back in her life, even if it meant things got more complicated while settling reaper-Saint affairs.

Elise bit her lip, still staring down at the letter. "It makes me sick, thinking my father, or Valeriya made her write those fake letters to me. I thought she was safe, with everything she needed."

Layla lifted a brow. "She didn't have you."

Sighing, Elise turned her focus to Layla. "She could. When I find her, I want to go to France and never look back."

"Hmmm…" Layla looked away.

Elise cleared her throat playfully. "Paris has some incredible research underway for reaper cures. You should come see them for yourself."

"You know I wouldn't only follow you to France for a cure, right?" Layla asked. She pushed off against the desk and stood behind Elise, draping her arms around her shoulders.

Elise nodded. "I know. Speaking of cures…" She spread the rest of the post across her desk, her throat going dry when she saw the newspaper headline:

THE DAWN OF A NEW AMERICA: HOW ONE MAN WILL RESTORE THIS NATION'S WONDERFUL FOUNDATION.

Layla narrowed her eyes. "Are they talking about *this* America? Because when has it ever been wonderful?" She turned the page and laughed. "Oh, look, they talked about how pitiful Stephen Wayne looked when he got out of the hospital. He even said that Tobias Saint is weak and not to be trusted."

Elise hissed. "My father will hate that."

432

Turning the page again, Layla glared. "How is England calling the United States the 'root of all things abominable'? Are they not the kettle?"

Elise blinked. "The what?"

"The kettle? Calling the pot black. Oh, this is even more sick and twisted than I previously imagined," Layla muttered.

Soft laughter escaped Elise. She pulled the newspaper away from Layla and sighed. "You're so funny, love," she said warmly.

Layla's eyes brightened. "Am I? That's fine." She jabbed her finger into the papers and hissed. "This is *not* fine. This man will start another world war."

Elise groaned and covered her face with her hands. "Arendale will be mayor soon. Since people found out about his desire to weaponize Stephen's poison, they've only endorsed him *more*. With him as mayor, it won't just be humans against reapers soon, it will be his reapers turned weapons against the whole world."

"What if we used these other countries' animosity to our advantage? If they had the evidence behind Stephen Wayne's plans, they would have to do something to stop them."

"It's a start. Thalia had contacts in Europe because her mother is still there. I could publicize her research and Stephen Wayne's crimes." Elise nodded. She pulled the notebooks Layla had retrieved from Thalia's office in the lab days ago and let out a shaky breath before meeting Layla's eyes. Her heart stumbled through its rhythm when she saw the concern in them, the usual brightness replaced by a dark despair. "I need to do this right."

433

A gentle smile stretched across Layla's mouth. "I believe in you, Saint."

Elise pouted. "Don't call me that."

"Elise," Layla said in a wistful voice, leaning in to kiss the corner of Elise's mouth. "Elise Saint, my beautiful best friend, I believe in you."

The Cotton Club sat like a corpse in the heart of Harlem. It had been completely gutted, every room cleaned out, furniture and decor gone in the wake of its sale to a new owner. Layla was surprised it had not taken too long to sell considering the incident that made it a sinister spectacle in the neighborhood. Only dust and sequins remained. Remnants of the life the club had once hosted, its blood and bones, now swept away and tucked into the darkness forever. Every sanguine sin and confetti charm that had been formed between the walls dissipated. It was difficult to imagine the crowds that had once filled the place in the silence it now bore. But Layla could still smell the depravity.

"Whatever alcohol remains, I will be taking it off your hands, because there is a chance it's tainted by Stephen Wayne's poison," Layla said. She followed Jamie to the back room, where he insisted leftover alcohol had been stored.

"I'm good at hiding my stuff; there's definitely some left," Jamie said. He pushed in a loose panel on the wall, and the whole thing came sliding out. Behind the wall was a compartment full of shelves.

Jamie glanced up at the stacks of wooden shelves, his face twisting with confusion. "Oh, brother," he muttered.

Layla sighed. "What is it?"

Jamie turned to her, one hand on his hip, his other hand rubbing his chin. "It appears that the booze has vanished," Jamie said.

"Oh?" Layla swallowed her frustration. "Jamie, are you being honest right now?" She snapped, glaring. Already, she felt her fangs digging into her gums and just a slight parting of her lips revealed them to Jamie.

Jamie's face went pale with fear and he hissed. "Okay, I sold it. When I found out the club was going under, I passed all the liquor off to someone else."

"Who?" Layla demanded.

"To be fair, I didn't know there was anything wrong with it until you told me—"

"Who did you sell it to, Jamie?" Layla pressed, sharper this time.

"She said her name was Rome, but I'm almost positive that's an alias," Jamie said.

Layla blinked. So many new burdens piled on her shoulders, she almost couldn't sort through her racing thoughts to make an informed decision. "We're going to have to find out who she is and get the liquor back before it's distributed—"

Jamie held up his hands. "This was not even my supply to begin with. I only took over for the Diamond Dealers. And if the alcohol was really tainted, then wouldn't everyone who came to the club have been poisoned?"

Layla let out a sad sigh. "Stephen Wayne sold reaper venom to the Diamond Dealers to ruin the products he knew would go straight to the dancers. They got infected. He tried to pin his plans on Dr. Harding, but the truth is, Stephen Wayne was the one who wanted to hurt us and make us hurt everyone else so we were to blame."

"Sinister man," Jamie muttered.

"It's not long before another fan club comes along for him. One Klan out, another one in. But this time with biological warfare." Layla turned away from the hideaway and stalked back to the main room of the club.

Jamie stopped by her side, a slight frown tugging at his lips. "I might be able to help you," he said.

Layla cast him a sideways look, but said nothing.

"I already have control over a lot of distribution in this area, but I can secure more. That way we'll have eyes on any malicious intent and we might be able to prevent the spread of this poison." Jamie nodded to her. "Would you trust me?"

Layla laughed roughly. "Are you proposing an official alliance?"

Jamie lifted a brow, smiling. "What do you say, Quinn? Should we bring gangsters and reapers together?"

"Sounds like hell." Layla grinned and reached for his hand.

44

"IS THERE A REASON WHY YOU'RE HERE, MISS SAINT?" Valeriya asked in a low voice.

Elise watched her trace her finger over the edge of her crystal glass, which was full to the rim with blood. A bitter taste rose in Elise's throat and she looked to Layla, who stood by the door of Valeriya's study. "Layla let me in. But I think you want me here."

Valeriya lifted a brow. She took a sip of her bloody cocktail, then smiled, her teeth scarlet in the flickering candlelight. "You want your sister. Tell me, Elise, what would you do for her?"

The gun on Elise's hip suddenly felt very heavy. She twisted the water glass in front of her, noticing the plain fear and anger etched into her reflection. "I would kill your entire clan for her."

Layla shifted by the door. "Elise—"

Valeriya lifted her hand, stopping her. "Oh, tension between the new lovers already." She chuckled. "You are so easy. So predictable.

Tell me, Saint. If you had to pick between your darling sister and your beloved Layla, who would you pick?"

Elise's free hand twitched by her side and her fingers closed over the gun handle. Her other hand gripped her water glass. "What do you want?" she hissed.

"I want you to choose. You cannot mix humans and reapers. I was there when the first venom was spilled. The Saints continue to spread it and you will regret your role in aiding that spread," Valeriya said.

"I no longer wish to vilify reapers. You are victims of a system that is bigger than all of us. We all are," said Elise.

Valeriya scoffed. "And you wish to *fix* things?" Before giving Elise a chance to respond, she laughed, her voice sharp against the room's silence. "There's no fixing what this country was built with."

Elise's finger trembled on the gun's trigger.

"Careful now, Elise. If you kill an ancient reaper, you will have hell at your door," Valeriya whispered.

Layla sighed. "This isn't worth it, Elise. Let's go—"

Valeriya interrupted, "I'm not sure that's true. Her own father loathes her for being unable to save his firstborn after that brutal reaper attack. Now she could very well be saving her baby sister's life. Josephine is an angel for now. But I could turn her against your grimy Saint—"

The glass exploded in Elise's hand. Breaking the glass had taken less force than she had anticipated. Glass shards now sank into her palm and fingers, spilling her blood across the table.

Layla was at Elise's side in an instant, pulling her to her feet. "You need to leave *now*."

But Elise stopped and watched as Valeriya dipped her fingertip into the blood, then brought it up to her mouth, sucking it delicately. Her eyes filled with light and for a moment, Elise's heart skipped a beat.

"Humanity truly is so weak. I can almost taste the futility," Valeriya muttered.

Elise glared. "You think of yourself as a god, but you bleed just like a mortal."

Valeriya flashed her a sharp smile. "My blood saves lives."

"And yet your penchant for human blood will get you killed," Elise spat.

Another sly grin crept onto Valeriya's lips, but it was interrupted by the slow trickle of blood from her nose. She wiped her upper lip, her breath catching as she noticed the blood. "*What have you done?*" Valeriya hissed. She tried to bare her teeth at Elise, but her fangs were gone. Instead, a painfully human whimper left her lips as Valeriya's features adjusted to show the years behind her age. Wrinkles cleaved her face and arms, her back curved as her bones creaked, and she stumbled away from Elise, limping slightly.

"I took an antidote that canceled out perfectly with the remainder of Layla's blood and venom in my system, so it did not affect me. But it seems like my tainted blood was too much for you. I thank my friend Thalia for her knowledge. She left behind a lot of useful information. The antidote alone is toxic for reapers, but when mixed with human blood, it's pure poison. No longer a delicacy for you," Elise said.

Layla's eyes, stretched wide, followed the older reaper to the massive window. Valeriya's breath grew ragged. She reached for the shelves to steady herself, knocking books onto the floor as she went. Her eyes locked on Layla, and the reaper tried to go toward her mentor, but Elise held her back.

"*No!*" Layla screamed.

Blood still trickled down Elise's fingers, but she ignored it. Her glare pinned on Valeriya. *No one threatens my sister and lives.* So when the ancient reaper turned weakling human lost her balance and crashed through the window, Elise felt no remorse. It wasn't until she noticed the storm in Layla's eyes that the cage around her heart fell away and guilt pressed into her chest.

"*What the hell,*" Layla hissed. Cold fury stirred in her voice. Before Elise could utter anything, Layla lunged for her, backing her against the wall, fangs bared.

Pain lanced through her cut hand and Elise whimpered. "I had to do it."

"*Be quiet,*" Layla snapped. Her eyes were bright, pupils dilated. "You must leave now. If you show your face here again, *you will die,*" Layla whispered. "I will cover for you—"

"Your clan will hate you—"

"I can live with that. But you..." Layla swallowed and pain broke across her face as she backed away. "You need to go."

With one last look at her, Elise ran off into the storm.

Rain plastered Layla's hair to her head. Her knees were stiff from sitting in the same position in the courtyard for hours, her clothes soaked all the way through, but she kept her hand on Valeriya's chest. It was impossibly still, and despite having been sitting with her hand over Valeriya's heart for hours, Layla still was not used to its absence of life. It took every ounce of her will to not internalize that her second chance at a family was gone, dead before her eyes.

"Layla," someone said gently through the rain.

"I already said no. She stays here," Layla snapped. Her clanmates had emerged every hour or so to suggest giving Valeriya a proper send-off. But Layla could not bear to say goodbye. Not yet. There might have been animosity, but Layla could focus on nothing but Valeriya for long enough to be sure. A few cursed Layla for having involvement in Valeriya's death, but they were too afraid to move against her. If they believed Layla was the one who killed an ancient reaper, then she would have power over them until someone challenged her for the now-open spot of clan leader. For a while, tears had stained her face, but then the rain started and Layla lost track of time as well as her emotions.

"Forgive me, but I do not recall that conversation." This time, Layla picked up on the unfamiliarity of the voice.

She looked up to see a tall human woman with long dark hair beneath a wide-brimmed black hat and umbrella. Her face was almost completely in shadow, but Layla saw the curve of red lips beneath the gloom. She scrambled to her feet, fangs already emerging. "Who the hell are you?"

The woman tilted her head to the side. "I know Vex. You can trust me," she said gently. A thick accent rode her words.

Layla's lips twisted with confusion. "Trust you for what?"

Water dripped from the woman's hat as she leaned forward, finally making her green eyes visible. They flickered over to Valeriya's body. "You have no idea how valuable this original reaper is, do you?"

"Valeriya—"

"*Sena*," the woman corrected her. "She was one of the first reapers. Her venom could change the world and she had no idea."

Hearing that name again was like a punch to Layla's heart. The letters were to no one. Valeriya had been signing her own name on those letters so she did not forget it. She swallowed. "You want to sell her remains?" Her voice hardened. "Are you working for Stephen Wayne?"

"My country hates what that man is doing. His ignorance of Sena and our knowledge of her keeps us one step ahead of him. Back home, we have evolved, and it's getting grim. We need your help and I promise, we can return the favor."

Layla narrowed her eyes. "We?"

The woman lowered her umbrella, and Layla gasped.

The second the fading sunlight hit her skin, it melted into an ashy gray color, her once high cheekbones sliding and sagging.

Those brilliant green eyes turned red, and her hair went limp. The hand that held the umbrella became nothing more than gray bone and black talons. If decay was a person, this woman embodied it. She gave Layla a wicked smile and fangs peeked out from behind her lips. "I told you. *Grim.*"

45

ELISE HAD NOT HEARD FROM LAYLA IN DAYS. Resisting the urge to show up at the Clarice made her anxious enough to go to Jamie's apartment instead, hoping she was hiding out there.

Jamie shrugged in the doorway of his apartment. "Sorry, kiddo. I haven't seen her in days—"

A cat's hiss sounded from behind him, followed by a curse. Elise gasped and shoved past Jamie. She found Layla almost instantly, her focus locking on her small form by the window. "Layla—"

"I can't talk right now, Saint, I'm busy fighting the devil," Layla hissed. She tried to walk away, but Elise cornered her.

"I know what I did upset you, but you promised me we were in this together," Elise said sharply.

Layla glared. "That was before you went behind my back—"

"She took my sister. You have to understand—"

"Well, I don't! I don't understand anything now." Layla almost shouted.

There was a haunted look to her eyes that Elise had not noticed before. She took a few steps back and sat on the couch, gesturing for Layla to sit. "Talk to me."

"There have been some developments since Valeriya died."

Elise sat back and nodded, encouraging Layla. By the time she finished, Layla was twisting her fingers in her lap. Even Elise had no idea what to make of the news.

"The news, while extremely mystifying, is not what I was asking for." Elise placed a gentle hand on Layla's knee, feeling her tension melt away beneath her touch. "I want you to talk to me about how you're feeling."

"I'm not sure how I feel. I just feel...empty." A shadow passed over Layla's eyes, and she pulled away. When Elise's hands closed over empty air, she almost regretted her own tenderness. "Valeriya was the closest thing I had to a mother since my own died." Layla paused. "Before her, when we were best friends, you were the only one who knew how to ground me. I'm not sure how to live anymore." She said it so nonchalantly, but Elise saw the hard-edged sadness in her eyes. She wondered, if forgiveness was tangible, would it spring up between them right now, like a field of flowers, waiting to be picked and fawned over? Or would it be like a bridge, finally falling into place over the abyss that had existed between them for five years?

Old, familiar emotions rushed in so hard and fast, Elise couldn't stop the tears that rose in her eyes. "You are," she whispered.

Layla's brow wrinkled. "What?"

"You said we *were* best friends. But you *are* my best friend," Elise said quietly.

Layla fell silent for a moment. Her teeth dug into her lower lip and she looked away as her smile faded. "You're only saying that because you have no one right now."

Hurt lanced through Elise's heart. She looked down, swallowing. "I'm sorry."

Layla drew closer, her shoulder bumping against Elise's until she looked up. "Remember when I said a reaper's fears and desires don't just disappear when they turn?"

Elise nodded.

"Well…I miss a lot from my old life. I miss not being looked at like I'm a monster. I miss even the mundane things, like getting excited about a home-cooked meal and inviting people to share it with. But most of all—" Layla took in a deep, shuddering breath and locked eyes with Elise. "I miss my sympathy."

Elise's heartbeat quickened. "Reaperhood didn't take that from you," she whispered.

"No, but time spent with the darkness did." Layla tilted her head to the side and her expression turned cold. "I cannot live in the dark anymore." She looked away.

Elise understood the reference to her going behind Layla's back. She touched Layla's hand and nodded. "I won't apologize for killing Valeriya, Layla. But as long as I have you, I promise, I will never harbor secrets against you again."

Layla's jaw went tight, and when she looked at Elise again, her gaze was full of sorrow.

Elise's voice hardened. "Do I have you?"

Elise felt no sense of home when she returned to her family's estate. But Mr. Saint stood on the stairs with Sterling next to him. She stopped, cold, in the middle of the pathway leading to the house.

Her father spun something small and shiny in his hands while he sneered down at her. "My pearl has come back to me."

He looked awful. Bruises lined his neck and eyes, still slightly swollen over a week after the attack. Elise swallowed as Sterling's lips curled. "You're still wreaking havoc, aren't you?" he spat.

"*Where is Josi?*" Elise demanded.

Her father lifted a brow. "I see that collaborating with an ancient reaper worked in my favor. You've killed her for me." He gestured to the estate around them. "I did all of this for us. It hurts to know that my own family would have a hand in my downfall. Josephine will not be happy to know you hurt me, Elise. How do you think she'll feel when she returns to a broken home?" His voice went hard as he closed his fingers over the metal. Josi's ring.

"Where is she!" Elise tried to step forward, but Sterling intercepted her with a hand on his gun, body braced in front of the hallway. "And where is my mother?" Elise demanded.

Mr. Saint's calmness told Elise all that she needed to know. He wanted Elise to snap. He wanted her to come running back to him with no other options so she was forced to kneel before him and beg him for help. "They're safe. They have always been safe here, in my city."

"*Where—*"

"You don't get to know that yet, Elise. You still owe me," Tobias Saint muttered fiercely.

Elise no longer saw her father, but a man made into a monster. The defiance in his eyes while he threatened her made her feel sick.

Elise blinked back tears and wiped her hands over her face. The Saint ring on her finger felt tight all of a sudden, and her chest ached—she couldn't breathe. "You—you've ruined everything—"

"*I* ruined everything?" Her father looked incredulous. "You truly know nothing." Tobias Saint gave her a smug smile. "I did not kill the Harlem reaper clan leader. *You* did. A threat against Josi made you go crazy and now you've driven a wedge between you and your only ally. That Quinn girl will never fully trust you again. Now…me trusting Stephen Wayne…" He tilted his head to the side and sighed. "That might have been a misjudgment on my part. But we live and we learn. Right, Elise? You can learn from your mistakes, right?" Mr. Saint's expectant gaze bored into her.

Elise's heart thudded so hard in her chest, she thought she would collapse. Her focus slipped. All she could think about was Josi and Layla. The two beings who she had pinned everything onto. Everything she had done had been for them and she had still let them down.

"My Josephine would never do this to me," her father said. He frowned at his daughter. "Oh, Elise. You're a member of this empire, but you still don't get it."

Elise recoiled. Her chest constricted and she backed away from her father, glowering. He wanted a pawn—to weaponize her devotion. Elise would be condemned to ruination if she accepted his cruelty. To love boundlessly, as a girl who the world intended to devour, was an act of defiance. She would not stay in the darkness with him. No matter how perfect she made herself, she could not fix him, nor could she reverse the scars he inflicted.

"No," Elise muttered.

"Pardon me?" he asked.

"I want no part of it." Elise ripped her family ring off and threw it at her father's chest. "I hope all your goddamn Saints fall."

Seething, she turned, and tore out of the yard before her father could properly react to her denunciation. Fury clutched her throat and heart with scorching fingers. She welcomed the jagged blade of her feelings, reveling in the roar of her pulse in her ears.

With moonlight guiding her path and pure determination driving her forward, Elise Saint left the Saint estate.

And she did not look back.

ACKNOWLEDGMENTS

Writing is often a solitary activity, but luckily for me, I had several people come along the journey of turning this story into a published book with me. Despite me being a writer, I frequently struggle to articulate my emotions, so bear with me as I thank everyone who has had an influence on me and this book.

Thank you to my lovely agent, Emily Forney, for believing in this book and me. You helped make one of my biggest dreams come true, and I feel so honored to call you my champion. I know my stories are safe with you, and I truly feel so lucky to be privy to your genius that makes my stories stronger.

Thank you to my editors, Wendy McClure and Natasha Qureshi, for seeing something in this book and taking a chance on me. I still smile when I think about how Tash read this whole book in one sitting and the first calls I had with you both to discuss this book and its potential. This book has transformed into something beautiful because of your incredible editorial visions and I'm excited to do something even better with book two! Thank you also to the rest of my Sourcebooks Fire team for working so hard to bring this book into the world: Thea Voutiritsas, Jessica Thelander, Jenny Lopez, Michelle Lecumberry, Karen Masnica, Nicole Hower, Delaney Heisterkamp.

Thank you to Margeaux Weston, Breanna McDaniel, and the We Need Diverse Books Black Creatives Revision Workshop. This program and Margeaux's mentorship gave me such valuable insight into the publishing industry and took this book to the next level in preparation for the query trenches.

Thank you Dr. Jen Ferguson and Dr. Julia Lee, my incredible professors and mentors. It was in Dr. Lee's Black Women Writers class (and all her classes, really) where so many of my ideas for this book were born and conversations with Jen that completely rearranged my brain chemistry. You both encourage me and inspire me endlessly. Dr. Lee, you nominated me and mentored me for a fellowship that allowed me to prioritize my writing. Jen, you were the one who convinced me to query and offered invaluable advice throughout the whole publishing process. I can confidently say this book might not exist without either of you, so I owe you everything.

To my best friends who have been there from the very beginning, ever since we stumbled across each other in various ways on the internet, I adore you. Cath, you were one of the first people I told about this book idea and one of the first to read it. The way your mind works needs to be studied (because you're a genius). I don't think there's anyone who believes in me more than you. You somehow always know how I'm feeling even when I'm a literal rock, and I'm so grateful to call you my best friend every day. Cassidy, you are one of the hardest workers I know, and I'm endlessly inspired by you. I appreciate how you're always one of the first people to offer to read my books, even when you're extremely busy. From the days when we were commenting on each other's BookTube videos to us traveling various countries, it makes me emotional thinking about how far we've come! I cannot wait to see more of the world with you. Alexandra, this book was born from a voice message conversation with you in the middle of our demon thread. Even thousands of miles apart, we have some unexplained connection, and it's wild to think that we've gone from talking about our current reads in Twitter messages to you reading the very first draft of this book (and most of my books) and believing in it so wholly. Thank you for reading eagerly and always being there for me. Spencer, if I had a dollar for every time you lifted me up whenever I was doubting myself, I wouldn't even need to worry about selling my books. I look forward to talking to you every day, whether it's about Beyoncé, food, or horror movies. Thank you for talking me down from so many ledges (especially when I'm panicking about my career). You're my hilarious voice of reason, and I'm so happy to have you in my life. Night, you're like my literary partner in crime, always the first to ask about me sending you my book before the ink of the first draft has even DRIED. I appreciate your thoughtful notes and ideas and unhinged, yet funny comments every single time. Nova, I swear you were Layla and Elise's biggest fan before you even read this book. I've never felt so lucky to know someone who willingly spends so much time and effort making art and loving my words. You've been there since DAY ONE. Brittany, you were one of my first friends on the internet, and you remain one of my oldest writing buddies. From ranting about the publishing industry and the writing process to sharing new ideas with each other, I'm so proud to call you my oldest writing friend. I can't wait to do another 10k word day with you. Thank you all for being my biggest supporters, my first critique partners, and for making me laugh and curbing my overthinking when I fell into misery. I cannot wait until all of our books are on shelves together.

Thank you also to Cooper for listening to me ramble on about my writer dreams and my very first book ideas. I still remember you keeping me company while I wrote or filmed a writing update video, and you being absolutely astounded that I won NaNoWriMo in less than two weeks. You carrying around a hard copy of my first book in a paper bag and having a personal vendetta against one of my main characters at the time remains one of the highlights of our friendship and my writing career. Thank you for always cheering me on. Thank you also to June, who is my ride-or-die, my best friend since day one. My life (and this book) would not be the same without you. You've shaped me as a person and the writer I am today. Thank you also to Erica for bearing with me whenever I stayed out late on the couch in our living room during sophomore year and for driving us to get midnight snacks and just overall being one of my biggest supporters during my struggle years (college).

Thank you to Ms. Powell, Mrs. Bond, and Dr. Bradley for your incredible feedback on my creative work in class. I still remember your kind comments encouraging me to pursue writing professionally after reading my work. It's those comments that I always think of whenever I hit a rough patch, and they've motivated me for over a decade now. Thank you also to Ms. Anthony for teaching me (and helping me teach everyone) the importance of details while writing. I was an incredibly shy child, so it was mortifying when you came up to me on the playground and told me I'd have to stand up in the middle of class and shout, "DETAILS, DETAILS, DETAILS," whenever you spoke the word in class, but I do think it ended up helping me, so I appreciate it (also it gave me a funny memory to look back on).

Mom, Dad, Josh, and Jordy, this all started with you. From the time before I even learned to read when we would all sit in bed together and tell each other stories to write in our family journal, to you all just accepting that I would be a writer, constantly up late at night and asking for updates on my book. Even if I don't show it, I appreciate your interest (and concern). Whether it's reminding me to eat earlier than midnight or offering to be my agents (both literary and film) and editors, your input never goes unnoticed to me. I'm grateful every day that you are my family. Darcy, I know you're not with us anymore, but you were witness to most of my late-night writing sessions. You kept me company, whether it was curled up on my feet under my desk or next to me in bed. I cherish those memories and miss you so much. Thank you for sending new companions, Luna and Daisy, to keep me company while you're away.

Last, but certainly not least, to my readers, thank you, thank you, thank you for being here and picking up this book. Whether you've been here since my BookTube days, where I shared my journey of writing my first book, or since deciding to read this book, I adore you. Because of you, I've always felt like I could get to this point, where I have a book to share with the world. So, thank you, reader, for choosing this book.

ABOUT THE AUTHOR

 Hayley Dennings is a recent graduate from Loyola Marymount University, where she double majored in English and French with a concentration in diversity and inclusion. She currently lives in the Bay Area, where she was born and raised. When she isn't writing or reading, she's working her editorial plus marketing day job in tech, spending time with her dogs, painting, or baking. You can find her on Instagram and Twitter @pagesofhayley, or check out her website at hayleydennings.com.

sourcebooks
fire

Home of the hottest trends in YA!

Visit us online and
sign up for our newsletter at
FIREreads.com

....

Follow
@sourcebooksfire
online